Impulse

THE FREED BILLIONAIRE
SPENCER CHRISTMAS TRILOGY
BOOK TWO

Z.L. ARKADIE

Copyright © 2019 by Z. L. Arkadie

All rights reserved.

No part of this book may be reproduced in any form or by any electronic or mechanical means, including information storage and retrieval systems, without written permission from the author, except for the use of brief quotations in a book review.

ISBN: 9781942857754

❀ Created with Vellum

CHAPTER ONE

JADA FORTE

CHRISTMAS EVE

Spencer and I stood outside my parents' front door. Lots of cars were parked in the circular drive, probably belonging to dinner guests, who were mostly my parents' colleagues.

I took a deep breath, vaguely noticing the changes my parents had made to the front of the estate. The fountain in the middle of the driveway was different. There used to be a fat, stone cherub who spouted water out of his mouth, surrounded by perfectly trimmed shrubbery, but now there was a cluster of squares, triangles, and circles mounted on top of one another. Water fell through each. I tilted my head, scrutinizing the display. It was a very contemporary choice for my parents, who had classic tastes.

My shoulders rose and dropped with my next breath. That second breath settled me. "Are you ready?" I asked Spencer, looking into his eyes, which appeared more pensive than normal.

His smile was tense, as it had been since before we boarded our flight to California. I felt the corners of my mouth pull downward and wondered if perhaps there was a conversation to be had before we joined the party. He'd barely spoken during our private flight from Jackson Hole to Santa Barbara. The night before, he didn't even come to my bed after spending all day in the space under the ranch house, chiseling at a cement wall.

I hadn't seen him until an hour before our flight was scheduled to take off, and thinking he might have abandoned me, I'd considered making an alternate flight plan. Once Spencer and I were sitting beside each other on the airplane, I asked him for probably the tenth time if he was okay.

Spencer wrapped an arm around me. "I'm fine. I'm just disturbed by something."

I felt relieved that he was finally revealing what was troubling him. "Does it have to do with what's beneath the house?"

"Yes."

"Did you find what you were looking for?"

His lips were parted as he stared deep into my eyes. Finally, he swallowed. "Yes."

I could sense his grief, and that feeling made my insides constrict. "Are you ready to tell me what you found?"

He kissed me on the forehead. "Soon enough."

"Why not now?" I asked, annoyed by my whining tone.

"I need to wait. It's important I not make mistakes."

I felt my eyebrows pull some more. "What sort of mistakes could you make?"

His eyes narrowed just a bit. Then he removed his arm from around my shoulders and scratched his temples. "I want to keep this to myself for now. I need you to respect that decision."

We stared at each other for a long moment. I loved his sincerity and how respectfully he asked for things he wanted from me. I acquiesced by nodding gently. We kissed again tenderly. Spencer lifted the armrest between us, and I pressed my head to his chest. Since I'd hardly gotten any sleep during the night, worrying about why he wasn't joining me, I was out like a lamp. I closed my eyes and didn't wake up until the plane had landed and we were ready to disembark.

A hired car drove us to my mother's house. Spencer spent the entire ride texting on his phone. Whatever conversation he was having, it made him look more miserable with each response. I asked him whether he was texting about the business beneath the ranch.

He kissed me tenderly. "Yes."

After that kiss, he'd seemed fine, but now that we were standing on my mother's patio, he was back to appearing sour, and it worried me. We were already at a disadvantage with my mom hating that we were a couple. If she perceived even a small crack in our relationship, she would agitate that fissure until we split apart.

Spencer cupped my chin and lowered his mouth to kiss mine. "Let's have fun," he whispered against my lips.

Everything inside me tingled, and for that reason, I felt as if I had no cause to doubt him. "Okay."

He kissed me more passionately. His tongue indulged in mine, making up for leaving me lonely in our bed the night before.

"Hello, Jada," my mother's voice blared in surround sound throughout the front porch.

Spencer and I ripped our mouths apart. I looked up and around, searching for the source of her voice. Spencer focused on the doorbell.

"Please come inside already," she said.

Then I saw the camera fastened near the right-hand corner of the veranda. The mechanism was also new. My parents hadn't had cameras on their property when I used to live at home. However, back then, my mother wasn't senate majority leader either. A lot had changed since then—she had changed the most.

Spencer opened the door, giving me space to pass. I looked at him with raised eyebrows as I walked by him. I tried to convey a warning, letting him know to get ready to tolerate the shit show. The way he smiled back told me that he understood my nonverbal message, and that put me slightly more at ease.

As soon as I entered, I noticed that my mom had renovated since the previous year. The foyer had been torn out, and now guests walked right into her grand living room, which had the necessary picturesque view of the lit city at the bottom of the sprawling hill. The flooring was shiny off-white marble, and the furniture was red velvet and built in an art deco style. I frowned at the triptych of women from the 1920s with long necks and smoking long cigarettes. Then I found myself wondering if my mom had changed it up so drastically to make me feel guilty about being away from home too long. I tried to dismiss the accusation as being self-centered. However, changing the decor in order to jar me was an action that was totally in my mother's wheelhouse.

I hadn't looked at the guests long enough to get an idea of who was present. However, I could feel their eyes on us as the volume of chatter lowered. We hung our coats on the rack as Sinatra crooned Christmas songs. Spencer and I grinned at each other. I could tell whatever had burdened him earlier was still on his mind, but he was choosing to put it aside for our first public appearance as a couple.

When we faced the crowd together, it wasn't me they were all staring at—it was him. Spencer and I had been cooped up in our mansion-sized love nest for so long that I'd forgotten how famous the Christmases were. The fascinated expressions on the faces of the other guests reminded me that

Spencer was arguably one of the richest men in the world.

"Jada, is that you?" My dad was standing in a circle with two other gentlemen I'd never seen before. They were my parents' age and had the worn, worried faces of people who had worked too late and too hard for far too many years. The men looked back and forth between Spencer and me as if they couldn't figure out which one of us to focus on.

"It's me, Dad," I sang. I threw my arms around him, erasing the distance between us, and hugged him tightly. It had been so long since I'd seen him that I made sure to breathe deeply. My father always smelled the same, like sweet mint with a tab of oranges.

"You look different," he said.

I examined him as I let go of him. "So do you." I leaned back and widened my eyes to get a better look at him. He had dyed all the gray out of his hair. The cream-colored turtleneck sweater paired with nicely fitted black slacks was an outfit I never would have thought he'd wear. He'd always been thin and frail, but now he had muscle mass, just the right amount of it to make him physically fit.

"Well…" I rubbed my hands together. "All the

changes around here are making my head spin. And, Dad, where are your glasses?"

Keeping a steady smile on his face, he pointed to his eyes. "Lasik surgery." He sounded proud to tell me.

"Oh…" He looked ten to fifteen years younger, and oddly, I found that unsettling. *Heck*, he almost looked like Spencer's peer. Then I remembered that I wasn't alone, and I turned to face Spencer, who was maintaining a gracious smile.

I gestured proudly toward my new lover. "Dad, this is Spencer. Spencer, my dad…"

"You're Robert Forte," Spencer said.

They shook hands.

"Spencer Christmas," my father said as if he'd said my boyfriend's name a million times before. "I have a lot of money invested in your company."

"Yes, you do," Spencer said.

"Well, it's nice to meet you in person."

Finally, they released their handshake. Spencer looked around the room, not pausing to acknowledge all the eyes that were fixed on him. "You have a nice home."

My father smiled tightly. I recognized the expression—he was avoiding saying something. I was still studying my dad when he slipped his arm around my waist. "Sweetheart, your mom is waiting for you in the terrace room." He glanced up at Spencer. "How about you go say hello?"

I suppressed the desire to roll my eyes and say that if my mom wanted to see me, then she could find me. It was obvious that she had enlisted him in the task of separating me from Spencer so that she could drive a stake through my mind with her hammer of a tongue.

Spencer winked, stretching his lips into my favorite irresistible smirk. "I'll be fine, Jada."

My lips parted as I stood in confusion. I still wasn't sold on the idea of leaving his side. He was my lifeline to a universe that existed beyond my mother's control. I felt that if I left him, she would catch me and manipulate me, and I would forget who I was becoming and fall back into the person she wanted me to be.

"Go ahead," my dad said. "I'll keep Mr. Christmas company."

"Call me Spencer," Spencer said.

"Maybe we can talk about improving my investment portfolio," my dad added.

I gazed wide-eyed at Spencer. "Are you sure?"

He planted a tender kiss on my lips. "Yes. Go."

I groaned—not because I worried about leaving

my boyfriend in my father's hands. My dad was sane. I was going against my gut, which warned me to stay the hell away from Patricia Forte as long as I could. Regardless, I kissed Spencer one more time before setting off to see what sort of scheme my mom was cooking up.

When I made it to the terrace room, I took a minute to admire the space. It was the area that was generally used for cocktail parties no matter what time of the year because the roof was retractable. If it was too hot, she could close in the space and air-condition it, and if it was too cold, she could heat it. I raised the palms of my hands and lifted my face to the sky. The temperature was perfect, so the roof was half-open, and the killer view of the valley was lit up. There were roughly twenty guests that night. Tall cocktail tables with high chairs were placed throughout along with clusters of oversized silk Christmas bulbs.

There was a different sort of ambiance in that room than in the living room. My parents usually kept their colleagues separated—business people up front and politicos in the terrace room. The politicos had a more mercurial energy.

My mom watched me intently. If only I could have delayed the moment a few seconds longer...

there was something about the way she focused on me that made me feel as if I'd suddenly lost my autonomy. No wonder I always made sure there was ample distance between us. Her attention felt like a vise.

She patted the shoulder of a young guy with sharp facial features and dark slicked-back hair with a prominent widow's peak. He had the looks of a movie star, like one of those good-looking guys in an action flick who always played the villain.

"Jada, over here," my mom called, her voice blaring as she waved me over, wiggling her fingers.

Along the path, I said hello to Carlson Quayle, Dana Cox, and Roma Lyles, political associates of my mom's whom I'd known for years.

"You have her in our room this year," Nelson Lyles said. He was Roma's husband and campaign manager.

Everyone chuckled. It was common knowledge that my parents competed to pull me into their respective professional circles whenever they combined their populations into one house—my mother's political colleagues and my dad's technology-business associates. Mostly, my dad won.

When I reached my mom, she hugged me loosely, which was a sign that she wasn't happy with me. She smelled good, though, and was as beautiful as usual with her long wavy auburn hair pulled back into the neatest chignon on the planet. Her matte skin was as flawless as a porcelain doll's, and it seemed lit up against her orange silk shift dress. My mom's uniquely feminine beauty didn't play well at the ballot box on its own, which was why she never forgot to put on or take off her tough-as-nails performance. However, on special occasions, she would turn on a charm so irresistible that even the oldest, most isolationist curmudgeon of the opposing party couldn't keep himself from fawning over her. She once said that she never forgot to remind certain constituents that she had a vagina and was putting it to use. One visual that was hard to conjure was that of her and my dad fucking. But here I was in the flesh, a product of their consummation, so as long as my mom claimed they were fucking, I had to believe her.

"How are you, Mother?" My tone was appropriately formal.

She pointed an open hand at the young man with slick hair. "This is Jimmy Lovell."

I smiled graciously and nodded once. She'd already mentioned him in our phone call, and I could sense how anxious she'd been for us to meet, so much so that she hadn't answered my question. I would have been satisfied with a simple "I'm fine."

"Jimmy's running for Congress, representing the state of Rhode Island. He'll be one of the youngest senators in history once he's elected." She winked at him.

I kept my smile pasted on at the appropriate height and level of enthusiasm. "That's great." I really didn't care and found myself thanking my lucky stars that I didn't live in Rhode Island or ever plan to move there.

"But he needs you on his team, Jada. You'll be a solid public-relations manager. On top of that, Jimmy knows that you love the East Coast, and you've set solid roots there, so voters won't look at you as a West Coast outsider. Plus, donors know you're my daughter, and you've done a phenomenal job building your reputation in your field. Well, that was until your little sidetrack gig…"

My hand shot up, gesturing for her to stop. "Sorry, Mom, but I like my sidetrack gig very much." I wanted to mention the pay, but I knew if I did, she'd take the opportunity to make a carefully crafted insult, alluding to how my bloated salary disappointingly included sex with my boss. "And

I'm sorry—I'm very confused. Am I running for office, or is he running for office?"

She opened her mouth to say something.

"And how is PR related to donors?" I added.

Patricia's painted-on smile outshone mine. She had done it so often that she'd perfected it. "We'll talk about the details later." She set her focus solely on Jimmy. "However, as I said, she's just an assistant for a businessman who's gone adrift. She's under contract, and he doesn't know if he's coming or going from one day to the next."

A bitter laugh escaped me, accompanied by a hard eye roll. "Mom, stop."

Jimmy's keen gaze shifted between my mom and me. "You know, Jada," he said as if he was used to saying my name, "I would love to hire you. Patricia said you'd been managing her image since before you were in diapers." He laughed at his failed attempt at flattery.

I made my smile even faker. "And not by choice, might I add."

He grunted while smirking weakly. That was a good thing. I was pretty sure my carefully crafted insult hadn't gone over his head. At least he was sharp enough to get it.

"No decisions have to be made this evening,"

my mother said. "But the two of you are close in age. You come from the same stock—decent families who have made themselves beacons in the eyes of the public." She rubbed my back like she used to do when I was younger and she was giving me a heroic speech. "That's why we serve the public, darling. And it's your duty to serve the public too."

My insides wanted to take off in two different directions. The way her hand buffed my back, all motherly and nurturing, made me want to hop on her bandwagon and take up her cause. The other part of me wanted to run as far away from her as possible.

"Beacons, huh? That's a lot of self-appointed duty you have there, Senator," Spencer said.

His arms wrapped around me, and I quickly looked up to see his handsome face. Spencer's presence felt as if someone had called in the cavalry and I had been saved.

"Spencer Christmas," my mother said coldly.

"Good evening, Patricia. Thank you for inviting me to dinner," he replied, remaining formal and classy.

My mom pressed her lips together in a pained smile as she shrugged. "My daughter insisted, but you're welcome."

I felt my skin burn hot because I was embarrassed and infuriated. *How dare she insult the man I'm falling in love with?* I wanted to tell her exactly that, but almost everyone was watching us, and I didn't want Spencer to see me behave like an insolent brat. He was such a strong and powerful human being. I needed him to believe I was a mature woman he could rely on in tough situations.

"So, Jada, you went to Redmond College?" Jimmy asked, watching me with glittering eyes.

I did not welcome his change of subject, even though it was necessary. "I did," I barely said.

"I went to Spruce Arbor." That was the all-male partner institution of Redmond's all-girls college.

I found myself grunting thoughtfully, Spencer style. He was sure rubbing off on me, and I was happy about it.

My mom shook a finger at us. "Yes, you have that in common as well."

Jimmy folded his arms, regarding me shrewdly. "What side of the political spectrum are you on?"

I wanted to laugh. But I also wanted to turn around and make out feverishly and inappropriately with my new lover just to let Jimmy and my mom know whose bed I was sleeping in and that no matter where Spencer went, I would follow.

Spencer wrapped me a hair tighter, and his dense bulge pressed against my ass. I let out a sigh and raised my finger. "Could you excuse us?"

"Not in the middle of a discussion," my mom said.

"I understand, Mother, and still, excuse us." I took Spencer by the hand. I loved how his nearness gave me the courage to defy my mother that I could never muster when I was alone. That was another reason my entire being needed him.

As I turned, I caught Spencer nodding at my mom and casually excusing himself before allowing me to lead him out of the terrace room. There was no need to articulate how much of a bitch my mom was being and explain that she was usually more genial than that—or at least that she knew how to be. I had a feeling Spencer had already formed his own opinion about my mother, and it had nothing to do with how he was currently experiencing her.

Dinner guests watched as we rounded the corner. I led him down the long hallway and past a powder room and the reading room, and then we headed to a back door. Once we were there, Spencer tugged me against him, and we made out feverishly.

"Self-appointed duty," I said breathily against

his mouth before my tongue dove in and lapped his. He tasted so delicious.

He grabbed me by my hips and nailed my mound against his rock-hard cock, sending a tingling sensation through my sex. "You liked that?"

"Umm…" I wrapped my legs around him as he lifted me off the ground. "Yes. Both things," I said with a moan. I liked both how he stabbed me with his erection and how he took the wind out of my mom's sails. I hated that I was wearing panties.

No one would be able to see us by the back door unless they were looking for us. We were not going to make it to the second guesthouse, where there was a big comfortable bed to fuck on.

Our tongues swirled hungrily around each other. He cupped my ass tighter and kept holding me as if it were no effort at all. His strength turned me on even more.

"Where can I take us?" he finally whispered.

I glanced over my shoulder and saw the door to what I hoped was still a storage room. My mom was always knocking out walls and creating new spaces. It was her way of bringing newness in her life, the sort she could control fully. I'd once asked her why she didn't just get a dog. She said her staff already had a lot on their plates and there was no need to pile taking care of animals on top of all their other duties. That made a lot of sense, considering that I'd had several nannies throughout my childhood. I couldn't remember most of them, but I did remember hating all of them for no other reason than that they weren't my mother. It was Maria Vasquez, the lead housekeeper, who I gelled with the most. When I turned twelve, I asked my mother to "ix-nay the nannies" because Maria and I could take care of each other. I got no pushback from Patricia, who agreed to the idea. And that was the end of the trail of nannies.

I pointed. "That way. Door on the right."

Spencer immediately pushed the door open so hard that it hit the wall, then he slammed it shut. "Unzip me," he said, and then his tongue slid up and down my neck as his teeth grazed my skin.

I leaned back, and my fingers shivered from pure need as I unbuttoned his pants, tugged down his zipper, and reached into his underwear to free his rock-solid erection. I ran my finger around the glistening tip. *Shit*, I needed it in my mouth, but it was too late. Once he was exposed, Spencer shifted the crotch of my panties to the side, sat on the only chair in the room, and lowered me on top of his swollen manhood. I moaned as he pushed through me. Our gazes stayed locked on each other as he shifted my hips back and forth, going at his desired speed.

He closed his eyes and sucked air. "Shit…" The pace of his shifting increased, and he made sure to sink himself deeper inside me.

"Umm…" I moaned and held my lower lip between my teeth, riding his dick like a wannabe cowgirl on a mechanical bull.

"I want to make you come, baby, so tell me how it feels," he said with his mouth against my ear then sank his tongue inside, the erotic sensation of his wet tongue making me shiver. "Did you hear me?"

"I heard…" I said with a sigh.

Spencer gripped me tighter by the hips and started shifting my hips in a circular motion. "Do you remember your spot?"

I nodded while going for a ride on his lap.

"If you're going to enjoy this, I need you to speak."

"Yes," I said breathlessly, already directing my hips to match his thrusts.

We fucked like a well-oiled machine, never losing eye contact. Never had I been so turned on. Fucking in my mom's house filled with fake people attending her special dinner added fuel to my fire. I felt like a rebel, not a good daughter.

Spencer raised his eyebrows, and when he lowered them, he licked his bottom lip. "Umm… you feel so damn good."

His expression grew increasingly tense. Experience had taught me that he was fighting to stave off his orgasm.

"Shit." I leaned back farther so that he could better stimulate the most sensitive spot inside my pussy. I moaned as soon as his cock agitated that spot. The extra loudness let Spencer know that he had found what he was looking for and was bringing me closer to release. Since I had a tendency to ride away from the pleasure to give myself some relief, he held my hips in place and continued stimulating my hot spot. I inhaled sharply, losing all control of my body. He did not let up.

I felt intoxicated, as if my head was spinning round and round.

He would not let up.

I whimpered and moaned, not caring how loud I was or who could hear me.

He would not let up.

I tossed my head back, crying out, experiencing

currents of orgasm streaking through my pussy like pleasure being pushed through veins.

"Damn, I can feel it," Spencer whispered, thrusting into me with short bursts of his dick, prolonging my enjoyment. Then, not letting it simmer any longer, he moved my hips rapidly against his cock, taking all of my pussy for his own enjoyment. In a haze, I kept my gaze clamped on his face. I loved to watch him enjoying me. Never had I seen a human so enraptured by engaging with another during sexual activity.

Then he announced that he was going to come, and he held me close against him and exploded inside me.

SPENCER AND I SAT STILL FOR A LONG TIME, holding each other, his dick still inside my ever-increasing wetness.

"Why didn't you come to my bed last night?" I asked. "We were overdue for what just happened between us."

Spencer chortled. "We *were* long overdue." He leaned back to get a complete view of my face. "I missed your body last night, babe."

I could feel the stars dancing in my eyes at the sight of his gorgeous face—so open, so happy—up close. "I missed yours too."

Spencer's lips gently kissed mine, and our tongues brushed indulgently. We continued with our kissing, enjoying the high.

"We should get out there," I finally whispered, pressing my forehead against his.

"Your mom is a pill."

I chuckled. "A pill?" I scoffed. "She's like a whole bottle of Vicodin."

We both laughed, then I turned serious, knowing my mom had meant to disturb and destroy our relationship by the end of the night.

"But listen, Spencer…"

He was looking steadily into my eyes.

"We can't let her get between us, okay? We stick together."

Spencer smirked. "Don't worry about your mother. I know how to handle her."

I pressed my lips together pensively, positive that he didn't indeed know how to deal with Patricia Forte when she was in full-throttle mode. Nobody did—not my father, not me, not even the president of the United Sates.

"I hope so," I replied. I truly hoped so.

CHAPTER TWO

JADA FORTE

Spencer and I cleaned up in the closest powder room, narrowly avoiding going another round. When we made it to the dining room, there were already approximately forty people around the long white-marble farm-style table, seated in dark-red velvet high-back chairs. The way everyone watched us, I was sure they could see the sex we'd just had written all over our faces and feel it in the energy we brought into the room. My mom had tried to play with the seating arrangement by putting me on one end between her and Jimmy Lovell, who seemed ecstatic about the placement, and Spencer at the other end of the table next to a woman with platinum blond hair who was showing way too much cleavage. I split my attention between Spencer, who was speaking to the woman, and my mother.

"Excuse Jada for being inappropriately tardy," she said. "It's only Christmas dinner with our family and friends." She chuckled as if that was a joke, but I knew it was merely her way of trying to shame me in front of her friends.

I didn't know who exactly my mom was speaking to because I'd just locked eyes with Spencer. I smiled at him, and he smiled back. He stood and walked in our direction then stopped behind a man named Turner Agnew and asked to switch seats. I glanced at my mom, who looked as if she was close to blowing a gasket, especially when Turner gladly obliged. He seemed as happy as a lark, galloping past the other guests and situating himself in the seat beside the siren. I studied her with narrowed eyes. She looked out of place, not like someone who would be connected to a politico or people in the technology industry. I wondered who she was and where she came from. During the after-dinner mingling, I would be sure to find and grill her.

Spencer winked as he situated himself in his new seat, not displaying that he was at all upset by the stunt my mother had pulled in separating me from my date. The fact that he was so easily able to rectify the matter made him even sexier than usual.

"Yes, you may sit elsewhere," my mother said, sarcasm saturating her tone.

Spencer narrowed an eye. "You're welcome, Senator Forte."

My smile wavered as I detected something bitter in his tone. It was clear that my mother and my lover were in a personal war. It would have been great if they'd gotten off on the right foot. However, I knew it was all my mother's fault. She was the agitator, and what made me nervous was that he was showing that he wasn't just going to lie down and take it.

Food service began, starting with the first course, which was soup. The creamy pumpkin-colored liquid tasted delicious and looked pretty. I couldn't concentrate on the chef's explanation of what it was, exactly, because I was keeping my ears trained on the conversation my mother was having with Marilyn Rain, one of her campaign organizers. They spoke about Marilyn's daughter, who used to be a good friend of mine until the fifth time she stole one of my boyfriends by offering him the sex I wouldn't.

"Mr. Christmas, it's an honor to meet you,"

Turner Agnew's wife said, batting her eyelashes at him. She wasn't the flirtatious type, but with a man like Spencer beside her, I supposed she couldn't help herself.

They got into a discussion about his brother Jasper and how Trish Agnew had met him once at a fundraiser. Spencer kept an even expression as she explained how Jasper had given more than everyone's donations combined.

"That sounds like my brother," Spencer said. "When he's in, he goes all out."

Trish giggled as if that was the funniest thing she'd ever heard.

"So, are you going to join my campaign?" Jimmy asked. I'd forgotten he was sitting beside me.

"Yes, she will," my mother replied.

"Stop," I warned her under my breath.

She pressed her lips into a tight smile and looked out over the table as though just remembering that she had other guests. Suddenly, she clapped her hands as if she were the great queen of the evening. "Everyone," she said, immediately commanding the attention of all the guests except Spencer, who I caught making eye contact with the Marilyn Monroe look-alike.

My stomach tightened as I wondered what in the hell that was about.

"Thank you for joining us this evening." Mom raised her glass of wine, and everyone followed. "This is a season for family and friends, old and new, but especially old." She flashed Spencer an impish smirk, and I instantly wondered what else had she done. "Sharing the table another year with my husband and our only daughter makes me feel so blessed."

"Humph," Spencer said, barely audible and with a bitter smirk.

"I'm sorry, Mr. Christmas. Are you feeling ignored? You are, of course, the most famous person at our table." She turned her head slightly. "And for many reasons of course."

"You would know," he said.

My mouth fell open and my ears started to ring. My mother glared at him, eyes narrowed to slits. She was behaving oddly aggressive toward my new boyfriend, and I was beginning to wonder, with the cryptic jabs they were throwing at each other, if there was something between them that I needed to know about.

"Yes, well… this is not the circus act you're used to, so mind yourself," she said.

I heard a few sharp gasps.

Spencer's eyes burned with rage as he folded his arms on his chest. "You're sharing a table with your daughter—that's nice. Does she know about you and your husband?"

My mom's gaze darted toward my dad.

"Spencer?" I said in a low voice. In my mind, I spoke his name louder. However, my curiosity made me unsure about quieting him. Deep down inside, I wanted to hear what he had to say.

My mom lifted her chin as she glared at Spencer. "I'm so sorry. I knew you were coming for dinner, and I thought you'd have a better time tonight, seated next to your old friend, Gina." She was threatening him. One had to be familiar with the cadence and tone of her voice when she was engaged in the act to notice it.

"Let's see… you and your husband have been separated for—what, fifteen, sixteen years? And when are the two of you going to tell Jada that she has a brother?" Spencer pointed at my mom. "And that you're not the mother?"

Gasps sounded off throughout the room. My mom's mouth fell open, and then she closed it. Since she was avoiding looking at me, I turned in shock to my father, who was staring at Spencer with a strange sort of unaffected look on his face.

Spencer slipped his napkin off his lap and tossed it over his soup. He fixed his eyes on my mom. "Do you want me to keep going, Senator Forte, or should we stop here?"

"Dad?" I said. One thing I'd learned about Spencer was that he didn't make up shit. He spoke only about what he knew.

My mom bared her teeth. "Get out."

I raised a hand before Spencer could move. "Mom?"

My mom flung her arm toward the door, pointing. "Get out!" she yelled like a crazed person.

Spencer stood casually. I felt so lost looking into his eyes.

"Sorry, Jada, I wanted to tell you. But I wanted to give her the chance to prove she cared about you more than herself and tell you first."

I felt as if I were dreaming. The only thing that proved I was awake was the very real feeling of shaking my head.

"Are you coming?" he asked me.

My brain tried to absorb what he'd said. I couldn't stop shaking my head as I looked from my mom to my dad and then to every set of pity-filled eyes at the table. By the time my confused gaze rested on Spencer, he was already confidently walking out of the dining room, perhaps knowing he had won that battle with Patricia Forte even though I'd been a casualty of their skirmish.

My feet wanted to take over and run after Spencer, but my heart felt so betrayed by everyone I loved, including him, that I wouldn't allow them to take me to him. How long had Spencer known about my parents? At least now all his strange reactions whenever my mother was mentioned made sense. I closed my eyes, remembering how Bryn had clearly believed I had a brother when we were having dinner. Even she had known!

No one moved a muscle as the servers, who had no idea what just happened, entered with the second course. I noticed that tears were rolling out of my eyes.

"Jada, please go clean your face and then return to the table," my mother said, smiling as if what had just happened never even occurred.

I shook my head at her and looked over at the blonde, who was watching me with a sad smile. I opened my mouth to speak but then closed it. Since so many other secrets had been revealed, I wanted to ask her who she was and how she knew Spencer, but I didn't want to be in that room a second longer. I'd lost my appetite, and I wasn't sure if that included my hunger for my new boyfriend. Spencer had a lot to answer for, that was for sure, but so did my parents.

"Jada, go," my mom demanded.

Then I brought my hands in front of my face and knew exactly why she wanted me out of sight of all her guests—I was shivering uncontrollably.

I didn't remember the walk, but I took the stairs and ended up in my old room. My body was still shaking as I kicked off my shoes, stripped out of my clothes, and climbed into bed. I felt embarrassed by the way I was handling my agony. A small part of me wanted to get up and figure out how to make it to wherever Spencer was as fast as I could. Instead, I pulled the covers over my head and bawled my eyes out.

CHAPTER THREE

JADA FORTE

TWO DAYS AFTER CHRISTMAS

"Jada?" a female voice said, sounding like someone from another lifetime—one in which I was younger and my mother was the smartest person I knew, the one person I needed to please above all others. Then the woman called my name again.

"Huh?" I squirmed.

The mattress beneath me was firm but not as comfortable as the one I'd been sleeping on for the past three weeks. I had tried to blink until I was fully conscious many times before, but when I remembered what happened at the dinner table, I'd quickly fall back to sleep. But this time, I stayed awake, recalling how Spencer revealed that my parents had been separated for many years and that I was not my father's only child and that my mother had planted the blonde as some sort of secret shame from Spencer's past. I was still lost as to why she thought the blonde would make me question Spencer's integrity and respect for me. Was I supposed to be jealous? Had she thought Spencer and I never talked about the hard, deep shit that made us tick?

As more light began to ease my brain into complete consciousness, I groaned and pressed a forearm over my eyes. I wished Spencer hadn't humiliated my parents in front of their guests. He was wrong for doing that. My mom might have deserved it, considering that she had agitated the situation, but my father didn't.

But what about me? How do I feel?

I wasn't embarrassed. I wasn't angry. I was conflicted. I wished I'd run after him so we could talk. We needed to talk.

I sat up quickly. "My phone." I had left it on Spencer's airplane. "Shit."

"Jada, you're up?" Maria said.

I whipped my face around to focus on her,

standing in front of the window seat. She had been the person calling my name.

"Maria?" I was happy to see her even though I didn't sound like it.

These days, Maria was the house director. She managed the other housekeepers, handled house bills, and dealt with maintenance issues as they arose. My mother paid her handsomely but not because of the mountain of job duties she was assigned, which often included managing me when I was around, since I never forsook a phone call from Maria or tried to hide from her. I always believed Maria knew where the bodies were buried.

I massaged the back of my aching neck. "How long have I been asleep?"

She calmly picked up a canvas bag off the floor and brought it to me. "This is for you."

I took it and looked inside. It held my cellphone and purse. I closed my eyes and swallowed gravely. "Did Spencer bring these?"

She pressed her lips together sympathetically as she nodded.

Then, recalling how important Maria was to my mother, I asked, "Did you know?"

She turned her head. "Did I know what?"

"About my parents' separation? About a brother I supposedly have somewhere in the world?"

Her eyebrows crumpled as she made a slight grimace. She couldn't say yes or no and still be loyal to her boss. Many times in the past, when I asked Maria a question that involved my mother's motives or actions, she would show me that same face, telling me that I knew the answer without her needing to articulate it. That expression had always been a way in which she communicated to me.

If I'd thought she would answer, I would probably have asked if she knew his name and where he lived. I would have asked if she knew what sort of woman his mother was and whether she was softer, kinder, and less narcissistic than my mother. Instead, I transferred my focus to the items Maria handed me.

My sinuses tightened, and my eyes filled with tears. But the sadness was something I knew to push deep into the back of my mind. My mom had taught me how to do that. Plus, I had no room in my life to think about a brother who had been the result of an affair or perhaps a sanctioned relationship my father had had with another woman. Spencer was still my happy place, so I gave my heart over to one promising action.

"He came back?" I whispered.

"Yes, Jada," Maria whispered and cupped my chin affectionately. "And he's a nice man. I like him."

"Then you spoke to him?"

She grunted and raised her eyebrows. "Not long, but I know energy. And his is good."

Even though I was disappointed that Spencer hadn't told her to convey to me that he loved me and was waiting to hear from me, I smiled anyway. "Thank you, Maria. By the way, I'm so happy to see you. And I'm sorry I'm in such a sour mood."

She kissed my forehead. "You don't need to apologize to me ever, even if you slapped my face. But I know you would never do that!"

We both chuckled. She was right. I would never do anything to hurt her. I loved her with every bit of my heart.

Maria breathed deeply in through her nose, and her expression turned serious. "Your mother wants you downstairs for breakfast."

"Breakfast?" That meant it was still early.

"Yes. You slept two nights. Go downstairs and eat. You need your strength."

"Then my mother's downstairs?"

"Yes, she is," she replied, looking me right in the eye.

I groaned, feeling the anguish of seeing her again.

Maria shook her head. "No, you are strong." She pointed to the door. "Now, go. Remember, you have your life."

I felt my forehead bunch as she kissed me one more time and walked out of my room. Maria was right. I couldn't crawl back into bed and allow sleep to take me away from my problems. I had to stand and deal.

I decided to call Spencer and make sure all was okay with us, but with one ring, I received a message that said his phone was no longer accepting calls, which made me wonder if he'd blocked my number. I tried him again, and the same thing happened.

I closed my eyes and sighed gravely. I couldn't help but feel as if our hot yet serious love affair had officially ended. Maybe he'd planned to out my parents at dinner all along. Maybe my mother was his foe, and that was why he'd hired me and seduced me in the first place. The possibility made me sick to my stomach. If I'd had food in my belly, I would have thrown up.

I sat very still and replayed how I'd come to know Spencer Christmas. I applied to work for him. He didn't seek me out. If he'd orchestrated our initial contact, he would have needed spy equipment not even available to the government. No, it was by chance that I applied to his job. He'd admitted that he hired me because I was my mother's daughter—I was fine with that.

But I wondered whether he'd performed his research on my parents before he hired me or after. The Christmases ran in an elite circle. Perhaps among people of their stature, my parents' trespasses were common knowledge. When I replayed the reactions of other guests, I realized that not many of them had appeared shocked by what he'd revealed. They seemed more appalled by how it was all playing out. Maybe they'd already known that Robert and Patricia weren't really a true couple and were only hosting the annual gathering together out of habit and obligation.

The next thought that came to mind made me sit up straight, back stiffened: I wasn't surprised either. I wasn't shocked. My parents had never loved each other as far as I could tell.

I pressed my hand over the bottom of my neck

as I gasped. I'd forgotten to breathe while admitting that to myself.

I STILL HAD CLOTHES IN MY DRAWERS AND CLOSET. I put on a fresh set of underwear, jeans, and my red-and-white Redmond College sweatshirt. I looked positively California casual, a style that I hadn't slipped on since my first year of college. Very early in my freshman year, I'd easily adopted the other girls' overtly sexy sense of fashion. But when I graduated and entered the professional realm, I'd traded the mounds of makeup, cascading curls, tight jeans, and crop tops for top designer suits, skirts, blouses, and sweaters—all bought on a budget. Now that I was back in my old garments as my new self, the style that I had grown up with felt right—very right.

My stomach growled. Hunger had finally caught up to me. For some reason, I felt more powerful than I had at the party, as if I could withstand any mind fuck my mother was about to lay on me. As I practically ran downstairs, hungry enough to eat a cow, I kept my mind focused on the fact that I had planned to advocate for myself and no one else. I would get some food in my belly and then figure out my next move with Spencer. He definitely needed to apologize for making a scene at my mother's table. I also wanted to castigate him for abandoning me. I could have left with him had he given me a moment to pull myself together. If we allowed ourselves to be inadvertently broken up, then Mom would win, and she'd be able to boast about how Spencer gave up on me just as she'd known he would from the start.

I stopped in my tracks when a voice deep down inside asked, *Then why are you still here?*

Perhaps I owed Spencer an apology for not being faithful and mature enough to handle our setback like an adult.

The vitality of my pondering had been weakened by the alluring smell of hot breakfast intermingled with the scent of fresh coffee. I started walking again, and when I saw my mother at the table with her pet, Jimmy Lovell—who stood up as I walked onto the patio—my feet brought me to an abrupt halt.

"Oh," I said, and my lips remained stuck open.

"Jada." My mother sipped her coffee. "Sit."

My feet didn't want to carry me into whatever trap she was setting. But a buffet-style breakfast spread fit for a king, which sat in the middle of the table, convinced me to enter as fresh meat would into the lions' den. What I loved about eating on the balcony was that my mom had citronella, mint, lavender, and rosemary in planters around the edge of the space. The aroma kept insects away.

"Good morning," Jimmy simpered. "You look nice."

I narrowed my eyes at him as I took a seat. "Good morning," I said, keeping my tone formal as I took a plate off the top of the stack and started serving myself a stack of pancakes. "Mom, I thought we would have a talk about the other evening without company present." I sat down and reached for the blueberry syrup.

"Jimmy needs a PR manager of your caliber immediately," she said, ignoring my last statement.

I shook my head as I poured the syrup over my pancakes. She was a fucking piece of work, and I wanted to say it to her just like that, but I knew better. "I have a job."

"Jada, I'm certain that job is no longer available to you." She spoke as if she had knowledge of what she was talking about.

I rolled my eyes. "Spencer hasn't fired me."

"He brought your bag to the door yesterday. He sure as hell wasn't seeking reconciliation." She threw her hands up, showing me her palms. "And that's just fine, Jada. The Christmases are blue-blood trash, and Spencer Christmas is the worst of them."

I felt my eyebrows pull to the extreme and forced myself to swallow what was in my mouth. "He's not trash, Mom. And you're the one who taught me that human beings can't be trash, remember? Or were you being a lying hypocrite?" I meant for that to sting her deeply.

She leaned back in her seat as her eyes narrowed to slits. "I'll let you get away with that"—she held up a finger—"one time, because I know you're angry about what your ex-boss said about your father and me."

Actually, I wasn't angry, but I decided to use what she'd said to my advantage. If she was talking, then she might be inclined to expose shit she would normally keep secret. So I folded my arms. "Is it true?"

She turned to Jimmy and then back to me. "Your father and I have had an arrangement for many years. But our arrangement has not affected how we parented you. Our relationship is our relationship. You're an adult. We are adults. Don't have a child's reaction to something you can't control."

I shook my head continuously. "Do your constituents know about *your* adult relationship?"

My mother turned her head slightly. "I was hoping you could help with that."

I jerked my head back and grimaced. "How?"

"You're a PR specialist. How would you make our voters understand our predicament?"

"Who the fuck is 'our'?"

My mom's eyes expanded. She wasn't used to me cursing in front of her, but I didn't give a fuck anymore. Especially since we were all now "adults."

"You're the only one whose name is on the ballot, Mother. This is your predicament, not mine."

She inhaled deeply through her nose, and when she let the air go, her fake smile was displayed in full force. "As I said, you are a PR specialist. In your professional opinion, what would you suggest *I* do?"

I chuckled bitterly. "Being that you lied to those who supported you for thirteen or fourteen years, I'd say you do what's expected of five-year-olds and tell the truth."

Her fake smile didn't waver. "And by use of what methods?"

I swallowed the food that I'd just chewed. I was feeling better, which meant I was less angry. I slid back in my chair. "Two people who are no longer in love or in a relationship should get a fucking divorce and worry about the fallout later."

"We're divorced," she said.

I jerked my head back so hard that I nearly tumbled backward in my chair. "What the fuck, Mom?"

"Do not say 'fuck' at my table."

I snarled as I considered whether or not to comply with her demand.

"But that's only for the ears of those who are right here, right now," my mom calmly added.

I looked at Jimmy, who didn't look shocked at all. He knew!

My mom shrugged indifferently. "But you're right. We'll tell everyone the truth."

I snorted bitterly. "Your version of it at least."

She smirked cunningly. "My version is all they need to know."

I shook my head. I so wished I'd been surprised by what she just said, but I wasn't.

Suddenly, my mother put her forearm on the table and shifted her body toward me. "Jada, Spencer Christmas is gone. You liked what you did in public relations. This is a great opportunity for you. And I'm starting to understand that Spencer

Christmas didn't share all that he is with you either."

I rolled my eyes. "You have nerve, that's for sure." I shoved more pancake into my mouth, proud that I hadn't let her ruin my appetite. Marta had said I was skinny. Suddenly, I understood that it was because every time I received a phone call from my mother that I didn't answer, I felt too anxious to eat. Patricia Forte had taken my appetite from me on so many occasions that I couldn't count them all. *But not this time—not this time.*

My mother sat back calmly and folded her arms on her chest, watching me, her eyes daring me to continue defying her. "Jimmy, show her."

Jimmy readjusted in his sat as he cleared his throat. "Jada, I have proof that Spencer Christmas is a sicko."

That did it. I released my fork and shot to my feet. "I'm done here. Goodbye."

"Sit down," Mom roared, her voice booming in my head like thunder. Without a pause, I sat. I didn't want to, but I couldn't make myself not do it.

Something satisfying glowed in Jimmy's eyes, which matched that slight grin of his, as if that moment had proved I was no better than he was.

"Jimmy, tell her," my mom ordered.

He cleared his throat and took on a man-meaning-business sort of posture. "Kids like Spencer and me used to hang out in St. Tropez every summer or so…" he said, sounding like one of those manly guys in a cowboy movie. I realized someone had taught him that he had to sound like that to be taken seriously.

I folded my arms, but once I saw I'd taken the same posture as my mother, I unfolded them. "Every summer or so? What does that mean? Either it's every summer, or it's not." I knew my argument was weak, but I just wanted to throw a monkey wrench into his presentation.

He went rigid and looked at my mom as if he had to remind himself of the reason for his carefully crafted nice-guy act. "Right, yes," he said, scratching the side of his face. "We kids would have parties. Spencer Christmas would attend, high on something very bad."

He pressed his lips together and looked at me like a schoolteacher scolding a naughty child in a 1950s TV show. I blurted a laugh, and again, he gave my mom that look. His skin was turning red, which meant deep down he was fuming.

"Jada, do a better job listening. You want to hear this, I promise you," my mother said.

I didn't want to hear it, but the expression on her face made me pay better attention.

"Maybe I should just show you already." Jimmy picked up his phone and pushed a button to activate the screen. "Everyone usually tried to do their dirty deeds behind closed doors for this very reason." He turned the screen toward me.

I refused to look. "What were your dirty deeds, Jimmy?"

"Jada, look at the screen," my mother ordered.

I folded my arms defiantly. "Was your dirty deed taking videos of people when they weren't watching?"

"Jada!" my mother shouted.

I jumped. She and I locked eyes. I was the one who looked away first and then slowly turned to view Jimmy's video. He pushed Play. I narrowed my eyes to get a better view of a woman with platinum blond hair. Her face was bruised, and blood was on the front of her white dress. Her features were familiar. "I've seen her before," I said, still studying the action.

"She was at dinner on Christmas Eve. It's Gina." My mother said the name as if it was her favorite note in a song.

Gina was laughing diabolically. Then Spencer,

who looked enraged, appeared on the screen, shirt-less. He grabbed Gina by the arm, dragged her into a room, and slammed the door behind them. The other people present started chuckling. Someone off camera said Spencer was a sick fuck and so was his whore.

I turned to look at my mom, who had replaced her smug smile with a look of concern. "That, darling—that's your new boyfriend. That's who he is in reality. I want better for you, even if you don't want better for yourself. I spoke to Gina. She said he starts off kind and loving and then the next thing you know, you're meeting his fist. You're in the honeymoon phase with him. I don't want you seeing him anymore. I taught you to be strong and never be victimized by someone with Spencer Christmas's instability. Let him go."

Her words shattered my heart into a million pieces. I felt sleepy again all of a sudden. I needed to dream away this moment.

"Now…" my mother said as if we were getting back to real business. "Jimmy needs a professional PR manager. I see no reason why it shouldn't be you."

CHAPTER FOUR

SPENCER CHRISTMAS

A MONTH LATER

I stopped to get a read on what Mita thought about what I'd just revealed.

"Continue," she said calmly as if she knew exactly why I paused.

"All I know is she was a woman and I was pounding her face with my fist. She was laughing and telling me to do it again. I didn't want to, though. She could have told me to stop, but she wouldn't because she was getting off on my pounding my fist into her face. And then…" I covered my face with both hands. "Then she became Jada. I was hitting Jada." I hung my head in shame. I didn't deserve to look at the face of any woman, including Mita. "I don't know what the fuck is wrong with me."

"Spencer?" Mita's voice was steady and strong.

I looked up. My eyes burned, and my vision was blurry. Self-loathing wanted to choke me.

"Were you aroused by your dream?" she asked, her voice steady.

I jerked my head from side to side. "No fucking way."

Mita picked up her notebook and started flipping the pages. It used to bother me when she did that, but it didn't anymore. I knew my past was contained in her hands. Now that I was back in New York, I'd upped my sessions, meeting with her three times a week, so I wouldn't lose my fucking mind. She'd been using those pages to show me how far I'd come since the first time I sat down with her, brutalized by the shame and the pain of growing up a Christmas.

She stopped on whatever page she was looking for and readjusted her position. "Remember how we talked about violence and sex and how both stimulate similar nerve centers in the brain?"

I sat up straight, wondering where in the hell she was going with this line of questioning. "I remember."

"We talked about how your brain was pretty volatile when Amelia introduced you to the practice of using sex and violence to stimulate arousal." She raised a finger pointedly. "You spent eleven months in a clinic to recondition your brain. Do you recall how similar dreams used to affect you pretreatment?"

I remembered—my dick would be hard, and I would shamefully rub one out, hating every moment of it. "I didn't get hard this time."

Mita pressed her lips into a gentle smile. "I'm glad you noticed that." She narrowed an eye. "So, if your dream didn't arouse you sexually, then what do you think is the root of your emotional reaction to it?"

I swallowed hard.

"Take your time," Mita coached in a soothing voice. "Close your eyes and think about it. Why are you having this particular emotional reaction to hurting a woman that you say you love?"

I took a deep breath and shoved my shoulders back, trying to relax. Then I closed my eyes and saw Jada's face and her sexy body, and my throat tightened.

"Now, connect your brain to your heart and your heart to your core. At the completion of the process, tell me what you feel." Her voice was tranquil as if she was leading me into a hypnotic state.

"Anguish."

"Why?" Mita asked.

"I miss her."

Mita grunted thoughtfully. "You said Jada's mother had dug up your past and invited Gina to Christmas dinner. How did seeing her make you feel?"

That was easy. I opened my eyes. "As if I can't outrun my past. But Gina and I are friends. At the table, she said she didn't know I would be there, and she was hired as Robert Forte's escort for the night." I scratched my neck as something else came to mind. "I think…" I narrowed my eyes. *Shit.* I didn't want to say it, but it was true. "I think Jada's taken her parents' side over mine, and that makes me fucking angry. Her mother is a liar like my father was. She doesn't know how to put Jada's interests before her own, and in the end, she'll try to destroy every ounce of happiness Jada could have—with me or anyone else."

"You sound sure of this."

I set my jaw and smashed my lips together. There was no way I could reveal all that I knew about Patricia Forte. She was a snake living in a swamp. She was the worst of the worst.

"When I finally got to know Jada's character through and through, I was shocked she wasn't as fucked as my sister and brothers and me. Then I got it. Her parents had been playing her as if she was a voter and not their daughter. But then I thought…"

Mita waited patiently for me to finish. My eyes darted from one side of her office to the other. Now that I'd known my therapist for a while, I was aware that her minimalistic office decor was intentional. She didn't want her clients knowing anything about who she was. For the longest time, I'd wondered why, but now I knew—she'd removed a second layer of judgment. I didn't know what she believed in. I didn't know if she had children or a husband. I didn't know what she thought about that kind of stuff. I only knew that she was my therapist and was there to help me.

"You thought…?" she said leadingly, bringing me back to the conversation.

"I thought Jada had a choice, and she chose to stay with her mother."

"Well, you are certainly still in a relationship with her. Are you aware of that?"

I felt my eyes narrow. I knew it, but instead of saying so, I shrugged.

"Your last encounter with her left you unsettled. Perhaps you should seek an ending that's best for both of you."

The thought of ending anything with Jada made me sick to my stomach. I'd tried to call her dozens of times, but I received a message telling me her phone wasn't taking calls. She had a habit of keeping her device in airplane mode. I remembered she used to do it to manage calls from her mother, but I knew she was living with Patricia and working for that weasel Jimmy Lovell. Working in political PR meant she had to be constantly on the phone. Plus, she was living with her mother. There was only one valid explanation for why she hadn't answered my calls.

"She doesn't want to speak to me," I said.

"You won't know the truth unless you have a conversation with her. Are you willing to do that?"

I pushed a forceful breath out of my nose. I recalled how fucking good it had felt to out Patricia Forte for being a liar. However, given the opportunity, I would take it back, especially on the heels of her most recent infraction. There was no way I could convince myself to be oblivious to Jada's mother's muck. But I loved Jada. I never thought I'd fall in love with any woman.

"I'll talk to her," I said.

Mita nodded as if satisfied. "Now, how about we talk about your discovery?"

I grunted as one side of my mouth stretched upward. "That's the part of my life I have under fucking control."

CHAPTER FIVE

JADA FORTE

A WEEK LATER

I sat alone at the front of the private airplane. At the moment, all I could hear was the rumbling of the engine. There were seven campaign staff members and one questionable candidate flying from California to Rhode Island, all of us focused on the large screen, which was airing a special report.

It was Spencer Christmas at his ranch in Wyoming. I was pressing my palm over my heart in a feeble attempt to slow the pounding. I hadn't seen his face since the evening he walked out of my mom's house. He was still the most handsome man I'd ever kissed, with his dark hair, light eyes, and strong jawline. I couldn't believe he hadn't attempted to contact me since then. I truly thought we had something special. I thought perhaps my mom was right, and after Spencer had exposed her farce of a marriage, he considered his work done and had cut and run. But now I was watching another explanation for why I hadn't heard from him and he hadn't taken my calls.

He was down in the darkness beneath the main ranch house. Cameras were capturing the wall, which was a mosaic of cement and human bones. At the bottom of the screen was a message that said, *previously recorded*, which made me wonder where Spencer was at that very moment. As the scene played out, none of us spoke a peep, not even Jimmy, who was used to making sure none of us ever forgot he was in the room.

"It's brave of you to show us this. Do you believe this discovery further tarnishes the Christmas family's legacy?" famed reporter Hannibal Newton asked.

Spencer frowned to the point of looking sick to his stomach. "I don't care about a family legacy, and neither do my siblings." He set his jaw.

"The hell you don't. All you Christmases care

about your fucking image," Jimmy yelled from behind me.

I rolled my eyes and clamped my teeth together, fighting the urge to tell him to shut the fuck up.

"Do you have any idea who these remains belong to?" Hannibal asked.

Spencer pursed his lips, pausing, and I knew what it meant when he did that. "We'll learn soon enough."

"But you have no idea who these people could possibly be?" Hannibal asked again in a different tone, perhaps hoping to get a direct answer this time.

"As I said, you'll know once the DNA testing is complete." Spencer squeezed his eyes shut and rubbed the inside corners. "But I'm certain the remains belong to young girls whose families have been looking for them for a long time." Spencer stared at the wall. "I want to get them returned to their loved ones and buried in a more peaceful final resting place."

My heart swelled. That was the Spencer Christmas I'd fallen in love with, who couldn't be the sort of man Jimmy and my mother tried to convince me he was.

"Is one of them possibly your mother?"

Hannibal asked. He had a reputation for sneaking in questions the interviewee hadn't seen coming.

Spencer glared at Hannibal as if he wanted to rip the man's head off. I knew him well enough to know he wasn't as angry as he appeared, and I was certain Spencer wasn't aware of that look on his face.

"Here's what I want to do." Spencer cleared his throat, which took some of the sting out of his expression. "I want to make amends for what my father has done." He quickly turned away from the camera to hide behind his forearm for a second. Then he took a deep breath and regained his composure. Of course, the lens pulled in, and his face—all emotional and so very gorgeous—filled the screen. "My father was a *bleep* fiend."

He cleared his throat. The whites of his eyes were red and the skin beneath them puffy. I'd seen the Spencer who hadn't gotten enough sleep many times before, and he looked worse than that. Not only that, but he was thinner. *When was the last time he ate?*

"And he was a *bleep* piece of *bleep*." Spencer twisted his mouth and nose to sniff. "I called you here because I want the world to know that I'm deeply ashamed, and I know the rest of my family is too. I'll do whatever it takes to bring these girls some justice and make amends for what they endured to get…" He shook his head.

"Your father's dead, nitwit," Jimmy yelled from behind me. "Justice? What are you going to do, go to prison for him?"

Again, I had to keep myself from yelling at him to zip it.

Hannibal pinched his chin, frowning intently. Anyone who watched him interview important people knew that when he did that, he was about to ask a rug-pulling question. My mouth fell open, and I gradually leaned forward in anticipation.

"But you also partook in the prostitution ring."

Spencer narrowed his eyes at Hannibal. Then his Adam's apple bobbed as he swallowed. "When I was younger, my father made me *bleep*. I sure as hell didn't want to do it. I've been working on the part of my soul that was wounded because of that. That's why I was here, looking, and was able to find this."

Hannibal leaned back and glanced at the camera. It was clear he hadn't expected Spencer to be so candid. "I see." He cleared his throat. "I'm sorry," he said, his voice cracking. "We all have our demons, don't we?"

Spencer turned to glare at the wall. "But we don't have to keep them."

"Yes, yes, yes," Hannibal said, nodding.

I could tell that Spencer's words had thrown Hannibal off his game. He put his hand on Spencer's shoulder. "Thanks for giving us the exclusive on this." He turned to the camera. "This is a special report. Now back to Stan Rochester in the studio."

"Turn it off!" Jimmy Lovell said.

As usual, Ron Wesley, Jimmy's campaign manager, told Riley, an assistant, to fulfill the request. Suddenly, the back of my seat was pushed, and I shifted forward. Then Jimmy's face appeared beside mine. "That was a bullshit publicity stunt your ex was pulling, and don't you forget it."

I felt that if he remained there a second longer, I would burst like a balloon that had too much hot air inside it. After one month, I'd already had my fill of Jimmy Lovell. My initial opinion of him was right on the money. When he gave interviews, he always sounded as if he was whining about the opposition's position on a political matter. Twice, when I'd been to lunch with him, a waitress complained he'd groped her ass, even though none of us saw it. He was a sneaky fucker—not to mention entitled as hell. He was the sort of person who would send back food because it was a tad bit too cold or too hot and never left even a dime as a tip. I'd never hated anyone in my life, but Jimmy was starting to change that. When my mother was around, he behaved like a golden son. But when she wasn't, he acted like a sniveling brat. So far, he'd made my job extra hard, since it was difficult to sell the world on someone I had zero confidence in. Two nights before at a fundraiser, I'd blurted a laugh in the middle of my introduction because I couldn't believe I'd written on my note card that he was an intelligent, strong millennial with the drive to be a force that would lead our country into the future. Sure, I'd gotten seven hot-button words into one sentence, but none of them were true of Jimmy Lovell.

"Got it?" Jimmy said right dead in my ear.

I inhaled deeply through my nose. "Get away from me." I was still holding my breath.

"Not until you tell me you got it."

I felt my eyes narrow to slits. "Move. Now!" My voice blared through the cabin.

He played drums on the arm of my seat, further annoying me. "All you have to do is say yes."

"How fucking old are you?" I shouted. "Get

away from me." My body cringed with anger. I felt strong enough to rip him into shreds.

"Jim!" Ron called. "Leave her alone."

Ron knew that from day one, I'd had both feet out the door, waiting for the rest of me to follow. He was always watching me like a hawk, keeping Jimmy off my back as much as he could. When Ron spoke, Jimmy mostly obeyed—suppressed daddy issues, I supposed. Ron was a handsome fifty-three-year-old with white hair and youthful skin. He had no wife or children but had been running the sort of campaign that got politicians elected since he was twenty-five. So far, he'd been ten for ten. Jimmy was his eleventh. After November, Ron's average was likely to change to ten for eleven. Or maybe not. Ron's tactics were cutthroat—he tended to destroy the competition and make his stinky candidate smell like a rose. And Jimmy smelled like a pit bull with bad gas.

Once Jimmy stepped far away from me, I tried to fantasize about being in my bed with Spencer back at the ranch, but I couldn't.

"I said ice water," Jimmy barked at the flight attendant.

"Sorry, Mr. Lovell, but the water does have ice in it." I couldn't see her face, but I could hear her trying to be genial without making him feel like the idiot he was.

"One, two, three cubes? You call that ice water?"

Instead of Spencer's beautiful face, I visualized Jimmy's pinched expression staring up at her, waiting for a reply to his stupid question. I massaged my temples.

"I apologize, Mr. Lovell. I'll get you another glass of water."

"And with how many cubes of ice?" he asked in a condescending tone.

The heat blazed through my throat as I shouted, "Will you fucking leave her alone about the fucking ice water?"

It was quiet, like it had been when we were watching Spencer on TV. Not even the tiniest part of me wanted to apologize for my outburst. I wasn't sorry, and I wanted him to stop hassling the flight attendant at every turn and behave like something other than a spoiled, entitled, whiny brat for once. For that reason, I didn't turn around.

"Thank you, Rachael," Ron said in his usual voice of reason. My mother had somehow convinced him to tolerate me too. *Hot damn*, I wanted to be fired. But now that the outburst was over, they all went back to going over the logistics for that night's donor event as if I hadn't chastised the snobby marquis of shit sticks.

FOR THE REST OF THE FLIGHT, NO ONE ASKED ME TO join the planning meeting as they should have. As my mom had wanted, I was tasked with the job of convincing special donors to buy into Jimmy's image enough to pay a lot of money and see the value of him being elected to Congress. I tried not to think about what to say to sway them. Once the moment arrived, my green light would turn on, and I'd usually put on the performance of a lifetime, complete with fake smiles, chuckling, and lies galore. Just thinking about it made me queasy. It wasn't that I didn't like the job. On the contrary—I preferred my current job duties over the ones performed while working for Spencer. Other than my burst of laughter the other night while reading my own words, I'd been pretty successful pawning the little shit's contrived image to voters and donors. When it was time for him to turn on his public persona, he mostly did what I said. We were still working on eliminating the way he whined when he spoke. He thought it was effective and named a number of loser politicians who employed the same tactic. Jimmy was probably right, but it annoyed me to no end, so him talking without whining was nonnegotiable as far as I was concerned.

When our flight landed, we all got into black SUVs with tinted windows and headed to Washington, DC, to our hotel. The fact that I ended up in the car alone with Ron wasn't by accident. I'd long known we had a conversation on the horizon.

"Okay, spill it," I said as soon as the vehicle started moving.

Ron studied me. I felt the hardness in my expression and in my heart. I liked Ron as a person. He wasn't a bad guy, even though he was a dangerous one. In just a short time, I'd figured out that the worst kind of politician was one with no fucking belief system whatsoever. And those were the sort of losers Ron made into winners.

"It must have been difficult to watch the interview with Spencer Christmas."

He leaned back to study my reaction. He had a way of making a statement that wasn't quite a question but nonetheless inspired an answer. I pressed my lips shut, determined to not give him what he was fishing for.

He shifted in his seat, signaling a change of strategy. "Jim's an asshole. We all get it."

I folded my arms. "Then why are you trying to make him a congressman?"

"Because he'll be an ally for your mother."

I cracked a shrewd smile. What an angle he had chosen. He went straight to the reason why I had to endure a cross country flight with the last person in the world I wanted to be around.

"Yes... my mom knows how to get what she wants, I'm learning," I said.

Ron raised his eyebrows. "Learning? I'm pretty sure you've always known."

I felt my eyebrows draw inward. I was pretty sure he was right, and I was still trying to come to grips with that. My mom had wanted to take me away from Spencer, and she'd succeeded. She'd wanted me on Jimmy's campaign, and here I was. Buckling to my mom's will wasn't new to me, although it was only recently that I was seriously trying to wrap my mind around why I did it.

"Listen..." He adjusted his sitting position again. I had long ago realized that was his strategic way of jolting the other people's brains to accept whatever brand-new angle he was using to try to convince them to see things his way. "You're very talented at what you do, Jada. I like you on our team. The fact that Jim gets under your skin and you still do your best on his behalf says a lot about your work ethic and your abilities." He paused to pick apart my expression. I continued to show him my poker face, but *damn*, he was good—I was chomping on his every word as he inspired something new inside me. Even though I wanted out, I could securely say that I was one hundred percent back on the team and ready to do the job.

"You have Alice and Howard Templeton on your radar tonight?" His tone was highly inquisitive. I took note that Ron knew he had gotten through to me. I had no idea what gave me away. He must have seen my emotions reflected in my eyes.

I cleared my throat. "Yes."

"Their support of Jimmy would be major. They'll open opportunities for him that other candidates won't have. Have you figured out your pitch to the Templetons?"

I sighed forcefully, and suddenly, I wanted to be far away from Ron and my mission for the evening. I hated that he'd played me and had won. As I thought about his question, I felt forced to come up with a different answer than the truth—which was that normally, unless I was giving a speech, I was more effective if I winged it as far as Jimmy was concerned. I'd discovered that the worst thing I could do was spend time thinking about how to peddle a walking, talking shit show to donors.

"I'm going to sell Jim to them through my mom's eyes," I said instead.

"Tell me more."

Shit. I sighed. My eyes darted to the right. I had to come up with something quick. "Alice is loyal to my mother. So I'll hint that Jimmy's her boy and what he does for Patricia, he'll do for Alice."

He nodded thoughtfully and winked. "I like that strategy. Make them believe support for Jimmy is the same as support for Patricia."

I released a sigh of relief. "Yeah."

Ron nodded sharply. "Good. Very good." He slid his cellphone out of his jacket. I watched him closely as he focused on the screen. He was finished with me, I presumed. In his mind, I'd been successfully handled. I wondered how much of what he'd said regarding needing me on the campaign had been bullshit. Jimmy certainly needed my mother's support to win. And Ron needed to make my mother happy to keep his job. It was the emotional circle of life, filled with assholes who did whatever it took to get what they wanted.

Ron made a phone call to the event coordinator, doing more listening to her than talking, mostly saying, "Yes... uh-huh... no... maybe." He was definitely the sneakiest individual I'd ever met.

Maybe not...

Finally, he glanced at me and flashed a tight smile. I didn't look away. There was something else I knew he was aware of. The illumination of it struck me in the brain. He knew I didn't believe in my mom, which was why he had to be careful during his phone calls. I wasn't truly on the team. I used to believe in my mom, but I wasn't sure if I did anymore. I was sitting in the back seat of the SUV with Ron, which testified to the fact that I was still one of her sycophants, but maybe I wasn't one to the same degree as all the other people associated with Patricia Forte.

Ron winked at me. I winked back. He cocked his head as if he hadn't expected me to respond that way. But that was when I knew he could be defeated. It wasn't that I planned to oppose him, but I felt safer knowing I could make him break from all his carefully crafted responses.

WE LOOKED LIKE A CARAVAN OF IMPORTANT PEOPLE as all our vehicles pulled up to the valet station, one behind the other. I very much disliked the spectacle, but everyone else seemed to thrive on it. The inside of the hotel was simply spectacular. It felt as if we'd stepped into the foyer of Kensington Palace. On top of that, the staff was super attentive in a way that said they were used to dealing with politicos and dignitaries. The concierge, a young man in a black suit complete with tie and vest, passed out our keys not long after we stepped into the lobby.

The others were making plans to hang out at the bar to see if they could make some pre-event connections. It was clear I wasn't going to join them —not only because I hadn't taken the time to make soulful connections with my campaign team members but also because the less I had to sell people on the idea of a possible Senator Lovell, the better. As soon as I had my keycard in my hand, I told everyone that I'd see them later and headed to the elevator.

"Hey, Jada," I heard when I was a few steps from my destination.

I braced myself then turned around. "Yes, Jimmy." The smile I gave him was even too fake for my comfort, so I released it some.

He walked faster, checking over both sides of his shoulders as if he didn't want anyone to hear what he was going to say. "I apologize for what happened on the plane," he whispered.

He had a way of searching people's faces while he was being insincere to see if they were buying his bullshit.

"Let me get this." I started counting down on my fingers. "You're apologizing to *me* for being an asshole to the flight attendant." I squished one side of my face as I tilted my head. "Ummm... that just doesn't add up, Jimmy."

"What? A guy can't ask for extra cold water?" He was whining again.

"Yes, a guy can ask for extra cold water. It's about how a guy asks for extra cold water that makes him either tolerable or an asshole."

His eyes widened. I'd seen that expression from him often. My words were hitting whatever emotional wall he'd erected inside of himself to not absorb what I was saying.

"I came over to say I'm sorry. That's all," he said.

I wanted to ask him if Ron had put him up to the apology, but it wasn't Ron's style. "See you later." I turned my back on him.

"That's it," he said loudly.

I turned around again. "Okay… apology accepted." I didn't mean it, but I had no problem throwing a dog a bone so that he would go away to fetch it.

He cracked a smirk, and my heart sank because I knew what was coming next. "How about we grab a drink or something before the event? Let's finally get to know each other better." His eyes ventured down to the very small amount of cleavage I was showing in my black knee-length sheath dress.

First I scoffed. Then I said, "Later, Jimmy." And this time, when I whipped around, I had no intention of looking at him until I absolutely had to.

CHAPTER SIX

JADA FORTE

I felt more refreshed after showering. The flight, Jimmy's immaturity, and Ron's mind fuck during our ride to the hotel had all washed down the drain. I'd changed into an elegant black spaghetti-strapped cocktail dress that wasn't too sexy. The last time I'd led with my tits while working, Spencer was my boss. I had a few more minutes before showtime, and I used them to sit in front of the window and gaze at a nighttime view of the Capitol Building. I debated whether or not to call Spencer. Lately, whenever I called him, I didn't even get the message informing me that his phone wasn't taking calls—the call merely rang once and ended. Begging for the affection of a guy who was no longer into me wasn't my style. But after seeing

Spencer with Hannibal Newton earlier, I wondered whether he'd been too distraught to reach out to me. Before I could totally pardon Spencer of the offense of loving me and leaving me, I remembered Carol's warning about him eating me up and spitting me out.

"Maybe not," I muttered.

Maybe so.

On that note, I slid my phone into my cocktail purse, slipped on my way too-tight two-inch heels, along with my warm black cardigan, and headed out.

THE EVENT WAS PACKED. JIMMY WASN'T THE ONLY candidate seeking financial donations from the ultra-wealthy people in the room. The fastest way to get through the night was to start working immediately. When I located Alice Templeton, she was already watching me expectantly. Alice, who was in her seventies, had a majestic appearance that made her stand out in the company of mere mortals. She and I had once had lunch together, about a week after I moved to New York, and she told me all about how she used to be a fashion model who booked gigs from Manhattan to Milan, strutting the runways for some of the world's top designers. Before she met her husband, Howard, she dated dignitaries and royalty. Even though she herself came from old money, Howard was something like thirty-sixth in line for the throne. Of course, he would never be king, but that didn't stop him from behaving as if he was responsible for the well-being of the entire world.

I first met Alice when I was a teenager at one of my mother's fundraisers. "She's a stunning beauty," Alice had said to my mom and then met my eyes. "I can see why she's here."

No matter what, I always remembered her saying that. At times, I'd run away from those words, but that was only when I was on the precipice of grasping the meaning of them. The older I got and the more events I attended, the more I pretended I had no idea what Alice had meant. I was a pretty, smart, and wholesome daughter. My mother used me to sell donors and voters on the idea that she was the purveyor of the American dream.

Alice nodded, and I knew that was my cue. I walked over and took the coveted seat beside her.

"Jada, your mother finally has you officially in

her stable," she said after we kissed each other on both cheeks.

I remembered to make the right kind of smile. If it was too high, my insincerity would show, and if it was too low, I would appear unenthusiastic about my job and my goal to get her money.

"Well…" I was going to say I wasn't there on my mother's behalf, but Alice knew good and well that my mother was on the menu for the night. She was letting me know she knew the truth—Jimmy was a representative of my mother's interests. That thought put a heavy feeling in the pit of my stomach. "I'm up for trying most things at least once." I smiled, and this time it was sincere.

She leaned away from me, studying my expression as if taken aback by my response. Finally, she grunted thoughtfully. "Then let's hear it. How can I help your candidate?"

I intensified my shrewd grin. "Give him money, of course."

Alice chuckled. "You're taking the direct route." She shook her finger. "It shows how green you're pretending to be. I need to hear more bullshit before you stick your hand in my pocketbook, darling." She was grinning, loving the dance to separate her from her cash. "However, I am curious

—what do you think of your mother's divorce campaign?"

She was too damn blunt, and I couldn't hide my surprise. After a minute, I closed my mouth and swallowed nervously to gather my bearings. "My mother is doing what she feels is right." *Shit*. I was defending her. I'd promised I wasn't going to do that, despite the fact that it was my advice she was following—although I was positive she'd been planning to take that approach long before I mentioned it.

"I didn't ask how she felt. I wanted to know what you thought about it," Alice clarified.

I sighed, almost feeling ambushed by her question. "I'm going on thirty, Alice. Truth be told, I always knew my parents weren't that much in love. They've always been partners, and that was much to my detriment—the way they would tag-team me." I chuckled, and Alice smiled. "The good thing is my mother never sold me on the illusion of marriage. So I really don't care if they're divorced."

She leaned toward me. "And your father's son?"

Her question shook me like the first jolt of an earthquake, which I gathered it was designed to do. I hadn't actually given it much thought. First of all, I hadn't seen my father since Christmas dinner.

He'd been conveniently traveling around Europe and Asia on business. But basically, when it came to my father's love child, I'd been actively engaged in a classic case of avoidance.

I shrugged. "I'll cross that road when I get to it." I knew my smile was rather smug, and I didn't care.

Alice studied me and then shifted abruptly in her seat. "Your candidate is too young, darling. My tastes are more seasoned."

I was actually prepared for her to say that, and I felt relieved. I scooted my chair closer to hers. "A wise woman once taught me to always know why I do what I do and, no matter what it is, know why I do it. I could feed you the BS about Jimmy Lovell being able to speak to the younger generation, but Jimmy has no concern about his peers. You support my mother, don't you?"

She narrowed an eye astutely. "Russ Connor, Macy Young, Jill Matthews, and Patricia Forte. Which one did you vote for in the previous midterm elections?"

A sense of panic raced through me. *Why would she ask me that question? Does she know?* Since the first time I stepped in the ballot box, I'd never voted for Patricia Forte. When I was nineteen, it was because

I was angry with her for choosing politics over being a good mother. Since then, it was because I loved my mother but simply didn't like her very much.

Just then, the emcee, Bob Mayberry—who looked and sounded like a seasoned game-show host—called everyone to their seats. I asked Alice if we could talk later. She said she was looking forward to my answer. I definitely needed time to form a response, one that wasn't quite a lie but got me what Jimmy's campaign needed from her.

When I stood, my gaze connected with Ron, who was sitting at the table behind us. There was a look of warning in his eyes. Perhaps he knew, just as I did, that I was losing Alice's support.

As I sat at the large round table with my party, I was still processing Alice's question, wondering whether I should tell the truth or lie outright. I was beginning to think that in these circles, lying was a strength and perhaps she was waiting for me to tell an enormous whopper. As the emcee told us all to prepare to be served dinner, my eyes roamed the room. I paid closer attention to what was actually going on. Nothing looked off. I'd been to countless events just like this one. I'd accepted what I saw and my interactions at face value. However, this evening, I couldn't help feeling as if there was a deeper reality that was occurring beneath the surface. There were lots of conversations. It was my job to talk to all the donors in the room, which meant I had a lot of socializing to do before the night ended. Not one benefactor was disengaged. Rachel Corwin, a woman notorious for kissing ass, had taken the seat beside Alice that I had abandoned. She caught me watching her, and she smirked right before I looked away. My curious gaze fell on Jimmy, who was already staring at me. I wasn't sure he knew he was giving me way too much eye service. After a server set his plate on the table in front of him, he actually said thank you, but it was part of his performance. Only at events like this would he show that he indeed knew how to behave as if he had manners and respect for others.

He smiled at me, perhaps looking for a sign that I was happy about what I was sure was his one and only thank you of the day. I cut my eyes off his face and planted them on Mayberry.

"Thank you all for attending tonight's dinner," the emcee said.

As he went into a spiel about putting the focus

on issues that mattered, which was why we were all gathered together, my mind was still trying to make sense of the recent examination. The room was full of people engaged in competition or seeking respect. It was all extreme, like an Olympic sport. And there I was, someone who actually liked the game but loathed playing it for my candidate.

"While you all enjoy tonight's great dinner made by the hands of celebrity chef Pierre Colbert, you'll hear from various donors who'll tell you what issues facing our great nation are important to them and why. And first up is Charles Buck."

Mayberry stepped away from the microphone, and up walked a round, balding man with horn-rimmed glasses who kept his focus on the page he was reading from as he spoke. His tone was just as lackluster as his performance, which made it easier to tune him out even though it was my job to listen to him intently. He wasn't really saying much other than stringing together sentences full of clichés and hot-button words. As I raised my eyebrows in delight at our first course—a micro-greens and pear salad with organic honey, cinnamon walnuts, and pecans—I realized his code words didn't match the ones Ron had so rigidly made sure I inserted into every speech, letter, or introduction. Instead of further assessing Buck's speech, listening for whether I should take a chance and approach him, I chose to relish every bite and debate with myself whether or not I'd ever eaten a salad so delicious.

"I want to cut to the chase," another next speaker said. I hadn't heard his name, but his voice sounded familiar, so I forced my attention off my next bite and twisted all the way around to see who it was.

My jaw dropped. *What the hell?* My head felt floaty, and my eyes widened past their normal limit. It was Spencer, and he was the only man in the room who wasn't wearing a suit. Instead, he had on a red button-front shirt and black slacks that fit him as if they were made by Brioni or Armani. He didn't look like a donor or an ass-kisser. However, his presence demanded that all eyes turn to him.

"Each year, I receive the same invitation asking me to join you at this…" He narrowed his eyes to slits and held them in that position for a long, suspenseful moment. "Shindig. I never attend, mainly because I know how you all operate. But I happened to be in town today. The feds had questions about some of you who are here." He paused to absorb the murmuring. I almost passed out when his scowl landed on me. He kept it there when he said, "Recently, I hired someone who was sharp as a fucking tack. She uncovered a scheme perpetrated by a guy named Dillon Gross. Does that name ring a bell to any of you?" As he paused to glare at the guests, I wanted to see who exactly he was looking at, but I couldn't take my eyes off him. He looked well, and that made me happy. But more than that, he looked yummy, and all I wanted was to catch a whiff of him before he left the room. The fact that I was the employee he thought was as sharp as a tack hadn't gone unnoticed either. I was very curious about what I'd done that made the FBI want to question him.

Spencer went on to slowly explain how campaigns were setting up foreign investment funds where the dividends paid to shareholders were actually donations made by foreign actors who worked in the interest of hostile governments. I gasped along with everyone else as I recalled how Dillon had attempted to use flirtation to convince me to fast-track documents that needed Spencer's approval. My intuition warned me he could possibly be up to no good, so I'd decided to add supporting details to give Spencer a more complete picture of what Dillon was asking for in his request for a signature. Spencer was now calling out names, outing those who had accounts in that illegal investment fund.

Whispers filled the room.

He stopped to glare at our table. I was sure he wasn't looking at me, which was why I turned to look over my left shoulder. I measured his line of sight again. Spencer had set his focus on Jimmy. Then he called his name.

I gasped, not because I was shocked but because I felt as if Spencer knew he was my mother's guy and was, once again, punching her in the face as an act of retaliation. Part of me felt she deserved it. The other part wished Spencer had figured out a way to first confide in me.

Someone yelled, "Enough of this."

Another person yelled, "Get him off."

Bob Mayberry approached Spencer, who threw up a hand, warning him to keep his distance. Bob stopped in his tracks, and Spencer continued naming names.

"Rand Lovell, Chris Lovell, Doug Nelson, and…" He was glaring at me, and there was no doubt about it.

My heart felt as if it was beating out of my chest. I knew who was on that list. Would he say her name?

"Boo," someone from my table called. I quickly turned to look at Ron, who had his hands cupped around his mouth. "Boo. Get him off."

Soon everyone at the table had joined him—all but me. The lack of decorum my counterparts were showing in the face of what we had just learned was shocking. I would have recommended we play it differently by keeping coolheaded, but I was learning that my way was far too decent for people like those who were present. I wanted to run up to the microphone and position myself at Spencer's side.

He remained standing tall with his focus solidly on me as he calmly folded the page he'd just read from and slipped it into his pocket. "I gave your names to the authorities. Do what you will with this warning."

Ron continued the booing as Spencer strolled past the tables of stunned guests and out the exit. I quickly stood, and so did Jimmy.

"Don't you run after him. If you do, you're fired," Jimmy said, once again the inherent douchebag, breaking his Academy Award-winning performance as a kindly candidate.

The dare in his eyes made me quicken. It was something new from him. He had always been an entitled twat but never a transparent bully. Now he'd given me another reason to dislike him. I shrugged indifferently, glaring at him with my lip curled. Then I snatched my cocktail bag from the back of my seat, along with my cardigan, and ran after Spencer.

The hotel felt grander than I remembered as I raced up the hallway. I made sure to look into every empty room or corridor. By the time I reached the lobby, I was breathing heavily. I stopped where I had a clear view of most of the grand space. He wasn't sitting on the sofas or standing at the front desk. I scurried over to the hotel bar. He wasn't seated at the counter or any of the tables. I ran outside, searching up and down the carport. A black SUV with tinted windows had just made a right onto the busy main street, and something deep inside told me that that was him. My shoulders curled forward. Spencer was gone.

AFTER I WALKED BACK INSIDE, I STOOD IN FRONT OF the revolving doors, eyes closed, scratching my temples. I didn't want to go back into the ballroom, even though, regardless of Jimmy's empty threat, I still had a job to do. I seriously didn't want to do it anymore. I shook my head, deciding to return to my room and think about how I would proceed as far as my job went. I had money in my account since Spencer had paid me for six weeks. On top of that, I'd been paid my monthly salary from my current shitty job. After paying off all my credit-card debt, I still had a pretty healthy bank account. I could quit my current job, but if I did that, then what? My heart raced as the elevator doors slid open. My hopes were thwarted when I didn't see Spencer inside. Deep down, I'd been hoping for one of those cinematic moments where the man I'd been chasing suddenly appeared.

I moved back to give four people space to walk out, and then I stepped in. My finger was on its way to hit the button for the sixteenth floor when an arm of someone wearing a red shirt stopped the doors from closing. I forgot to breathe while looking into Spencer's eyes, up close and personal, once again.

CHAPTER SEVEN

JADA FORTE

Spencer stepped into the elevator car and stood in front of me. The heat and energy from his body made me feel dazed. A young couple entered behind him.

"Can you push eighteen?" the man asked.

Spencer kept his smirk on me as he quickly did what the man asked.

"Wait, I recognize you," the man said. "You're Spencer Christmas."

"Oh my God," his female partner said. "It is him." She pressed her hand over her mouth. "I saw your interview. It was moving, and I'm sorry about…" Her eyebrows squished together.

Spencer frowned at her, and she instantly

retreated into the safety of her mate's arms. Finally, Spencer nodded briskly. "Thank you."

The couple looked at each other, perhaps trying to figure out whether the energy Spencer was giving off was hostile or not. I remembered being in their shoes. It was certainly a confusing place to be. They looked relieved when Spencer and I stepped out of the elevator, their eyes shifting between us.

He and I were now alone in the long hallway, gazing into each other's eyes. I felt so many things going on inside. I was afraid that he would disappear into thin air, or worse, that he was only a figment of my imagination.

"That sure was a bombshell you dropped downstairs," I finally said, hoping my words didn't send him running for the hills.

His lips parted, and he swallowed. "It had to be done."

I felt my eyebrows pull. "Did it?"

"Yes." Spencer wrapped his arms around my waist and put his mouth near my ear. "Now, take me to sixteen twenty-one."

My soul fluttered. "Wait…" My head spun. I had a question I'd been wanting to ask him ever since he made it to the end of his list of offenders. I looked at him and felt as if he was speaking with his eyes.

"What?" he whispered and gently kissed me on the lips.

I swallowed the moisture in my throat. "You said, 'and.'"

He pulled back, frowning. "When did I say 'and'?"

"You had one more name on your list."

"I had plenty more names on my list."

I jerked my head. "Are you really going to do this right now? Just say it, Spencer."

All of a sudden, he tugged me against him, and his tongue was in my mouth. His taste, the feel of his lips against mine, the way his hair felt between my fingers—the familiarity was back.

"Yes, your mother," he whispered and sank his tongue deep into my mouth again.

I felt starved for Spencer Christmas and satisfied that he'd exposed Patricia Forte only to her daughter. I moaned like a lost kitten as our kissing deepened. I took backward steps across the red carpet as Spencer guided me to my room. Not once did I stumble, or our lips break contact. I pulled his shirt up by the hem so I could feel his skin. Finally we stopped in front of my door.

"Key," he said in a fiery whisper and sank his tongue into my ear.

The erogenous sensation made me cream as I fumbled to open my purse. Thank goodness I didn't have much in it besides my wallet, cellphone, and room key. As soon as I had the keycard in my hand, he took it and opened the door.

SPENCER LIFTED MY DRESS OVER MY HEAD. I STOOD before him in only my panties, no bra, and he certainly liked the sight of my bare chest because he muttered a string of expletives before taking my left breast almost completely into his mouth while guiding me down onto the bed.

I whimpered and sighed, feeling his nibbling and the whirling of his tongue around my nipple as his fingers dove in and out of my pussy. Then he raked his teeth across the tip of my other nipple before sucking it into his hungry mouth. He went from right to left, consuming my body as if starved for me.

Then suddenly, he stopped. When I opened my eyes, Spencer was staring at my face. The seconds mounted, and we couldn't look away from each other.

"I missed you," he whispered.

"I missed you too. Why didn't you return my calls?"

His frown deepened. "You called me?"

I felt my brows pinch. "So many times I can't count."

Spencer tilted his head thoughtfully. "Oh…" He flung himself next to me on the bed and rolled onto his back then covered his face with his hands, laughing into his palms.

"What is it?"

"I should've fucking known."

"Known what?" I asked, completely lost about whatever he could mean.

"Your father did something that disrupted communication between our devices."

I shook my head ardently as I sat up. "No way. My dad wouldn't do that."

Spencer rolled off the bed to stand. "You think your father's a saint?"

I felt my face squeeze into a frown. "Well… he's not like my mother."

"Your father does whatever your mother says,

even pretending to be married to her to preserve her image."

"That's not fair, Spencer."

He rammed the hem of his shirt back into his pants. "And he never told you that you had a brother. Doesn't sound like an honest stand-up guy to me."

My mouth was caught open, my mind unable to absorb the awful things he was saying about the only ally I had in my immediate family. Spencer's expression was hard and detached. We'd had difficult conversations before, but this time, I felt as if my opposing position made him dislike me.

"Are you leaving?" I asked.

"Why didn't you just come back?"

I felt exposed, so I crossed my arms over my tits. "What do you mean?"

"You could've gotten on a flight and flown back to Wyoming, but you didn't."

"Why didn't you ever tell me about my parents?"

"It wasn't my job to tell you about your parents."

"But you had me investigated?"

Spencer studied me carefully. "From the first day I

met you, I knew you were a fucking parent-pleaser. I knew it because I saw myself in you. Instead of flying back to Wyoming to resume your job, here you are in this fucking hotel, working for your mother. The only reason I didn't say her name in front of those donors is because of you. But now I'm questioning my decision not to expose her for the political parasite that she is."

His words made me cringe, but I tried not let him see it. Of course, he was right, but I couldn't detach myself from whatever unknown thing tethered me to my mother.

A new revelation hit me. "Then you told the FBI?"

"I had to, yes."

All I could picture was my mom in handcuffs and an orange jumpsuit, and the vision made my heart sink.

Spencer sniffed sharply as he turned his back on me and walked to the door.

"Spencer," I called. He stopped but didn't turn around. "You're right. I could've gone back to the ranch and resumed my job, but..." I closed my eyes. "You didn't have to out my parents at the dinner table in front of their guests. I think I was upset about that, but I'm not anymore." I squeezed the sides of my head, knowing I should have kept all that to myself.

Spencer turned to glance at me across his shoulder. Then without another word, he opened the door and walked out, leaving me all alone.

I LAY ON THE BED FOR A WHILE, TRYING TO FIGURE out what in the hell had just happened. I went over and over our conversation. Honesty hadn't done me any good. No wonder people lied. Then I realized why he'd had to leave. He knew he couldn't love me if I kept choosing my mother.

The tears rolled. I pressed my forearms over my eyes, increasing the pressure, attempting to push myself into the mattress and disappear.

Knock, knock, knock.

I sat up, sniffed, and wiped the tears from my face. He knocked again.

"Give me a few seconds," I called as I rushed to put on my robe, deep down believing for certain it was Spencer, returning to accept my apology—one I was willing to give—and then make mad passionate love to me.

I swung the door open, and my big smile turned upside down. "Mom?" I said, surprised.

"Why aren't you downstairs at the dinner?" Patricia said.

I stood in the middle of the threshold. Since I got my height from my dad, I towered over her.

"Mom, what are you doing here?" I felt spent and sounded that way too.

She shook her head as if thoroughly disappointed in me. "You have a job to do, darling, and it's downstairs and not in here." She tried to barge into my room, but I continued using my body as a barricade. "Move out of the way."

"Mom, again, what are you doing here?" I made my tone clear.

"Move out of the way, Jada," she said, enunciating every syllable.

I knew what I had to do. The drive to do it took over my mind, my heart, and my limbs. I let whatever was going on inside me energize me, saturate me. I did step back but only to do one thing—slam the door in her face. The sound blasted loudly in my room. Next, I locked the door and waited. My mom didn't even call my name. She was probably just as shocked by my actions as I was. I felt powerful and wished

Spencer was there to see it. That old familiar tug wanted me to open the door and let my mom into my room so that I could apologize profusely. However, I squeezed my eyes shut, fighting the yearning.

"No," I whispered. "No way."

As long as my feet were walking in the opposite direction of whatever Patricia Forte wanted, I decided to let them keep taking me away.

CHAPTER EIGHT

JADA FORTE

"Ma'am? Miss Forte?" a man called. My heart raced. I was halfway inside of the cab, following my luggage, which I'd stuffed into the back seat before me. I plopped my buttocks onto the seat and was just about to close the door when I saw the concierge running toward me, shaking an envelope. "This is for you."

I hesitated before taking it. "Thank you," I said with a sigh, feeling totally drained.

I couldn't open the letter as long as tension remained in my body. Not until we were off the property of the hotel and rolling up the main avenue could I relax. While packing my things, I'd called Hope and asked if I could stay with her for a few days until I figured out other living arrangements. She gasped dramatically and said I could stay in her place for as long as I needed and she'd pick me up from the airport—all I had to do was text her my flight details. Hope also said she had something to tell me but didn't want to say it over the phone. She asked me what happened—"Why the mad dash out of DC?"—and I told her I didn't want to recount the details of the evening over the phone either.

To my dismay, there was traffic on the main streets. The driver explained that the gridlock was the result of several rallies earlier in the day and planned roadwork. I looked down at the envelope in my hands. Hoping it was from Spencer, I ripped it open, careful to not damage the contents.

I pulled a typewritten letter out of the envelope. It read,

Jada,

This is Alice. Meet me at Constantine's on 7th Street NW at 10:30 p.m. I want to talk to you, darling, but not about Lovell.

My hand fluttered to my neck as I wondered what in the hell she wanted. I checked the time on my cellphone. She wanted to meet in twelve minutes. I liked Alice. But she was a friend and a trusty supporter of my mother. It would have been just like Patricia to use my affection for Alice to trap me. I didn't know what to do. Was I afraid of my mom? No. Truth be told, I wasn't finished battling it out with her. I had this newfound feeling of empowerment, and if she was at Constantine's with Alice, attempting to ambush me, she'd better be ready for a fight.

"Excuse me, but could you please take me to Constantine's on…"

"I know the address." The cabbie whipped a right at the next corner.

WHEN I ARRIVED AT THE BAR, I WAS SHOCKED TO only see Alice waiting for me. Alice must have seen me walking toward her through the mirror behind the bar because she spiraled around on her stool and watched me, her expression brightening.

"Hi, Alice," I said, smiling faintly but wishing I had the motivation to be more of a bitch.

She pointed to the empty stool beside her. "I saved you a seat."

I climbed up on the tall chair and looked at her, waiting for her to explain why she'd asked me to meet her.

"That was some event, wasn't it?" she asked, grinning.

I grunted, raising my eyebrows. Then the bartender, grinning from ear to ear, asked if I wanted to order a drink. I wouldn't have noticed his expression if I hadn't felt annoyed that it was the direct opposite of what I felt. Regardless, I ordered club soda with lime.

"No cocktail?" Alice asked.

"I have a long night ahead of me."

She just smiled. "I see… you didn't return to the event." Her tone was leading me to explain.

"And my job, Alice. I'm no longer affiliated with Jimmy's campaign."

"Your mother doesn't seem to believe that."

"Well, my mother is free to believe whatever she likes."

The bartender set my drink in front of me. I thanked him, and he winked at me. His apparent flirtation made me lean back a hair. I never used to notice such behavior from the opposite sex.

Alice leaned toward me. "He knows a true beauty when he sees one."

I smiled tightly, feeling way too antsy to discuss the guy behind the bar. "I'm sorry, but why am I here, Alice?"

She took a sip of her martini with an olive while regarding me shrewdly. "Do you know Spencer Christmas?"

I felt my frown intensify. "Yes."

"Intimately," she added.

I cocked my head. "Are you asking or making a statement?"

"The latter. He played very well in the media recently, exposing what Randolph did to those poor girls."

"Then you knew Spencer's father?" I asked because her tone indicated a familiarity with the subject.

"Randolph? Yes. You couldn't be associated with politics and not know Randolph Christmas. He had magnificent aspirations for his son Jasper. But after Randolph died, he chose to go in a different direction. Spencer Christmas, however…" She flexed her eyebrows twice. "His interview with Hannibal Newton is everywhere."

I looked off. For some reason, I felt a pinch of jealousy. I wanted Spencer to go undiscovered until I was sure his heart belonged to me and mine to him.

"I take it you didn't know the clip had become so popular."

I caught a glance of my grimace in the mirror and evened it out. "No, I didn't."

"Were you his media advisor?"

"No," I said with an edge. "His reaction was not a performance coached by me or anyone else. That's not Spencer's style."

She grunted thoughtfully. "Then that's good."

I took a sip of my drink, waiting for her to say more. We were almost done as far as I was concerned.

"Has he ever considered running for office?"

"Ha!" I said loudly.

"That would be a no."

"He doesn't like politicians, Alice. By the way, how deep are you in with my mother?"

A tiny smile formed across her lips as her eyes narrowed. "Why do you ask?"

I shrugged, feigning indifference. "Just curious."

"Well…" She chuckled. "I'm not deep into anyone, darling. Your mother is a strong ally. Patricia is great at getting the things that need to be done completed."

"Such as?" I quickly asked.

Alice placed her forearm on the bar and leaned into it. "I never took you for one of those black-or-white kinds of individuals, Jada."

I frowned, showing her that she needed to explain what the hell she meant by that.

"Life is complex, darling, and people even more so." Alice took a drink. "He loves you, which is why he didn't call her name."

"Sorry?" I said, frowning.

"Spencer Christmas loves you, which is why when he called the names of all who had been naughty, he left your mother off the list. Your mother…" She set her nearly full martini glass back on the bar. "She's a natural at winning. Patricia understands that all is fair in love and politics, which is why she'll do whatever it takes to keep her advantage. However, unfortunately, with her divorce tour and now this…" Alice closed her eyes as she shook her head. "I'm afraid she's tarnished. I need another ally in Washington."

I was shaking my head. *Who in the hell is this woman sitting beside me?* She'd lost her prim-and-proper posture. She looked like a poker player who was trying to win a high-stakes game, and for that reason, I knew I'd be a fool to trust her.

"You're going to trade her in just like that?" I asked. "You're not even going to give her the opportunity to make things right?"

She dipped her head to the side, grinning cleverly. "Darling, I've been around a long time. Knowing Patricia, she'll put up a valiant fight, but she's already lost."

Alice's splintering loyalty to my mother, a person she'd known for a very long time, was making me angry. And that was energy I didn't want to give the ordeal, because after thinking about it twice, I didn't care. So I hung the strap of my purse across my shoulder. "Spencer and I are no longer involved. You have to find another way to get to him." I slid off the barstool. "Good night, Alice." My voice was firm and lacked affection.

Alice gracefully dismounted her barstool. "When you see Mr. Christmas again, mention my offer to him and let him know that if he has my support, he'll win."

I felt as if my insides would explode. "Didn't you hear me? Spencer is not…"

She shook her finger. "Isn't he from the same state as Jimmy?"

My neck jutted forward. "Huh?"

"He would clobber Jimmy in an election. I have a feeling you would love to see that." Alice kissed me on both cheeks. "Lovely seeing you again, darling." She stared into my eyes. "You've certainly grown into a beautiful swan. I bet your mother never knew what you would become, because if she had, she would've tried something else."

She turned to walk out, and I suddenly remembered something. "Alice?" I called.

She stopped and turned all the way around to face me. "Yes, darling?"

"I voted for Macy Young."

Alice chortled. "That's what I figured."

I was completely flummoxed as I finished observing her exit. It was pretty impressive, actually, the way she'd flipped the moment to her advantage. But the part of me that admired such craftiness was quickly admonished by the part of me that hated the bullshit.

When she was gone, I sat back on the stool and signaled the bartender that I wanted to order a drink. "Vodka and cranberry, please," I said, needing something stronger after that encounter.

There was no way I would present her offer to Spencer. After one of our lovemaking sessions, he'd told me his theory about politicians. He said the best ones were ideologues. The worst ones loved the taste of power like a lioness loved the taste of blood in her mouth. The bloodthirsty ones were the majority. After he'd said that, I wanted to make love until I reached a state of oblivion. He was smart. I bet that he'd always been smart and his father never wanted to acknowledge it. Perhaps that was what Alice's last cryptic comment was about. My mom thought I would forever be her little drone—she would control my mind and would be the one I fiercely protected no matter what. I was that person, but I knew it was my responsibility to work like hell not to be that way anymore. If I kept waiting for Patricia to loosen her grasp and release me into complete independence, then I would never move an inch. I had to do it for myself.

The bartender leaned on the bar in front of me, grinning with his face close to mine. "Hey, so... I was wondering if you want to grab a late dinner. I'm off in ten minutes."

"The beauty part. What the hell did she mean by that?" I whispered to myself.

He smirked. "You are beautiful."

I could barely focus on the man's face. The stranger serving the drinks was cute but a mere mouse in a world where Spencer Christmas could be my man.

I dug into my purse and slapped a twenty on the lacquered wood. "Keep the change."

Only when I got to the door did I realize I'd forgotten to let the guy down gently. So I rushed back, but when I got close enough to him, he was already asking another woman out to dinner. I shook my head, chuckling, before heading to my final destination—back to Manhattan, my favorite city in the world.

CHAPTER NINE

JADA FORTE

Instead of waiting all night in the airport for a six a.m. flight to JFK, I rode the direct line from DC to Manhattan and arrived before four a.m. Hope still insisted on picking me up, even though I could have taken the subway to her apartment. She swooped in and picked me up on Thirty-First Street. We hugged before she tossed my suitcase in the trunk of her brand-new sleek silver car.

"You never told me you bought a new car," I said.

Her face was alight. "Hurry up and get in," she said impatiently.

From the passenger seat, I took in a deep whiff of the new-car smell. "What is it?" I asked once she was behind the wheel.

Her eyes were still shining. "Guess what?"

"What?" I said, happy to play along because it felt so good to be in her presence again.

Hope raised her hand, flashing me the ring on her finger.

My eyes grew wide. "What the hell? Is that an engagement ring?"

"I'm getting married!" she shouted, honking the horn in celebration like a madwoman.

My jaw dropped. "To whom?"

"Perry."

"Who's Perry? Because that's not the name of the district attorney who was driving you crazy between the sheets and in the courtroom three months ago."

She clutched the steering wheel, checking to see if the road was clear. "No. He was a pathological commitment-phobic douchebag. But Perry..." Her smile grew as big as the moon. "He's my one, and I'm his." As she guided the car along the street, she told me how the district attorney was one of those guys who fucked a girl until he was ready to move on to the next. "But you know what, Jada? Instead of crying over it or calling all guys horny scumbags with one-track minds, I decided to look in the fucking mirror." Even though the car kept racing forward, she turned her entire face in my direction. "Like, I literally looked in the mirror."

I pointed at the windshield. "Please look at the road."

She snapped her eyes forward. "And you know what I saw?"

Again, she looked at me, and once again, I pointed at the road. "What?" I finally said when she was facing in the right direction.

"I saw someone who picked assholes. So the next day, I was in court, getting my ass beat by Aaron, the DA I used to fuck, and when court adjourned for the day, I felt like shit, so I decided to go to Ben & Jerry's and buy a trough of Milk and Cookies to binge on while watching back-to-back episodes of *Fixer Upper*, and that's when this guy walks up to me and says, 'I know how it is when all you need is Milk and Cookies,' and then he paid for my ice cream."

"Wow," I said, trying to picture what she was describing.

"So, as I was standing there with my bag of ice cream, he was walking out of the shop, and I decided to run after him and ask if he wanted to grab dinner sometime."

I jerked my head back. "Whoa. You asked him."

She smiled proudly as we entered a parking garage. "Pretty progressive of me, right?"

"It is." I readjusted my position. "But how long have you known him? Because only three months ago, you were having sex with Aaron."

She rolled her eyes and shook her head. "It doesn't matter how long I've known him."

I squished my forehead. I looked at her doubtfully. "Well, it kind of does."

She grunted. "Don't fucking rain on my parade, Jada. I love him."

"Okay, then who is he?"

She pulled into a parking spot and stopped the car. "He's a real estate developer."

I shook my head. "That's what he does. Who is he?"

Her forehead crumpled. "He's kind, funny, and thoughtful."

Hope and I had been besties since our days at Redmond College. She'd dated a lot of guys but never anyone with those three adjectives attached to him.

"And fun," she sang. "He's so fun. I've seen this city in a different light ever since I met him. Everyone who works for him loves him. I really hit the jackpot here, Jada. So again, please don't rain on my happy parade. Please." Her eyes pleaded with me to accept her in her happy place.

I smiled in the sincerest way possible. I really wanted her to believe what I had to say next. "Hope, your guy sounds lovely."

Her eyebrows furrowed and then released. "Thank you."

THE INSIDE OF HOPE'S APARTMENT WAS SPOTLESS and felt as if it hadn't been lived in for quite some time. I was about to ask whether that was the case, but she quickly told me she'd been living with Perry in his penthouse overlooking Central Park East for three—going on four—weeks. And for that reason, she said I could stay in her place for as long as I needed and didn't have to worry about paying rent or utilities. She asserted herself by saying she wouldn't take a dime from me as long as I lived in her apartment.

"Wait until you find another job, then we can work out an agreement for rent."

We shook on the deal, and then she helped me unpack my suitcase and invited me to wear anything of hers that was in the closet or the drawers except for her underwear. It didn't take long to get settled. I didn't have much and had been living with very few possessions ever since I moved to Wyoming to work for Spencer and then got stuck in Santa Barbara with my mom. Now I was down to the bare minimum.

After I put on a set of Hope's pink satin pajamas, we made ourselves comfy on the sofa, and I told her all about what had happened at the event in DC.

"Wow, Spencer Christmas did that? He must've been very angry about what happened at Christmas dinner," she said.

My shoulders curved as I sighed. "He was." Then I filled her in on what happened after I walked out on the dinner and my job.

Hope looked at her wristwatch. "Jeez, Jada, sounds like a whole lot of drama. How do you plan to simplify your life?"

I fell back against the arm of the sofa. "I don't know yet. Maybe I forget them all. My mom, Spencer…"

Suddenly, she squeezed my foot. "Oh my God, have you seen the video of Spencer with the wall of bones? It's a classic."

"I've seen it." I'd more than seen it. I watched it

nearly twenty times on my train ride from DC to Manhattan.

"The story's gone viral, and he's looking like a good guy. What a way to change your image—expose your father's graveyard."

"Humph," I said contemplatively, remembering Alice's offer. "Maybe I shouldn't forget Spencer." My eyes expanded. I hadn't meant to say that out loud.

Hope stood. "I don't think you should." She checked her watch again.

"Leaving?"

"I want to get more sleep before my first court session. I tell you, this lawyering shit is for the birds."

"Oh," I said, shocked by her revelation. I'd never heard her express that before. I thought she loved her job.

Then her eyes brightened. "Hey, why don't you join Perry and me for dinner tonight? It might do you some good to get back into the New York social scene."

I groaned as I sank deeper into the sofa, thinking about how much I missed Spencer and dreaded ever seeing my mother again.

"Come on, Jada. Let's get you back in the swing of things. Remember how that felt?"

It felt like decades since I'd walked the streets of my favorite city, sat on a stool at my favorite bar, and chatted it up with someone I met probably two months before at another bar, who just so happened to be at the same place as I was that night.

I sat bolt upright. "Okay, why not?"

All I had to do for the rest of the day and night was sulk until I came up with a plan for how to proceed with my life. Plus, it would be nice to meet Perry sooner rather than later.

I TOSSED AND TURNED FOR HOURS, TRYING TO SLEEP. After one abrupt movement, I was sitting on the side of the bed, massaging my temples while intermittently staring at my cellphone, which sat on top of the dresser. It was seven in the morning, and I didn't know whether Spencer was in New York, DC, or back in Wyoming. I wondered whether he was asleep or awake. He hadn't slept much at the ranch. Sometimes, I would wake up in the middle of the night, and he'd be sitting up against the headboard, staring at nothing in particular.

"A penny for your thoughts," I once said.

Instead of telling me what he was thinking, Spencer had mounted me and commenced to fucking my brains out.

"Shit," I muttered.

He had discovered human remains at his ranch. The bones belonged to women his father had murdered. What a heavy discovery, and it explained why no matter what Spencer presented on the outside, he emitted the vibe of someone with a deeply tortured soul.

Like a snake striking, I rose and swiped my phone off the dresser. Then I paused to ponder whether it was still unable to connect with his phone.

Instead of calling, I sent a text message with one simple word: *Hi.*

I dropped the phone on top of the bed as if the device was on fire and stared at it. There was no way he would respond anytime soon, so I lay back down and closed my eyes, thinking perhaps it would be easier to sleep now that I'd gotten that off my chest.

Ding.

I sat up swiftly and picked up my phone.

Where are you? he replied.

"Shit," I whispered, gathering my hair into a bunch and then letting it go.

"Why are you asking that?" I said, using voice-to-text software.

Then I deleted my reply. I didn't want to sound snippy. However, I did wonder if he'd returned to my room later that evening and discovered I'd left and that was why he was asking where I was.

"New York," I said into the microphone and pressed Send.

I sat with bated breath. The seconds kept mounting and then—*ding!*

Why did you leave DC?

I was ready to gush my answer and tell him all about the run-in with my mother, but instead, I replied, *I quit my job.*

Again, I waited for his response. Fifteen minutes went by, then half an hour. Before the hour ended, I'd fallen asleep.

CHAPTER TEN

SPENCER CHRISTMAS

AN HOUR EARLIER

The old chair I sat in kept creaking, and that bothered me. I made a swift adjustment, which ended with my foot on my knee. That was a hair more comfortable.

I stared at the last message from Jada: *I quit my job.*

Which job is she referring to—the one I gave her or the one her mother manipulated her into taking? The night before, when I left the hotel, I hadn't been sure how I felt about her. I knew her mother better than she did. Patricia Forte didn't have a conscience.

I stared at Jada's message some more. She'd left DC because she'd ended her association with that sniveling asshole, Lovell. I knew him from my early years. He was a competitive son of a bitch with zero fight or smarts. Therefore, he resorted to sinking to levels everyone else was too decent to drop to. I wasn't surprised he got hooked up with Forte. Taking money from foreign adversaries in return for political favors was right up both their alleys. I'd felt a brazen sense of satisfaction in turning both of their names over to the feds. I, of all people, understood the power a parent could have over a child. Patricia Forte was a sort of black widow who would fight to the death to keep her daughter stuck in her web.

But Jada quit.

I sniffed, smirking. "Good girl, babe. Good girl."

I was on the verge of typing that out in my reply when the door to Nestor Finley's office finally opened, and he peeped his head out into the hallway.

"Sorry for making you wait, Spence." The door opened wider. "Come in."

Every muscle in my body tightened as I stood. "Do you have good news?"

He raised his eyebrows and shrugged. "That depends. Come on in."

I walked, but each step was heavy, as though

Nestor was a doctor about to tell me I had a terminal illness rather than one of the best private investigators in the world. Nestor's services didn't come cheap, although one couldn't tell by looking at the hovel he chose as an office. The building was old. The hallway smelled like mildew. But his office was clean and orderly and smelled fresh and new, like an alternate universe from the rest of the building.

"Sit." Nestor settled into his chair on the other side of the desk.

"Let's get to it," I said, not at all interested in small talk.

I'd been to his office many times before. Investigators had already identified all the bones found in the wall and contacted living relatives. It was a fucking tragedy, parents finally knowing what had happened to their daughters. Most of them had been runaways or drug addicts. Some of them were prostitutes. Three of them weren't even American.

I'd started a fund to cover funeral costs. There was no cap on what I would pay. I also created a fund for restitution. It wasn't publicized. I didn't want the families to feel ashamed to take money from the man whose father had done that to their loved ones. There were seventeen bodies in that wall, and each of those women's families would receive no less than twenty million dollars.

"Irina Petrov is one of the seventeen," he said.

I sat up straight. I'd asked him to let me know if the name Petrov came up amongst the dead.

"I take it you don't know who that is?" he continued.

I shook my head. The tension in my face was giving me a headache. "Do you?"

He dipped his head to the side, which let me know he had some information I'd want to hear. "She's been on the FBI's Most Wanted list for twenty-three years. Her specialty was human trafficking."

I had to work not to show how what he'd just revealed socked me in the gut, taking my breath away. I wondered if my father had at some point made me engage in sexual behavior with any of those girls. *Who am I fooling, anyway?* I couldn't throw money at this nightmare, and I couldn't get back into my mother's womb to be born into a different family. At the moment, I hated them all—Asher, Bryn, and Jasper. But the emotion was fleeting. After all, we had all been born into the most debased circumstances.

"Is that it?" I asked, ready to go straight to my

brother's office and have a chat with him about anyone he might know who was associated with Irina Petrov. Perhaps there was someone still alive, other than Arthur Valentine, whose days were numbered, who could shed some light on who my mother might be.

"There's more," Nestor said. "Irina has a sister in Toronto."

He explained how the woman in Toronto went by an alias. He was able to connect her to Irina by following the DNA and getting closer to first-cousin connections until he found one of her relatives, who lived in the Republic of Georgia. It was Irina's grandmother, who had been grieving the loss of her granddaughter for years. Without much prompting, the grandmother revealed that Irina had a sister named Nadia who now resided in Toronto. Nadia went by the name Sarah Caldwell and owned a café downtown. She was single and had no children.

"Then she's hiding?" I said.

He nodded once. "I don't have a DNA profile on Nadia, but I'd sure like one," he said as if he were just musing. "Regardless, the grandmother said the sisters were close. I'll fly to Toronto to talk to her…"

"No," I said. "I'll do it."

Nestor shook his head. "I'd prefer to handle this one. She could be hostile and…"

"I've got it. And I'll get you your DNA sample for testing."

He scrutinized me with a frown. There was a reason why I needed to talk to her. I'd never told Nestor about Arthur Valentine's involvement with what I'd discovered at the ranch. However, when I overheard my father and Valentine when I was a kid, Valentine had mentioned Petrov specifically. He was the one who wanted the woman dead. And I wanted to know why.

Finally, Nestor sighed, surrendering to my will. "All right, then. But keep me informed."

I told him I would, and he gave me the address of her café and home. Before leaving his office, I said, "Also, thanks for fixing our phones—my girl-friend's and mine."

Nestor raised his hand. "Anytime."

———

As soon as I walked out of the musty building, I decided to put off going to see Jasper and called Jada instead. I needed to hear her voice and be near her body. I wanted to ask if she'd fly to Toronto with me. I planned on making love to her sexy body all the way there and back. As I was thinking about that, my phone rang in my hand, and I leaned back when I saw who was calling.

"What the hell?" I muttered and answered the call of someone I hadn't spoken to for far too long.

CHAPTER ELEVEN

JADA FORTE

The atmosphere around me is opaque. I'm walking. It's cold. Somewhere in the darkness, I'm sure Spencer exists. He's my goal. I need to reach him. I hear a click, and then light pushes against the blackness from an open door up ahead.

A woman giggles, and a man murmurs. I incline my ear to their sounds while moving toward the light.

"Feels good to be free, doesn't it?" he says.

Suddenly, I stop, recognizing the voice.

"Dad?" I call, but my words don't project, so he can't hear me.

I rush toward the room, but with each step, the doorway stretches away from my reach. I break into a sprint, and the entrance moves away from me faster.

"Dad?" I scream at the top of my lungs.

"Now we can be in love," a woman says and giggles. She's certainly not my mom.

"I killed Patricia for us, for Jada," my father replies.

"Killed." I stop and grab my heart, feeling the loss of my mom. *Oh, the pain.* I could not have heard that right. My dad did not kill my mom. "Why?" I shout.

I take off running again, this time gaining ground even though the hallway is still stretching. "Mom!"

When I reach the doorway, I'm momentarily blinded by the light, but I blink until I'm able to see my father sitting on a silk chair fit for a king. His mouth is attached to a woman's nipple, and milk is running down the sides of his chin. The woman he's breastfeeding from is Gina, the prostitute.

I'm lost for what to do next.

Ring…

Ring…

Ring…

I gasped as I sat up. The room was dark, and the faint sound of traffic mingled with the ringing of my cellphone. I brushed the mattress, feeling for my device in the dark.

Then my hand made contact, and I quickly answered the call. "Hello?"

"Donnie's, East Village. Dinner flipped to party, so move your ass now and hurry up and get here!" Hope hung up before I could say anything.

Talk about a hit-and-run. I shook my head. My best friend was probably certifiable. And there was still no message from Spencer. I wondered why he'd gone silent on me. *What did I say to make him do that?* I scrolled through our latest texts. The last thing I told him was that I'd quit my job. I didn't know whether he approved or disapproved.

My cellphone said it was eight thirty at night. I'd slept for more than fifteen hours. Working for Jimmy's campaign had really exhausted me mentally. I thought about that dream I'd just had with my dad sucking milk from a prostitute's tit and saying that I was now free because he'd killed my mother…

I squeezed my eyes shut as I massaged my temples, wondering what sort of trippy shit in my subconscious would cause me to have that kind of dream.

But I didn't have time to come up with an answer. I bounded to my feet and went to get showered and dressed for the night. I had no idea what Hope meant by "Dinner flipped into party," but I was up for it. I kept my fingers crossed that whatever sort of shindig Hope had invited me to would have lots of cocktails, good food, and the caliber of men to help me get over cryptic, crazy Spencer Christmas.

WHAT I FOUND OUT, ONCE I PULLED THE CURTAIN from over the window, was that snow rested on top of everything it could settle upon and was still falling. I hadn't brought a coat strong enough to endure such elements, since my starting point was California. Fortunately, Hope had a cute wool trench coat in her closet and plenty of angora scarves. Once I was all showered, dressed, and appropriately bundled, I headed to the subway station.

I loved feeling like a New Yorker again. I'd learned I had to be quick and assertive without being a bully to make my ride on the train as comfortable as possible. I had to know how to put space between me and the guy who wanted to rub his erection against my ass and the chick who wanted to dig into my purse. How green I'd been when I first came to the city after graduating from Redmond! In the first thirty days, my ass had gotten some guy off three times. I made the mistake of getting into an empty subway car twice. And I'd learned the hard way that on the weekends, anything went, as far as the subway schedule was concerned.

I grinned as I flopped down in a window seat. I'd learned all the tricks of the trade when it came to navigating the city. I was sure I'd never leave New York again, especially after the train made it to my stop without a blip.

When I walked into Donnie's, loud, awful pop music was playing. It sounded like the cheap music played in strip clubs, featuring a nasally girl rapping, and made me want to walk back out into the cold. But I kept moving forward. The after-work professional crowd was represented in droves that night. People had their ties loosened, jackets off, and shirts unbuttoned and were swaying or dancing to the music wherever they stood and appearing to be having a good time in general. I found Hope at the bar, chatting it up with our friends Angela and Laura, who I was so thankful to be laying eyes on again.

Angela screamed loudly when she caught sight of me, but Laura got to me first. "You're back," she sang, tugging me from side to side with her embrace.

"I am," I said jubilantly.

Next, it was Angela's turn to do the same. "Don't you fucking leave us again."

"I won't!" I shouted at the top of my lungs, suddenly feeling euphoric, and grabbed them both to pull them in for a three-person hug.

Hope watched us with a smile, and I gave her a hug too. "What happened to dinner with you and your new fiancé?" I shouted.

"We decided to make it an engagement party instead since the wedding is this Saturday!"

I jerked my head back. "This Saturday?"

"We're eloping!"

Laura and Angela were already looking at me with deliberately wide eyes, nodding as if they agreed with me about how crazy it sounded that Hope was getting married so soon.

"Uh, uh, uh…" Hope said, shaking her finger.

"No naysayers tonight." She waved over the bartender and ordered all our favorite drinks and then announced that the drinks were on Perry, there was buffet-style dinner in the back of the room, and dancing was wherever we were standing.

I didn't want to let it go. Something was off about this new relationship of Hope's. I could feel the confusion forming on my face and wondered whether I should continue pushing for answers or let it be for now.

Finally, Hope raised a hand. "Perry!" she called, waving wildly.

I whipped my face around to see this mystery man who had made my best friend sacrifice her common sense just for him. *That couldn't be him*, I thought. When Perry stood next to Hope, who at five foot ten towered over him, I thought I'd walked into the twilight zone.

He wore spectacles, and his curly brown hair was mussed. On the bright side, he had a sweet face with exotic pale-blue eyes. But Hope had never done *sweet*. Her guys had always been the classic scruffy, good-looking, hard-to-catch rebels with five o'clock shadows and eyes that flirted with every girl in the room. No way had that short, sweet-looking man worked his voodoo on Hope Callaway.

"Perry, this is Jada," she said proudly.

I shook his hand. He had a firm grip.

"Jada, I heard a lot about you. Nice to meet you in person."

I smiled, forcing myself to not say anything insulting like, *Never heard anything about you before Perry, and gosh, you're shorter than how Hope usually likes them.*

"Nice meeting you," I replied.

"Sorry to hear about your recent hardships," he said.

I tilted my head, frowning. "My recent hardships?"

"What happened in DC. Hope put you up at her apartment, but there's room at my place if you like, and it's a lot more comfortable. Any friend of Hope's is a friend of mine. As a matter of fact…"

Hope shook his shoulder. "Honey, the manager is calling us. Could you go see what she wants?"

Perry stiffened like a guard dog who'd been called into action as he looked to where Hope was pointing. I doubted the manager was really looking for them. Hope wanted him to stop talking. Regardless, once his eyes spotted the person she'd indicated, Perry kissed Hope on the cheek and started to move in that direction. Before he got away, she grabbed him by the arm and pulled him to her, and they tongued like two people who needed to get a room. I watched them as if I was in a movie theater and it was their scene. When the kiss was over, Perry slid his hand under his unbuttoned shirt and put it against the fabric, making it appear as if the kiss made his heart beat out of his chest. Hope laughed like a little girl. *Holy shit.* Now I knew why she'd fallen in love with him.

"By the way, babe, ask Rhonda to put out some more food while you're over there," she said.

I smirked, knowing she was covering up for fibbing about the manager looking for them. However, seeing how they were together, I decided to drop my doubts and let their love be. Whatever they had together would either fail or succeed, and regardless of how it went, I would be there for my friend.

Hope traipsed off to mingle with more of their guests, and I caught up with Laura and Angela. Nothing much had changed in their lives. The men they dated still sucked. Laura was still a marketing director and Angela a business-journal editor, and both of them articulated that the only thing they liked about their jobs was the money.

"It's always the money, isn't it?" I said, realizing

money was the reason I'd met Spencer in the first place.

"I take it you're not working at the mystery job anymore?" Laura asked.

"Nope." I pursed my lips. Frankly, I didn't want to say anything more about it.

"Well, who were you working for?"

"Mm… I think it's private," I said.

Angela rolled her eyes. "You think it's private?"

I twisted my mouth thoughtfully. "I guess I'm not working for him anymore and he's done with his special project. And he and I are…" I clamped my lips shut, figuring I was about to go a step too far.

"You and him are what?" Angela asked.

"Was it someone famous?" Laura asked.

"Sort of," I said. "I guess I can tell you."

Laura craned her neck toward me expectantly as Angela shrugged.

"Who?" Angela asked.

"Spencer Christmas."

Laura gently shoved my shoulder. "Get the hell out of here. No way."

I nodded.

"No fucking way," she said again.

"Yes fucking way," I said, still nodding.

Then Angela reached out and wrapped her hand around my wrist. "The video... have you seen it?"

I had to give my heart a moment to slow down because her question had taken me by surprise. "You're talking about the wall with the dead bodies in it?"

"Yes, but his reaction too. Oh my God. It's one for the history books. He's so hot. Is he single? Because if he is, could you introduce us?"

I stared into her eyes to make sure she meant what she'd asked. Her expression didn't break. She meant it.

"I can't believe you didn't tap that," Laura said, making me rip my confused gaze away from Angela. "Or did you?" She wiggled her eyebrows.

"No way—not Little Miss Muffet," Laura said.

I twisted my neck to look at her, snarling. "Did you just refer to me as Little Miss Muffet?"

"All prim and proper and virginal, yes." Laura shook her head as she rolled her eyes. "Oh, don't look so stupefied, Jada. We all know you're a virgin. It's nothing to be ashamed of. I mean, I wish I would've kept my pussy to myself until I was almost thirty too."

I now remembered that Laura was one of those

friends I liked most during the first two minutes of interacting and after that stopped feeling much of a connection with. This time, she'd stirred something within me, speaking as if she knew me on some intimate level when she didn't.

I turned my head toward my raised shoulder. "I fucked him." I felt like a rooster proudly strutting around the yard.

Laura scoffed as she rolled her eyes. "And pigs are flying." She hopped off her barstool. "Now," she said loudly, indicating that she was changing the subject, "I'm going to check the full scope of the man scene."

My mouth was still open as she walked away.

Angela chuckled, and I turned my stunned expression on her. "Forgotten how much of a bitch she can be, I see."

I shook my head, wanting a redo of what had just happened between Laura and me.

"But really, you fucked him?"

I blew a brisk breath through my nose. "Repeatedly."

"Shit, he's the king of studs. How was it?"

I wanted to say, "Unlike anything I'd ever experienced," but I decided to get some food to cool down. My head was banging to the beat of the loud music, and being angry with Laura reminded my body of how low my blood sugar was.

"Yeah… Excuse me." I stomped off toward the food table and loaded my plate with lasagna bites, savory cannoli, and assorted ravioli. After polishing off that plate of food, I made another.

"Your appetite is sexy," a man said. He'd stepped up beside me out of the blue.

I didn't recognize the guy, but he had the typical Wall Street look—suit, dark hair stiffened by gel, young face. He was sort of cute but definitely no Spencer Christmas.

"Thank you." I stuffed another cannoli into my mouth.

The guy touched his chest. "I'm Daniel."

I finished swallowing what I was chewing. "I'm Jada."

"Daniel and Jada. I like the sound of that," he said, his eyes shining with pure delight.

I wished I could feel weird about some guy I'd known less than ten seconds trying our names out together, but I was back in New York City, a place where all kinds resided.

"So what do you do for a living?" he asked.

I sighed at the dreaded question, one popular among young professionals from coast to coast.

Since I wasn't in the mindset of appealing to another man besides Spencer, I had no problem saying, "I'm between jobs." I popped a ravioli into my mouth.

"Then you're unemployed," he said as if *unemployed* was a dirty word.

"Yep," I replied proudly.

He threw his hands up. "Well, what did you use to do?"

I was almost disappointed that my answer didn't make him find an excuse to go away and hit on someone like Laura who was looking for a guy like him.

I sighed. "Well… I worked for a politician that my mother wanted to…" I realized I was on the verge of saying too much. The cocktail I'd drunk was strong.

"Wait? Your mother's a politician?" he asked, frowning, confused.

I was pretty sure I hadn't said that, but I couldn't remember exactly what I had said. *Note to self: if you decide to have another cocktail, watch the bartender and make sure it isn't so potent.*

"Yeah, Mom's a politician, but I wasn't working for her, at least not directly. I was working for her puppet, a real asshole who can kiss my ass."

"Oh yeah… I like politics. Who's your mother?"

At a different point in time of my life, I would not have given him my mom's name, especially after all the shit I'd just said about working for a politician who she was puppeteering. "Patricia Forte." I twisted my head, watching him closely to see if he recognized the name.

"Get the fuck out of here—the senator?"

I nodded. "Yep."

"Fuck! She's pretty hefty. Let's dance!"

I had no idea why what I'd said made him want to dance, but I needed the exercise to help ease my buzz. "Okay!" I shouted over the horrible music.

Suddenly, the song changed to one I liked better. I let my mind be full of music as David or Daniel—or whatever his name was—took me by the hand and led me to where people were mostly dancing. I caught a glimpse Hope boogying down with her new beau. I still could hardly believe what I was seeing. However, I wanted to stay focused on the dancing, not thinking or feeling anything about Spencer Christmas or Hope's quick trip to the altar. My feet started to move, and my hips gyrated. I wanted to be sexy, so I put my arms in the air and waved my fingers to the beat, swirling my body like a sexy snake. My dance partner's eyes grew as they took in all of me.

Then I felt two hands clamping around my waist, a hard body against my back, an erection pressing against my ass, and hips moving in unison with mine. "Who the fuck is that guy?" Spencer whispered in my ear.

I gasped, suddenly completely sober. Then he spun me around, and I was looking into the eyes of the man I loved.

CHAPTER TWELVE

JADA FORTE

Endorphins flowed as we stood face-to-face, my lips on his, our tongues gently swirling around each other, tasting, dancing, indulging. My arms were wrapped around his neck, fingers freely playing through his hair. The music was faster than when we were moving. I'd completely abandoned my other dance partner, who I was certain had gotten the message.

"What are you doing here?" I asked between kisses.

"Perry's my friend. He told me you would be here." His tongue plunged deeper into my mouth.

My head felt as if it was running in slow motion above the atmosphere. "Perry's your friend?" I was shocked, but I was too dazed to ask more than that.

"Yes," he whispered and then did my favorite thing, sinking his tongue into my ear. "Let's get out of here."

My panties got even wetter.

I would have been concerned about leaving my best friend's engagement party, but I suspected Hope had something to do with Spencer Christmas being here, and I felt sure she'd understand that I wouldn't have the willpower not to go somewhere else and give my body what it had been craving since the other night when he'd left me hot and bothered on the bed in the hotel room.

I nodded, and Spencer took my hand. I caught a glimpse of Damon, or whatever his name was, watching us in awe as we passed by him. Spencer led me out into the cold dark night. He opened the passenger door of a midnight-blue luxury SUV. We kissed again before I got in. My desire burned for him.

I watched his manly frame standing in front of the car, looking up the road as if he had to guard the one he loved with his life. It was like a good dream, the best dream in the world, when he got in and looked me in the eye.

"Is this really happening?" I asked, immediately feeling like a doofus for letting that slip out.

Spencer's face brightened, and he smiled in a way that I'd never seen before. "You know, I love that about you."

I felt confused. "What do you mean?"

"How you say whatever the hell you're thinking, even though you're the kind of person who's cautious about what she says."

I sniffed, amused. I loved how he noticed all the quirks about me that I hadn't known existed.

"And yes, I'm here for real." Suddenly his expression turned serious. "Sorry about how I left you at the hotel. I was fucking butt hurt because I want you to always choose me."

"I choose you," I said, feeling an urgent sense of desperation.

"I know, baby." Spencer started the engine, pulled away from the curb, and then reached out to take my hand. I rested the side of my face on the back of my seat, unwilling to take my eyes off him as he drove us to our next destination. I didn't ask where we were going because I didn't care. Spencer Christmas could take me to the depths of Hades for all I cared. As long as we were together, I was in pure bliss.

WE ENDED UP AT ONE OF THOSE MODERN HIGH-RISES in Chelsea that had its own car elevator that took us up the building. When the SUV stopped on one of the high floors, he told me to stay put. He was being commanding again, which meant that sex would soon follow. I sat very still, my nerves jittering, my pussy anxious, my lips in need of his.

As soon as he opened the door, he fulfilled at least one of my longings and pressed his eager mouth against mine, kissing me deeply. Spencer muttered against my lips about how badly he wanted me before maneuvering me out of the vehicle, opening the back door, and setting me on the edge of the seat, my knees facing out the doorway.

"Lay back," he said, flexing his eyebrows.

My toes curled as I did what he said. Spencer pulled off my ankle boots, and I heard them drop on the ground. I twisted, moaning with anticipation, as he snatched off my pants and then my panties.

"Shit," he said, unzipping his pants with unrestrained impatience.

His dick sprang forward. He didn't pause for a second as he lifted my thighs up to his waist. Instinctively, I wrapped my legs around him, and he slammed his overgrown erection into my drenched pussy.

"Fuck!" he shouted, tossing his head back slowly, indulgently, and shifting his dick in and out of me.

"Umm…" I bit my bottom lip as I propped myself up on my elbows, feeling every inch of him, watching what I'd been longing for, my pussy swallowing his glistening cock, moistened by my desire.

"You like that," he said, watching my face.

"Yes," I sighed, trapped in euphoria as I let my head fall back and fingers grip the seats and then released a deep breath from the back of my throat.

"Your face is so sexy, baby," he whispered.

I brought my head forward again, and my hooded gaze matched his. He slowed the pace of his thrusting, rounding his dick inside me and, by the look on his face, enjoying every second of it. Then he licked his thumb and pressed it against my clit, circling it around my hard knot, applying the right kind of pressure for immediate impact.

I clung to the seat and tightened my body, inhaling sharply and moaning. Spencer was an expert at handling the lower part of my body as if I was his favorite plaything. My body was light as air in his grasp. He was so strong, so sexy, watching me intently, knowing I was enjoying it. My tense hips rose toward his stimulation, chasing the sparks of orgasm.

Then the sensation became strong. And stronger.

I cried out, overcome by the most powerful orgasm ever, watching myself sigh and moan. It was like an out-of-body experience. Then Spencer bent over to sink his tongue into my wetness and rolled it around my clit some more, doing it over and over again. He was slowly taking me there again, and he never took his eyes off me.

I braced myself for what was soon to come while bearing the silky stimulation of his wet, warm tongue. All sorts of sounds were leaving my mouth as my thighs quivered and pussy throbbed. The more I tried to squirm, the firmer he held me in place. There was no getting away, no decreasing this pleasurable mugging. One sensation led to the next, and then my pussy was engulfed by another orgasm.

Spencer stood. My eyes lapped up his hard-as-steel dick, but before I could reach out for it, he slammed it inside me again. My body wouldn't stop trembling as he lifted me out of the vehicle. I wrapped my legs around him as he carried me past the automatic sliding door and into his apartment. My head felt balmy as we kissed, the scent of my sex around his mouth intermingled with new house smell. I was too dazed to notice much of my surroundings, but soon my backside came into contact with a bed and a furry black bedspread. Spencer, standing beside the bed, clutched my ass and pounded my pussy until he roared, erupting inside me.

I thought he would call this sex session to an end, but he didn't. Spencer wrapped me up in his arms and lay on top of me, and we made out feverishly, rolling around on top of his soft bed. We didn't stop kissing until he was hard enough to be inside me again. Spencer did me every way possible, experiencing our pleasure from different angles —with me on my knees and him pounding my pussy from behind, my body twisting this way and that, or me sitting on top of his dick as he bounced me on his lap while squeezing my tits and pinching my nipples. He would change our positions abruptly. At times he would slow down until the need to explode passed and then start over again.

Spencer was lying against my back, dick in my pussy, with my thighs together to seal him inside me. In, out, in, out, faster, faster, rapidly...

"Ah!" I screamed, grabbing a handful of furry bedspread. The best kind of orgasm ignited inside me, and then his detonated, and together, our bodies quaked and shivered as we shouted each other's names.

Spencer and I glistened with sweat as I laid my head on his chest. He stroked my thick hair and seized a handful of it to gently guide my head back and kiss my forehead.

"You were dancing with that guy. Why?" he asked.

"Huh?" His question was out of the blue and hours too late.

"If I hadn't shown up, what would've happened between you two?"

I squeezed him tighter. "Nothing. I was just dancing. That's all, Spencer." I chuckled. "I couldn't remember his name to save my life."

He fell silent. "I want you, Jada," he finally said.

I ran my tongue around his nipple, and he quickened. "You have me," I said.

"I want you to be mine only, but..." He spoke

breathlessly, perhaps still feeling the remnants of my stimulation.

I waited patiently for him to add whatever he was going to say. The silence continued.

"But…?" I finally asked, controlling my excitement as I guessed what he would say next. After what had just happened between us, I remained optimistic that Spencer would make it clear that I was his girlfriend. No more bullshit. We were a real item.

"I have to take a trip to Toronto. Would you like to come?"

"Oh." I was surprised and was pretty sure that wasn't what he'd really been about to say. I raised my head off his chest and looked at his gorgeous face. "Then you want me to be your girlfriend," I said, getting back on subject.

"I do, but…"

"But…?"

"I'm barely holding it together right now." He placed his forearm over his eyes. "I love making love to you, Jada. Enjoying you sexually. But these moments are tough."

I frowned at him severely. "What's so tough about them?"

He took a deep breath. "The shame," he whispered.

I closed my eyes to endure the gravity of what he'd just revealed. "You're ashamed of me?"

He removed his arm. "That's not what I said. You heard me wrong. I'm ashamed of the pleasure. It's fucking me up. My interactions with women are supposed to hurt, not feel this fucking amazing."

I gently smoothed the side of his face. "But it is supposed to feel this amazing."

Spencer seized my hand and drew me against him again. "Babe, please don't take this personally. I'm being honest with you. I'm fucked up right now in many ways." He pushed my hair off the back of my neck and kissed it. "I never thought I'd enjoy sex this way. I never wanted to love a woman as much as I…"

Again, I waited for it. No doubt, he wanted to complete that sentence but couldn't. I sighed gravely, feeling so sad. I'd never wanted a man who couldn't say he loved me, especially when it was clear he did.

Spencer sucked the back of my neck. "You taste so good, baby." His blossoming erection was hardening against my ass.

"But if I let you make love to me again, then

you'd feel shame again," I said, feeling so sad to have to say it.

We endured another long silence. "I'm working through it, Jada."

I sat up straight, breaking body contact. "I don't understand, Spencer."

Now he sat up. "You wouldn't, but I'm trying to be honest with you. Do you want me to continue to lie to you like your parents did for sixteen years?"

Rage swelled inside me, and I wanted to scratch his eyes out for saying that. I could feel my expression getting more pinched by the second.

"Baby," he said, touching my thigh.

I pulled away from his hand. "What are you trying to do, Spencer? Put distance between us? Because I've dated that sort of asshole before and…"

"God damn it." He jumped out of bed, his new erection sticking straight out. "I can't have a real conversation with you. It's got to be fucking butterflies and flowers and happy shit all the time with you. I'm telling you the truth here. I'm not fucking perfect, so I don't want you to fuck me and fall in love with the perfect man, because that's not who I am or will ever be." He sighed hard as he grabbed the sides of his head and closed his eyes. "But you're the perfect woman, and I love you."

My jaw dropped. He'd said it. He'd actually said it.

"I love you too," I said.

He opened his eyes, and the expression of the man looking back at me was scared as hell.

CHAPTER THIRTEEN

JADA FORTE

O f course, we made love again. This time, it was soft and indulgent with lots of kissing and caressing. At times, my heart felt as if it would explode. At times, tears filled my eyes as I could hardly believe this was happening in real life. At times, I answered his, "Damn, I love you, Jada" with the same confession. At times, we'd be kissing deeply, and his cock felt so good inside me that we'd have to stop and stare into each other's eyes until we were smiling at each other. I knew it was the same for him as it was for me. The sex between us was fantastic, but it was our hearts and minds that created the love between us.

We slept through very little of the night, unable to keep our hands off each other. By the middle of the new day, when we were both zonked from kissing and stroking each other almost nonstop, we finally got out of bed. I put on one of Spencer's T-shirts, which nearly swallowed me whole, and a pair of his boxers, and he gave me a tour of his condo.

His place was upwards of three thousand square feet, each room designed in the modern and sleek contemporary style suitable for a man's tastes. However, he kept using the word *our* for each room. "Our bathroom… our guest bedroom… our living room… our library." I wanted to ask if he meant the two of us, but for some reason, I was afraid of what the answer might be.

When we made it to the kitchen, he told me to sit on one of the stools while he made us breakfast.

"You sure know how to handle a knife," I said, impressed by how he cut up the onions and bell peppers for potatoes au gratin. Feeling guilty for letting him cook by himself, I slid off my stool. "Let me help you."

Spencer pointed to my seat. "No, babe. Sit."

I stiffened. "Really?"

"Yes."

I sighed, conceding. "Okay, then." I hopped back on my stool. "So you like cooking?"

He poured olive oil into a cast-iron skillet. "I

do." He chopped the vegetables easily, as if he could have done it in his sleep.

"How does a guy like you, so busy and rich, learn to cook?"

Spencer tossed his head back to laugh. "My father used to hire some of the best chefs in the world. Those guys were into what they were doing and didn't mind teaching me the tricks of the trade."

"Would you rather be a chef than what you are now?"

He shook his head adamantly. "No. I like what I do. I'm good at business, especially now that my head is finally clear."

I grunted, intrigued. "What do you mean by that?"

He dropped the two chopped potatoes into the hot oil with the sautéed onions and red, yellow, and green bell peppers.

"For a long time, I was stuck in survival mode. Now I'm in thriving mode," he said over the crackle of frying.

I grinned from ear to ear, mulling over what he'd said as he cracked fresh eggs into olive oil and sliced garlic. Perhaps that was my problem. For so many years, I'd been surviving and not thriving.

What would thriving even look like for me? I didn't know.

As the eggs cooked on a low fire, Spencer came over to kiss me tenderly. "What are you thinking?"

I twisted my lips and sighed deeply. "I like what you said about surviving or thriving. When I'm with you, I feel as though I'm thriving, but then there's the rest of my life." My shoulders curved.

Spencer kissed me again. "You're thriving, babe. You want to know how I know this?"

I nodded, filled with bliss to think he believed I wasn't stagnating.

"You're here and not in DC or wherever your mother wants you living under her thumb."

He winked, and I sat, mesmerized by his sexy physique, as he walked over to the large oven to see about our eggs. Then he announced that they were done and began plating our food as if we were eating in a five-star restaurant.

My first bite and every chew thereafter made me feel as if I'd died and gone to food heaven. "Um…" I kept saying. "Oh my God."

Spencer watched me eat with a look of lust in his eyes. After I consumed my last bite, he waved me over with two fingers. "Come here," he whispered thickly.

He must have smelled my horniness. I sprang to my feet and walked seductively to his side of the table. Slowly, I straddled him. He freed his erection from his boxers, and I sat on top of it. He took a sharp breath as his manhood pushed through my slippery walls.

"I'm getting used to this," he whispered against my lips.

We kissed as I started shifting my hips back and forth.

Spencer whimpered and clamped his hands on my hips, stilling me.

He shook his head. "I want to get used to being inside you." He sucked air between his teeth. "Could you give me that, baby?"

Our foreheads pressed against each other. The warmth from his breath lingered on my lips. "Yes," I whispered. "Yes."

The longer we sat like that, the more natural our closeness felt, although I tingled with want. We kissed tenderly, never losing eye contact, as if Spencer was my new appendage. I could only hope I was his. At times, he'd moan and stiffen, controlling his desire.

"So…" he finally said and chuckled.

"So…" I laughed too.

"So your friend is marrying Perry?" He laughed at how we were trying to concentrate on something else besides wanting to bang it out.

I licked my lower lip. "Uh-huh."

"Don't do that," he admonished me.

"Don't do what?"

He drew my lip into his mouth, indulging in it. "That," he whispered.

"Oh," I said with a sigh.

"Perry's a good guy."

"Is he? Last night was the first time I met him."

His lips parted as his body tightened. "Um, he's, um… a good guy."

"I know. You said that already."

He squeezed his eyes shut. "Oh, I did."

I nodded. "He's short, though."

He chuckled. "But I heard he has a big dick."

We both laughed.

"You have a big dick," I said.

Then, lightning fast, Spencer shifted me back and forth on his lap, grunting and breathing, harder and faster until he wrapped me up tightly, coming to a sudden stop. "Not yet." His tongue dove into my ear, making me still as my pussy tightened around his dick. Back and forth, he nailed me deep.

"Shit," he whispered heavily as his body quaked against me.

Spencer and I continued holding each other tight. All I could do was hope he wasn't ashamed about what had just happened between us. When he leaned back to look at my face, he was smiling.

"That was nice," he said.

My mouth was first to devour his, but as soon our tongues connected, he took over. We didn't move—we sat like that, kissing more, getting used to being so close, him not turning away when the pleasure consumed him.

Then we finished eating and went back to bed. As the time progressed, we embraced each other, made out feverishly, and made beautiful slow-burn love, Spencer learning with each blast of climaxing that he deserved my body and the intimacy I so freely gave him.

The night arrived. Even though we slept, we couldn't keep our hands off each other when one of us woke up, rousing the other until my legs were parted and he was inside me. Our lovemaking had certainly changed. It wasn't about how many orgasms we had and how many ways we could have them. Our sex was about closeness. I wanted to disappear into his body, and he voiced that he felt the same. Now, during the moments of our interactions, our bodies and souls were made one.

WHEN MY EYES OPENED AGAIN, THE CURTAINS WERE pulled back and the muted light of a dreary day had settled in the room. Spencer was gone, but he'd left a note on the pillow beside me: *Working on some things. You can find me in my office.*

"Hmm…" I simpered, twisting as I yawned.

I slid off the bed. My whole body ached from the exercise of so much sex. The view called me to the window, and I appreciated how the haze settled over and between the skyscrapers beneath us. I could have stayed locked in Spencer's condo with him forever. I moaned with delight at knowing he was all I needed.

Then out of the blue, an image of my cellphone popped into my mind. I'd neglected it since arriving in Manhattan. I was sure it was loaded with messages from Mom and the campaign. I couldn't help but feel the thrill of knowing my mom had no idea where I was. I wanted to keep it that way, but deep down inside, I knew I couldn't.

Holy shit—I have walked out on my job. Will Spencer

hire me again? Can I even work for him? I couldn't help but feel as if I'd abandoned Little Jimmy Lovell. But then I realized it wasn't Jimmy I feared abandoning —it was my mom.

Don't do it, my inner voice warned. *Don't call her.* Thank goodness we'd left my purse in Spencer's SUV.

Spencer Christmas… I seized my lower lip between my teeth as I remembered how he'd sucked, chewed, and kissed it.

I hugged myself tight. "My goodness, Jada, you're in love," I whispered. That was the excuse I was looking for. There was no immediate need to hop through my mother's hoops or even exit the love shack I'd made with Spencer.

"Jada?"

I quickly turned to see Spencer standing in the doorway, fully dressed in an expensive suit and a black overcoat. He looked like the real-life version of the sort of man Armani ads attempted to capture. His gaze roamed my naked body. "I have to leave." He coughed to clear his throat.

I jerked my head in surprise. "Leave? I thought we were going to Toronto together?"

"Something else came up. I have to take care of that first. I've been wanting to surprise you, however…" He sighed and stared at my nakedness again.

I tried to control my excitement. I would never confess to myself that I'd wanted to hear Spencer reaffirm that he wanted me around him forever and ever.

"Surprise me with what?" I asked, beaming.

"I want you to stay here, live here. With me. So I had your things shipped from the ranch." He pointed to the hallway that led to the large dressing room near the bathroom. "Your clothes are hanging in the closet, and I had them put in some of the drawers. And all of your toiletries are in the bathroom."

I could hardly believe what I'd just heard. I practically leapt into his arms, and we kissed madly. A phone chimed, and Spencer impressively multitasked, not letting up on our kiss as he dug his device out of his pocket.

"One second, baby," he whispered.

He scowled at the screen and then pressed the answer button with his thumb. I was amazed how light I felt in the one arm he was using to hold me. The fact that he was so strong still turned me on, so much so that I vowed there was no way he was leaving without fucking me again.

"Yeah," he said sharply, looking down at the floor and then, after a few beats, at me. "She's here."

I leaned back to study his concerned face.

"Wow. Really? Okay. Thanks for calling." He ended the call and looked at me with a searching expression.

"Who was that?" I asked sharply.

"Perry, calling on behalf of Hope."

"Well, what did she want?"

He did something between a grunt and a sigh as his entire face collapsed into his most intense frown yet. "It's your mother."

CHAPTER FOURTEEN

JADA FORTE

I still couldn't believe what Spencer had implied. I smashed my hands on my waist. "Are you suggesting my mother is behind her own shooting?"

The news report said Patricia Forte was shot in the shoulder after returning home from a trip to DC. She'd been ambushed in her driveway, and the assailant was reported to have called her a traitor before shooting her. The authorities believed the attack was tied to the recent announcement about her and several other politicians being tied to a scheme that allowed them to take campaign money from hostile foreign governments, but they weren't sure, which was why the investigation was still ongoing. I wasn't concerned with why it had happened, but Spencer was.

He frowned impatiently, checking his watch. "Jada, slow down, take a break, and think this through."

Earlier, I'd scrambled around the room, putting on my garments as I found them. My heart was beating out of control. I couldn't get to California fast enough.

"I have thought it through!" I shouted, trembling.

"Listen… stay here. I'll be back later tonight and…"

"No." My eyes roamed the room. I was looking for my purse but then remembered it was in his office.

Suddenly, Spencer took me by the shoulders, forcing me to meet his gaze. "Think, Jada. Doesn't this seem too convenient?"

"No," I said, shrugging out of his grasp. "I'm going to the airport."

I knew Spencer didn't have the capacity to be my ally just then, and I didn't blame him. My mom hadn't shown him anything but the worst side of her. However, what he was insinuating about her was abominable. I barely believed she'd willingly participated in the campaign-finance scheme. My mother had a lot of people working for her. A guy named Jason Sands handled her campaign finance. I was willing to bet my bank account on the idea that he was the bad actor in that situation.

I rushed down the hallway to Spencer's office, found my purse on top of his desk, and fished out my phone. My fingers shook as I tried dialing my mom. After one ring, the call went to voicemail. I left a message letting her know I was on my way. Then I tried my dad and got his voicemail too. I tried to work out how I'd get to the airport.

My phone dinged in my hands. I had a message from Spencer that read, *Do what you will. I have to leave.*

I stood very still, feeling the latent shock of Spencer leaving without even saying goodbye. I was even more surprised by how relieved I felt about it. My brain had gone into a mode that I recognized— in moments of crisis, my mom came first, no matter what. I didn't need to slow down and think about it.

"Hope," I whispered but then remembered it was Tuesday, which meant she was probably in court.

I left her a text message about leaving for California to see my mother. I scrambled around

Spencer's apartment in search of anything with the address, found a junk-mail sales flyer in the trash can, and arranged for a cab to pick me up.

The driver would meet me in fifteen minutes in front of the building. I figured I could book a flight in the car and then go to the counter to purchase my tickets. In the past, I'd been able to save a lot of money by doing that.

Soon, I had my coat and was walking out of the large apartment doors, which closed behind me. One thing was for sure—there was no going back. I walked up to the hall but didn't find the elevator. I panicked because there wasn't much hallway space in the opposite direction. Since I was already locked out of Spencer's place, I could possibly be trapped in the hallway.

As I walked past Spencer's apartment again, the door opened, and I jumped, spooked. With my hand over my beating heart, I looked at the man in a black suit and chauffeur's hat.

"Miss Forte," he said.

Take a breath to calm down, I nodded. "Yes." My voice was shaky.

"Mr. Christmas has arranged a ride for you to the airport as well as a flight to Santa Barbara, California."

For one second, I wondered if I was dreaming. However, he held the door open for me, and I reentered Spencer's apartment and followed the man down a hallway that I had totally missed, which led to a private elevator. Once we reached the lobby, I canceled my cab ride—the driver was stuck in traffic, anyway—and soon, I was in Spencer's midnight-blue SUV and on my way to Teterboro.

THE WHOLE PRIVATE-AIRPLANE-AND-PERSONAL-DRIVER arrangement made me feel as if Spencer was with me the entire trip. No busy airports and no long layover before flying into Santa Barbara. I arrived in my hometown after five hours in the air. I slept for the entire flight. Before takeoff, I texted Spencer to thank him, and after landing, I still hadn't received a reply. It was just like Spencer to remain gentlemanly while still being too angry to communicate with me. I'd read in the book and during my Internet research of him that he'd been a major douchebag. I often wondered if they were talking about the same person I was in love with.

I rented a car for two days. I couldn't shake the foreboding feeling of never being able to return to

New York as I drove to the hospital. At one stop-light, my mind tried to convince me to turn the car around and run away from Patricia Forte as fast as I could. The light turned green, and I spied a right turn that would allow me to get back to the airport fast, but my cellphone, which I'd hooked up to the speaker system, rang, and I drove forward.

The name *Hope* came up on the screen. I hit the answer button. "Hey, darling," I said.

"Really, Jada? You went to Santa Barbara without Spencer?"

I tipped my head to the side. "Who told you?"

"I couldn't get in touch with you because you were on the airplane, so I asked Perry to call Spencer to ask where you were. He said you were on your way to Santa Barbara, and you were alone. Come on, Jada. You know you can't take on your mother without someone there to go to battle with you. I mean, goodness gracious, you just left her in DC. And to tell you the truth, Jada, I don't think you're strong enough to withstand her manipulation. I mean, what if Spencer's right?"

I squeezed the steering wheel so tightly that my wrists ached as I yanked my head back. "Excuse me?"

She fell silent, which she meant she must have heard the anger in my tone.

"Calm down, Jada. He's not offtrack when it comes to the shit your mother pulls that you're blind to."

Like any lawyer worth her salt, Hope backed up her claim with evidence. I felt only a few short breaths away from hyperventilating as she reminded me of the time when I was supposed to travel to Europe for two months with her, Ling, and Rita. But two days before our flight, my mom called to say that my dad was having a major procedure and she was worried that he was afraid of going through it alone. She said doctors would be searching for cancer in his rectum.

"I mean, I remember counting ten hot-button words she used in her calculating explanation. Like *blood*, *cancer*, *die*, *procedure*, *treatment*…"

I sighed forcefully. "I know, Hope. I remember."

"And do you also remember that his procedure ended up being a routine colonoscopy? But once you were home, your mom roped you into attending two state dinners with her and got you all excited about renovating the guesthouse so that you could live in it. Heck, at one point, I thought we'd lost you forever."

I wanted to squeeze my eyes shut, but I couldn't. "I understand what you're saying, Hope, but this is different."

"Oh, really? What about the time she—"

"Stop!" I shouted like a crazy person.

"Jada, I know this is hard to hear, but…"

"I'm hanging up."

"Don't hang up on me," she warned.

"Goodbye, Hope—love you," I sang and ended the call. Before reaching the next light, I'd powered off my phone.

I drove the rest of the way to the hospital in a daze. I couldn't blame Spencer for relaying his fears about my mother to Hope—Mom could be very convincing, and he was merely concerned about me. As far as Hope was concerned, she didn't have to keep listing my mother's infractions. I remembered every single one of them, but I'd never thought the day would come when Hope would throw them all in my face—that wasn't her style. However, rushing to the altar with some Joe Blow who used to be a friend or acquaintance of the unreformed Spencer Christmas wasn't her style either.

My eyes darted from left to right and then back to the road ahead. I felt ashamed of my thoughts.

The only thing I could do was prove to Hope and Spencer that they were wrong about my mom in this instance. She would never go so far as to have herself shot and hospitalized in order to control me. That would make her beyond certifiable.

Spencer and Hope were the two people in the world I loved just as much as I did my parents. By the time I'd driven into the hospital parking lot and parked my car, I was dead set on proving them wrong.

THERE WERE A LOT OF PEOPLE IN THE LOBBY. I still hadn't spoken to either of my parents, which meant I didn't know where my mother's room was. As soon as I set my glare on the reception desk, someone said my name, and within seconds, I was being swarmed by a constantly increasing number of people bombarding me with questions. My legs turned weak, and I didn't know which way to turn.

"How's your mother?"

"Is she still afraid for her life?"

"Are you afraid of the threatening letter?"

Then another person asked me about the letter,

which apparently threatened my life as well. "Are you afraid?"

I was still absorbing their questions when I saw Clinton, one of my mother's bodyguards, exiting an elevator and heading in my direction. The reporters shuffled to one side or the other, giving the burly man room to pass.

"Jada," he called, his gruff voice possessing the power of a roaring lion.

He waved me over, and only then did my feet allow me to move away from the action. The questions kept coming as I ducked my head. When I reached him, Clinton put his arm around my shoulders, keeping me safe from the ravenous horde of reporters. He expertly swept me into an elevator.

"Your mother didn't know you were coming," he said now that we were alone and riding up to a higher floor.

I was still trembling, so I folded my arms. "I guess she didn't get my message. I couldn't reach her or my father."

He nodded, letting me know he accepted that answer. "On the way out, take the private elevator down."

"Okay, but where is it?"

"I'll escort you to it when you're ready to leave."

I nodded and frowned. "By the way, what's this business about my life being in danger?"

"You don't have to worry about that. As long as someone from our security detail is with you, you'll be safe."

I touched my temples as I closed my eyes, battling my thoughts. This entire ordeal was feeling wonky. "I still don't understand why my life is in danger."

The elevator doors opened. "Your mother will explain."

I shook my head adamantly. "No. I want to hear it from you."

He shrugged. "I'm sorry, but your mother insists on telling you about it."

I narrowed my eyes to slits. "Then she knows I'm here?"

His frown intensified. "Sorry, Jada. I'm just doing my job."

I opened my mouth to ask him what specifically he was apologizing for, but instead, I thanked him for saving me in the lobby. His facial expression was severe as he nodded again and stopped in front of a closed door of a corner room. I'd looked at Clinton's face hundreds of times and never before noticed what I was seeing—he, too, was her puppet, and for that, I suddenly lost trust in him.

I untwisted my mouth and thanked him again without looking into his eyes then entered my mother's hospital room. The scene was not at all what I'd expected. First of all, the space was large and had two comfy armchairs facing a queen-sized hospital bed. A pair of modern floor lamps with bent necks spread pleasant light throughout the space, and alluring black-and-white stills of Santa Barbara were tacked to the wall. On the way to California, I'd visualized my mother in a hospital bed with tubes attached to her and the breathing mechanism in her mouth. In my thoughts, she was vulnerable and needy and it was my sole responsibility to take care of her. But Patricia Forte was sitting up in bed, skin glowing and a patch of gauze taped to her exposed left shoulder. She was speaking to someone on her cellphone, which meant she could have easily returned my call or texted me to say she was fine.

I stretched my lips into a wide fake smile, forcing Hope's warning out of my mind. "Mom," I whispered, unable to make myself sound concerned.

She raised a finger, which was her way of telling

me to wait for a moment. "Yes," she said, using her official voice. "I see... I understand." Her wide-eyed expression settled on my face and then slowly morphed into a look of concern. "Yes, she's here." She nodded. "That sounds fine." Finally, she set her phone on top of the bedside table. "That was Felix, one of my aides. He said the police are still investigating the shooting, so we have to remain cautious." Her eyes softened again. "But I'm happy you're here. Are you alone?"

I wanted to lie and say that Spencer was with me, and I also wanted that to be the truth. Something was happening inside of me, and I had to struggle to step back and figure out what it was.

"Yes," I finally said and walked to her bedside and kissed her forehead.

"Well, I want you around for the next couple of days until all of this is resolved."

I smiled tightly. "You look rather well. How are you feeling?"

My mom adjusted her position. "I look well because I have to be well. I have no time to be bedridden. Congress is in session next week. An important vote is hitting the floor, and there are still a few people I have to convince to see things my way. I might need your help with that."

I worked like hell to contain my shock. *Shit, she isn't wasting any time.* Surely, she must have known I wasn't interested in doing her bidding, especially after I'd quit Jimmy's campaign and gone straight to New York to resume my life.

I looked at a spot at the foot of her bed, wanting to sit there but also not wanting the weight of my body pressing down on the mattress to hurt her. I opted to remain standing. "What happened exactly, Mom?"

Her expression was pinched. "Did you hear what I said?"

I inhaled deeply through my nose, but it hardly contained the rage I felt. "Of course I did, Mom. I'm standing right here beside your bed. But I'm asking you a different question, and I would like you to answer." I felt tense and shaky.

Her eyelids fluttered as if she was trying to absorb what I'd just said. "A maniac shot me in the shoulder—that is what I know. The same maniac is threatening my family—that is also what I know. If you don't mind, I want to keep my daughter safe." I opened my mouth to respond, but she raised a finger. "And don't ever speak to me that way again. I am your mother."

I set my jaw and rubbed the back of my neck.

So many emotions and impulses were warring inside me. "Sorry," I finally said in a strained voice. "I'm just concerned about you."

"It's not your job to be concerned about me. It's my job to be concerned about you. I also can't believe Spencer Christmas let you travel across the country alone, especially after someone tried to hurt me."

Her eyes... there was something about them. They seemed as if they had never known fear, not because she was brave but because she was defiant. They smiled slightly, too, in that way a person does when she knows she's getting away with something.

"Do you remember meeting Thomas Norton?" she asked.

She'd taken on a brand-new tone, and I decided it was in my interest to play along. "Sure," I lied.

"I want to send Clinton with you to Washington, and I need you to have lunch with him and explain to him why he should vote on a certain bill that needs to get passed in the House."

"That's a pretty hefty task, Mom. Why would he listen to me? He doesn't know me, and I was fairly new to politics before I quit." I turned my head slightly. "You do remember I quit?"

"It's just one lunch, my darling." That naughty

gleam was in her eyes again. "Thomas is a hand-some young man. He would appreciate you being my messenger."

I felt my face collapse into a frown. "And why is that?"

"Because you're my daughter, sweetheart, and I'm sending him my best."

My heart swelled and deflated. I folded my arms against my chest as nerves gripped me. I checked over my shoulder—I didn't even remember closing the door. I wanted out of the room and away from her, but I also wanted to fulfill that one last request of hers.

"Mom, where's your staff? You rarely leave home without them. I can hardly believe they're not all surrounding your bed right now."

"They're at home, where it's safe."

"And Dad? Where is he?"

Her pinched expression was back in full force. "I don't know where your father is."

I yanked my head back. "You two are divorced, but you're still friends, aren't you?"

"Of course."

I didn't want to show her that I detected the lack of warmth in her tone. I knew my dad very well. If he thought she was hurt, he'd be right at her side. I wondered if Spencer's suspicions regarding the entire incident were valid. I forced myself to control the impulse to yell at her and try to make her address those suspicions. If she'd arranged her own attack to bring me back into her fold, then she was sicker than I could ever imagine. Not only that, but I was possibly fucked-up beyond repair for falling for her tricks for as long as I could remember. I wanted answers, but I knew I wouldn't get the truth from her even if she were being tortured.

Finally, I sat down on that spot at the foot of her bed. "Okay, Mom, I'll meet with Thomas Norton."

And right on cue, that wicked gleam in her eyes returned. Patricia Forte believed she'd gotten what she wanted.

I RESENTED THE BLISS MY MOTHER SEEMED TO FEEL as she told me all about Thomas Norton. She explained that hefty bill, how she'd helped author it, and the fact that her reputation would be on the line if it didn't pass. I engaged my ears differently. Sure enough, we'd been in this place many times before. She had me exactly where she wanted me and was happy as a lark. She talked about her career and how successful the divorce campaign was, never mentioning Spencer's accusation against her and other politicians. And even though I wanted to bring it to her memory, I chose not to simply because I knew exactly what I needed to do next and didn't want her to suspect that I couldn't give a damn about her career and was certainly not going to fly to Washington to meet with Thomas whatever-the-hell-his-name-was on her behalf.

"You never explained what happened between you and Spencer Christmas," she said out of the blue.

Just the mention of his name made me miss him more. I felt nervous. I knew if I paused too long, she would detect deception.

I sighed deeply. "We had a fight."

There was that dancing in her eyes again. "Honey, it's for the best. There is a predictable factor to human behavior."

I felt my eyes expand and skin warm as I fought the urge to shout at her about her own behavior on the one hand and soak in her every word as the stone-cold truth on the other.

"Randolph Christmas was a Goliath of a monster. There's no way Spencer Christmas escaped him unscarred. The question isn't whether he will turn into the same sort of creature his father was but when it will happen. And look what he did to me. Not only has he manipulated my daughter, but he also disrupted our annual Christmas Eve soiree with his lies and the Annual Centennial Benefit with that performance of his. I wonder what his motivation for that was."

My lips were pressed together so tightly that I thought they would merge into each other. I'd been doing so well in keeping up the facade. I desperately wanted to remind her that everything Spencer had said at the dinner was the truth and perhaps she shouldn't denounce his "performance" at the benefit as a lie.

"Yeah." I made myself cough to take the shakiness out of my voice. "He was always strange."

"He's more than strange, He's dangerous, and I don't want you around him."

I yawned on purpose, and to my benefit, there was a soft rattling on the door. Then a nurse entered. I rose to my feet and smiled at the nurse, who announced that she was checking my mother's vitals.

"Mom, I'm a little jet-lagged. Someone told me there's a room for me to sleep in here. I think I'm going to get some rest."

I could see her thinking before she smiled. "That's a good idea. Don't forget to come check on me, though, at some point."

I stepped slowly and softly out of the room, trying to convey that I was harmless. I had one goal in mind, and it wouldn't be easy to fulfill it. First, I had to handle Clinton, which meant I couldn't just slip out. When I looked to my left, he was already watching, being the good soldier he was.

I made my smile beyond pleasant to convey that everything was just A-OK between my mother and me so he wouldn't have to worry about whether or not I would fall in line. Clinton stood a hair taller as he watched me approach.

I thumbed over my shoulder toward my mother's hospital room. "So Mom is fine and is going to get some rest. We're both famished from all of our catching up." I pointed ahead of me. "The nurse said there's an empty room around the corner. I'm going to go there and get some rest. I'll come back to check on my mom when I wake up." I made myself yawn.

Clinton nodded. "Sleep tight."

I already knew he wouldn't insist I have an escort. I was no longer in the business of deluding myself. My life was not in danger. I smiled tightly as

I walked past him and then turned around. "You're going to get to rest at some point, aren't you?"

"Hugh will relieve me in about an hour."

"Ah," I said, smiling. "Is there anything I can get you until then? You must be famished."

Ever so slightly, his eyes veered down to my tits and back to my face. "I'm fine. Thanks for asking." He stared straight ahead again.

I was sure he perceived that I'd noticed him lusting after my breasts and the fact that I was grimacing. I was still processing what had just happened when I reached the end of the hallway and looked up and down it, trying to reorient myself and understand where in the building I was. When I turned to glance at Clinton, he was still looking straight ahead.

A woman in scrubs was close to passing me, and I asked where the private elevator was. She watched me with narrowed eyes, perhaps realizing that if I was on this high floor with its grandiose rooms, I might indeed be a VIP visitor. She pointed at the space behind me, and I quickly turned and walked in that direction.

I reached an elevator and stood there, waiting for it to arrive, feeling like a sitting duck. If Clinton abandoned his post to check on me, he would discover me attempting to flee the scene. I nervously observed my surroundings until I spotted an exit sign above the door to a stairwell. Without another second of deliberation, I entered the vestibule and practically ran down the steps.

At some point before reaching the end, I exited through a door on the third floor. From there, I went in search of another stairwell near the rear of the hospital. When I found what I was looking for, I scurried down the steps and entered a different hallway. When I walked out into the cool night, there was no one around. Relieved that I had successfully escaped, I freed my hair from the high topknot, took off my coat, tucked it under my arm, and walked quickly to my rental car.

EVEN THOUGH THE PORCH LIGHT WAS ON, MY MOM'S home still looked lonely. I had a key to the house, but my mother constantly changed the security code to disengage the alarm. I drove cautiously to the rear of the house and parked my car in front of the garage of one of the guesthouses. Time was of the essence. Every second, I feared my mom would ask Clinton to fetch me. He would then search for me and uncover the lies I'd told him, and my mom would become suspicious.

It was going on eleven o'clock, and it looked as if whoever was staying in the guesthouse that night had already gone to bed. Sometimes Maria would sleep there if she were working long consecutive days. Mostly, Luz and other house-services team members would stay in one of the three bedrooms after they'd completed their tasks for the night. I decided to first try the back door that the house staff often used. To my relief, it was unlocked.

I padded up the hallway, passing my mother's office. She never kept anything she didn't want anyone to find in there. I kept going past the utility closet Spencer and I had banged in on Christmas Eve until I reached a door that led to the basement.

Because I was their only child, my parents made sure I stayed engaged in activities outside the home, such as ballet when I was very little and tennis practice once I convinced my mom that twirling and toe pointing wasn't my style. Then the activities kept multiplying—community theater, debate club, swim team, and yearbook. My mom attempted to talk me into running for student government, but that idea put a bitterer taste in my mouth than ballet had. One afternoon, Maria picked me up from the tennis courts after practice, and as soon as we entered the house, I went my way and she went hers. Usually, on Wednesdays, my mom didn't come home until after dinner, due to regularly scheduled city council meetings. I followed my regular routine to a T. I was on my way to the laundry room, ready to strip out of my sweat-soaked tennis outfit and stuff the garments, including my underwear, into the laundry basket. Maria never understood why I had to do all that in the laundry room, so I'd explained to her that I just didn't like the smell of athletic sweat in my bedroom. She'd rolled her eyes, shaken her head, and muttered about how crazy that sounded, but she always left three fluffy white robes for me to change into on the rack next to the dryer.

As I rounded a corner, leaving one long corridor for another, I caught a glimpse of my mother leaving a space that we called "the throw-away room" because it contained all the shit my mom bought on a whim while traveling, like mugs, ceramic pots, tablecloths, and silk flowers—stuff she kept to dole out as gifts to her staff for their birthdays or Christmas. My mom was so engrossed in whatever was on her mind that she didn't see me. I opened my mouth to call to her, since she was walking toward the terrace room, but something stopped me. Once she entered the terrace, I continued walking up the hallway but stopped in front of the throw-away room. Something was off about my mother's demeanor, and I'd never even thought she visited that space. It was Maria who maintained it. My mom had an uncanny ability to remember all the junk she ever bought, so there was no need for her to scan the shelves—all she had to do was explain to Maria exactly what she wanted, and Maria would find it, wrap the gift, and leave it on my mom's office desk.

On that day, I walked right past the space and continued, still planning to strip out of my clothes before heading up to my bedroom. However, while I tried to finish my homework, and even before bed, I couldn't get the picture of my mom skulking out of the room off my mind. So I decided to go figure out what in the world she could have been doing in there.

My search of the throw-away room started slowly, with me picking up each object and putting it back down. Then I saw a closet and opened it. There were boxes stacked on top of each other. My curiosity made me open the top one, which had envelopes inside. They were neatly lined up in rows.

I casually lifted one out and saw that it was a hand-written letter addressed to Patricia Forte from someone named Gunther Boudreaux. Once I dug in there a little more, I saw that all the letters were from Gunther. My heart sank deeper into my chest, and I instinctively knew that whatever was written was not for me to read and that the letters were deeply personal to my mother. Another box had more mail, accounting ledgers, and other documents. I even found my birth certificate. Before I searched through boxes that would take more effort to look inside of, I'd called off my exploration, concluding that all that was there was more personal shit of my mother's.

Over the years, I thought about the closet, but I never went back inside it or told my mother what I'd done. I suspected she never guessed that anyone, even Maria, would invade whatever she wanted to keep secret. After all, we'd been trained to keep her secrets and articulate her concocted version of the truth. But that night, it was that room and that closet that I found myself inside of.

The boxes were still there, all piled up high. I wasted no time opening those that were easiest to access and combing through the contents. I had no idea what I was looking for—perhaps something that looked suspicious. My mom wasn't stupid enough to keep secret evidence in her closet. However, I wanted to find something that proved she was the sort of person who would arrange to have someone shoot her.

The letters to Gunther were gone. Now that I was older, I understood the ledgers were accounting for campaign spending. I scanned each page, looking for Dillon Gross's name. It didn't take long to figure out that line items were salary payments.

My eyes were becoming tired as I picked up another ledger, but I made a bargain with myself to look through two more boxes before writing off my suspicions as feeding into Spencer's paranoia about my mother. That was when some folded pages fell out of the book.

I felt dizzy as I swiped the pages off the floor and opened them up to give them the obligatory scan. Slowly, my mind began to uncover what I was seeing—photocopies of cashier's checks for thousands of dollars, all made out to "Patricia Forte for Congress." But what made my jaw drop was the fact that the payments came from Christmas Industries. I examined the year of each check. Since my mom was a career politician, I could recite senatorial election dates going back the last twenty years and beyond off the top of my head. The checks had been issued a year before each election year.

I shook my head continuously. I'd discovered the last thing in the world I thought I would find. My thoughts were muddy, so I took a deep breath and gave the pages a more in-depth examination. Payments were definitely made by Christmas Industries. The last three checks, all made seven years ago, were for one hundred thousand dollars each.

I closed my eyes, thinking about *The Dark Christmases*, which I'd binge read back at the ranch. *When did Randolph Christmas die?* I drew my phone out of my purse and turned it back on. My device beeped, letting me know I had voice and text messages. Spencer had called me once earlier. I wondered if he knew anything about the payments to my mother.

The papers fell out of my clutches as I opened my reading app. When I bent down to pick them up, I saw a note scribbled on the back of one of them. It was definitely in my mother's handwriting. My head spun as I read the three words, and I thought I would hyperventilate.

Knock, knock, knock.

My heart raced as I turned to the door. "Hello,"

I called as I stuffed the pages into my purse and placed the ledger back in the box.

"Jada, is it you?" Maria asked.

"Um, yes." I tried to keep from sounding shaken.

Maria told someone in Spanish that all was fine. "I'm coming in," she announced to me.

She was the last person I wanted to see me. Maria knew me better than my mom and had the ability to see past any sort of performance I could put on. Before I could ask her to give me a few seconds, the door opened. Maria's curious eyes shifted from the open boxes to my face.

"Are you okay?" she asked.

I smashed my lips together as I nodded.

She dipped her head and closed the door behind her. "Your mother doesn't allow anyone in the closet. Not even me."

I cleared my throat. "Are you going to tell her?"

She studied me with narrowed eyes. "Is what you're doing a secret?"

"Yes," I blurted out as if my mouth had a mind of its own.

"Then I will not say anything."

I felt my eyebrows furrow as I thought about how my mom might react if she detected that someone had searched through her private documents.

"Well… if she asks, then you tell her it was me. But maybe soon she'll know it was me anyway."

Maria heaved a sigh before walking out of the room. She didn't have to say another word. I'd always known that even though my mother paid her salary, she was more loyal to me.

ONCE I PUT EVERYTHING BACK EXACTLY HOW I'D found it, I went back to my rental car and drove off that property as fast as I could. There was no way I would return to the hospital. I had no proof, but I didn't doubt Spencer was right about my mom. Something fishy was going on with her being shot in the shoulder. The farther I drove down the hill, the fuzzier the world became. Then I perceived that tears were rolling down my eyes like a leaky sink. I couldn't stop them. The pain in my heart was too deep for that.

I was crying so hard that I had to pull over to keep from crashing. I guided my car over to the side of the road and then collapsed against the steering wheel, my face buried between my arms, and wailed. All the pain in my heart was way too much to bear, and I knew I needed to call Spencer. I wished he were with me. I wished I'd stayed at the apartment in Manhattan—then I would never have discovered the note my mom had written that said, *Hush for girls.*

My cellphone rang. I jumped, but it wasn't her. It was him. I snatched the phone off the seat and answered it.

CHAPTER FIFTEEN

SPENCER CHRISTMAS

EARLIER THAT DAY

This time, as I walked down the dark passageways, I felt taller, stronger, more in my body. My footsteps echoed around me. It was cold between the cement walls. I'd never seen the cracked white paint coated with dust that had accumulated on the walls through the generations. My brother Jasper had installed recessed lighting not too long ago.

"Before I set foot in those fucking tunnels, I needed to light them up," he'd said earlier that morning. He called before Jada awakened to tell me that he had a buyer for the home we'd grown up in.

My muscles tightened as my head drew back stiffly. "I didn't know it was for sale."

"You're just now starting to answer phone calls, Spence."

I sighed heavily. "Then you tried to inform me?"

"Many times."

"What about Bryn and Asher?"

"Asher's MIA."

I cocked my head. "And Bryn?"

Jasper went silent.

"Did you get Bryn's permission?"

"I don't need Bryn's fucking permission or yours either," he blared.

"Then why the hell are you calling me?"

He muttered, "Fuck." Then he cleared his throat. "Sorry about that, Spence. You know Father's mind fuck. He put me in control to keep me imprisoned."

Shit... I pinched my nose between my eyes. I used to resent Jasper because of that. The fact that I didn't anymore was miraculous. Instead, I felt sorry for him.

"I know, brother," I said with a level of empathy that even surprised me.

"Bryn wants it. But she's in the hospital again. What's this, the fourth time?"

"Third," I said, hoping it was enough to make Jasper give her some sympathy.

"If you ask me, she needs to let it go. That fucking place has something inside it, and you know it."

I knew what he meant. The heavy and sad energy always disturbed me, especially when I was asleep. It was the girls. I was sure of it. They'd moved through the shadows of the hall, the darkness absorbing their angry, abandoned, destructive spirits. And what they left behind became ghosts hell-bent on destroying their tormentor's family for everything he had done to them. He was right—Bryn should let the place go. But I knew she wouldn't.

"Listen, Spence." Jasper went into his all-business voice. "The fucking buyer won't sign the papers unless you meet her at the house to talk."

I tilted my head back to pause and process what Jasper had just said. "What?"

"Yeah, I know. It's fucking crazy."

"What's the buyer's name?"

"Alice Templeton. You know, she used to…"

"I know who she is," I said, recalling how she'd

ARKADIE

wanted Jada to convince me to run for office. "And if I don't show up?"

"Be there, Spence."

As always, Jasper was used to ordering me around. "And if I don't fucking show up?" I asked more slowly, pronouncing every syllable so he'd get it through his fucking head that I had a choice in the matter.

"I want you to show up," he said in a gentler way.

He'd been working on changing his tone for the better ever since he'd married Holly Henderson and they'd had their first child.

I asked him to give me a few minutes, and I hung up without hearing his reply and called the hospital to speak to Bryn. When they heard I was her brother, they went to get her. Then I told her about the sale. She darn near broke down, crying for me to please not let it happen.

When I called Jasper back, his cellphone had been transferred to his assistant, who told me he was already on his way to Newport and expected me to arrive at ten in the morning.

I came up with a solid line of curse words before deciding to charter my helicopter out to Newport and nip the entire sale in the bud.

Jasper's copter was there, but he was nowhere in sight when I landed. I remembered what he'd told me about adding lights to the secret passages and decided to see for myself. I told Bruce, my pilot, that if my brother came looking for me, he should let him know I was in the narrow halls.

Bruce grimaced. "The narrow halls."

"He'll know." I started toward the mansion. The closer I got, the harder it was to breathe. I reached down to loosen my tie, but I didn't have one on. "Shit."

I sighed briskly, deciding to shake off the thoughts of how the spirits that haunted the mansion could smell me coming a mile away and were already fucking with me. However, when I reached the hallways, I found that the macabre feeling had been drained from them just by the addition of lights. *Who would've guessed? All we ever needed were lights.*

"Spence," I heard Jasper call before I picked up the sound of his heavy steps.

I rotated to get a look at him and grinned, glad to see him in the flesh. It had been way too long. As usual, Jasper's expression indicated that he was all business. I recalled the days when I used to get off on disturbing his composure. The more intense and serious he'd been, the more unpredictably I behaved. I was never comfortable with the role I chose to play—the unreliable Christmas brother who couldn't get his shit together to save his life— but it was the only way I could get Father to acknowledge me. He seemed to like that I didn't have any discipline. It had made him believe I was more like him than I actually was.

"Hey, Jasper," I said as we shook hands and hugged.

He folded his arms and widened his stance, taking ownership of the moment, Jasper style. This time I didn't shrink before his commanding presence as I would have in the past.

"Alice is running late. She'll be here soon," he said.

I pushed my gaze up and down the hallway until I found what I was looking for. I had a memory from when I was twelve or thirteen—it was hard to recall my exact age when I thought about childhood. I used to like to lurk in the passageways, looking for something, although I never knew what I wanted to find. However, on this one occasion, I heard footsteps. Usually, I'd wait to see if they belonged to Bryn or Asher, who also liked to play in that particular hallway. But the footsteps were a mix of heavy and light, which meant they belonged to an adult and someone younger. I ducked into a vestibule that separated the part of the house that was visible from its secret passageways. When I was sure the visitors had passed, I entered the hallway again and found myself locking eyes with a girl who my father was dragging by the wrist.

I remember hearing mumbling. The girl was silent and her eyes vacant. Only as an adult did I realize the sound had to have come from my father, but at the time, I had no idea where it came from. I thought it was the ghosts who haunted the passageways. The tone was gruffer than my father's normal voice and almost demonic. The girl heard me, but my father didn't. He was too intent on getting her to where he was taking her. The girl, though... she didn't look afraid, and I thought she should have been. I was. She wasn't even curious. Her gaze haunted me for decades, appearing in my dreams or coming to mind whenever I looked at a girl her age.

After my sister-in-law's book was published, I had a hard time with reporters, who wanted my take on what had been written about me. The problem was, I'd never read the damn book and didn't want to. Then one night, the girl appeared in my dream again. I woke up shaking. I felt paranoid and could barely breathe. That day… the way she'd looked at me. I finally knew what she was conveying to me without words. She was pitying me. She would go upstairs into my father's den and let him do whatever he did to her, but then she would leave, and I would have to stay and live with and seek love from the sick old man.

When I woke up from her visit, I felt the deprivation of being Spencer Hunter Christmas. The next morning, I walked to the bookstore and bought my sister-in-law's book. Then, with the help of a bottle of whisky, I peeled open the pages of the book and read them. It took me two days to get through it. I hardly slept or ate. When I read the last page, it wasn't my sister-in-law I hated for exposing my father's sins or my brother for letting her do it—it was myself for having Randolph's blood coursing through my veins. I hated that I was a product of his fucking seed.

"The light changes the mood in here, doesn't it?" Jasper asked.

I forced myself back into the present as my mind still tried to put the past in the right perspective.

"Yes, it does," I confessed and gave the hallway another once-over.

He said he would have preferred to bulldoze the house, but he couldn't because it was a historical monument. Then he said he'd considered setting it on fire but couldn't bring himself to do it.

"I think you should let Bryn have it."

My brother frowned as if he was chewing on lemons. "Bryn doesn't know what's good for her."

"She's the one who brought Holly into your life. Remember that?"

His forehead ruffled.

"Listen…" I put a hand on his shoulder. "There's something about this godforsaken place that she finds redeeming."

"She's wrong," Jasper barked, but it wasn't as strong as usual, and that meant deep down he was considering Bryn's request, as he rightfully should have.

"Let her decide, then." I dropped my hand from his shoulder.

After a moment, he huffed and glared up and down the hallway. "Can you believe this is where we grew up?"

"Ha," I said, trying to picture my older brother as

a boy. He had always been a man to me. Our father didn't let him be a child. He'd always had to be serious. For the first time ever, I saw a unique quality in his eyes—something softer, tempered with fulfillment. He had been able to connect with Amelia's side of his family. Jasper didn't feel like a Christmas on the inside. He was a Hollander. He'd spent every holiday with those people since the day he found them. I used to hate him for it until I came to the realization that if I'd had the same opportunity, I would have done the same thing. *Fuck Randolph. Fuck the Christmas name.* And now I could see as clear as day how connecting with their kind of normalcy had given my brother what Randolph had stripped away from him.

"Jasper, give Bryn full control of the mansion. Let her decide its fate."

His frown intensified. "I don't think that's…"

"What the fuck do you care, anyway?"

"I care about Bryn."

"She knows how to get help for herself if she needs it. And we'll be here for her. I'll be here for her. Hell, you're more Hollander than Christmas, anyway."

"The hell I'm not," he roared and put his hand on my shoulder in the same manner I'd just done to him. "You can't say I'm not a Christmas. You can't say that shit."

I gulped, keeping the tears that flooded into my eyes from falling. Finally, I nodded jerkily.

"I'll give it to her." He sighed. "Let's see what Bryn can do to this fucking monstrosity."

Completely unexpectedly, Jasper hugged me, and for the first time, our hug wasn't loose and manly. We were holding on to each other tightly, brother to brother.

Once we let go, I checked my watch. "Listen, I don't want to see Alice Templeton. I have to get back to Jada."

Jasper folded his arms. "The senator's daughter?"

"Yeah." I sighed heavily, thinking of the senator.

"Then you two are close?"

"I love her."

His eyes narrowed to slits. "Does she know about the connection between Randolph and her mother?"

I scowled as I rubbed the back of my neck. There was no use in telling Jasper about what had happened during Christmas Eve dinner. What I knew about Patricia Forte had been bothering me since the day I'd laid eyes on Jada. I hadn't even told Dr. Sharma what I knew about Jada's mother.

"No," I said.

"You have to tell her," Jasper said.

"I know."

"No!" I roared after reading Jada's text message.

My airplane had landed, and now I was standing at the top of the ramp, replying to her.

One second passed, and then a few more. I waited long enough, so I called Jada and reached her voicemail.

"Fuck!" I shouted even louder.

I made a big mistake, not telling her everything I knew about Patricia Forte. I ran down the ramp as fast as I could. Jada was about to do something dangerous—and I had to stop her.

Read *Bliss*, book three of **The Freed Billionaire Spencer Christmas Trilogy** now!

Made in the USA
San Bernardino, CA
10 May 2020

71161013R00124

M000081898

Waiting for You

Waiting for You

A PINE VALLEY NOVEL

Heather B. Moore

Mirror Press

Copyright © 2018 by Mirror Press, LLC
Print edition
All rights reserved

No part of this book may be reproduced in any form whatsoever without prior written permission of the publisher, except in the case of brief passages embodied in critical reviews and articles. This is a work of fiction. The characters, names, incidents, places, and dialogue are products of the author's imagination and are not to be construed as real.

Interior design by Cora Johnson
Edited by Cassidy Wadsworth Skousen and Lisa Shepherd
Cover design by Rachael Anderson
Cover image credit: Deposit Photos #102039262
Published by Mirror Press, LLC

ISBN-13: 978-1-947152-38-0

PINE VALLEY SERIES

Waiting for You

Gwen Robbins loves her job waitressing at the Pine Valley resort restaurant, and as a single woman she has no trouble turning down offers of dates from the restaurant patrons. Even when her boss, Seth Owens, shows interest in her, she's not tempted in the least, no matter how strong their attraction.

But when Seth helps her through a crisis, she begins to see him in a different light. He's not the rich and privileged business owner she first makes him out to be, but a man who's making huge sacrifices to follow his own dreams. As Seth encourages Gwen to mend the divide with her family, she realizes her heart is slowly opening toward a better future.

One

"Fourth of July isn't until Thursday," Alicia told Gwen.

Gwen smirked at the image of her friend on FaceTime as she put on her American flag earrings and necklace. The Fourth of July might technically be on Thursday this year, but Gwen Robbins loved holidays, and she decided Monday wasn't too early to start celebrating.

Gwen pulled her blonde hair into a messy bun. "Are you coming to the homeless shelter with me tomorrow?" she asked Alicia.

"I have to take my mom to a doctor's appointment," Alicia said. "I'm bummed to miss out on those Fourth of July cupcakes you ordered for the shelter, though."

"I'll try to save you one," Gwen said with a smile. "No guarantees."

Alicia laughed. "That's all right. I should probably cut

back on desserts anyway. Chef Pierre sends home way too many leftover desserts with me, since my mom is always hitting me up."

Gwen knew Alicia's mom had some dependency issues, but Gwen had never pried too deeply about it. As far as she was concerned, Alicia was a saint.

"All right, I'd better go," Gwen said, holding up her hands to inspect her fingernails. "I think I need to touch up my nails."

"Can't wait to see how creative you get with them."

Alicia hung up, and Gwen grabbed her box of nail polish. She had to be to work in about an hour, which was just enough time to redo her fingernails with tiny stripes of red, white, and blue. She'd ordered miniature flag decals online the week before, too, and would add them to each ring finger.

She and Alicia Waters had become fast friends when they both started working at the five-star-resort Aspen Lodge restaurant. To some, Gwen might be simply a waitress, but with Pine Valley quickly becoming a premium resort town, Gwen's take-home pay rivaled that of her friends who had college degrees and annual salaries. Besides, she was a night owl.

Alicia was the hostess, and she usually took off the same day as Gwen to go to the homeless shelter, but this week Gwen was going to the shelter on Tuesday instead of her usual Wednesday.

The only thing that pulled her out of bed before noon was her volunteer days at the homeless shelter in the next city over. Gwen thought it would be fun to bring a little patriotic cheer to the shelter residents, so she'd put in a huge order for Fourth of July themed cupcakes at the Main Street Café. The cost would be a strain on her waitressing budget, but her homeless friends were worth it and deserved a special treat once in a while.

Gwen used an Insta-Dri coating on her nails; then she went to her bedroom to get dressed. She pulled on her black slacks, then buttoned up her standard white blouse that made up her uniform. Last, she attached her name badge. *Oh, one more thing.* Her outfit wouldn't be complete without some dark red lipstick. Was it weird that Gwen was as excited for holidays as an eleven-year-old kid?

She grabbed her purse and hurried out of her apartment, then locked the door behind her. She drove a total beater car that she'd nicknamed Marge. If the saying "running on a prayer" was ever to be proved true, Marge could be exhibit A.

"Come on, Marge." Gwen slid onto the cracked vinyl seat. The car had a cassette tape deck that didn't work, so Gwen used her cell phone to listen to music. As she drove toward the ski resort and the Aspen Lodge she passed plenty of luxury cabins. She rarely wondered about the lives behind the blinds and curtains. She knew. She'd grown up in an affluent home and neighborhood, but she was more happy in her small apartment than she'd been surrounded by luxuries.

Now her vacations consisted of a couple of days off in a row, which she then spent at the homeless shelter. She'd once joined a group of college girlfriends on a vacation to Cancun. After watching her friends party for three straight days, getting puke drunk and not caring which guy ended up in their beds at night, Gwen had vowed never to go on a vacation again with those girls.

In fact, she'd become tired of the whole privileged Ivy League college mentality and had dropped out of Stanford and ended up at Pine Valley. Big change. But Gwen had never been happier, or at least mostly happy. Her parents had given up on talking her into returning to school, and their communications had been reduced to letters since she'd told them to never call her. All the letters were from them though, letters that Gwen didn't open.

Marge puttered up the final incline to the lodge, and Gwen coasted into a parking place. The car died without Gwen having to turn off the ignition. That wasn't a good sign, but nothing that hadn't happened previously. By the time Gwen got off her shift later that night, Marge would be cooled off and start up fine. She just didn't like the summer heat.

Gwen climbed out of her car, re-tucked in her blouse and walked across the parking lot. Her usual shift was 5:30 p.m. to closing, but she liked to arrive at 5:00 to make sure all the tables had been set right.

Another car entered the parking lot, its motor an elegant purr compared to Marge.

"Oh no," Gwen muttered. "Not him." She picked up her pace to avoid any one-on-one conversation with the driver of the black Mercedes.

But she wasn't fast enough—mainly due to the fact that Seth Owens had a reserved parking space near the top of the lot. So, by the time she reached the lodge, his path intercepted hers.

"Hi, Gwen."

She couldn't pretend she didn't see him. She looked over at Seth—technically her boss—but really, he was just a rich kid whose dad owned the lodge. Well, Seth was a *man*, not a kid, but Gwen had no doubt he'd been the typical frat boy during his college years. Weekend drinking binges. A string of girlfriends. No credit card limit. And Pine Valley was the perfect place for him to keep living out his ski-bum aspirations.

Now, she eyed Seth. His blond hair was darker than hers, and his hazel eyes were the kind that even women envied. Gwen suspected he spent his frequent days off golfing or waterskiing to keep his torso trim and those shoulders and arms of his well defined. Not that Gwen wanted to notice these things about her boss. But when you worked with someone on a regular basis—even if that someone only barked orders at you—you started to notice things like how his nails were always trimmed and clean, and how he never shaved on weekends so that by Sunday his scruff made him look even more the ski bum he was.

Today he wore gray slacks and a pale-green button-down shirt with a tie. Gwen may or may not have noticed how his shirt made his eyes look more green than brown. He always dressed professionally at work, but the slight muss of his hair made it obvious that he was one of those guys who only dressed up for his job.

Even though Seth's dad had crowned him the manager of the restaurant, Gwen doubted Seth had any real-world work experience. Seth was just good at delegating—another classic personality trait of the wealthy. Why do something yourself when you can pay someone else to do it for you?

"Your name's still Gwen, right?" Seth asked.

Gwen realized she hadn't returned his greeting. "Oh, hi. Sorry. Long day."

He looked her up and down, wearing that crooked smile of his that always made her skin heat whenever it was directed at her. She might hate everything Seth Owens stood for and represented, but she wasn't immune to a good-looking man's appreciation. Not that she ever wanted to mix with his kind again. She'd had her fill growing up among the privileged.

"Saving the world again?" he said.

His comment hadn't been sarcastic, or had it? She wasn't

5

quite sure, but just in case, she decided to take him down a notch. She stopped walking and turned toward him, folding her arms. "I sincerely regret ever telling you about my volunteer work. What I do during my off hours is none of your business and is certainly not up for discussion."

His eyes were extra green in the light of the fading day, and at her retort, they widened. "Hey. I didn't mean to offend."

She narrowed her gaze. He was so hard to read, but she couldn't tell if he was being serious or teasing. Was there a glimmer of amusement in those baby greens? Typical frat boy. Seth had to know how much he got under her skin, and it was as if his sole purpose at the restaurant was to push her as far as he could. Gwen had complained to Alicia more than once, but Alicia said Seth acted the same way around all the other employees.

Okay, so maybe Gwen *wasn't* being singled out, and she shouldn't be so sensitive, but keeping her mouth shut wasn't one of her virtues.

"Don't flatter yourself, boss." She moved past him, and he barely stepped out of the way, avoiding a collision, as she reached the front doors of the restaurant. The valets had yet to arrive, and Alicia probably wasn't here yet either. So Gwen would busy herself wherever Seth wasn't being busy himself.

Before she could open the door, Seth reached around her and pulled it open.

She hated that he was one-upping her. And she hated that he smelled good—a mixture of spice and pine and just . . . fresh—like he'd showered recently. After his all-day golf game, of course.

She walked through the doors, ignoring the way her pulse drummed at his nearness. They hadn't touched at all, but his close proximity always put her on high alert. It was like her drop-out-college-girl-self was forming a protective bubble against the stereotypical guy she'd always despised.

First thing, in order to distract herself, she walked to the hostess stand and opened the reservations folder. She liked to be somewhat familiar with the evening's patrons and know if there were any *who's who* coming into the restaurant so she could pre-plan the seating arrangements.

While she was looking at the reservation list, Seth continued toward her, on his way to the kitchen, where he'd taste test the various sauces that Chef Pierre would be stirring up. Seth acted as if he knew the difference between basil and rosemary, but Gwen thought he was one-hundred percent winging it, trying to impress, for whatever reason.

Another thing on her list about Seth Owens to be annoyed about.

"By the way," he said as he moved past her, his voice low, "love the earrings."

Gwen didn't move, and likely didn't breathe, until Seth had disappeared through the double swinging doors that led to the kitchen. She wouldn't let his compliment cross off any of his many faults. Besides, how could she be sure he wasn't making fun of her? Although, he'd rarely made comments about her appearance—not like her co-workers did. No one had been negative, but it was more of an affectionate teasing. The restaurant patrons were the ones who were most likely to comment on the pattern of her nails or her choice of earrings.

"Hi," Alicia said, coming in through the front doors.

Gwen smiled at her friend. "Hey you, you're early."

"Yeah. My mom was in a bad mood, so I came over." Alicia joined Gwen at the hostess stand. "Distract me, please."

"New dress?" Gwen asked.

Alicia looked great in her black, fitted dress. She rotated

through a few dresses for her hostess position, but Gwen hadn't seen this one before.

"Yeah, got it on Amazon, if you can believe it," Alicia said with a smirk. "Forty bucks." She had the perfect appearance for a hostess of an exclusive restaurant. She was tall, elegant, well-spoken, and had a sereneness about her that Gwen envied.

"I love a good bargain." Gwen rubbed a hand over her collar bone in a nervous gesture. "Here's the reservation list. It looks like the city mayor is coming in with a group."

"Good to know." Alicia took the reservation list, then her gaze went back to Gwen's. "What's got you all flustered?"

Gwen furrowed her brows. "What do you mean?"

"I can just tell."

"Oh." Gwen gave a short laugh. "I already had a run-in with the boss. Nothing I can't forget after the next six hours on my feet. Tomorrow can't come soon enough."

"Yeah, helping at the shelter always puts things into perspective," Alicia said.

"Yep." Gwen's phone chimed. She'd forgotten to turn it off. "Although I wish I could have gone on my usual Wednesday to deliver the cupcakes—closer to the holiday, you know."

"I'll be working Wednesday too," Alicia said. "It's already booked solid." Then she did a weird buggy thing with her eyes, and Gwen got the hint that Seth had just come out of the kitchen.

"I'll check on the tables." Gwen turned from Alicia and hurried into the dining area.

She didn't know if Seth had heard her, but she wasn't sticking around to find out.

Two

The night at the restaurant seemed to drag for whatever reason, and maybe the reason was that Seth Owens had determined to speak to Gwen after their work shift. He thought luck had found him when he arrived in the parking lot before her shift earlier that night. But she was obviously bothered about something that he decided to wait to bring up helping him at the barbeque.

His parents were hosting a private barbeque the night of the Fourth, and he wanted the food catered from the Aspen Lodge, to promote the restaurant. The place didn't normally cater, especially since the dinner reservations on the night of the Fourth had been booked out for weeks. Patrons wanted to be able to eat steak and sip wine while having great views of the fireworks show.

The view would be spectacular from Seth's parents' place

as well. But he needed help to pull off his plan. He couldn't really afford to pull any of his employees off the job. But Gwen could easily fulfill the role of both hostess and server while Seth managed the food—and that way he'd only need to understaff the lodge by one person. Some of the food would be from Aspen Lodge's kitchen, but Seth planned to make a few of the dishes himself. Not that his father would approve, but Seth didn't plan on telling anyone until, well, he was in the kitchen doing the preparations on the morning of the Fourth. By then it would be too late for his father to complain.

Seth's father had practically disowned him when Seth accepted a culinary internship a few years ago in Paris. He'd been halfway through his hospitality and restaurant management degree when one of his professors handed him the application. Seth had loved to cook all his life, it seemed. But it wasn't until college that he'd learned the science behind cooking and begun to experiment with different recipes.

When the year in Paris was over, his father said if he wasn't offered a head chef position, then he needed to return to California and finish his degree. Politics and seniority status meant that Seth was at the bottom of the employment chain no matter how good of a chef he was. After swallowing a big piece of humble pie, Seth returned to the States and finished his degree.

After graduation, he'd worked his way up in management at one of his dad's restaurant chains in Sacramento, and when the Pine Valley opportunity opened up, Seth had bought into the ownership. It wasn't like he'd done much with the money his years of salary had brought him. He'd rented an apartment with a couple other single guys, splitting rent and utilities, and saved money.

"Seth?" Alicia came into the manager's office, where Seth

had started the night's accounting to make sure the receipts matched up with the intake.

Seth never shut the door, wanting to be accessible to the employees. "Yeah?"

"One of the customers is throwing a fit about the price of the wine on her bill," Alicia said.

Seth rose to his feet. "Whose table?"

"Rob, but he left early because his kid was sick," Alicia said. "I called him, and he says he's sure he quoted her the price before she ordered it."

Seth walked out of the office and joined Alicia as they headed toward the dining area. "Who's on the table now?"

"Gwen."

Gwen was no pushover, so the patron must have a fairly strong personality to put up such a complaint. "Okay, I'll go find out what we can do," he said.

It didn't take Seth long to determine who the unhappy customer was. Sure, she was sitting in Rob's section, but the woman was with a party of other women, and they all looked a bit dull-eyed with drink. Gwen stood a couple of feet from the table, her arms folded, as if she was just barely managing to hold in her frustration. Gwen was excellent with customers, but she wouldn't put up with much.

Sometimes a simple change in waiters would put a patron on edge, and he wondered if that was the case now. Gwen saw him approach, but her expression didn't change.

"Hello, ma'am," Seth said to the customer. "I'm the manager here, and I wanted to see what I can help you with."

She looked up at him, her giant fake eyelashes touching her eyebrows. "Thank you." Her tone was far from conciliatory, though. She held the receipt in front of her. "I was told by the other waiter that this bottle of wine is forty-five dollars, but here it says sixty dollars."

Seth took the receipt. "This wine is forty-five percent off this month," he said, glancing over at Gwen who looked stone-faced. "Which does make it sixty dollars. It's normally $110.00."

"That's what she claimed, too," the woman said, pointing at Gwen. "I think this restaurant has some sort of coup going on. You quote one price, then charge another, hoping that the customers don't check the receipts."

Seth practically felt Gwen bristle behind him. He didn't feel much better.

"That's not the case, ma'am," he said in as even a tone as possible. "I'm willing to discount the wine further tonight due to the misunderstanding, but our servers are trained to always quote the direct price, even if there is a discount. Rob would have told you the discount in addition to the final price."

"Well, if he did, he didn't tell it to *me*," the woman protested.

Seth only nodded, refraining from what he really wanted to say. "I'll be back in a moment with the corrected receipt," he said. At this point, it was always better for him to handle the customer personally until he got them out the door. Otherwise, customers like this would continue to act disgruntled toward their servers.

Gwen caught up with him by the time he reached the sales register positioned behind the curtained-off section where they kept the extra serving trays.

"You know she's playing you," Gwen said in a low voice.

He looked over at her, and as he'd predicted her blue eyes were more gray, like there was a storm brewing. "I know." He showed the woman's credit card to Gwen. "Tell Alicia to flag her name. The next time she comes into the restaurant, I'll give her table to you."

"Um, thanks?"

"You'll keep her straight, I've no doubt." Seth ran the credit card and printed out the new receipt, although he doubted the woman would add any gratuity.

"Why do I get the nightmare customers?" Gwen moved closer.

At this proximity, Seth could swear he smelled lemons on Gwen. Had she been slicing the lemons herself for the drinks? He liked lemons. "Because I know I can rely on you, and because you aren't a pushover, no matter how rich and famous someone might be. You don't let flattery go to that pretty head of yours."

Her blue eyes only turned darker as she narrowed her gaze.

"See? You get angry when someone compliments you."

"I do not," Gwen said. "I can spot fake from a mile away, and most compliments are fake."

"Fair enough." Seth took a step away from her. He had to get the unhappy customer out of the restaurant ASAP. "Rest assured that I'm never fake."

She opened her mouth as if to reply, then shut it. And that was probably wise for both of them. He left the curtained section and headed back into the main dining area. He presented the modified receipt, then thanked the ladies for coming to the restaurant. Instead of returning to his office, he hovered near the kitchen doors to ensure that the ladies left without further incident. You'd think that a fine-dining restaurant wouldn't encounter much drama. All in all, Seth had only involved security twice in the past year.

The women left, and Seth remained in his spot a while longer, watching Gwen. She had an easy way with the customers, was very attentive, and it all added up in her tips. She made the most money out of all the other servers in the place. Not that anyone would guess by the state of her car. It

13

was like she'd hung onto her high school car and never replaced even the tires. He wondered how she'd made it through the winter coming up the winding pass on snowy days.

It wasn't like he could ask her any personal questions, though. Every time he tried to move forward a step with her, she pushed him back two. She either acted annoyed with him or ignored him, and Seth wasn't sure why. And for some reason, it only made him more curious about her. How such a vivacious and a beautiful woman like Gwen was unattached, and didn't seem interested in dating anyone, he could only guess. She never really flirted with any of the male servers, or male customers, for that matter. She received plenty of attention from men, but she mostly brushed it off good-naturedly. If she needed to put someone in his place, she would. Seth had witnessed her set-downs more than once.

Her appearance drew attention, sure—her blue eyes framed with dark lashes, her flawless skin, those lips she painted dark red or deep pink, and her fingernail art . . . all of which he'd noticed. But she also made the customers feel like she really cared about them. It seemed that by the end of the night, they'd become old friends. In fact, some who made regular reservations often requested to be put at one of Gwen's tables.

Yet . . . there was something Seth couldn't quite figure out about Gwen. She was friendly with all the restaurant patrons, but he'd overheard a few digs about "wealthy people" she'd made to Alicia. He knew Alicia was helping her mom out, and this job wasn't so much to make money but to keep a balance in her life. Apparently, she'd left a decent job to come help her mom. Gwen . . . he hadn't figured out. But if he hadn't seen her car, he'd have thought she'd grown up well off. It was just the way she carried herself with confidence and the attention to detail she put into her appearance.

Where some other women were a mystery, Gwen was an enigma.

Seth straightened and headed into the kitchen. He didn't want to be caught staring at Gwen; eventually someone would notice. He didn't always stay through all the cleanup because the final receipts only took half an hour to reconcile after the last customer had left, but tonight Seth pitched in, helping the bus boys clear the tables. He knew Gwen was usually one of the last ones to leave, so he'd wait it out until she was finished.

After the restaurant closed, the employees left one by one, calling goodbyes to each other. Gwen cast him a couple of curious looks—well, one might have been a glare—but Seth wanted to wait to talk to her when they were completely alone. When she finally headed out the door, Seth locked his office door, then walked out after her.

She was halfway across the parking lot by the time he came out of the doors. Had she been running or something? Within moments, she'd be inside her car, backing out. He had no choice but to call out to her.

She glanced over her shoulder but kept walking. With a half-wave, she said, "Goodnight, boss." Then she did start to run.

What in the . . . Seth broke into a jog. Maybe she was more upset about him giving into that customer than he realized. But it wasn't like the discount would affect Gwen.

"Hey, Gwen, hang on."

"I'm in a rush." She had reached her car and unlocked the door.

Seth found it sort of funny she'd even bother to lock such a beat-up car. He caught up with her, but the look on her face told him he had about five seconds to spill what he wanted to speak with her about. "I need to talk to you about working the night of the Fourth—"

"I know, I'm working already," Gwen cut in. "Can't this wait until later? I've got to get to the grocery store before it closes."

It had to be after eleven already, and even though Pine Valley was a booming resort town, there was no way the grocery store was open this late. "I think it's already closed. Do you want me to Google the hours?"

Gwen pulled out her cell phone from her pocket. "Damn. It's later than I thought."

The numbers on her phone clearly read 11:05. Gwen groaned and braced her hands against her car, then dropped her head.

Seth didn't know what to think. "Can I help you with something?"

She shook her head and sniffled.

"Gwen?" he moved closer. Was she *crying*? "Seriously, what's wrong?"

Lifting her head, she wiped at her cheeks.

"Hey, let me help you." He had no clue what would make Gwen Robbins so upset. He'd never seen this side of her.

She inhaled, then rubbed a hand over her face. "Unless you happen to have twenty boxes of cupcake mix, I don't think you can help me."

Three

Seth stared at Gwen as if she'd grown a second head. And perhaps she had. All Gwen knew was that her entire plan to bring her homeless friends cupcakes tomorrow had been completely foiled. Around 8:30 p.m. she'd received a voice-mail from the manager at the Main Street Café saying that their ovens were down, so they wouldn't be able to fulfill the cupcake order until likely tomorrow afternoon. But that would be too late. Gwen needed the cupcakes in the morning so she could deliver them for the lunch hour. If she waited until the dinner hour, she wouldn't be able to drive back at night. She didn't trust Marge driving that far in the dark. If she broke down on the highway leading to Pine Valley, Gwen would be stranded.

"Sorry, I don't usually cry over cupcakes." She took a deep breath. "I was going to take Fourth of July cupcakes to the shelter. The oven is down at Main Street Café, so now I need to make them tonight." She hated that her voice was trembling.

Seth wasn't saying anything, and she wondered if he thought she was a crazy woman. He did look like he was concerned, and she kind of hated that expression on his face. It made it harder to be annoyed with him.

"I'll figure it out," she continued. Her voice was steadier now, and for that she was grateful. Surely she could buy cupcakes somewhere in the morning, but then they wouldn't be decorated. So her attempts at decorating would have to be simple and quick. Maybe she could dye the frosting blue and then use red sprinkles? But . . . what grocery store would have that many cupcakes for sale?

"How many cupcakes are we talking about?" Seth asked.

"Two hundred," she said. "There's not that many at the shelter, but no one wants just one cupcake. I'm planning on at least two per person."

"When do you need them by?" he asked.

He was leaning against her car, watching her intently, and Gwen could hardly believe she was having this personal of a conversation with him. "I planned to leave around 9:30 in the morning so I can get there by 11:00 and help set up the lunch line."

Seth straightened from the car. "We can make the cupcakes at my parents' place. They've got two ovens. I'll just need to borrow some of the flour and eggs from the restaurant. And probably powdered sugar and butter—assuming you want to decorate them?"

Gwen stared at him. "I can't . . . I mean, you're talking about making the cupcakes from scratch?"

Seth raised an eyebrow. "It won't take much longer than the boxed version. Plus—"

"I can't show up at your parents' in the middle of the night," she said. "And I don't expect you—"

"Gwen," he said, putting a hand on her arm. "It's not a problem. We've got all the ingredients right inside the restaurant, and my parents are out of town."

Gwen stepped back from him, partly because his hand on her arm was making her feel . . . light, comforted? She didn't have time to define it. And he was not acting like Seth Owens, Mr. Boss, should be. She didn't know what he should be doing right now, but it wasn't offering to make cupcakes with her.

She exhaled and pushed a few strands of hair behind her ear. "Look, Seth, I appreciate the offer, but I think I can find cupcakes at the store tomorrow. Slap on some frosting, a few sprinkles, maybe find those tiny paper American flags to put on . . ."

He started laughing.

Gwen didn't know if she'd ever heard him laugh in such a way before. Maybe she'd heard him scoff, or snicker, but not a full-out laugh. Now she was annoyed. She folded her arms. "Why are you laughing?"

"I . . . just . . . you . . ." He continued laughing.

"All right, whatever." Gwen yanked her car door open. She slid into the seat, praying with every part of her being that Marge would start. The only thing that could make this night worse was Seth having to jump-start her car.

Before she could even turn the ignition, Seth grasped her shoulder.

"Wait," he said, his voice barely recovered from his laughing fit. "Please, wait. I didn't mean to laugh."

She looked up in to his eyes . . . that were filled with amusement.

"Come into the restaurant with me, and we'll get the

ingredients," he said. "Seriously. You'll have your two hundred cupcakes in no time."

Gwen told herself it wasn't the way he was looking at her, or the feel of his hand on her shoulder, or the fact that even after a long shift at a restaurant, he still smelled great . . . No, she was making this decision for the homeless people who were depending on her. Whether they knew it or not, they needed some sugar-holiday-happiness tomorrow.

"All right."

Seth grinned, and Gwen couldn't find it within herself to be annoyed with him. Of course, that would change in a few moments. Of that she was positive.

Seth moved his hand and stepped back so she could get out of the car. His mouth twitched, and she knew he was still holding back some laughter. But right now, she had cupcakes to make—from scratch, no less.

She headed toward the restaurant, and Seth joined her.

"Do you think Pierre has his recipes written down anywhere?" she asked.

"I know a few recipes."

Gwen looked over at him. "You do? Like . . . off the top of your head?"

He shrugged and shoved his hands in his pockets.

Well, then. She was tempted to ask him where he found time to memorize recipes when he was on the golf course. Maybe he was an avid Pinterest fan or something. But she was trying to be nice right now, especially since he was doing her a pretty big favor. Although it could very well turn into a disaster. She wasn't much of a "scratch" baker.

Seth opened the door for her, and she was struck with déjà vu from earlier that evening. They went into the kitchen, and he flipped on the lights. The place seemed different, and so large, with everyone gone. And that fact made her realize how she was completely alone with Seth for perhaps the very first time. Her pulse thrummed with awareness. He was just being a nice guy, right? This wasn't some master plan of his to get another notch in his belt. Not that she thought he was attracted to her, but some men weren't picky about their conquests.

Seth moved toward the cupboards and pulled them open. He started collecting ingredients—which was good, because Gwen wouldn't have known where to look. She did know where the eggs would be. She crossed to the refrigerator and opened the door. The egg cartons were stacked on the lower shelf. "How many eggs do we need?"

"Three dozen," Seth said without hesitation.

She looked over to where he was picking up what looked like small bottles of vanilla extract. She gathered three egg cartons, set them on the counter, then said, "What about butter? How much?" Since apparently he did have a recipe in his brain.

"Five pounds," he said again as if he didn't even have to think about it.

Who was this guy? A walking recipe calculator?

"Five?" she clarified.

He turned to meet her gaze. She wondered how he could look even better late at night than right before work. Her appearance usually morphed into scraggly hair, tired eyes, and worn-off makeup. Oh, right. *He* was a guy. Guys got all the luck.

"We're making two hundred, right?"

"R-rrright . . ." She waited. But he didn't ad lib.

"I think that's everything." He held up a package of cupcake liners. "Let's box it all up."

So they did, and with Seth carrying the box full of

ingredients, and Gwen opening doors for him, they made it to his car. Seth loaded everything into the trunk, then turned to her, brushing off his hands.

"How about we ride together, then I'll bring you back here after?"

"No," Gwen said immediately. She didn't want to put him out any more than she already was. "I can follow you and then get out of your way when the cupcakes are done."

Seth shut the trunk, then said, "Well, here's the thing. My parents' driveway is pretty steep. So you might have to park at the bottom of the hill, since I'm not all that sure your car—"

"—I'll ride with you," Gwen said.

Thankfully, Seth didn't laugh. Gwen headed for the passenger door and opened it. Sliding onto the cool, interior leather seat that smelled like someone had oiled it with orange-scented polish, she finally allowed herself to hope that her crisis might be diverted after all. And . . . it seemed Seth was gaining quite a few points tonight. He might possibly reach the scale of "sometimes helpful and decent boss," which was a huge step up from "pampered-pansy boss."

Seth opened the driver's door and sat down, then started the engine. Keyless. Of course. Gwen's car didn't even have automatic locks or windows, but she was proud of Marge. Every dented and rusted inch of her. Gwen had paid for the car herself after her parents had confiscated the Audi they'd given her. Perhaps they thought they were teaching her a lesson, and that would somehow convince her to return to college and her drunk roommates. But no one should ever underestimate the power of Marge . . . or overestimate her. Which was why Gwen was sitting next to Seth right now in his million-dollar Mercedes.

She knew it didn't cost a million dollars, but she had to

admit, she *felt* different sitting in such a nice car. It was as if there was no road at all, that they were literally flying through the air.

Seth was quiet on the drive, which, surprisingly wasn't awkward. She glanced over at him a couple of times to gauge his expression, but he stayed focused on the road. Gwen found herself scanning the line of his shoulders, that led to the definition of the muscles in his arms. They weren't bulky, but they exuded strength. And then she noticed the way his right hand wrapped around the steering wheel, and how his hands seemed like capable hands. *Look away, Gwen.*

Seth turned off the main canyon road and started up an incline. Gwen hadn't noticed this turn-off before, but she wasn't usually driving above the lodge. Seth was right, the hill was steep, and by the looks of how far they were driving, she would have had quite the hike to his parents' house.

Then, a sudden thought occurred to her. "Do you live with your parents?" Perhaps she shouldn't have blurted it out, because Seth actually flinched.

Then his shoulders and arms relaxed again. "I do."

That was it? No explanation? She didn't know what she'd expected, but wasn't it hard for a frat boy to, er, entertain his lady friends in the same house he lived in with his parents? Not that she was thinking of him bringing back other women to the monstrosity that seemed to rise out of the mountain slope before her.

Gwen couldn't stop the words that escaped from her mouth. "Oh. My. Gosh. This is your parents' place?" She'd seen it in a magazine once but hadn't realized the sheer size and magnificence until she viewed it at midnight glowing with lights on the multi-story decks. It was the most gorgeous cabin Gwen had ever seen. The place was like a fairytale castle set in the woods, but with giant wooden beams, and pine trees, and knotty pine double-doors.

"Wow. Just wow. This is an architect's dream on steroids." Gwen gushed. "I don't even know what to say."

Seth chuckled. "I think you've already said it."

Gwen ignored him. Her gaze was glued to the mansion, and she turned her head to look up through the window as Seth pulled up closer. He stopped the car in the circular drive made of *cobblestones*. That alone took her breath away. Okay, so her parents were well off, but this was another level entirely. Like ten more levels up, or a hundred.

"It's amazing," she said. "Amazing! Is that bear—" She clapped her hand over her mouth.

Seth waited, settled back in his seat, probably laughing again at her. Well, she *was* giving him quite the show.

The grizzly bear standing on its hind quarters next to the entrance was fake—it had to be. It might have once been alive, but now it was dead. And stuffed. But still kind of scary. "Seth," she said, turning to him and grabbing his arm. "I'm sorry for implying that you are any less of a man because you live with your parents. Because if this was my parents' house, I might still be living with them too. Or at least talking to them."

This time Seth did laugh. But it didn't bother Gwen. She was gazing back at the house. "I've no doubt that your parents have at least two ovens." Then she bit her lip. "Are you *sure* your parents will be okay with this?"

"I'm sure," he said with another chuckle. He opened his door and climbed out, and that's when Gwen realized she'd still been holding his arm. With him out of the car, she had to snap out of whatever spell she was under. Make cupcakes. Go to the homeless shelter tomorrow and try to reconcile the living conditions of what she saw before her now with those she'd be feeding tomorrow. Could anything be more juxtaposed?

How did people really live this way? They must be super-human, or something. But Seth had been acting so . . . *normal* tonight.

Her door opened, and Seth stood there, looking down at her, that crooked smile on his face. "You can check it out, you know." He held out his hand.

She swallowed because she was suddenly second-guessing this making-cupcakes-from-scratch-with-Seth-Owens thing. Then she thought of her homeless friends: Jerry, Ricky, Bo, Maddy, Silv, Declan . . . Gwen put her hand into Seth's and let him pull her to her feet. She let go as quickly as possible, telling herself for the umpteenth time that he was only being a gentleman.

Then she took a deep breath and followed him into Wonderland.

Four

Seth placed the box of ingredients on the large granite counter, then moved to the double ovens. He set the temperature on both to preheat. Even though he'd told Gwen they should get the first batches of cupcakes into the oven, and then he'd give her the grand tour, he hadn't seen her since he'd pointed her in the direction of the bathroom while they were carrying in everything.

Well, women could take a while in bathrooms, so he really shouldn't worry. But as he gathered mixing bowls and measuring cups and spoons and set them out on the counter, he began to wonder. Maybe she was sick? She hadn't acted sick, though. She'd been distressed, yes, but he thought they'd come up with a pretty great solution.

And it had only taken one small lie. His parents would *not* be okay with him bringing home a woman to their house for an all-night bake fest. In fact, his mom was still holding out hope that he and Cynthia would get back together, even though it had been a full year since their breakup. Their families were close friends and business associates, and both sets of parents had been more than thrilled when he and Cynthia had started dating their senior year in high school.

Seth had always liked Cynthia, perhaps even loved her, but he'd never really felt she was his *one and only*—as far as love legends went. Not that he was an expert by any means, or expected some sort of fantastic happily-ever-after; but he supposed he'd given into the family expectations for Cynthia and him. His parents had what he considered a good marriage, yet marriage was tough. Families were tough. Seth's older sister Emmy had gone through a divorce and was now in a great relationship with a new guy. But things were really complicated in her life as she dealt with custody issues with her ex-husband and their four-year-old son.

It might not be such a coincidence that Seth had called off his relationship with Cynthia during the same time Emmy had filed for divorce. He and his sister had had many late-night heart-to-hearts that he'd never told his parents about. But it had changed his whole way of seeing relationships. And he knew from that moment on that he was fooling himself into believing he could keep things up with Cynthia.

His sister's famous words were something like, "I knew things weren't right with Marc when I realized that every time he walked into a room, I wanted to leave. I didn't want to talk to him anymore. I didn't want to hear about his day. I simply stopped caring about his well-being. I know it sounds harsh, but we'd spent our whole marriage focusing on things about *him*. His career, where he wanted to eat, whether he was in the mood for intimacy, or if he felt like going on vacation or staying home. One day, I realized I was living *his* life. And I wanted to live *our* life."

His sister had suggested marriage counseling with her husband, but Marc had refused. And now . . . Seth was happy for Emmy and her new relationship with Jed. Seth could see the difference in his sister when they'd come out for Memorial Day weekend. She was happy and at peace. Life was still hard, but she had someone to fully share it with.

"Did you know there's a waterfall in that bathroom?" Gwen said, coming around the corner and into the kitchen.

Seth had been so involved in his memories and sifting the flour with baking powder that he hadn't even heard her footsteps. He looked up to see that Gwen had that star-struck expression as if she'd met someone famous.

"Of course you know there's a waterfall, you live here." Her voice trailed off as her brows drew together and created that small vertical line on her forehead. Seth wondered if she knew about that line.

"Look at you," Gwen continued.

Well, her quiet streak in the car was clearly over.

"You're like . . ." She tilted her head as if she was trying to come up with something nice to say as opposed to her usual jabs. "I'm not sure *what* you are, but how did I not know that you can cook?"

Then she blushed, and Seth wasn't sure what to make of that.

"Technically, it's called baking," he said.

Gwen stared at him, and he decided he liked her close scrutiny. He was so used to her trying to avoid him, that this was a nice change. "What kind of flavored extract should we use?"

"Flavored *extract?*" There was that line again between her brows. "Do you mean vanilla?"

He pointed to the container of extracts he'd brought along. "There's lemon, mint, almond—"

"Like those gourmet cupcakes at specialty shops?" She walked to the counter on the opposite side of him and pulled the container toward her. "I don't think the Main Street Café even gets this fancy." She picked up a couple of the extracts and read the labels. "Are you serious about this? I was thinking vanilla cupcakes with frosting and sprinkles, and we'd be good to go."

"With flags."

Her mouth lifted into a smile. "With flags."

Seth loved the way her blue eyes sparkled, and how they were more blue than gray right now. He wondered what she'd say if he mentioned it. He should probably keep it to himself.

"Let's try lemon for one batch." She picked up the bottle and walked to where he'd finished sifting the dry ingredients together. "What are you doing with the eggs?"

Seth looked to where he'd set the eggs in a pan of warm water to take off the chill. "The cupcakes will rise better and be more moist if the eggs are warm when we mix the dry ingredients with the wet."

"Hmm." Gwen set the lemon extract on the counter, then folded her arms. "What's going on here?"

Seth arched his brows. "What do you mean?" He knew what she was getting at, but he was going to make her work for the information. It wasn't like she ever let *him* off easy.

He started to unpeel the butter squares, not looking at her.

"Seth." Gwen put her hand on his arm, stopping his movements. "Do you have a secret life?"

He laughed, but Gwen kept staring at him, her blue eyes intense. "Here," he said, handing her a square of butter to unwrap. "The butter's easier to unwrap when it's cold."

She released his arm and took the butter. "I'm not leaving here until you tell me how you are suddenly Mr. Chef when all you do at the restaurant is arrange everyone's schedules and tally up the receipts at night."

Seth wanted to laugh again. "I do a little more than that."

"Right." Gwen set the unwrapped butter into one of the mixing bowls. Not Seth's preferred place, but he'd let it go for now. "And you calm down irate women who were overcharged for their already discounted wine."

"Yep." He reached for the pot of warm water and took out two eggs. He held them out to her and said, "Do you want to do the honors?"

"Sure." She took the eggs and cracked them against the batter bowl that he slid over to her. Then he picked up the bowl and set it in place on the Mixmaster. He turned it on, and once the eggs were whisked he added the sugar and one of the butter squares.

"You didn't even measure the sugar," Gwen said, coming over to the mixer and peering inside. Her shoulder brushed against his arm as she leaned in to look. When she straightened, they were standing so close they almost touched.

Seth didn't move, and when the realization dawned in Gwen's eyes, she stepped away.

"The amount of sugar doesn't need to be exact," he said. "Just salt."

"I know about salt," Gwen said. "Too little, not enough taste. Too much, too salty. But you . . ."

His gaze connected with hers, and he was pleased with what he saw. She didn't have that guarded look she usually had around him. Maybe it was being at the house instead of at work?

He snatched the bowl of dry ingredients and slowly added the contents to the mixing bowl. He loved watching

31

how everything blended with each rotation of the electric beaters. "Time for the lemon extract," he said as he turned the speed down.

She grabbed the extract. "How much?"

"Maybe ten or twelve drops."

So Gwen added the extract, and the scent of lemon wafted up from the batter as it spun around. "Mmm. Smells good." She closed her eyes and inhaled.

He couldn't help but smile when he watched her. "Smells like you."

Gwen's eyes flew open. "I smell good?"

"You smell like lemons," he said.

Gwen smiled back. "You're not who I thought you were, Seth Owens."

He turned off the mixer, since he didn't want to overmix. That would be almost worse than undermixing. "Who did you think I was?" He threw an arched glance in her direction before he pulled out a stack of muffin tins. There were four of them, and that would be a good number to rotate through the different batches.

Gwen followed him to the counter, and they started slipping the cupcake liners into each opening of the muffin tins. "Well, you're one of those frat boys. You know, a guy who comes from wealth and privilege, gets a high-paying job handed to them, takes out a different girl every weekend, coasts through life with the biggest stress of the week being whether to choose the lobster or the top sirloin at whichever $1,000-a-plate benefit you're attending."

Seth set down the cupcake holders and braced his hands on the counter.

She paused and turned toward him. "Too much?"

He could respond in several ways. Nothing she said he hadn't heard before. It was the battle of the classes. And basically it was true . . . but there was a lot she was missing. He didn't really feel like giving a rundown of how much his parents contributed to things like clean water in fourth world countries, and the endless hours his mom put into humanitarian work. No, this wasn't really about his upbringing. He had no say in that for the most part.

"Do you know why I live with my parents?" he asked.

"Um . . . because this place is freaking gorgeous?"

If there was one thing about Gwen, it was that she spoke her mind. Even when her words stung. And to be honest, Seth liked that about her. Cynthia was more of the passive-aggressive type—and he was never sure whether she was upset about something or truly enjoyed something.

"The first reason is that my parents are gone a lot, probably about twenty days out of the month, so I'm mostly a house sitter." He picked up the mixing bowl of batter and methodically poured it into the cupcake liners. "The second reason is that I needed to move someplace rather quickly after a breakup with my girlfriend. My parents had just finished building this cabin, so I thought I'd check out Pine Valley. I liked it enough to talk my dad into selling me the restaurant. So, the third reason I'm currently living with my parents is that I'm trying to pay off the business loan I took out to buy the restaurant."

Gwen was so silent that Seth looked up.

Her cheeks were pink, but he didn't know if that was from the heated ovens only a few feet away, or because he'd been a little too direct.

She opened her mouth, then shut it. Then opened it again. "Okay. So I think I owe you an apology. For a lot of things."

Hmmm. He could live with that. He picked up one of the muffin tins, crossed to the first oven, and slid the tin inside.

33

Then he set the timer. He turned back to grab the second tin, but Gwen was on her way with it to the second oven.

"Fourteen minutes?" she asked, having seen him set the timer on the first oven.

"Fourteen to start," Seth answered. "It might be a little longer. First batches always take longer."

"Of course they do." Gwen turned to add cupcake liners to the next set of muffin tins.

"Ready for the tour?" Seth asked.

She glanced at him, and that line between her brows was back. "Look, um, that's really sweet of you. In fact, this whole thing is amazing, and I'm grateful. But I'm going to pay you back for all these ingredients, and I'd like to compensate you for your time. Because obviously you're like some sort of mysterious master chef—"

"Gwen," Seth cut her off. "You're not paying me for helping you, and as the owner of the restaurant, I'm not going to charge you for a little flour and sugar. Come on. Let's go see the house. We've got . . . thirteen and a half minutes."

She hesitated, and he started to walk out of the kitchen, motioning for her to follow.

"You don't want to miss seeing the pool deck at night with millions of stars glittering overhead." He took a few more steps. "Not to mention the greenhouse full of lemon trees."

The line of her shoulders relaxed just slightly. "You have *lemon trees?*"

"If any were ripe, we could add lemon zest to the frosting."

Gwen glanced over at the ovens that were counting down the time. "Okay, but really quick. I don't want your head getting too big over how much I love everything about this house."

Seth chuckled, and he led the way to the back door that

opened onto a massive wooden deck. A cooling breeze had picked up, and it felt nice to be outside. He flipped on the outdoor lights, and the backyard illuminated in an ethereal glow.

"Wow." Gwen brought her hands to her heart. "I feel like I'm standing in a painting."

Seth stood back as she walked around the deck, commenting on everything from the elegant wrought-iron deck chairs to the planters overstuffed with flowers and greenery. He agreed that the place was beautiful, but seeing it through Gwen's eyes brought on a new appreciation as she noticed details he hadn't paid attention to before.

She smoothed her hair back more than once as the breeze tangled through it, and he was about to ask her if she was getting cold when she said, "Is that the greenhouse?"

"Yep. Ready to see the lemon trees?"

"I am." Gwen smiled at him.

Seth wondered what it would be like to have Gwen smile at him every day, because the way she was smiling at him right now made him feel like he could find beauty in any place if she was with him.

As he neared her to take the steps to the lower yard with the greenhouse, she said, "Hey, I'm really sorry about all those immature accusations earlier."

"Don't worry about it." He reached up to tuck a piece of her blowing hair behind her ear. "Nothing you accused me of was entirely untrue, although I think you'll find some surprises."

Five

$\mathcal{G}$wen didn't know what was happening to her. When Seth had tucked her blowing hair behind her ear and she'd felt the warm brush of his fingertips, she'd wondered if swooning would ever come back in fashion. Not that she was about to faint, but her boss was hitting her with too much, too fast.

First, he *baked*? Like *Top Chef* baking. Gwen hadn't even tasted the final result, but she'd only seen his method of assembling ingredients in one place: television. Not even Pierre baked without measuring first.

And Seth had had a steady girlfriend, one whom he'd had to move away from to get over? Her frat-boy image of him had been pretty much blown apart. And why in the world did he need to get a bank loan to buy a restaurant that his dad already owned? She had a million questions, but there were probably only a few more minutes on the oven timers, and she really wanted to see the greenhouse. Gwen had a small affinity for lemons. Okay, so a rather large preference, since most of her bathing product choices were lemon-scented. The scent of orange was a close second.

She smelled the lemon trees the moment Seth opened the door to the greenhouse.

The place was illuminated only by the moonlight and stars, but that was enough for walking among the young lemon trees. Gwen was pretty much speechless as she walked around the small trees, then looked at the table with rows of potted herbs. Another table held what looked like rose bush starts.

"Do you have a green thumb as well?" Gwen said.

Seth was inspecting the herb pots as if he was some sort of master gardener too.

"Not really." He looked up, and even in the dimness of the greenhouse she could feel the warmth of his gaze.

Gwen shook that thought away. Seth did *not* see her like that, and she wouldn't even allow her brain to go there.

"This is actually my dad's hobby, although my mom has come to enjoy growing as well." He brushed his hands off. "This table of herbs was my idea, for, you know, cooking. But my dad loves to interbreed roses."

"And the lemon trees?"

"My mom." Seth smiled. "It appears you have something in common with her."

"Hmm." Gwen tried to act dismissive, but in truth, her pulse sped up. So what if Seth's mom liked lemons enough to actually grow lemon trees? Gwen walked to the table of rose bush cuttings and bent down to smell a couple of them. "I suppose you do the watering when they're out of town?"

"We have a gardener," he said. "But I'm the one over-seeing these herbs. They can be finicky."

She felt his gaze on her, but she wasn't quite ready to meet it—not in this place of heady fragrance and moonlight.

"We should probably check the ovens." Seth moved to the door of the greenhouse.

Yes. How could she have forgotten about the cupcakes for even a minute? With Seth holding the door for her, she hurried out of the greenhouse.

The temperature outside was markedly cooler than inside the greenhouse, bringing much-needed clarity of mind.

Once they were back inside, Gwen smelled the sure scent of baked goods.

Seth beat her to the first oven, and he whipped out the first batch of cupcakes before Gwen had even reached the counter.

Thankfully, they were lightly browned and not burned.

"Perfect," Seth declared. Then he took out the second batch from the other oven and set the muffin tin on a cooling rack. Of course he would. Apparently, he didn't do anything subpar when it came to baking.

Gwen watched him for a moment, marveling at how he could be so cool and collected, and at ease, even though it was nearly one o'clock in the morning. The bright lights of the kitchen made Gwen realize that she probably looked like a ragamuffin. After working a long shift at the restaurant, her go-to was a long bath, then straight to bed.

"So, should we use a different extract for the next batch?" Seth asked, his hazel eyes zeroing in on her from across the counter.

Gwen shook her head, mostly to clear her straying thoughts.

"No?"

"No, I mean, yeah, let's try the almond," she said.

He smiled. "Sounds good to me."

When he smiled at her like that it only made her feel guilty for how snarky she'd been to him. *Mean*, truthfully. Why did he have to agree with her put-downs, and why did he have to be rich *and* talented *and* good-looking *and* generous with his time?

"Should I put the eggs into the mixer?" she asked.

"Yep." Seth was already adding up another batch of dry ingredients—flour, salt, and baking powder—to a bowl. Without measuring.

Gwen cracked the two eggs and turned on the mixer, then added the butter and reached for the sack of sugar. "Um, how much sugar again?"

"About a cup," he said, glancing over at her.

She began to tilt the bag, and he crossed to her in two strides and put his hand over hers with a chuckle. "Easy, there, it's all going to come out at once."

So, with his hand on her wrist, they poured sugar into the mixing bowl as it rotated, beating the eggs and butter.

"Looking good." Seth released her and moved away, taking his warmth with him.

Gwen stared down at the mixing batter, trying to refocus her thoughts and slow her breathing. She was *not* developing a crush on her boss. And when had the kitchen become so hot? Weren't these fancy ovens supposed to contain their heat? Finally, she turned toward the island just as Seth turned toward her, holding the bowl of dry ingredients.

"I'll put that in," she said, and he handed her the bowl. "Any special method I should be aware of?"

"The slower the better," he said with a wink.

Gwen knew she was about to blush, and she covered it up by turning toward the mixer and dumping in the dry ingredients. Judging by the puff of flour that escaped, she'd probably poured it in a bit too fast.

40

She sneaked a glance over her shoulder to see if Seth had noticed. He had a slight smile on his face while he took out the cooling cupcakes and put in more clean liners. Something struck her then—she'd never seen Seth in a home environment. And although this was a gorgeous cabin with a professional grade kitchen, Seth seemed perfectly at ease.

She'd never seen him so . . . relaxed. And, dare she suggest, content? Maybe even happy?

"Do you want to try one?" Seth lifted his gaze to meet hers.

"Try one?"

His mouth quirked. "A cupcake?"

How did he do that? Make her feel like he was teasing her and being sincere at the same time? "Um, we don't have frosting yet."

One of his brows lifted. "Do you require frosting on *all* your cupcakes?"

Gwen held back a smile because even though Seth wasn't exactly the man she thought he was, that didn't mean she was going to do a one-eighty. "I do, in fact. I don't even consider a cupcake finished without frosting. And sprinkles."

"Hmm." Seth pulled another muffin tin toward him. "I hope we have sprinkles then."

"If you don't, I have some at my place," she said. "Along with the toothpick flags."

She knew he was trying not to laugh. She set her hands on her hips. "What's wrong with flags on cupcakes? Aren't you patriotic?"

He raised his hands. "I have no problem with it. I just think it's . . ."

She waited, and when he didn't finish, she joined him at the counter and took over the job of putting in the cupcake liners. He was watching her movements, but she ignored him.

41

"It's sweet," he said.

She looked up at him, which was probably a mistake. Because they were standing a lot closer than she'd realized. And he was holding a cupcake, the wrapping peeled from it.

"Try it," he said. "Just one bite."

She exhaled. Then she leaned forward and took a bite out of the warm cupcake. The light lemon and sugary taste melted on her tongue. It was amazing. Without the frosting. She plucked the cupcake from Seth's hands and, ignoring his grin, took another bite. "Okay, you win this round."

He laughed.

"But . . . I know it will be better with frosting, sprinkles, and a flag."

Seth took the half-eaten cupcake right from her fingers and popped the whole thing into his mouth, a gleam in his eye. "It's pretty good for having to use the ingredients that were available in the restaurant kitchen."

"*Pretty good?*" Gwen said. "It's amazing!"

"Have you always gone all out for holidays?" he asked.

Gwen lifted her shoulder. "Yeah. My mom decorated to the hilt for holidays, and I guess it just stuck with me. It's probably the only real thing I appreciate about her." As soon as she said it, she wanted to take it back. She didn't talk about her parents with anyone, not even Alicia. It was like their friendship was all about sharing work experiences and escaping their family issues.

"Where do your parents live?"

"Sacramento."

"So . . . you're not that close with your mom?"

Gwen walked to the mixer and turned it off, then brought the batter back and filled up the cupcake holders. She wasn't nearly as suave as Seth had been with the first batch, but she could manage the task just fine. When she finished, Seth took the first tin over to the oven and set the timer. She set the second one in the other oven.

She turned, and there was Seth, leaning against the counter, his arms folded, his gaze on her. Waiting . . .

"Um, I haven't exactly seen my parents for over a year," she said. "I'm not proud of it, and I wish it could be different. But until they accept my choices in life, it's too painful for all of us to even be in the same room together."

Seth scanned her face. "Are you a felon, or something?"

"Ha." Gwen leaned against the opposite counter. "That might be easier. I'm a college dropout."

Seth's brow rose. "And . . . ?"

"And that's pretty much it. I dropped out of Stanford my sophomore year."

He didn't look shocked or disgusted, just curious.

"For some parents that's worse than a teenage pregnancy or a drug bust," she added.

Seth nodded. He wasn't going to tease her or ask her a million questions? Despite this guy's hidden talents at baking and growing herbs, he was still a frat boy, wasn't he?

"My dad credits his heart attack to my year at culinary school in Paris," he said. "Dad had a miraculous recovery when I told him I'd return to the States to finish *my* degree."

Gwen's mouth dropped open. "*Ouch.* But . . . Paris? Culinary school? You've totally held out on me and the entire restaurant. Does Pierre know?"

His mouth twisted into a half smile, and he straightened from the counter. "No one in Pine Valley knows except my parents, and they want to keep it that way."

"Wait, why?" Gwen said. "I mean . . . who doesn't want a chef in the family? That's almost as good as a doctor."

"Ouch." Seth pressed a hand over his heart.

"Oh, my gosh. Don't tell me your parents wanted you to be a doctor?"

He nodded.

"Sorry." Gwen didn't think he looked too upset by her comment, more like amused. Obviously, all of this chef-doctor-restaurant-owner had been reconciled with his parents, since he lived in their huge cabin.

"It's okay," he said. "I only cook when my parents are gone. You know, to keep the family drama to a minimum."

Gwen couldn't believe any parent would discourage their kid from becoming a world-class chef. "I have all kinds of things to say about your parents, but I'm going to hold back because I think we should get that next batter going, or we'll be here all night."

"Right." Seth moved back to the island. "Although my schedule is wide open tonight, so I don't mind."

Gwen scoffed. "Everyone's schedule is open in the middle of the night—because they should be *sleeping*." She looked over at him. "Thank you, by the way. This is more than I would have ever expected—"

"Are you going to talk about me being a frat boy again?"

"I've repented of my preconceived opinions of you," she said.

"Really?" His gaze looked hopeful.

Gwen decided to ignore the butterflies flitting around inside of her. "Well, *mostly*."

"That's more like it." Seth chuckled as he mixed up another batch of unmeasured dry ingredients. "Mint?"

"Why not?" She picked up the extract and set it on the counter by the mixer.

Over the next two hours, they settled into a routine, and Gwen hardly noticed the passing time or the fact that she should be dead on her feet. Somehow, she still had energy, although she refused to analyze if the reason was because she was excited to deliver the cupcakes at the shelter in the morning. Or maybe it was because the more time she spent with Seth, the more interesting she found him.

Six

"And that's it." Seth turned off the oven timer and pulled out the final batch of cupcakes. He didn't know what type of reaction he expected from Gwen, but it wasn't total silence. He looked over where she was sitting at the counter. She'd laid her head down on her folded arms.

"Gwen?" he said in a quieter voice.

She didn't answer.

He walked over to her and moved to the side where her face was turned. She'd fallen asleep. Seth exhaled. It would be another hour before the newest batch of cupcakes was completely cooled and ready for frosting. They'd decided to do all the frosting at once when all the cupcakes were finished.

But Seth didn't have the heart to wake her up. A quick glance at the oven clock told him it was 4:30 a.m. Yet, if Gwen continued to sleep like this, she'd have a sore neck. So Seth did the only logical thing he could think of.

"Gwen?" he said, nudging her shoulder. "Do you want to sleep on the couch for a while?"

She mumbled something but didn't move.

"Gwen?"

Nothing. So he slid one arm under her knees and pulled her against him with his other arm. He lifted her up and carried her to the couch in the adjacent great room. The leather couches were overstuffed and oversized. Gwen barely stirred as he set her down. He left her there and went to find a blanket in a closet. He grabbed a couple of blankets and returned to the great room.

Gwen hadn't even moved. For such a vivacious woman, she sure slept deeply. He draped the blanket over her, then grabbed a throw pillow and tucked it under her head. He stood for a moment, watching her sleep, as a myriad of thoughts flooded through him. Tonight had been unexpected, and he hadn't even asked her the original question he'd meant to in the parking lot.

He yawned and decided he'd catch a little sleep. The sun would be up in ninety minutes, and he could sleep until then. Frosting would only take an hour with Gwen's help, and she could be on her way well before her deadline of 10:00 a.m. Just in case, he set his phone alarm for 7:00 a.m.

Seth took the second blanket and went to change before settling on the other couch. He felt wired as his mind replayed the events of the evening, and he wondered if he'd fall asleep.

"Seth," someone was saying.

"I'm sleeping," he mumbled. Then he realized the woman's voice wasn't his mom, or his sister.

He blinked his eyes open to find he was in the great room. And the place was flooded with the morning light.

Gwen was standing next to the couch, her arms folded, as she peered down at him.

Seth sat up and looked behind him at the massive windows. "What time is it?"

"It's 7:30," Gwen said. "What happened last night? How did I get on the couch?"

It took Seth's brain a moment to catch up. He scrubbed his hand through his hair. "Um, you fell asleep sitting on the barstool."

"I did?"

Seth pushed the blanket aside and rose to his feet. When Gwen simply stared at him, he remembered he wasn't wearing a shirt. He'd changed into gym shorts last night after he'd carried her to the couch.

When he met her gaze, Gwen flushed.

"Did . . ." She paused. "Did anything happen last night?"

"What do you mean?"

"I mean—between us." She took a step back, her arms still folded. "You're, uh, not exactly dressed."

"I changed before I crashed on the couch. I didn't want you to wake up and not know where I was." He grabbed his cell phone, wondering why his alarm hadn't gone off. He'd accidentally set it for 7:00 p.m. instead of 7:00 a.m. "I didn't mean to sleep so long."

Gwen nodded and, avoiding his gaze, said, "It looks like all the cupcakes are done. I can frost them really fast and then be on my way. Do you have a pastry spreader?"

"Uh, sure." Seth didn't like how things seemed so awkward between them this morning. Last night, or should he say, earlier this morning, they'd gotten along great. "I thought we'd use decorator tips. I've got some you might like." He headed toward the kitchen. "And breakfast. I'm starving."

He supposed Gwen was following him, but when he reached the kitchen, she was still standing in the great room. "What's wrong?"

She blew out a slow breath. "Okay, I need to ask you to put on a shirt. I'm sure you're well-aware that you have a chick-magnet bod, and I can appreciate it as well as the next woman, but I've got two hours to frost two hundred cupcakes, get back to my car, drive to my apartment, shower, and get on the road. So, I'd appreciate it if you'd do me this one, small, final favor."

"Decorate," he said.

Gwen blinked. "What?"

"We're going to *decorate* the cupcakes," he clarified. "Frosting sounds like you're going to slap some Pillsbury pre-made frosting on the tops."

That line between her brows appeared.

"I'm only running on a couple of hours of sleep here," she said at last. "Can we just cut to the chase?"

"With me putting on a shirt?"

"Yes."

Seth smiled. "All right. I'll be right back. Sorry to throw you off-kilter."

She didn't meet his gaze, just gave a little shrug.

Apparently, she did not warm up with teasing in the morning. He crossed through the kitchen and walked to the stairs that led to the lower level and his bedroom suite. Last night between batches, Seth had showed her the entirety of the house, well, except for his bedroom. Gwen had announced that she didn't need to see every room in the house, and Seth had conceded.

Now, in his room, he changed into jeans and a T-shirt. He wished he could take time for a shower, but he'd wait until after he took her back to her car. Although, now he was wondering how she'd fit all the cupcakes into her small car.

When he returned to the kitchen he was surprised to see

Gwen standing by the counter. He at least expected her to be furiously whipping up some frosting to meet her deadline.

He decided not to comment on her slow start. She was probably exhausted. For some reason, he wasn't feeling all that tired. Well, first things first. "Hungry?" he asked.

"Maybe just some coffee."

"I don't think so." Seth moved past her, trying to rid his mind of the thought of how she looked sweet and vulnerable when she'd just woken up. He opened the fridge and pulled out the eggs and cheese. He slid the block over to Gwen, then grabbed a cheese grater. "Can you grate some cheese?"

She picked up the cheese but looked confused, as if she wasn't sure what to do with it.

"Have you ever grated cheese before?"

Her blue eyes connected with his. Her makeup had mostly worn off, and all that was left were some gray smudges on her eyelids. This subdued Gwen was new to him, and he was intrigued.

"Yes, I've grated cheese before." Still, she didn't make a move to pick up the grater. "I'm sorry, but I'm not really a morning person, even when I've slept more than a couple of hours. Could we just skip straight to the coffee?"

Seth would go with Plan B. He cracked four eggs, then separated the yolks. He beat the egg whites and poured them into a small frying pan. With that heating up, he took over the cheese grating, then opened a can of black beans.

Gwen just watched him as he worked. He normally would have asked her to dice a tomato, but he decided not to. He'd forgo onions and peppers for the sake of time. Once he had all the ingredients mixed in with the eggs, it was time to put on the coffee.

"Thank goodness," Gwen mumbled.

Seth dished up two bowls of the food, drizzled a mild

chipotle sauce over the whole thing, and handed one bowl and a fork to Gwen. "Try it. Before your coffee."

"What is it?"

"Some version of huevos rancheros." He dug into his own bowl. Yes, food was good.

Gwen took a tentative bite. She wasn't a picky eater, was she? He wouldn't have guessed that about her.

"It's good," she said, then covered up a yawn. "Really good." She took another couple of bites, but everything about her seemed in slow motion.

"Hey," he said. "Here's a thought. Why don't you crash for another hour, and I'll get the cupcakes decorated. I'll save the sprinkles and flags for you do to when you wake up."

Seth was fully prepared for her to shoot down his idea and say no, but he was surprised when she said, "Are you serious?"

He held back a laugh. "I am. Believe me, I can handle a few cupcakes. I'm worried about you driving when you can't even grate cheese."

She was apparently too tired to even give him stink eye.

"Okay, but wake me up in an hour."

"Will do." Seth watched her rise from the counter, her bowl only half finished. He could refrigerate it and warm it up later for her. She seemed to have forgotten about the coffee too. He couldn't help staring at her while she made her way back to the great room. She lay down on the couch, adjusted the blankets and throw pillows, and that was it . . . She'd gone to sleep.

Seth had never seen someone fall asleep so fast. It reminded him of his sister's four-year-old son, who was jabbering one minute in the car, and the next instant was sound asleep. Seth finished his breakfast, then poured a cup of coffee and set to work with blending the icing. He didn't know which decorator tip Gwen would have chosen, so he went with the leaf design that also worked well for making a layered spiral. He used white vanilla extract when making the frosting so that the white would stay whiter, and then he did another bowl of red, and a third bowl of blue. Then he put all three colors into the decorator bag so that it would come out as a rainbow of red, white, and blue. Hopefully Gwen would like it.

He wasn't entirely sure how they'd transport all the cupcakes and keep them from getting squished, so when he heard Jon's truck pull up to begin a morning of yard work, Seth went out to meet him.

Jon was in his sixties, and he used to work at a local nursery until he had an injury. The nursery wouldn't let him go part-time and still keep his benefits, so Seth's dad had hired him.

"How are you doing this morning?" Seth asked Jon.

The man grinned. "Great. Just thought I'd get started before the heat of the day kicks in."

"Nice idea," Seth told him. "I wondered if you could do me a big favor. I'm kind of in a bind, and I need those kind of boxes that you put donuts in. Do you think you could go to the Main Street Café and pick up enough boxes to hold two-hundred cupcakes?"

Jon's bushy eyebrows shot up. "That's a lot of cupcakes."

"Yeah, it is," Seth continued. "You can add it onto your hours, and I'll reimburse you for the cost of the boxes, if they charge you at all."

"Sure thing," Jon said, spinning his keys in his hand. He climbed back into his truck and started down the hill.

Seth returned to the house and turned on some low music, hoping not to disturb Gwen. He suspected she could sleep through quite a lot, though. He wondered what had awakened her in the first place. Good thing she had gotten up, though, or he might have kept sleeping as well.

The next hour sped past as he worked on the cupcakes, and when Jon pulled up, Seth went out and grabbed the pink pastry boxes while Jon got to work on weeding flower beds. Seth loaded the counter with the boxes, and Gwen slept through all the commotion.

Seth got so caught up in the decorating that he didn't hear Gwen coming into the kitchen until she spoke.

"Wow, these look amazing."

He looked up from where he was working on the final dozen or so cupcakes.

She looked much more awake than she had earlier. A line from the pillow creased her cheek, and her hair was down around her shoulders.

"Do they meet your approval?" he asked.

She studied them, like she was truly analyzing each and every cupcake. "How did you get the three colors?"

He held up the frosting bag. "I add the three into the bag, so they only mix a little when the frosting comes out."

Gwen swiped her finger into the bowl with red frosting and licked it off. "Mmm. I definitely approve."

"Good," he said. "Because I'd hate to start over."

She swiped another bit of frosting, this time blue. "I don't think they're going to need sprinkles after all. But the flags are a must."

Seth smiled. "Of course they are."

"Hey, you got boxes too?" She stared at him. "Don't tell me you had them in your pantry?"

"No." He laughed. "I sent the gardener to fetch them from the Main Street Café."

Gwen tucked her hair behind her ears, and Seth watched

her movements. He probably should be finishing up the last of the cupcakes and not staring at her.

"So, I'll wash my hands, then load these up." She moved to the sink and turned on the water. "Sorry about falling asleep on you, twice."

"Not a problem. I can grab a nap this afternoon, or a five-hour energy."

Gwen looked over at him. "Those are terrible for you. I hope you're kidding."

"I've pulled all-nighters before, but technically I have today off." Seth straightened from the counter and began to put the cupcakes in boxes.

Gwen joined him. "I hope I'm not ruining your plans," she said. "I'll be out of your way soon."

"Do you want me to go with you?" he asked.

She paused and looked up at him, her blue eyes wide. "No. You've done so much already. I can't expect you to work the lunch line with me."

Seth wanted to push the issue, but he also knew that he was more tired than he was admitting, and he might not be making the best judgment calls right now. Because what he really wanted to do was spend the rest of the day with Gwen. And the night. And tomorrow. Some distance between them might be good.

"Then take my car," he said. He hadn't intended to make the offer; it had just come out. But now that he'd said it, he knew it was a good idea. Frankly, he'd be surprised if her car could make it as far as the homeless shelter.

"You're kidding." She shook her head. "Drive your Mercedes with all these cupcakes?"

"I'm not kidding," he said. "The boxes will fit in the trunk, and I can work from here today. Besides, my parents' cars are in the garage if I do need to go somewhere."

Gwen fell silent for a few moments. Then she said in a quiet voice, "Are you sure? What if I wreck it?"

"I have insurance, but I'm happy to drive you as well." He held her gaze.

She looked away first. "Okay, but only because Marge was having trouble yesterday and died in the parking lot. I'm not entirely sure she'll start up."

"I can have Richards come look at it—he owns that auto shop," he said. "If it's not an easy fix, they'll tow it to their place."

Gwen closed her eyes.

What was going on here? Had he pushed too much? He hadn't meant to, but he found that he really wanted to help her, and not because he viewed her as some damsel in distress. But because it felt important to him. *She* felt important.

She opened her eyes. "Tell me how I can thank you." She waved a hand toward the cupcakes. "This is above and beyond anything I could have ever imagined."

Seth folded his arms and leaned against the counter, studying her. "Tell you what: if you can help waitress my parents' Fourth of July barbeque on Thursday, we'll be even."

Seven

Oh, right. Waitressing. That's what Gwen did, and that's all the interest Seth would ever have in her. He was her boss, the owner of a restaurant, and she was his employee. "What about the restaurant?" she asked. "It's going to be a full night."

"I know." His hazel eyes focused on her. How did he manage to look so good in the morning after a night of little sleep, no shower . . . and a change of clothes into jeans and a T-shirt that made no secret that this man was regularly engaged in some sort of sport activity . . . His choice of casual attire wasn't any less appealing than when she'd seen him shirtless, but at least she could breathe now.

She really shouldn't be checking out her boss. "And your parents and all their fancy friends will be here?" she asked. "Oh, sorry, I shouldn't have said that. I'm sure they're all amazing people."

Seth smirked and leaned close. Scruff had grown on his

face overnight, and Gwen wasn't opposed to it at all. She *was* opposed to the way her heart now raced.

"They are fancy," he said, "but that's sort of the point, right? I mean, it's the Fourth of July. If you can't dress up for a holiday, when can you dress up?"

"Touché." She sidestepped away from him, because his nearness was becoming a habit of his, and she wondered what was going through his mind. About her. She slipped the tops of the boxes over the ones already filled with cupcakes. She'd leave them closed until she got to the homeless shelter, where she'd put on the toothpick flags she'd bought.

When the last box was sealed, she said, "Are you sure about your car? Marge is tougher than she looks."

Seth stacked a couple of the boxes. "I'm sure. But I'll give you my cell number in case there are any issues with the car. The tank's full, and it gets good gas mileage."

"Of course it does." Gwen hoped she didn't sound snarky. It was a hard habit to break. Seth didn't reply but led the way out the front door. They made another trip to get the rest of the boxes, and Seth carefully loaded them into the trunk.

Still, Gwen hesitated when he handed her the keys.

"It's okay, really," Seth told her. "It's just a car. Maybe a little faster than Marge, but there are a lot of similarities too."

"Like four tires and a steering wheel?" Gwen said.

Seth grinned. He really did have a nice smile. He opened the driver's side door and held it for her. So . . . she had to slide past him to sit in the driver's seat. It felt luxurious, and she hadn't even started the engine.

"Drive safe," he said, and their gazes connected.

Somehow, Gwen knew he wasn't saying it because he was worried about the car, but because he was invested in this project too. "Thanks, Seth."

He nodded and swung the door shut, then stepped back from the car.

Gwen exhaled. She could do this. She could drive this car and not get a scratch on it. Once she figured out how to start it. Even though Seth had given her the "keys," apparently it was still keyless. Her face heated up from the simple fact that Seth was still standing there, watching her, and possibly about ready to laugh. As soon as she drove away, of course.

She opened the door. "A little help here?"

Seth strode to her, trying not to crack a smile. "Step on the brake, then push that button."

Gwen did so, and the engine purred to life, barely audible.

"Got it?" Seth asked. When she nodded, he continued, "When you want to turn it off, put it in park and push the button again. You have my number, and you can call me for anything."

She tried not to read into that too much. "Got it." She put the car into Drive, then pulled forward along the circular driveway. Soon she was heading down the hill, trying not to freak out at the power she felt rumbling through the car at the slightest touch on the gas pedal. She kept trying to tell herself that it wasn't that much different than driving her former Audi.

Somehow she made it to her apartment all in one piece, and after she'd showered, dressed, pulled her hair into a wet, messy bun, she grabbed the box of toothpick flags. On the road again, she put in her earbuds and commanded her phone to call Alicia.

Her friend answered on the second ring.

"You're awake early," Alicia said.

The clock on the Mercedes said 10:00 a.m. "I'm on my

way to the shelter."

"Oh, that's right," Alicia said. "My mom's appointment is at noon. How did the cupcakes turn out?"

"Well, that's why I called you." Gwen merged onto the interstate, then said, "I have sort of a funny story. And I'm kind of freaking out here—so I need you to talk some sense into me."

When she finished telling Alicia everything . . . Alicia could only say, "Wow."

"I need a little more than *wow*," Gwen said. "I mean, I'm supposed to help waitress at his house on Thursday night . . . His parents will be there. His sister. All the fancy people of Pine Valley. You know how I hate this kind of stuff. All their pretentious conversations. The women with their boob jobs and butt lifts. The men with their hair implants and bleached teeth. The teenagers driving cars that cost more than most people's houses."

"I hear you," Alicia said, laughing and giving out no sympathy. "You do you know you wait on these same people at the restaurant every night of the week?"

"I know."

"Then what's the problem?" Alicia continued. "You find out that our boss Seth Owens isn't a total stuck-up frat boy, and suddenly you're turning down time-and-a-half at a gorgeous mansion?"

"He said he'd pay me double because I'll have a lot more responsibility."

"Sounds good to me," Alicia said. "Unless . . . Oh my heck!"

Her exclamation startled Gwen. "What? What happened?"

"You are crushing on him, aren't you?" Alicia said. "You

like Seth."

It was Gwen's turn to laugh. "Ha. Not even close. He's not as big of a jerk as I thought he was. I mean, he's pretty nice. Amazing, really . . ." She stopped talking.

"Gwen?"

She exhaled. "I didn't get enough sleep, obviously, and it's messing with my head."

"Um-hm." Alicia didn't sound convinced.

"I can't change my view of the world and the unfairness of class equality just because I'm attracted to one of the elite." She clamped her mouth shut.

Alicia had the good sense to not comment.

Gwen released a groan. "I need to turn down the Thursday job. I need to keep my distance. I need to figure out how to distract myself from what he looks like without a shirt."

"Too late," Alicia said, sounding like she was on the verge of laughter again. "And by the way, this explains so much."

"What do you mean?"

"First, it explains why Seth and Pierre clash all the time," Alicia said. "Seth really does know what he's doing in the kitchen, and it must be frustrating to him when Pierre screws something up. And . . . it explains why Seth is always watching you."

"Because he's my boss," Gwen said. "And he's kind of a control freak at the restaurant."

"True, but that's not why he's watching *you* . . ." Alicia said, drawing out her words. "And I don't think his offer to make two hundred cupcakes from scratch in the middle of the night was out of the kindness of his heart."

Gwen was afraid to ask Alicia to clarify. It turned out that Alicia went ahead and did it anyway.

"Don't you see, Gwen?" Alicia asked. "Seth Owens *likes*

you. As in . . . he's *interested*."

Gwen wouldn't let it go to her head, even if Alicia was right. "That just strengthens my theory that he's a party guy and looking for a fling."

"What about his girlfriend he had to get away from?" Alicia said. "Wasn't that a long-term relationship?"

"I'm not sure how long, but their parents are close friends," Gwen said.

"And he hasn't dated any of the waitresses or anyone, from what I know," Alicia said. "Maybe that's a clue right there."

"What clue?"

"You know what clue," Alicia said. "Tell you what, let's test my theory. Waitress for his family's barbeque on Thursday, and if he doesn't ask you out by the end of the night, I'll take back everything I said."

"And?" Gwen prompted.

"And I'll come with you next week to the homeless shelter."

"And?"

"I'll buy lunch on the way home."

"All right," Gwen said, smiling to herself. "That sounds like a deal." A few moments later, when she'd hung up with Alicia, Gwen realized she didn't really want Alicia to be right. Because if her friend was right, and Seth was interested in her, then that would mean that Gwen would have to turn him down. Dating her boss would never be an option, especially someone like Seth Owens. It would go against every principle she'd ever fought her parents on.

In the meantime, Gwen was enjoying driving Seth's car, but she told herself it was only a means of transportation, and temporary at that.

She pulled off the freeway and drove the rest of the way

to the homeless shelter. She could hardly wait to set up the cupcakes at the end of the lunch line. She pulled around to the back door of the building so she could unload the cupcakes by the kitchen entrance. When she pushed through the door, carrying the first box of cupcakes, Mac looked up from where he was stirring a big bowl of macaroni salad.

"You're early," he said. His dark brows lifted when he saw that she was carrying a pastry box. "What did you bring?"

"A surprise." Gwen set the box on the table and slid off the lid. "Ta-da!"

"Wow—did you make those?"

"Yeah, but I had help." A lot of help.

"Our friends will want you to replace me as cook," Mac teased.

"Never." She smiled back at him, then headed outside to fetch the rest of the boxes. Once she had all the boxes on the tables, she stuck the toothpick flags in each cupcake.

Then Gwen helped Mac finish preparing the sloppy joes that would go along with the macaroni salad. Less than an hour later, the patrons started coming inside the homeless shelter.

When Jerry saw her, he called out in his typical way. "There's my princess!" For a man in his seventies, he looked much older. His limp was more pronounced today, and Gwen stepped around the table so she could pull him into a hug. He didn't smell too great, but that didn't bother Gwen. As long as Jerry got something good to eat, she'd be happy.

"Ricky, you made it," Gwen said when the next man approached the lunch table. Ricky's shoulders were stooped from what Gwen suspected was a form of MS. But his gap-toothed grin made Gwen smile in response. He hadn't been around the week before, and that always made Gwen nervous.

The streets weren't always safe.

Bo and Silvia came through the line, and Gwen was pretty sure the two were sweethearts even though she guessed that Silvia was about five years older than Bo. They always stuck together.

Maddy walked into the shelter, wearing her usual bright red sweatshirt, which she wore rain or shine. Last year, Gwen had replaced it with a new red sweatshirt, since the first one had worn through at the elbows and hem. Maddy was a hugger, and Gwen moved out of the serving line to give the woman a quick hug.

"I like your earrings," Maddy said.

"Thanks." Gwen touched the flag earrings she'd been wearing for two days now. "I brought you a special dessert, so be sure you save room."

Maddy's brown eyes warmed. "I will. Thank you."

Gwen's attention was caught by the next man in line. He was one of the younger homeless, probably no more than twenty. And he wore a cast on his left arm. "What happened to you?" she asked.

Declan's blue eyes shifted way.

"He got in a fight," Maddy said. "Mac made him go to the clinic."

"Broken arm?" Gwen asked. "Sounds like a nasty fight."

Declan shrugged. He didn't speak much, but he paid attention to everything going on around him. Gwen served up his lunch, then said, "Are you okay?"

"Yeah," he mumbled, then shuffled away.

She wasn't bothered by his lack of communication. She knew he'd understood her concern. Mac had told her that Declan stuck around after most people went back into the streets to help clean up. That told Gwen right there that Declan wasn't self-involved. He cared about his environment, and he cared about others.

The cupcakes disappeared quickly, and when the lunch line had ended, only eight cupcakes were left. "Why don't you take these home, Mac?" Gwen told him.

"Oh, I'm sure more will wander in," Mac said, wiping down the long tables.

"Yeah, but your daughters would like them too," Gwen said. "Tell them they're from the crazy holiday lady."

Mac laughed. "All right. I will. They'll like that."

Once in a while, Mac brought his wife and two daughters to help at the shelter, so Gwen had gotten to know the family. She already knew that if she had a family of her own one day, she'd involve them in charity work as much as possible. Mac was her hero. He cooked at the shelter weekdays as a volunteer. Then he worked as a security guard in the evenings at a bank. He was one selfless man.

The type of man she hoped to end up with someday.

Eight

"What are you up to, Seth?" Emmy said, coming into the kitchen.

Seth glanced up at his sister. Her sandy-blonde hair was cut shoulder length, and she wore a blue skirt and red-and-white blouse. No flag earrings or decorated nails. "Just doing a little food prep. How was your drive?" Seth returned to rolling out the pretzel buns he was making for the barbeque.

"Oh no. You're not getting away with brushing me off." Emmy came around the counter, and despite the flour on Seth's hands and chef's apron, she pulled him into a hug.

"Hey, sis," he said, hugging her back with a laugh. "Great to see you."

"That's better." She drew away and scanned his face. "Mom's right. Something's going on."

Seth had already had this conversation with his mom,

and he didn't need a repeat. Obviously his mom didn't believe him that nothing was going on—that he only wanted to prepare some of the food for the barbeque tonight . . . and try out a few recipes.

"Where's the kid?" he asked. "And did you bring along Jed?"

"Jed came, and Ryker's probably peppering Dad with a million questions." Emmy folded her arms. "Is it true that Cynthia's coming tonight with her parents?"

Seth shrugged as he cut the dough into circles with a pastry cutter. "That's what Mom said."

"And . . . it doesn't bother you?"

He looked up, trying not to act annoyed. He and Cynthia had been over for a long time. There was no reason they couldn't be at the same event together. After all, they'd been friends long before they'd ever dated. "Not really. Why?"

Emmy's mouth twitched. "There *is* another woman. Who is she?"

"Why can't I just be happy and content without a woman involved in my life?" Seth asked, shaking his head but holding back a smile.

"You can," Emmy said. "But a woman adds something extra to your life. When Mom told me that you've been annoyingly cheerful the last couple of days, we both suspected something. Come on. Who is it?"

There was no way Seth was going to tell his sister that he simply had a crush on someone. She'd get a huge laugh out of that. Besides, he wasn't entirely sure how Gwen would react to knowing he was talking about her to his family. Yep. He had a crush on Gwen, and at this point, he wasn't sure if it was just because she was so different from Cynthia or any other woman he'd dated. She charmed him. She made him laugh.

She cared about things in a way he found endearing. She was also a mystery and entirely frustrating most of the time.

He was glad he'd been able to spend time with her on the cupcake project the other night, because she had lowered some of her barriers toward him. He never really thought he'd be interested in a woman who thought critically of him because he was ambitious and came from a successful family. In his world, those two things were admired. In Gwen's world, things like service and making the most out of holidays seemed to be at the top of the priority list.

And yeah, the whole boss-employee thing wasn't ideal; but they lived in a modern era, and *if* they started dating, and *if* the other employees found out, they'd just have to deal with it.

Tuesday afternoon, he'd awakened from a nap from the all-night-baking spree when he noticed his car was back in the driveway. And Gwen was standing behind it, rubbing it down with a cloth. He'd gone outside to tell her to not worry about cleaning up anything. She'd stopped, but she thanked him over and over as he drove her to her car in the restaurant parking lot. He'd waited to make sure the car started before going home to plan the menu for the barbeque.

That had been two days ago, and Seth had hardly talked to Gwen since. At the restaurant last night, she said maybe two words to him. Seth had expected a little more interaction, a little more warmth or friendliness; but she was back to her closed-off self. At least she'd committed to helping at the barbeque tonight, and Seth would hopefully have more alone time with her in the kitchen.

"Wow," Emmy's voice cut into his straying thoughts. "You're really into her, aren't you?"

"What?"

Emmy laughed, then snatched his phone from the

69

counter. "Is she in your contacts? Maybe the most recent phone call or text?"

Seth reached for the phone, but his sister moved around the counter. "Why you never put a password code on your phone is beyond me. Hmmm."

He folded his arms as she scrolled through his phone. He'd never called or texted Gwen, although he did have her number saved.

"Alicia? Who's that?"

"The hostess of the restaurant," Seth replied. "She called last night to tell me she'd be late."

"It's not Alicia," Emmy said. "There was nothing special in your voice when you talked about her."

He scoffed. "You should be a detective. Go ahead, search my phone. You won't find anything."

Emmy set the phone on the counter. "So, it's new, then. Or . . . she doesn't know."

Seth opened a lower cupboard and pulled out two baking sheets.

"That's it! She doesn't know." Emmy laughed with what sounded a bit too much like glee.

"Fine." Seth set down the baking sheets on the counter a little harder than necessary. "She doesn't know."

Emmy clapped a hand over her mouth. Then she released a long breath. "This is a first. Seth Owens is crushing on a woman who has no idea what's about to happen."

"Nothing's going to happen."

"You always have a plan, little brother."

Emmy was right. He did have a plan, but Seth wasn't going to admit that.

"So, do you have a picture of her?" his sister asked. "Or can you tell me what her Instagram account is?"

"She's not on Instagram." Seth started loading the dough

onto the baking sheets. "Besides, I'm not telling you her name unless she agrees to go out with me." *Officially go out.* Baking all night didn't count.

"Okay," Emmy said. "So when are you asking her out?"

"Tonight."

"Great," she said. "I can't wait to hear her answer. Are you calling her after the barbeque or something?"

Seth hesitated, debating about what he should admit. But Emmy was the person he was closest to. Maybe it would be nice to share. "She'll be here, so I'm asking her in person. I'm sort of old-fashioned that way."

"She'll be *here*, at the barbeque?" Her voice rose in pitch. "Oh, my gosh. Does Mom know?"

"Of course not." Seth stared his sister down. "You'd better not say anything, or I'll never tell you about my dating life again."

"You know I'm good at keeping secrets," Emmy told him, a grin on her face. "I'm so excited! And you're sure it's not Cynthia?"

"Ha. Ha." Seth slid the first baking pan into the oven. He looked over at his sister. "This woman is about as opposite as you can get from Cynthia."

Emmy lifted a brow. "Which means it might actually work out."

Seth didn't respond. There was a very good chance Gwen would turn him down tonight. But he planned on asking her anyway.

The next few hours both sped by, or crawled, depending on how much Seth was distracted. His four-year-old nephew Ryker wanted to "help," which amounted to Seth handing the kid the multi-colored chocolate chips and having him put them into piles according to color. Seth loved his nephew, but the kid was a handful and had already had enough sugar to last him for the rest of the week by the time Emmy came and ushered him to another activity. Apparently "Grandma" had set up a water slide.

Gwen was coming at 4:30, and at 4:15 his cell phone rang. Seth was surprised to see that Gwen was calling him, but that surprise quickly turned to dread. Was she cancelling? He answered while he turned down the heat to the homemade barbeque sauce he had in the slow cooker.

"Hey," Gwen said. "I'm sort of in a bind."

No . . . Don't cancel, please.

"Marge is having a rough day, and . . . well . . . she's not going to make it up your hill."

Seth exhaled. Gwen wasn't cancelling. *Hallelujah.* "I'm so glad you're not cancelling. My ex-girlfriend Cynthia is coming with her family. I need a buffer."

Gwen laughed. "Okay, I'll be your buffer."

"Great. I'll be right there." He looked about the kitchen as the oven timer went off. "Actually, I'm going to send Emmy—my sister—I don't dare leave the kitchen for even a few minutes."

"Are you sure?" Gwen asked. "I don't want to put out your sister. I can walk up the hill—I should have thought about that in the first place."

"No, stay put," Seth insisted. "Emmy will be there soon." When he hung up, he called out to Emmy. She came into the kitchen.

"Can you pick Gwen up at the bottom of the hill? She's one of my employees who will be helping out tonight."

"Sure," Emmy said, then turned to leave.

Seth breathed easier when his sister had left. He'd played it nonchalant, and she hadn't clued in. Lowering the temperature on the sauce, Seth reset the oven timer, then took out the veggie and fruit trays from the refrigerator. He'd ordered them from the restaurant, and they'd been delivered a couple of hours ago, along with the bottles of wine to be served at the bar.

"You *are* in the kitchen," a woman said.

Seth recognized the voice before he turned to face Cynthia. She was early, and Seth hadn't prepared himself mentally to see her yet.

"Hi, sweetheart," she said.

It irritated him that she called him "sweetheart," but he decided to let it pass. Gwen would be arriving at any moment, and he didn't want her to walk into an argument between him and his ex.

"Hi, Cynthia," he said, keeping it simple and neutral. She was obviously dressed to impress, and her dark blue dress clung to her slim body that she spent hours each day working on. Exercising, waxing, primping . . . the works. He could smell the scent of her expensive perfume above all the smells in the kitchen.

"You're looking good," she continued, her voice dropping into a low purr.

Seth tried not to scoff. He was perspiring from all the food preparation and would have to change his shirt before the rest of the guests arrived. He'd already planned on that, since his red T-shirt and white chef's apron had plenty of stains on it.

"Are you here with your parents?" he asked, keeping to his side of the counter.

Cynthia smiled. "Yep. They're talking to your parents. It's so great to have everyone together again."

Seth grabbed the long bread knife and began to slice through the now-cooled-off pretzel buns.

"It smells amazing in here," Cynthia said. "I didn't know you took up cooking again."

"I never abandoned it." Seth tried to keep the bite out of his tone. Then he heard the front door open and Emmy's voice—likely talking to Gwen.

"Your mom told me you were doing some of the dishes for tonight," Cynthia said. "That's so fun."

Seth nodded, not answering, his hearing trained to what Emmy was telling Gwen.

"And your mom said there'd be dancing," Cynthia continued as Emmy and Gwen rounded the corner. "I hope you'll come out of the kitchen long enough to dance with me."

"Oh, he'll be out of the kitchen soon enough if my parents have anything to do with it." Emmy walked toward the island, her smile on Seth.

Damn. She had that knowing look in her eyes. Had she guessed about Gwen? His gaze slid past his sister to Gwen, who had paused in the entryway to take in the scene. Her blue eyes didn't miss a thing. She was wearing her traditional waitressing outfit—white blouse and black slacks—but she'd pulled her hair back into a twist, and she had sparkly red and white stars in her hair. Bobby pins? Silver earrings dangled from her ears, and hanging at the end were tiny red, white, and blue stars.

"Hi, Cynthia," Emmy said, embracing her. Then she turned to Gwen. "This is Gwen. Gwen, this Cynthia."

"Nice to meet you," Cynthia said, holding out a rather limp hand.

Gwen's brows quirked as she shook Cynthia's hand. Gwen hadn't even looked at Seth, but he knew what she was thinking. *This is your ex-girlfriend?*

He wanted everyone to leave the kitchen so he could explain to Gwen.

"Nice to meet you as well," Gwen said in a carefully polite voice.

Seth exhaled, pulled his gaze from her so he wouldn't be caught staring. He knew his sister was watching him like a hawk, so he tried to keep his expression unaffected by the appearance of Gwen. "Glad you made it," he told Gwen.

And then her blue eyes were on him, and Seth felt suddenly too warm, despite the air conditioning.

Her red lips curled into a smile, and her blue gaze seemed to fire a dozen silent questions at him. She moved toward the counter, and asked, "Can I take out these platters?"

It took Seth a second to answer, and he had to clear his throat. "Uh, yeah, that would be great. There are several dips in the fridge too."

"I'm on it," Gwen said in a cheerful tone. She picked up the fruit platter closest to her. "Thanks for picking me up, Emmy. It was nice to meet you as well." Then Gwen turned and moved through the kitchen toward the back doors—she was already familiar with the layout of the house and yard from her tour, so Seth didn't need to give her directions.

It seemed that his sister picked up on that. Emmy's brows lifted ever so slightly, and she gave Seth another knowing look, pursing her lips as if she couldn't wait to drill him with questions. But Cynthia was talking to Emmy, so Emmy thankfully took her focus off Seth.

"Tell me about Jed," Cynthia said. "Your parents told my parents that you two are spending a lot of time together."

"He's great," Emmy said. "Want to meet him?"

"Of course." Cynthia followed Emmy out of the room, but not before Emmy cast a look over her shoulder to Seth that said, *We need to talk!*

Moments later, Gwen came back into the kitchen and reached for one of the veggie platters.

"Wait." Seth opened the fridge and pulled out the dips.

He began to put in the miniature serving spoons, and Gwen set the dip bowls in the center of the platters.

"From the restaurant?" she asked.

Seth met her gaze. "How'd you guess?"

"Only Pierre slices the black olives," she said with a smirk. "I prefer them whole."

"Me too." A beat passed, and Seth said, "Thanks for coming tonight. And sorry about your car. Did it overheat, or is it something worse?"

"It's just a hot day," Gwen said, touching her neck, and Seth's gaze shifted with her movement.

"Yeah, it is hot." Why were they talking about the weather? That was the last thing he wanted to speak about with her.

"Marge is temperamental, that's all." Gwen continued to gaze at him. She seemed to be looking right into his soul and trying to figure him out. It was kind of uncanny.

"Why did you name her Marge?"

Gwen shrugged. "No particular reason. It just fit her."

Seth smiled. "It does seem to fit her."

"She's pretty," Gwen said.

"Marge?" Seth wasn't sure he'd describe the old car that way.

"No, Cynthia."

Seth blinked. What did it mean when the woman you wanted to ask out told you she thought your ex-girlfriend was pretty? Cynthia *was* pretty. But Gwen was *real*, and that made her beautiful. "Cynthia is one of those women who puts a lot of effort into her appearance," he said. "I think everyone should just be themselves."

Gwen gave him a searching look. "It looks like we agree on two things. Olives and being yourself."

Seth nodded. "Three things."

"What's the third thing?"

"Come here, I want you to taste something." Seth opened the fridge and pulled out a tray full of miniature crème brûlées.

"You made those?" Gwen moved closer and picked up one of the small dishes. "What's with the red sugar on top?"

"Watch." He used a lighter to light the sugar on fire. It burned out within seconds, creating a small puff of red smoke.

"That's pretty cool." Gwen said.

"Here, see if you like it." He handed her a spoon, then watched as she dipped the spoon in the dessert and took a bite.

Gwen closed her eyes, and that's when he saw that she had blue sparkles on her eyelids.

"This is delicious." She opened her eyes. "Seth, you're *really* talented."

He'd been complimented by others before, but Gwen's words lodged themselves into his chest. He wished that everyone would find another place to celebrate the Fourth of July and leave him and Gwen in the kitchen alone.

"So, do we agree on three things?" he prompted.

Gwen took another bite of the crème brûlée, then grinned. "Definitely."

Nine

Okay, so was eating crème brûlée made by your boss considered flirting? Because that's what Gwen felt like she was doing. Flirting. Crossing the line. Letting herself be flattered and charmed by Seth Owens. If a warning light was to go off, it would be giant, red, and flashing.

Maybe it was seeing his ex-girlfriend Cynthia in that tight blue dress of hers that made Gwen feel like she wanted to capture and keep Seth's attention. She didn't take the time to analyze her motivations, but if Seth wanted her to try his dessert, she was going to try it.

"So . . . tell me again why your parents had a problem with you training as a chef," she said, leaning against the counter after taking her third bite of the crème brûlée. "I mean, *I* don't have an issue with it."

Seth laughed. "I can see that. By the way, it's all yours." He pointed at the dessert she was pretty much inhaling.

Then he winked at her and turned to open the fridge.

He's flirting back. Definitely flirting. In fact, if Gwen was to go by what Alicia said, he *was* interested in her. Even though Gwen might feel flattered right now, she knew Seth was still her boss, he was still the son of millionaires, and although he might flirt with or even date someone like her, he'd never be interested in her long-term. And to be honest, Gwen could never really date someone like Seth. It would be like backtracking four years and giving into her parents' hopes and dreams. The next thing she knew, she'd be enrolled at Stanford again.

Not for her at all.

"My mom wasn't necessarily against it." Seth opened a cupboard and pulled out empty sauce bottles. "My dad was okay with it as a hobby . . . for example, a Fourth of July barbeque . . . but not as a profession."

Gwen set down the bowl of dessert before she put herself into a sugar coma. "What's your favorite thing to make?"

Seth twisted off the caps of the sauce bottles, and Gwen reached for a couple of them to help. "Desserts," he said. "I like to change them up and experiment a little. Take an old stand-by and add something new."

She eyed the rows of fresh-baked pretzel buns and the simmering barbeque sauce. "I'd say you're pretty good at everything."

"Timing and fresh ingredients is the key to whatever you want to bake or cook."

"I think there's a little more to it than that," she said. "I mean, you have to be organized, which I was not expecting you to be . . . at least to this extent."

Seth quirked a brow.

"It's a compliment."

He paused, his hazel eyes completely focusing on her. "Are you going soft on me, Gwen?"

Hearing him say her name in that low voice of his sent a rush of bumps along her arms. "I'm giving you a bit of a break tonight, since I'm at your house." She picked up one of the veggie trays to carry outside.

"So, tomorrow it's business as usual?"

Gwen laughed and carried the tray to the back doors. It would be good to be outside for a few minutes, because she was on the verge of blushing.

She wasn't surprised that the backyard was gorgeous in the daylight, just as it had been the other night. Huge planters of flowers lined the deck, and soft music played from a massive speaker. The outdoor tables were set with china—for a barbeque, no less.

She continued to the serving table where she'd already put the fruit platters. A woman who had to be Seth's mother was speaking to the bartender on the other side of the serving table. Her blonde hair was scooped into a twist, and diamond earrings and a necklace sparkled against her skin, catching the light from the setting sun. She laughed at something the bartender said. Then she spotted Gwen.

"Hello?" his mother said. "Are you Gwen?"

"I am." Gwen set down the veggie tray and brushed her hands off, even though she didn't have anything on them. But Seth's mom didn't make a move to shake her hand.

"Seth told us he had help tonight," his mom said. "I'm glad he let at least one person come from the restaurant. I want him to be able to enjoy the night and not be in the kitchen the whole time." The words might have been disparaging, but she spoke in an affectionate tone.

Despite herself, Gwen found that she kind of liked that about the woman.

"Oh, there's my husband," she said. "You'll have to meet him, too."

"Whom do I have to meet?" a man said behind Gwen.

She turned, her heart thudding in anticipation of meeting Mr. Owens. She'd seen him from a distance a few times at the restaurant, but they had never actually met.

He gave her a cursory look, his expression unreadable. He was an older version of Seth, although Seth was taller, and Mr. Owens' eyes didn't have the friendly humor that Gwen appreciated in Seth's gaze.

"This is Gwen," Mrs. Owens said. "From the restaurant. She's here to help Seth tonight."

Mr. Owens shook his head. "We should have had it catered. Emmy will want to spend time with her brother, and Cynthia's whole family is here. Yet our son is playing in the kitchen, and he's got Dave on the barbeque."

Gwen didn't know if she felt hot with embarrassment or cold with offense for Seth.

"Dear," Mrs. Owens said, patting her husband's arm. "The food is wonderful, and everyone will be delighted with Seth's contributions. Once the food is served, he'll be mingling with everyone."

Mr. Owens tightened his jaw but didn't argue further with his wife.

Gwen guessed it was an old argument. She busied herself with arranging the fruit and veggie dips that went with the platters. As soon as she could, she'd make her escape back into the house. But right now, the Owens's were in her direct path between the serving table and the house.

"I came out here to tell you that the Feltons have arrived," Mr. Owens continued, walking a few paces away with his wife. "I don't care how much they try to butter us up this evening, we're not giving them the bid on the Sacramento hotel unless they meet all of our requirements and come in under the Colemans' bid."

"Yes, well, we should leave any business talk for the boardroom, anyway." Mrs. Owens' tone was light and soothing, but Gwen guessed the woman was frustrated. "I'll be sure to keep our conversations casual."

"Well, hello!" someone called out.

Gwen glanced up to see a couple coming around the side of the yard. They looked like they could model for the next cover of *Fortune* magazine. Gwen used the distraction to hurry past the Owens's and return to the kitchen.

She found Seth filling up the last sauce bottle. He smiled when he looked up to see her come in. Gwen silently commanded her heart to calm down a few notches. "More guests are arriving," she said, trying to keep her conversation with Seth neutral. She didn't want to return to their flirting. Gwen's life was complicated enough without being drawn into Seth's world of mergers, deals, controlling parents, and more money than any person should ever see in their lifetime.

"Are you okay?" Seth asked.

She looked over at him. Had she let her expression reveal too much? "I'm great. I just met your parents."

Seth chuckled. "That's an oxymoron if I've ever heard one. Did my dad ask you what your qualifications were for assisting me?" He wiped his hands and walked toward her.

"No, he didn't," Gwen said. "I guess I got off easy?"

Seth stopped a couple of feet in front of her so that she had to look up to meet his gaze. "You did," he said.

How did his eyes seem to draw her in? Their amused gleam made her want to smile along with him. Her stomach felt all fluttery at his nearness, but maybe it was just a sugar rush from the crème brûlée. She stepped back and snatched up two of the sauce bottles. "Table?"

"My cousin David should be out on the grill by now," he said. "Take two of the bottles to him. The rest can go on the serving table." Seth paused. "My parents didn't give you a hard time, did they?"

"Nope," she said. "Your dad seemed more concerned about some of the guests who'd just arrived—the Felters?"

"The Feltons," Seth replied. "Yeah, I won't blame you if you accidentally spill something on them."

"Sounds like there's a story there."

Seth opened his mouth to respond, when a woman's voice interrupted.

"Oh, here he is."

Gwen didn't need to turn around to know that it was Cynthia. Gwen moved past Seth, grabbed a third sauce bottle, and headed out of the kitchen as a conversation buzzed between Cynthia, Seth, and what must be her parents. All the "great to see you" and "how have you been" was something Gwen didn't need to be a part of. She hadn't left the kitchen fast enough, though, because she saw the unmistakable gaze of interest in Cynthia's heavily lashed eyes. Seth might claim that things were over between them, but it was clear that Cynthia would be up for reuniting.

Outside again, Gwen didn't know where she'd rather be—in the beautiful backyard as more and more guests arrived, looking like they'd stepped out of a *Chanel* catalog, or in the kitchen being bombarded by all things Seth and watching him talk to his ex.

Gwen could only hope the evening would go quickly. She gave a nod or smile to those whom she passed on her way to the serving table. She set down the sauce bottles, then looked for the grill. It didn't take long to spot it, because the scent of barbecuing meat had permeated the air.

She headed toward the massive grill on another level of

the deck, and a dark-haired man who looked to be around thirty turned as she approached. Although he was manning the grill, he was wearing what looked to be expensive slacks and a short-sleeved dress shirt, probably Gucci or Armani.

"You must be Gwen," he said. "I'm Dave." He stuck out his hand, and Gwen set down the sauce on the barbeque extension to shake his hand.

His hands were huge, and Gwen suspected he was into lifting weights, by the size of his neck and arms. He was also checking her out, a little too thoroughly for Gwen's taste.

Gwen raised a brow. "Finished?"

Dave grinned. "I like you already. You're not in a relationship, are you? Engaged? Married?"

"Uh, no." Gwen narrowed her eyes as she drew her hand away. "Why are you asking?"

Dave shrugged one of his massive shoulders. "Oh, just wondering why Seth told me to keep my hands to myself around you."

"Do you have a habit of randomly touching strangers?"

Dave bellowed out a laugh that drew attention from some of the guests. "It's an expression, sweetheart." He leaned closer and lowered his voice.

Gwen held her ground, curious, yet repelled at the same time.

"I think it's interesting that my cousin is marking his territory when it comes to you." Dave's blue eyes watched her closely.

She exhaled. This guy talked in riddles. He was also perspiring quite a bit. "Another 'expression'?"

Dave grinned. "It's whatever you want it to be. In fact, why don't you call me when things don't work out with Seth-boy?" His gaze dipped, then returned to her face.

Gwen had the sudden urge to slap this man. But there

already seemed to be enough drama going on as far as she was concerned. "Here's an expression for you, Dave," she said in a quiet tone. "There's not a snowball's chance in hell that I'd ever call you."

His laughter followed her as she walked back to the house. She hoped that Cynthia and her family were out of the kitchen. If not, she'd make a detour to the bathroom.

But as she rounded the corner leading to the kitchen, she found it completely empty. Seth must have taken out the rest of the food, since the counters were almost bare.

Gwen grabbed a cold water bottle from the fridge and guzzled most of it down. She could do this. She looked at the ornate kitchen clock on the wall . . . five hours. Six, tops.

Ten

Seth caught glimpses of Gwen throughout the night, and they shared some brief conversations, mostly about refilling this or that, or telling the bartender to stop mixing drinks for Dave. His cousin had had way too much and was about ready to get punched out, and that would be quite a feat, since the guy was at least twice as strong as Seth. Not that he couldn't hold his own, but Seth didn't spend three hours a day in the gym.

Gwen was deliberately avoiding Dave, and Seth had finally gotten out of her what Dave had said to her. She'd laughed it off, but Seth still didn't like any of the insinuations Dave had made. Yet . . . that wasn't the only problem of the night. His father had also had a few drinks too many, which was unusual for him, and Seth had overheard some cutting remarks. Not about the food—his dad could admit that it was all delicious—but about how "my son likes to throw away the good things staring him in the face. I offered him the job as assistant manager of the resort, but he wants to play kitchen manager. And just look at his ex-girlfriend. What man in his right mind would break things off with her?'"

If his mom hadn't intervened each time, Seth wouldn't have been able to hold back his own words—which would have certainly put on a show for their holiday guests. Something had been bothering his dad more than usual lately, and Seth wasn't sure what it was. Maybe it had to do with the presence of the Feltons, since he knew that a previous business deal had gone south, and his dad had to put some personal financing on the line to turn things around.

And if his dad's moodiness wasn't enough to deal with, Cynthia wasn't making any secret of her interest in "hanging out" again—as she termed it. Seth wasn't fooled, though. It wouldn't surprise him if somehow his parents and her parents were all in cahoots with each other. More than once during the evening, her dad had chatted with Seth.

Dinner finally ended, and with Gwen's help they set out the desserts: crème brûlée, mini cheesecake bites, two dozen Fourth-of-July cupcakes with toothpick flags—for Gwen's benefit, of course. She'd laughed when she saw them, but it felt as if she was growing more and more distant as the night wore on.

The easy banter between them was gone, and although Gwen served everyone with a smile on her face, Seth knew it wasn't a genuine smile.

Seth's dad took up the microphone set up at one end of the main patio once dessert was laid out. The sun had sunk already, and the outdoor lights glowed in the evening darkness, making the backyard look ethereal.

"Thank you all for coming," his dad said. "I hope you've

enjoyed yourselves tonight. In about an hour, the fireworks in the valley will begin, and we'll all reconvene in the front yard to get the best view. The dessert is now available, and my wife has reminded me to recognize our son Seth for his efforts in providing the food."

Scattered clapping sounded, but Seth couldn't relax. He had no idea what his dad might say next; he did seem more sober now.

"At the request of my daughter Emmy, we're going to have a dance," his dad said. "All ages are welcome, so get on those dancing shoes."

Emmy moved to the microphone and held out her hand, and thankfully, his father relinquished it. Seth felt relief rush through him as Emmy said a few words and then turned up the music on the speakers. The playlist sounded like a selection of 80's music, which was just fine with Seth. He wasn't planning on dancing.

"Remember this song?" someone said next to him.

Seth turned to find Cynthia smiling up at him. He wasn't sure what she was talking about, but he nodded anyway.

"Me too." She smiled and slipped her hand into his.

Seth was about to pull away when she said, "Dance with me?"

Her gaze was so hopeful, and Seth knew it would be beyond rude to tell her no. Besides, they were supposed to be friends, and over the years their families would continue to interact. He looked around to see that a few other couples were already dancing, including Emmy and Jed.

"Sure," Seth forced himself to say.

Cynthia's smile widened, and right there and then, she reached up and looped her arms about his neck. Seth rested his hands lightly on her hips as they swayed to some ballad he knew was familiar—but maybe that's because, like all 80's music, it still played on the radio.

"This is so crazy that we're dancing to our song after all this time," Cynthia gushed.

Seth vaguely remembered they'd picked a song once to define them as a couple, and it was probably good that he'd forgotten this was it. His neck prickled with heat, and it wasn't in a good way.

"I also can't believe that you're still single," she continued, lowering her voice. "It's ironic that even though we've been apart, we're both still single. Don't you think that means something, Seth?"

Not really. "I've been so busy with the restaurant," he said. "You and several others probably overheard from my dad tonight about how much work it's been."

"Yeah, but you have to be proud of yourself," she said. "I mean, you could have taken the promotion from your dad and made a lot more money. Instead, you're trying to do something on your own, even though it put you into a lot of debt."

Cynthia seemed to have heard an earful—from his dad, or maybe her parents, and that still would have come through his dad.

"I'm doing what I love and will eventually pay it off," he said.

"Oh, I don't doubt it," she said. "I mean, I've never doubted you."

Seth was surprised at her compliments, simply because he didn't expect them tonight.

"And it's not like your parents can't help you out if you get into a bind," she continued.

Seth's neck felt hot. Cynthia was right, but Seth living at his parents' house was about all the help he would accept.

Besides, they'd have to hire security or a house sitter if he moved out. But the fact that Cynthia saw his parents as a bail-out plan bothered him.

The song ended, and Seth pulled away from her. "I've got to make sure the clean-up is going all right. I can't leave Gwen to everything."

Cynthia laughed. "I'm sure it can wait until later. Maybe even until the morning. I don't get to see you very much."

Because we're not dating anymore, Seth wanted to tell her. "I won't be long. I don't want to miss the fireworks." He turned before she could say something else to make him feel guilty.

Seth threaded his way through the dancing couples and families, nodding a greeting as he passed by several of them. He entered the kitchen, and the quiet felt like a balm compared to the noise and music of the party.

He found Gwen in the kitchen wearing his chef's apron and scrubbing out the slow cooker. He couldn't help but smile, but he straightened his features when she glanced over at him. "I didn't know I hired a dishwasher."

Gwen arched her brows. "I can't leave you with such a huge mess."

Seth scanned the rest of the kitchen and saw that she'd already washed all the big stuff. Two loaded garbage bags were also tied at the tops and sitting next to the pantry door. He joined her at the sink and turned off the faucet.

"Hey, what are you doing?" she asked, reaching for the faucet to turn the water back on.

Seth grasped her arm and tugged her away from the sink. "You're not cleaning up any more. Come out and dance or whatever you want. The fireworks will start soon."

She pulled her arm from his grasp but didn't move away.

"When the fireworks start, I'll watch them from the front porch."

Seth moved closer and pulled at the apron so that the ties in the back released.

Her eyes widened, but she didn't say anything. So he continued pulling off the apron. Then he set it on the counter and grabbed a kitchen towel. "For your hands."

She hesitated, then took the towel. "I'm totally willing to help clean up. You'll be up all night, unless someone else is coming in to help? Maybe Dave?" Her eyes flashed with amusement.

"Dave's probably passed out by now on one of the hammocks," he said. "He told me you crushed his heart when you told him your heart was taken."

Gwen smirked. "I don't think that was the *exact* conversation." She folded her arms. "He seems to think you and I are dating."

"What made him say that?"

"*You* tell *me*." Gwen scanned his face. "It was one of the first things he said."

"Hmm, weird."

Gwen set her hands on her hips. "Look, you're my boss, and you know my opinions about all of this in general." She waved a hand as if she was including the entire house and property in her *all of this* comment. "Even if I did like you in that way, I still wouldn't date you."

Seth nodded. He'd expected such a response. "So, if I asked you out on a date, you'd emphatically say no."

"Yes."

"Why?"

She exhaled, her hands still on her hips, but she looked a little unsure now. "I just told you why."

"Because I'm your boss, and because my parents are wealthy?"

She blinked. "Yes."

"Do you have anything else on your do-not-date-a-man-with-these-qualities list?"

She took a step back and sounded a little breathless when she said, "I don't have a list. I don't need a list. I know what I want—or, rather, what I *don't* want."

She paused and braced herself against the counter behind her.

"I understand where you're coming from," he said in a low voice. "But I have to be honest with you. I was hoping to maybe break some of your expectations and possibly, maybe convince you otherwise."

She was staring at him.

"Here's the big confession," he continued. "I like you, Gwen. More than as an employee. I appreciate your good work, and of course your help tonight, but . . ." He slid his hands into his pockets. "I hoped that maybe you wouldn't be completely opposed to going out with me."

Gwen covered her mouth with one hand and turned away from him, facing the counter. Her shoulders shook, and Seth had a terrible feeling spread to his gut. Was she *crying*?

She dropped her hand and held onto the edge of the counter as if she needed the support.

"Gwen . . ." Seth didn't know what to say, but he hadn't expected this reaction. Then, he realized . . . "Are you *laughing*?"

She nodded, and then the laughter spilled out. Still, her back was turned to him, and she seemed to be trying to catch her breath.

"Really?" Seth folded his arms. She didn't seem like she was going to be stopping anytime soon.

"I'm sorry," she said with a gasp. She turned toward him. Her face had reddened. Then she turned back around and started laughing again.

"Are you okay?" Seth asked.

She nodded, taking another gulp of air.

He put a hand on her back. Yep, she was breathing.

She straightened and seemed to collect herself. He dropped his hand as she turned to face him again.

"Sorry," she said, waving a hand in front of her face. "I don't know what hit me. I mean, I pictured what your parents' faces would look like when you tell them we're going out, and I just couldn't stop." She made a valiant effort to hold back a smile.

Seth narrowed his eyes. "My parents have nothing to do with this."

"Oh, they do. I mean, you're *Seth Owens*. And I'm . . . well, *me*. I named my car Marge, and I'm a waitress at *your* restaurant. I'm a college drop-out, and I'm pretty much good at one thing: staying out of people's way." She took a breath and lowered her voice as if they were conspiring in whispers. "Don't forget that I met Cynthia. She's like—I can't even describe her. Suffice it to say we are complete opposites. And men like you might fool around with girls like me, but I'm not that type."

Seth rubbed the back of his neck. "What if I *like* that you're different from Cynthia?" he said. "There's a reason we're no longer together."

"You're probably the only one holding onto that reason."

She was right about that. "Eventually my parents are going to accept that there's no future for me and Cynthia."

Gwen wiped at her cheeks. She'd laughed so hard, she'd cried.

"Why is it so hard to think that we could date?" He took

a step closer, expecting her to scoot away. But she held her ground and gazed up at him with those impossibly blue eyes. "I think we have some things in common, and it wouldn't be so crazy to think we could have a good time."

Her brows flew up.

"*Not* what I meant," he clarified.

Her mouth twitched.

"I really don't get why you're so opposed to us going out." Another step. With the counter at her back, they were only six or so inches apart now. How did she still manage to smell good after several hours of bussing tables?

"You need to get your hearing checked, because I've given you plenty of reasons." She smirked. "I don't want to hurt your feelings, but it's not a good idea any way you look at it."

"What if I can change your mind?" he said. "I could make you more cupcakes."

She shook her head. "No cupcakes."

"Chocolate mousse?"

"No," she said, but it came out as a whisper.

He placed his hands on the counter on either side of her. He wouldn't be surprised if she could hear the hammering of his heart. His gaze was drawn to her mouth. "What if I kissed you?"

"I don't think so," she said, but a smile tugged at the corner of her mouth. "Unless . . . it was an amazing kiss."

His smile was slow. "I've no doubt that kissing you will be amazing."

"Seth." She put her hands on his chest, and he expected her to push him away, but then something shifted in her eyes. "Maybe just once," she whispered.

It was an invitation that didn't need to be issued twice. Lowering his head, he closed his eyes as he touched his mouth to hers. He wasn't surprised that she tasted of sweet lemon. He kissed her lightly, slowly, reveling in the warmth spreading through him. Gwen slid her hands over his shoulders, then moved behind his neck.

He rested his hands on her waist and drew her close. She pressed against him and threaded her fingers through his hair, making his skin prickle with warmth at her touch.

Kissing Gwen was like taking his car from zero to sixty in three seconds.

The first firework boomed outside, and Gwen flinched at the sound. Seth smiled against her mouth and kissed her one more time, then drew away.

Gwen's eyes fluttered open, and her gaze seemed a bit unfocused when she looked at him.

"Let's go watch the fireworks," he said.

She nodded, still looking dazed. Seth grasped her hand to lead her to the front yard.

Eleven

*G*wen's alarm went off at 11:00 a.m., but she was already
awake. Normally, after watching Fourth of July fireworks,
she relished sleeping in and eating whatever leftover treats
she'd made. But not today.

Gwen turned off her alarm and fell back onto her pillow.
The bright summer sun had already warmed her bedroom,
although she wasn't sure if the heat of her body was from the
sun or from the memories of Seth.

She'd agreed to go on a date with him. Today at 1:00—
for lunch—because they both worked nights at the restaurant.
After that kiss in the kitchen, she'd given in to his invitation.
One date, she'd clarified while the fireworks were exploding
across the valley before them, *and no more kissing.* He'd
laughed and drew her against him, then wrapped his arms
about her as they watched the fireworks.

If it hadn't been dark, and if everyone's focus hadn't been on the fireworks, she would have pulled way. But with the cover of darkness, she stayed leaning against Seth. She could admit that having his arms about her felt nice, very nice, but she still planned to keep her wits about her.

Spending time with him in broad daylight would surely bring more clarity to all his flaws. She'd already mentioned a few—the big ones—and planned to be on alert for the smaller flaws that would surely annoy her. She needed *something* to annoy her about Seth, because unfortunately the way her stomach was fluttering, even now, was making it hard to keep said wits about her. And she could not allow herself to crush on him. Crushes led to more flirting, more kissing, more relationship stuff . . .

Seth's life was beyond complicated, and Gwen was determined to honor her commitments to herself about keeping her life free and pure of the trappings of wealth and society's expectations.

Gwen closed her eyes and tried not to relive the way Seth had kissed her and the way her heart had thumped and the way her skin had hummed. The way his hazel eyes watched her with amusement. The way he laughed. Smiled.

A loud knock made Gwen's eyes fly open. It took her a second to realize she'd fallen back asleep, and that it was . . . 1:15. She groaned.

The knock sounded again, and the panicked jolt clenching her stomach told her it was probably Seth. *Here.* For their date.

She scrambled out of bed and hurried out of her bedroom, down the short hallway, past the living room and kitchen. She reached the front door and looked through the peephole.

Seth's head was bent as he looked at his phone. He'd

probably tried to call or text her, but her phone had been on silent. He lifted his head, and his hazel eyes seemed to look right at her. His disappointment was clear. For some reason, that set off the fluttering in her stomach all over again.

She watched as he turned and started to walk away. Gwen unlocked the dead bolt and cracked the door open. "Seth?"

He turned, surprise in his gaze. "You're here." His eyebrows lifted. "You were sleeping?"

Gwen closed the door a few more inches, realizing that she was wearing only a tank shirt and panties. It appeared that Seth hadn't missed that fact either.

"Yeah, um, I set my alarm, but I guess I fell back asleep." She exhaled. This wasn't exactly how she'd wanted to greet Seth. She wanted to be at the top of her game so she could think clearly. All she felt now was that she wanted to drag him inside and kiss him again.

"I can wait for you to get dressed," he said, studiously keeping his eyes on her face.

"It's not that simple," she told him. "I really need a shower. Maybe we should reschedule."

"Waiting for you is no big deal," he said. "I'm not in a rush."

Gwen hesitated. Going out today would get this over with once and for all . . . whatever *this* was.

"Okay, I'll try to hurry." She eyed him. "If you can give me a head start, you can come in and sit on the couch. But you have to promise to wait until I get into the bathroom."

He smiled, and Gwen was sure she was blushing.

"Cross my heart," he said.

So Gwen left the door open about an inch and hurried back through her apartment. She slipped into the bathroom and locked the door. It took her a few minutes to catch her breath. Then she heard the front door to her apartment shut and knew Seth was inside. She didn't know if that made her feel better or worse. She tried to think of what state of cleanliness her apartment was in. She wasn't a messy person, but she also wasn't used to having company over.

Well, if it scared Seth off, so much the better. She turned on the shower and tried to make record time . . . but she had to shave, and she had to wash her hair. Which meant she had to blow-dry her hair. And then she had to put on her makeup, because she didn't want to look like a total slob on her one and only date with Seth Owens.

When she finished in the bathroom and still had to get dressed, she cracked open the bathroom door. She couldn't see Seth from this far down the hallway, so she called out, "Are you still here?"

"I am."

The amusement in his voice was clear. "Are you still good to wait?"

"Yep," he said. "Take your time."

She frowned, wondering if he was the first man on earth to say that to a woman. He wasn't doing a good job at annoying her. Maybe that could be what annoyed her—that he *wasn't* annoying.

"I just need to get dressed," she called out, "then I'll be ready."

"No problem."

Gwen dashed across the hallway to her bedroom and shut the door. It might be kind of juvenile to not want him to see her in a towel, but he was still her boss; that fact hadn't changed, even though they'd kissed last night.

Safely in her room, she turned to her closet. Seth was dressed casually, so she'd follow suit. She sifted through her nicer blouses, then decided to settle for a V-neck white T-shirt and a pair of newer jeans that she hadn't worn much. Mostly because they felt too dressy for the homeless shelter. Once she was dressed, she paused in front of her dresser and debated whether to spritz on her usual body spray. It would be strong at first, and Seth would certainly smell it. She decided not to.

And now it was time to face her date.

Gwen paused by her bedroom door for a moment, going over in her mind why this would be the one and only date with Seth. Once she had her justifications firmly in mind, she grabbed her phone and opened the door.

She walked down the hall, and sure enough, there was Seth sitting on her couch, scrolling through his phone. He might look out of place on her cheap plaid furniture, but he definitely made it look better.

He looked up when she came into the living room and stood. "Ready?"

"Yeah," she said. "I hope this is okay, since it looks like you're dressed down too."

His gaze scanned her, and when his hazel eyes met hers again, he said, "You look great."

She gave him a half-smile. "Sorry I slept in."

"I'm glad you could sleep after a night like last night," he said.

She wasn't sure she wanted to know exactly what he referred to. Was it the barbeque in general or . . . them . . . kissing? "I enjoy my sleep, I guess." She wouldn't confess that she'd been awake for hours, and only after her alarm went off did she crash.

"So, what are you in the mood to eat?" Seth asked.

This made Gwen hesitate. "You want *me* to suggest the restaurant? Not with your eclectic tastes, I won't."

Seth grinned. "You tell me what you're in the mood for, and *I'll* suggest the place."

"Ah," she said. "That's more like it." She paused. "Pizza."

He didn't even blink. "Okay."

She laughed. "I'm kidding. I just wanted to see your reaction. I promise I won't make you take me to some hole-in-the-wall pizza joint."

"Actually . . ." Seth took a few steps toward her, closing the distance.

His nearness meant that Gwen could smell his aftershave.

"Sometimes hole-in-the-wall pizza joints are better than an upscale restaurant," he said in a low voice. He grasped her hand and linked their fingers.

Gwen's heart thudded at the warm, solid feel of his hand. Never mind the return of flutters in her stomach. "I'm assuming you know of just the place?"

He smiled and leaned down. With his other hand, he touched one of her silver dangling earrings.

His nearness made her think that it would be so easy to let him kiss her, to kiss him back, and to maybe skip lunch altogether. But her wits were strong. "Remember what I said last night?" She felt his gaze on her mouth as she spoke.

"I remember." But he didn't draw away. Instead, he inhaled. "You smell good."

Gwen tilted her head to look into his eyes. "You're standing really close to me."

"Does it bother you?" One side of his mouth lifted.

"It doesn't bother me on principle," she said. "Since I did promise you one date. But I'm starving."

He chuckled and squeezed her hand. "Okay, point taken."

Gwen tugged away from him, and he released his grasp. She walked to the door and opened it. She guessed she had to be the strict one, and that was fine with her. Seth had flattered her, and he could be quite charming, but she still stood her ground about his lifestyle versus hers. She wasn't interested in being part of his world. If she was interested, she wouldn't be estranged from her own parents.

She locked her apartment door, then walked with Seth to his car. "Are you sure you don't want to take an inaugural ride in Marge?"

Seth smiled. "Can I take a rain check on that? This pizza joint is a little way outside of Pine Valley."

"Ouch," she said. "I hope Marge didn't overhear that."

He laughed and opened the passenger door, holding it for her. Which meant she had to pass by him, closely, to slide into the seat. He shut the door, and as he walked around the car she had a moment to herself. The clean scent of the car reminded her of Seth, and there was hardly anything in the car except for a compass attached to the middle console. She'd noticed it before and wondered why he had what looked to be a cheap, plastic compass when the car had a built-in navigation system.

Seth opened his door and slid into the driver's seat. "Sorry, the car's hot." He started the car, and the AC blasted through the vents.

"Oh, so you're one of those guys who has to have the AC on full blast and turn everything to ice," she said.

He didn't miss a beat as he reversed out of the parking place. "And you're one of those girls who says she's freezing when it's ninety degrees outside?"

Gwen laughed. "Yep. I would have worn a sweater if I'd know about your habits."

He glanced over at her before pulling out of the parking lot. "I've got a jacket in the trunk. Maybe some emergency hot chocolate too."

"You do not!"

"Yeah, you're right," he said with a chuckle. "No hot

chocolate, but there really is a jacket. Do you want me to pull over?"

"How about we do this," Gwen said, turning down the AC. "Much better."

Seth shook his head, and Gwen decided that she liked his fancy car a lot better when he was driving it. When she'd taken it to the homeless shelter, she'd been a nervous mess about getting into an accident.

With the temperature more pleasant, Gwen settled back into her seat for the drive. They reached the main highway, and she said, "I meant to ask you why you have a compass in your car. Is it for an emergency?"

Seth glanced down at the compass on the console, then looked over at her. "It's from Paris."

"A souvenir?" she prompted.

"Something like that," he said. "Probably more a reminder to keep to my own course."

Gwen raised her brows. "Does that refer to your culinary skills?"

He didn't smile like she expected him to. Instead, in a somber tone, he said, "For the most part it represents the fact that I can make my own way in life. I've been born to privilege, which you've pointed out plenty of times. But although I'm grateful for all the opportunities in my life, I still need to make it my own."

Gwen watched his profile. "Do you think your parents will ever accept that?"

He shrugged. "It doesn't matter. They know who I am, and it's their choice whether to accept my choices."

"So . . . me giving you a hard time probably isn't all that helpful." Gwen felt the smallest bit of guilt. Not too much, though. She had her own reasons for her choices.

"I think if you hadn't grown up a privileged kid, too, I

might take it personally." Seth glanced at her. "I'm pretty sure I can handle your heat."

Speaking of heat . . . sitting in the car with Seth, on their way on their first—and only—date, was making Gwen feel plenty warm. She leaned forward and turned the AC up a notch. Seth didn't comment on this.

Instead he said, "So, what's your sad tale with your parents?" His voice was light enough that Gwen knew he was giving her an out.

And she took it. "Oh, no you don't. First-date conversation is all about favorite colors, favorite foods, number of siblings, funny high school stories, clarification on past divorces . . . not about family drama."

"That's your plan, huh?" Seth said with a laugh.

"It's a good plan."

"Um-hm." He turned on the radio and pushed *seek* a couple of times until he landed on a station he liked.

The music wasn't very loud, but it still sent a loud message to Gwen. "Are you kidding?"

"What?" Seth said in a way too-innocent voice.

"We're already at the listen-to-the-radio-because-we-ran-out-of-topics stage?"

Seth tried and failed to hold back a smile. "I already know all those things about you. Or can at least make an educated guess."

"Just because you're my boss and have my pitiful résumé somewhere on your computer doesn't mean you know me."

Seth said nothing as he pulled off the highway exit and steered the car onto a side street that looked like it housed a row of small business factories. Nestled between two gray buildings was a shop with the red letters *Valentina's Pizza* over the top of the door.

"We're here?" Gwen said in surprise. The drive was

shorter than she'd thought it would be. "Marge could have totally made this drive."

Seth parked, but instead of shutting off the engine and getting out of the car, he said, "Your favorite meal is seafood fettuccini, your favorite color is blue like your eyes, you're an only child, you hated high school so I'm assuming there aren't many funny stories, and you've never been married."

Gwen opened her mouth, then shut it. "My favorite color is red."

Seth's hazel eyes held hers.

"Okay, you're right, it's blue," she said. "But how did you know that? Did you track down my kindergarten teacher and ask her?"

"I'm just observant," he said. "It's hard to miss that you wear something blue every day. So, I assumed it's your go-to color. Even on Valentine's Day, you had blue-and-pink-striped nails."

Gwen stared at him. "What are you, a stalker?"

He cracked a smile. "I call it observant. Part of my job is to know my employees."

"What's Alicia's favorite color?" she asked.

"I have no idea." He raised his hands. "Okay, you busted me. I'm just observant about *you.*"

Twelve

As Seth walked Gwen into the pizza parlor, she asked, "How did you find this place?"

"My dad invested in a company a couple of doors down," he said. "I came with him on an inspection, and we ended up here to eat." He pulled the door open so that Gwen could go inside first. Immediately the aroma of hot bread and spicy meat surrounded them.

"Wow, smells good," Gwen said.

He couldn't agree more.

"My Seth!" Valentina herself came around the red-and-white counter, her arms outstretched for a greeting. "What a wonderful surprise!"

Seth stepped into the woman's embrace, and she proceeded to kiss him on each cheek, before drawing back to inspect him. "You're more handsome every day." Valentina looked over at Gwen. "Who's this?"

"Valentina, this is Gwen."

Valentina pursed her very red lips. "Welcome, Gwen." She turned back to Seth. "Where is your father, love?"

"He's not with me."

Valentina narrowed her eyes. "You're on a *date* with this woman?"

"I am." Seth grasped Gwen's hand, hoping she wouldn't protest. She didn't. "Are you still open for lunch?"

Valentina didn't miss Seth's action, and her nostrils flared. Seth wanted to laugh, but he didn't. Valentina was at least fifteen years older than he, and she'd always been flirtatious with his father, which his father was pretty much oblivious to, since his only thoughts were of the next pending investor deal.

"The booth in the corner is clean," Valentina said in a prim voice, waving in that direction. "I'll get your drinks while you look over the menu."

Valentina sashayed away, and Seth released Gwen's hand.

"Sorry about that," he said, leading the way to their booth.

"What was that all about?" Gwen said in a quiet voice after they sat down.

"I'm not sure." Seth rested his elbows on the table. "She's never acted like this before."

Gwen raised a brow. "Have you ever brought a woman here?"

"No." He picked up a menu. "But what should that matter?"

"I think she's marking her territory," Gwen said, reaching across the table and patting his arm. "Are you into her type?"

"An older woman?"

Gwen shrugged. "Oh, I don't know. Gorgeous. Italian. *Experienced.*" She lowered her voice. "She's kind of possessive of you."

Seth sighed and rubbed the back of his neck. "She's usually flirtatious toward my dad."

Gwen was watching him closely, her blue eyes narrowed. "She's charming your dad to get to you."

"No."

"Yes," Gwen said, smiling. "The oldest trick in the book."

Seth dropped his head and closed his eyes for a second. "I love eating here." He opened his eyes to meet Gwen's gaze. "I'm going to have to tell my dad this place is off limits now."

"I'm sure she's harmless."

Something clattered in the kitchen. Not like Valentina had dropped something, but had *thrown* something. Gwen's eyes widened.

Seth was feeling a bit panicked himself. "The food is amazing," he said, "but maybe we should go."

Gwen bit her lip, then said, "How about you come over here?" She patted the space next to her on the booth seat. "Cozy couples sit on the same side of the bench. When she comes out with the drinks, it will look better if we establish ourselves right from the beginning. We can, you know, hold hands, and . . . cuddle." The smirk on her face was a challenge.

Seth shouldn't have hesitated, but he did. Gwen might be able to fake her affection, but his would be genuine. Another clatter came from the kitchen, and Valentina called out, "I'll be there soon, love."

Seth scrambled over to Gwen's side of the booth, and she laughed when he scooted in next to her.

"Arm?" she prompted.

He set his arm across the back of the seat, and she grasped the hand near her shoulder and pulled him in closer.

Then she leaned against him. Under any other circumstances, his heart would be going wild, but right now it was more filled with dread about what Valentina would do to their order.

"Relax," Gwen whispered, placing her other hand on his thigh.

He nearly jumped. "Uh, that's not going to help me relax."

Gwen tilted her head and looked at him. "I can move over a little."

"No," Seth said, his voice sounding hoarse. He grasped her hand and linked their fingers, keeping her at his side.

"Here are your drinks, dears," Valentina said, in a tone that bordered on too sweet.

"Thank you," Seth answered.

Valentina set down huge water glasses with ice and lime. "And something special for you," she continued, producing a bottle of red liquid. "Grenadine." She poured a dash into Seth's glass but pointedly ignored Gwen's. "Are you ready to order, love?"

"I'll have the sausage—"

"Your usual, of course!" Valentina cut him off and beamed at him. "Right away, love. I wouldn't want you to go hungry."

Seth watched as she was about to turn away, not taking Gwen's order. "Valentina," he said.

She turned and cocked her hip. "Hmm?"

"Gwen would like to order."

Valentina's dark eyes slid over to Gwen. "All right. What will it be?"

Gwen set her menu down, then turned to Seth, and said in a Valentina-sweet voice, "I'll have what you're having." She ran her hand over his chest. "I'm sure I'll love it."

Seth wanted to laugh at her antics, but mostly he wanted to kiss her again. Even with Valentina scowling in the background.

"Fine." Valentina sashayed away.

Gwen didn't move her hand from his chest. "That was kind of fun."

Surely she could feel the thump of his heart. "It was," he agreed. "You almost had me convinced, too."

The blue of her eyes seemed to darken, and for a moment Seth wondered if she felt what he was feeling. Then she moved her hand and reached for her ice water.

Seth reached for his, too. The cold water was much needed. He kept his arm around the back of the booth in preparation for Valentina's next appearance, and Gwen didn't seem to mind.

After Gwen took a long drink, she said, "Okay, do you want to know what my real problem with you is?"

Seth blinked. "Why don't you tell me how you really feel?"

Her lips twitched. "Funny." Gwen took another sip of her ice water, then turned to him, so they were still quite cozy in the booth. "You live in a different world than everyone else. It's like you're purposely oblivious, although I'm not sure you even know it. Valentina is the perfect example. Sure, you've come here with your dad, but her interest in you didn't just start twenty minutes ago. She's more than obvious about it too, yet you act as if you're blindsided."

"So, I'm dense," he said. "Is that what you want me to admit?"

"You're not dense," Gwen said. "You're actually quite brilliant, but I think you try to act dense for some reason."

"What reason would that be?"

Gwen shrugged, eying him. "I haven't figured that out

yet, although I'm thinking it has to do with your parents and their expectations of you and how you are following your own compass—or whatever you said in the car."

Seth gave her a half smile. "I'm glad you're so interested in psychoanalyzing me." He leaned a little closer, because, in truth, he liked being near her. "So, what if I was oblivious to whatever fantasy Valentina has built up in her mind? How does that prove that I live in a different world?"

"You have this innate confidence that everything will work out," Gwen said. "Like you can charm everyone and anyone, do what you want, and things will fall into place."

Seth brushed back a bit of her hair that had fallen across her cheek.

"See? Just like that."

Seth's hand froze. "See what?"

Gwen captured his hand and moved it away. "You say you like me, and the next thing I know, we're on a date, even though you're the last person I want to go out with."

Her hand was still on his, so Seth tried to figure out how her actions belied her words.

"Yet, you agreed to come today."

"I did." Gwen moved her hand and sighed. "I swore I would stay away from guys like you, yet here I am."

Seth had been around Gwen enough over the months to know that she wasn't directing her comments to him, even though it might sound like it. "What happened? Was it a boyfriend?"

She gave him a sharp look. "Not a specific boy, no, but just the general lifestyle."

Seth could respect that, but it seemed that she needed to talk to *someone* about it. "Does Alicia know?"

Gwen shook her head, and for a moment Seth thought she might open up to him. But just then Valentina arrived with two pizza pies filled with cheese, sausage, and veggies. She set down two forks, knives, and napkins.

"Enjoy, love," Valentina said, her focus solely on Seth.

When she left, Seth noticed that his napkin had a heart and phone number written on it. "So, I think you're right. I was completely oblivious," he told Gwen.

"Um-hm." She picked up the knife and fork. "I've never eaten pizza with a knife and fork."

He waited and watched as she took her first bite. As she chewed, her eyes fluttered closed.

Seth smiled. "Good?"

Her eyes opened. "Amazing."

Their gazes held for a moment. Then she cut her next bite, and Seth dug into his own pizza pie.

For the most part, Valentina left them alone. In fact, she didn't even refill their glasses. At one point, Seth could hear her talking on the phone in the kitchen—in Italian—and by the sound of it she wasn't too happy.

He felt a little bad that he might be the cause of that unhappiness, but how was he supposed to react when she went all crazy that he'd brought a date to lunch? Speaking of his current date, Gwen continued to successfully dodge any questions about anything more personal than her favorite color.

She had been alternating between warmth and still holding her cards close. She had no problem speaking her opinion, but she always veered the conversation from getting too personal. It left Seth frustrated. But he knew he had to be patient. He'd been paying attention to Gwen for a long time, and it seemed that she was just barely starting to notice him. Securing this lunch date felt like a victory.

He'd take the baby steps.

When they finished eating, Seth called a goodbye to

Valentina and left a generous tip on the table. She could make of it what she wanted to, but this was likely the last time he'd eat here.

Once they were back in the car, Gwen leaned against the seat and smiled over at him. "Thanks for lunch. It was amazing, despite the livid owner."

"Sorry about her," he said. "If I would have known, we could have gone out for Chinese. Maybe next time?"

"Let's just focus on today," she said. But her tone was soft. And her body relaxed.

Seth took that as a good sign.

Thirteen

To hug or not to hug, was running through Gwen's mind as Seth walked her to her apartment door. She'd had a great time with Seth, and he was once again proving different than she'd expected. Although she didn't quite believe he'd been so clueless about Valentina, she decided not to get caught up on that point. Besides, if Gwen told herself it wasn't such a terrible thing to be friends with Seth, she could relax more around him. They were going to be around each other a lot, just by nature of their jobs, even though the dynamic between them had shifted.

She wasn't about to go on another date with him, though, because she could see herself letting her guard down inch by inch. And that would only lead to complication and disaster. They'd reached the end of the date—her front door—and before she unlocked it, she turned to face Seth. "Thanks, again. That pizza was divine."

Seth smiled. He'd put his hands in his pockets, which Gwen took as a very good sign. That took the good-bye hug off the table.

"I'm glad you liked it," Seth answered. "I've been thinking of adding a pizza pie offering to the restaurant menu."

This surprised Gwen, but it shouldn't have. "I don't have any objection to that."

His smile broadened. "Good. I'll talk to Pierre about it."

"Okay, well," she took her keys out of her purse, "see you in a few hours."

"Sure thing." He took a step back, his eyes on her.

Gwen felt an invisible pull toward him, but she forced herself to stay rooted to the ground while she unlocked her door. He waited until she'd opened it; then he walked toward the parking lot. Gwen closed the door and leaned against it, trying to steady her breath. She'd almost hugged him. She'd *wanted* to hug him.

What was wrong with her? She pulled out her cell phone and called Alicia.

When Alicia answered, Gwen said, "Emergency."

"Seth?"

"How did you know?"

Alicia laughed. "Um . . . you texted early this morning, remember?"

"Barely." Gwen crossed to her couch and plopped down on it. Maybe if she talked through it all with Alicia, she'd be able to start thinking straight—though Seth had just left, she sort of wished he'd stayed.

"Did you kiss him again?"

"No!" Gwen scoffed. "Besides, he's the one who kissed *me*. This date was completely platonic. Well, mostly."

Alicia laughed. "Sounds intriguing. Tell me more."

So Gwen did. She told her friend about how she'd been sound asleep when Seth arrived and how he'd waited while she'd showered. Then she told Alicia about the pizza joint and the possessive Valentina. Alicia found that quite funny, and now that Gwen thought about it, it was funny.

"So, nothing at the doorstep?" Alicia prompted. "No kiss or hug?"

"Nothing." Gwen fell silent.

"Uh-oh." Alicia's voice was filled was amusement. "Sounds like you're disappointed."

"No, it's not that," Gwen said quickly. "I mean, I hope it's not that." She ignored Alicia's laugh. "We did have a fun time, and I wasn't expecting that. I was looking for a personality quirk to annoy me—besides being my boss and one of those social-elite snobs—and I found nothing."

"I'm sure you'll find something," Alicia said, laughter in her tone.

"Are you on the schedule tonight?" Gwen asked.

"Yep, always on Fridays."

"I'll see you there."

"Can't wait," Alicia said. "Actually, I can't wait to see how Seth acts around you."

"Ha. Ha." Gwen said goodbye to her friend, then hung up. She sat on the couch for a while, thinking through the events of the date with Seth. She'd been surprised that he knew so much about her, and it made her wonder if she was the oblivious one. What had prompted Seth to ask her out, and how long had he wanted to do so?

She felt flattered on one hand, but the truth was that the thought of becoming involved with Seth was overwhelming. It might be too easy to fall for him. And if he truly did like her, as he'd claimed, how would their relationship work with her eschewing all things pretentious?

Gwen changed into her standard work clothes, then put on her sunshine jewelry set. She redid her nails to a white base and small sunshines on each nail. Once they were dry, she headed outside.

Marge was in a good mood and started right up, and Gwen took that as a decent sign of things to come. She just hoped the interactions with Seth at the restaurant wouldn't be too awkward. They could be friends and get along, and Gwen could stop giving him a hard time, maybe.

Once she reached the parking lot, she pulled into her usual space beneath a group of pine trees so that Marge would benefit from the evening shade as much as possible. Gwen checked her appearance in the visor mirror, trying not to analyze why it was important to do so when she hadn't on other work days. She climbed out of the car and walked through the parking lot, noticing Seth's car wasn't there yet.

Gwen continued into the restaurant to see that Alicia had already arrived. They chatted for a couple of minutes; then Gwen busied herself getting the tables ready and organizing the menus.

Even though she couldn't see the front entrance of the restaurant from where she stood, she knew the moment Seth came into the restaurant. It was like something in the air changed. Gwen stayed focused on the table she was setting and told herself she wouldn't turn around. It ended up that she didn't have to, because Seth joined her at the table.

"Hey."

She glanced up. "Hey, back." He looked great, as usual, but because she'd spent so much time with him that week, she noticed some smaller things. Like how the edge of his chin had a small cut where he must have nicked himself while shaving. And how his eyes were more green than brown when he wore his gray button-down shirt. And how his eyelashes were blond at the tips.

"Everything going okay?" Seth asked.

"Yep."

He looked like he wanted to ask something else, but instead he said, "I've got some extra accounting to do, since I didn't close up last night. But if you need help with the tables, just let me know."

"I'm on top of it."

He flashed a smile. "Of course you are."

He strode away, passing through the main restaurant, then stopped to talk to Alicia.

Gwen looked away. She didn't want to be caught staring after him. She sort of felt let down, although she couldn't pinpoint why exactly. Had she expected him to flirt with her? To ask her out again? To show some sort of preference for her? Apparently, he was going to treat everything like they'd never gone out, like they'd never kissed. Apparently . . . things were going back to normal. Just what Gwen had hoped, right?

The evening sped by, and for that Gwen was grateful. She didn't have time to keep track of Seth and what he may or may not be doing, or who he may or may not be talking to. The restaurant was fully reserved, so Gwen helped the bus boys to get tables cleared quickly and ready for the next group. Through it all, she kept her standard smile and cheerfulness; but inside she felt melancholy. *Ridiculous*, she told herself more than once.

She'd been the one to tell Seth she'd only go on *one* date with him. And that's what she got. So why did she feel like going home early and pulling out her emergency stash of red velvet ice cream from the freezer? Maybe she'd ask Alicia if she wanted to hang out, but before Gwen could act on it, she talked herself out of it. Alicia lived at her mom's, and although she hadn't said much, Gwen knew Alicia's mom waited for her to bring home food each night.

By 10:15 p.m., the restaurant had all but cleared out. Only one couple remained, and Gwen was about to go over and see if they'd changed their minds about getting dessert when Seth came out of the kitchen carrying one of the restaurant's to-go containers.

Gwen watched him head over to the couple's table. She paused to listen.

"How did you enjoy your meal tonight?" Seth asked.

"It was really good," the man said, although the woman looked annoyed that they'd been interrupted. "It's my girlfriend's birthday."

"Perfect." Seth grinned. "I've brought you a complimentary dessert to go, and all I ask is that you report back whether you liked it."

The woman perked up. "What is it?"

"I haven't named it yet, but if you like chocolate, you'll love it," Seth said with confidence.

The woman laughed. "Are you kidding? I love chocolate."

"Just fill out the comment form on our website and tell me what you think." Seth put the container on the table, then strode away.

The couple finally stood from the table, taking the container with them.

Gwen was curious about the dessert and admired the woman's resolve to not peek inside the container.

With the couple gone, Alicia closed the hostess stand. "Good night, Gwen," she said with a wave.

Sometimes they walked out to their cars together, but Alicia seemed to be in a bit of a hurry, and Gwen liked to make a sweep of the restaurant to make sure there were no menus under tables or other dropped belongings. Everything was all clear, and she walked across the restaurant to get her purse and keys from the employee cupboard in the kitchen when Pierre walked out of the kitchen.

He was a stocky, dark-haired man with whom Gwen had had little interaction, even though she was a waitress. Pierre nodded at her but said nothing. Gwen wasn't surprised. He didn't speak much to those he considered underlings.

Gwen pushed through the kitchen doors to see Seth at one of the counters, mixing something in a bowl. He didn't look up, and Gwen decided it would be better if she slipped away unnoticed. She opened the cupboard and picked up her purse. She turned to leave the kitchen, when Seth said, "Try this."

She turned to see him holding up a fork with what looked like chocolate cake.

"What is it?"

Seth just smiled.

"Your secret dessert you're handing out to customers?"

"I can't decide if I should infuse raspberry or coconut into the chocolate sponge," he continued. "So far, the coconut holds up better."

Well, if it was chocolate, raspberry, *or* coconut, Gwen was not opposed to staying a few extra minutes to try it. She crossed to the counter and took the fork. "Which one is this?"

"See if you can guess."

Gwen took a bite of the chocolate spongey confection. It was warm and literally melted in her mouth. She closed her eyes and let the taste spread through her senses. Raspberry. Definitely raspberry. She was pretty sure this beat out the *crème brûlée* from the other night. When she opened her eyes, Seth was watching her, a satisfied smile on his face.

"Here." He handed her a glass of cold water, then held up

a new fork with another bite of the dessert on it. "This one's the coconut."

She took the water and drank some, then set the glass on the counter and took the second fork. "New fork?"

"I don't want to mix even a crumb of the different flavors," he said.

She took a bite, and her eyes slid shut again. Maybe Gwen should have consented to more than one date with Seth. One in which he made her dessert.

"What do you think?" he asked. "Do you like the coconut better?"

Gwen opened her eyes. "I love them both. And I think you should serve them both, side by side. A slice of each."

His brows lifted. "That's a good idea."

"I should probably try them both again just to be sure." Gwen moved to his side of the counter. He didn't budge, so she had to practically reach around him to get another bite. The raspberry again. "Yep. You need to serve them together. They complement each other."

"Hmm." He was so close to her that she could smell his scent of spice and pine.

He wasn't wearing a chef's apron, so there were small specks of chocolate on his gray shirt. One spot of chocolate had made it to his jawline.

"Is this a recipe from Paris?" she asked to distract herself, because this heavenly dessert and being alone with Seth was making her question her resolve to not date him.

"No," Seth said in a low voice. "I came up with it last night after the fireworks."

And after he had kissed her.

"What does Pierre think?" Gwen asked. She'd had four bites now and should really stop.

"He knows who's boss."

Gwen laughed. "Oh, really? That's how it is?"

Seth's smile was crooked. "With Pierre. You're a different story."

The breath left her, and she had to look anywhere but at him. But he seemed to fill the whole room, her every sense. "Well, if I have a vote, I vote yes."

Seth nodded. "That's good news, because I'm naming the dessert after you."

"What?" Gwen stared at him. "Like Gwen's Brownie or something?"

"I was thinking more like She-Devil."

Gwen gasped, then smacked his arm. "That's mean."

He caught her hand before she could pull away. "It's mysterious and sexy."

Gwen was literally speechless. And she couldn't move, either, because Seth had threaded their fingers together, and she felt every beat of her pulse reverberate through her body.

Maybe it was the dessert, or maybe it was the way he smelled, or maybe it was how his thumb was lightly stroking her hand, or maybe it was because he was so infuriatingly patient, waiting for her to make the first move . . . that she finally cracked.

"You have chocolate on your face," she said.

"I do?" It was a question, but there was no surprise in his voice.

She placed her free hand on his solid chest and rose up on her toes. He didn't move an inch as she pressed her mouth against the edge of his jaw. She drew back slightly.

"Is it gone?" he whispered.

"Not exactly," she said as she rubbed a finger over the mark. "Now it is."

His other hand moved to her waist, his gaze holding hers. "Thanks."

"You're welcome." She couldn't look away now. His hazel-green eyes drew her in.

She wasn't sure who moved first, but suddenly they were kissing.

Seth trapped her against the counter, and she moved her hands around his neck and pulled him closer as she kissed him back. He angled his mouth over hers as he lifted her hips and set her onto the counter. Gwen wrapped her legs around him and let herself melt into his warmth, and touch, and taste. She wasn't sure when she'd changed her mind about Seth, but she now realized that she'd been hoping he'd kiss her again.

If she could gauge his interest in her by his intensity right now, she could pretty well guess that he'd been thinking about kissing her again too. His mouth was hot against hers, and he ran one of his hands up her back and tangled into her hair. It was falling out anyway. Then his mouth moved along her jaw and down her neck. She let her head fall back as she tried to catch her breath.

When his lips touched her collar bone she felt like she'd been ignited. "Seth," she whispered.

He lifted his head, their gazes meeting. The desire in his eyes was palpable and sent her pulse thrumming even faster.

"I know," he said, his voice hoarse. "We should stop."

She nodded because she didn't know if she could speak in a normal tone. He brought both hands up and cradled her face, then tenderly kissed her mouth again.

"I'll walk you to your car," he said when he broke away.

She nodded again. Seth drew back, and she only wanted to grab him again and pull him to her. To feel his mouth warm against hers, his hands holding her up, his scent surrounding her.

He turned and scrubbed a hand through his hair as if he was trying to regain his composure.

Gwen slid off the counter and straightened her clothing. Then she picked up her purse from the counter. Her heart thumped with nerves. Had she been too bold? Had she made herself vulnerable?

"I'll clean this up later." Seth turned back to her. His eyes scanned her face, and he gave her a soft smile. "Come on." He grasped her hand, and Gwen couldn't exactly explain why, but relief flooded through her. Whatever the kiss had or hadn't meant, Seth seemed to want to keep her close.

They didn't speak as they walked into the summer night and crossed the parking lot. They passed Seth's car along the way to Marge.

Gwen released his hand and dug her keys out of her purse to unlock the door. Seth held the door as she slid into the seat. She put the key into the ignition, then turned it. Marge started right up. *Thank you.*

"Gwen."

She looked up, and into Seth's gaze.

"If you, uh, change your mind about that second date, you have my number." He looked so assailable, standing there, that Gwen almost climbed out of the car to kiss him again. But she resisted.

"You're pretty good at changing a woman's mind," she said.

Seth smiled. He leaned down and brushed his thumb against her earring. "See you later, sunshine." He straightened and stepped back, then closed her door.

Fourteen

Waiting had always been hard for Seth. So he hoped he was making the right decision by waiting for Gwen to reach out to him. He felt they'd shared some pretty amazing kisses, and he even felt their connection when they weren't in the same room together. But it was more than the physical attraction between them. She gave him confidence to keep forging his own path. The problem was, Seth had no idea what Gwen was thinking or feeling.

The day after their kiss in the restaurant kitchen, Seth had debated whether to text or call her. He'd thought of a few scenarios. The boss scenario: *Just checking to make sure you're still good with the work schedule for the rest of the weekend.* The man-who-is-trying-to-get-to-know-you-better scenario: *How did Marge do on the drive home last night? If you ever have car issues, I can pick you up.* The guy-who-can't-stop-thinking-about-you scenario: *Want to grab a late lunch before work? I'd love your opinion on another dessert recipe.*

Instead, he did nothing. Well, he baked more desserts, since he had his parents' house to himself again. All that counter space was too tempting, and judging by the way Gwen had loved the She-Devil last night, he was definitely putting that on the menu. In fact, he'd already sent the new menus to the printer.

Wait . . . did Gwen kiss him *because* of the dessert? Had the chocolate made her feel amorous? He had to think about it for a moment. *No*, he decided. Gwen kissed him because, well, because she wanted to. She had to like him more than she was letting on. At least, he hoped so.

That night at work, Gwen was her usual friendly self, with *everyone*. Which meant with him too. She left before he was finished running the numbers for the night. Sunday she had off. Monday the restaurant was booked with a software users group, and Seth barely had time to say hi to Gwen. He'd noticed the line between her brows more than once when she wasn't interacting with a customer, and his instinct was to pull her aside to see if everything was okay. But he refrained. The consolation in all of this was that the She-Devil became the most requested dessert on the new menu. Next week he planned to introduce a pizza pie—he and Pierre just had to agree on the ingredients.

By Tuesday night, Seth was ready to break all promises to himself and call Gwen after all. But then he had an idea.

On Wednesday morning, he found himself driving out of Pine Valley to the homeless shelter where he knew Gwen visited each week. He hoped she wouldn't skip this week.

Less than an hour later, Seth pulled into the parking lot of the shelter. His Mercedes would stick out like a sore thumb, and he debated where to park. Finally, he chose a spot and climbed out of the car. He hoped the shelter accepted drop-in volunteers and that there wasn't some sort of government security clearance he had to apply for.

He pushed open the front door, and the first thing that greeted him was the scent of Italian food. Spaghetti sauce and meatballs.

"Hi, there," a man's voice said from the direction of what had to be the kitchen.

Seth walked farther into the building and saw a man leaning through an alcove that connected the main room and the kitchen. He was tall, with dark hair and a neatly trimmed beard.

"Hi," Seth answered. "I'm here to help for a few hours. What can I do?"

The man hesitated, although his gaze was assessing. "Have we met before?"

"No, I'm Seth Owens," he said, "Are you Mac?"

The man's thick brows lifted. "I am."

"Great. We have a mutual friend—Gwen Robbins."

Mac's dark eyes lit up. "You're friends with Gwen?" Then his eyes narrowed, and Seth felt like he was being scrutinized.

"Yeah, she usually comes in on Wednesdays, right?" he asked.

"Yep," Mac said.

When Mac paused, Seth continued, "So, what do you need help with?"

"Can you cook?" Mac asked.

Seth grinned. "Sure."

Mac waved him into the kitchen. "Spaghetti is already boiling. Meatballs are defrosting in the red sauce. You can start on the salad and garlic bread."

Seth made a quick scan of the kitchen—all basic stuff—

and the ingredients—even more basic. He got to work, ignoring the fact that apparently Mac used frozen meatballs. Seth would let that slide. "It's hot in here; doesn't the air conditioning work?"

Mac chuckled. "First time in a shelter?"

"Yeah . . . ?"

"Uh, air conditioning is the last thing the county wants to spend money on," Mac said. "Just being inside a building is enough luxury for some of these folks."

"Understood," Seth said. Next time, he'd wear shorts and sandals.

And although he was tempted to ask Mac about Gwen, he decided he needed to keep his head down and work. A line had formed by the time the meal was assembled, and still no sign of Gwen.

Two older women showed up to help, and Seth joined them at the serving table, taking on the task of adding the sauce and meatballs to the plates coming through the line.

One man, who looked to be about eighty, called out in a loud voice when he reached the table, "Where's Gwen?"

"Right here."

Seth turned to see Gwen coming into the center.

"Sorry I'm late, Jerry." Gwen crossed to the man and kissed his cheek.

Jerry smiled, making his wrinkles curve up.

When Gwen saw Seth, her mouth fell open.

"Hi, Gwen," he said. He turned back to the next person waiting for the sauce. His heart had started pounding the moment he heard her voice, but he had to play it nonchalant.

Gwen said something else to Jerry, then talked to a couple of other people, but Seth forced himself to focus on serving.

Then he smelled lemons and vanilla.

Gwen stood right next to him, taking over the salad job from one of the older women.

"Hi, Ricky," she said, and the man before them grinned.

Half of his teeth were missing, but the man's smile lit up everything around him. "You're late," Ricky said.

"I know," Gwen said with a laugh. "But I'm here now. How are you doing, my friend?"

Ricky shrugged his thin shoulders. "Same ole, same ole."

Gwen piled on the salad.

A woman was up next. She was skinny as a rail and looked as if she'd been out in the sun for weeks.

"Love the sweater, Maddy." Gwen stepped around the serving table and hugged the woman.

The sweater in question had probably once been red but now looked more like a maroon, with all the filth. Plus, wasn't it too hot for a sweater in the middle of summer? The kitchen was like a sauna as it was.

"And I love your earrings, Gwen," Maddy said with a wink.

Now Seth had to look. They were small, genuine diamond studs.

"Thanks, they were my birthday earrings when I was sixteen." Gwen touched her earlobes. "Still fit."

Maddy laughed.

Then Gwen took her place in line again and continued serving salad, chatting with everyone who came through. One man, named Declan, wore an arm cast, and Gwen fussed over him. Although the man wasn't very talkative, Seth could tell he appreciated the attention.

When the line dwindled to the last few people, Seth started to clean up, pitching in wherever it looked like help was needed.

"Can you handle this, man?" Mac asked. "I've got to get to my daughter's school choir performance."

"No problem," Seth answered.

"Thanks for your help," Mac continued. He turned to give Gwen a quick embrace. Then he was gone.

Seth turned to continue cleaning the kitchen, but Gwen stood in his path, hands on her hips. He wasn't exactly sure how to read her expression.

"Your sixteenth birthday, huh?" he said.

Her mouth twitched. "Are you stalking me?"

"I had a few hours to spare."

Her blue eyes didn't look convinced.

"Okay, so I was curious about where you spend your days off," he said. "So, yes, I knew I'd probably see you here, but I also thought it would be half-decent to help someone else for a change, being a spoiled frat boy and all."

Gwen didn't say anything for a moment, but her eyebrows had shot way up. "Okay, so maybe I was a little judgmental."

"Just a little?" Seth teased.

She smiled but seemed to be mulling something over. Seth hoped it was about him and that it was positive.

"Don't push it," she said.

"I'm not pushing anything." Seth stepped past her and loaded the pots into the sink to be scrubbed. While he worked, he felt Gwen's gaze on him from time to time. But he stuck to the chores while overhearing quite a few conversations between Gwen and the homeless.

He'd thought at first that Gwen came every week to do service, maybe to fulfill the part of humanity that seemed ingrained in her. But seeing her interactions and overhearing her conversations, Seth realized she enjoyed the actual people. They were friends of hers, and she cared about each one. Seth was more than impressed. Not many people from her station in life felt comfortable around the destitute and downtrodden. It was like they thought homelessness was contagious, and they'd only help them at arm's length by donating money or something equally hands off.

It was *time* these homeless people needed. Time, care, patience, love. And, of course, food and shelter.

Seth dried the last of the dishes. He set things back into the cupboards, guessing where everything went.

Finished, he looked around for Gwen. She was sitting at the table next to the woman with the red sweater. They seemed engrossed in conversation, and Seth didn't need to make a grand exit. So he pushed through the door that connected the kitchen to a back parking lot. He walked around the building to find his car. A few slots down from his Mercedes was Gwen's beater car. He was tempted to wait in his car until he could make sure her car started up okay.

Why she drove the thing was beyond him. She was the top-paid waitress at the restaurant, and Seth figured she could afford a low car payment even if she didn't have a roommate to split rent with. Maybe she was just hyper frugal . . . although she wasn't opposed to wearing diamond earrings to a homeless shelter.

Seth opened his car door and cranked up the air conditioning before shutting the door so the air could circulate a little quicker.

"Hey, Seth!"

He looked up to see Gwen hurrying across the parking lot toward him. He climbed out of his car, leaving it running. By the time she'd reached him, she was out of breath, which, to Seth, was kind of sexy in itself. But he shouldn't be letting his mind wander.

"Thanks for cleaning up the kitchen," she said. "And for helping today."

"No problem." Seth slipped his hands into his pockets. "Does Mac run the kitchen every day?"

Gwen smirked. "Don't you get any ideas. We're not feeding my homeless friends gourmet food."

Seth laughed. "That's not what I meant. I just wondered how he finds the time in the middle of the day."

"He works security at nights for some company," Gwen said. "Mac's here Tuesdays through Fridays. Someone else helps the other days."

"How did you get involved?" He hoped he wasn't asking too many questions, because he knew Gwen liked to keep things private.

She shrugged. "I Googled it and then called the shelter."

"Cool." Seth's gaze kept going to the sparkle of her diamond studs as they caught the sunlight. Surely there was a story there. "Hey, if you're coming next Wednesday, maybe we should carpool."

A smile tugged at Gwen's mouth. "You really don't like Marge, do you?"

"I worry, that's all," he said. "I mean, I'm sure she's great for shorter trips. But maybe she could use a break."

Gwen's smile bloomed. "I'll let you know, boss. See you tomorrow."

With that, she turned and walked over to her car. She gave a final wave before climbing in, and of course Seth was still standing there when she backed Marge out of the parking spot and pulled out. Marge was running just fine, so Seth climbed back into his car and left the parking lot himself.

He hadn't secured a date, but driving to the shelter together next week would be progress.

Fifteen

"I am not nervous," Gwen told her reflection in the bathroom mirror. It appeared she didn't believe herself. "No, really. I'm *not* nervous."

A knock sounded on the apartment front door, and she flinched. Seth was right on time. It was Wednesday again, and all week Gwen had been thinking about how she'd agreed to carpool with Seth to the homeless shelter. Spending more time with Seth made her both nervous and excited . . . although she wouldn't confess the *excited* part to Alicia.

Alicia was already teasing her enough, and it was getting harder and harder to act nonchalant around Seth at the restaurant.

Gwen ran her hand over her loose braid, then applied her lip gloss—she'd wiped off the pink lipstick earlier. She didn't want to be too gussied up. Next, she made sure her yellow-and-white, polka-dotted blouse was tucked into her navy capris. Ready. She just had to open the door now.

She could almost sense Seth wondering if he had to knock again, if she might have missed waking up to her alarm again. Gwen strode down the hall and opened the door.

And it happened again. Every time she'd seen him over the past week, her heart had flipped.

"Hi," Gwen said, unable to stop herself from checking him out. His dark blonde hair looked like it was still damp from a shower. He wore a light-red T-shirt that hugged his toned arms and chest. His shorts were khaki, and Gwen wondered if she'd seen him in shorts before. Only once, she now remembered, after she'd slept on his couch. His toned legs pretty much completed his perfect visage. "Don't worry, I'm ready this time."

Seth's green eyes filled with amusement. "I wasn't worried." He stepped back as she crossed the threshold and locked the door.

When she turned, he was sort of leaning toward her, and for a panicked second she thought he was about to kiss her. And when he straightened and said, "You smell nice," she was slightly disappointed he hadn't.

She really had to stick to her own resolutions. She couldn't be telling him she wouldn't date him, yet wish that he'd kiss her again. "Thanks," she said. "I like your shirt."

He chuckled as she walked past him. She refused to question why he was laughing, because obviously he was in a flirtatious mood and thought he had the upper hand since she'd agreed to ride with him. But when she slid into the smooth leather passenger seat, she was a tiny bit glad she'd agreed. Marge's air conditioner had been hit and miss all week, and it was everything Gwen could do to not arrive at the restaurant a sweaty mess.

Seth's Mercedes was in a different class, and Gwen knew she shouldn't allow herself to enjoy it, because then she might be allowing some defeat of her morals. But then again, her parents were Audi people. So she clipped on her seatbelt and leaned the seat back a few more inches.

When Seth climbed in, he adjusted the air conditioning to a lower level. "Is this okay?"

"Perfect." She noticed a small white bakery box on the middle console. "What's this?"

"Something new I want you to try." He backed the car out and pulled out of the apartment parking lot.

"Hmm." Gwen picked up the box and opened it. "A cream puff?"

"Yep, but it's not any ordinary cream puff." Seth glanced over at her and winked.

The wink pretty much sent goose bumps skittering across her arms. If Seth noticed, she'd claim it was the air conditioning. "Nothing you do is ordinary, Seth Owens."

He smiled. "Can I take that as a compliment?"

Gwen laughed. "Take it however you want. Before I taste what I'm sure is delicious, I want to know the story behind it."

"Story?" he asked, as if he was confused by her question.

She nudged his arm.

"Okay, so I woke up early this morning—like normal people." He cast her a sidelong glance, and she scoffed. "And when I was out running . . ."

Of course he ran—with those thighs—and probably lifted weights, too, since she doubted that his muscled shoulders came from decorating cupcakes. Anyway . . .

"I thought of the éclairs Pierre makes. They're delicious, of course, but pretty ordinary as far as desserts go." He steered the car onto the highway. "I started thinking about the She-Devil dessert and how you said to put a slice of each flavor on the plate. So I thought about how maybe the éclair could be paired with something."

Gwen took out the cream puff and held it up. "With this?"

"With that."

She took a bite, and a burst of orange inundated her taste buds. It was the last flavor she'd expected. Without saying anything to Seth, she took a second bite and closed her eyes, letting her head fall back against the seat. "This is like orange heaven, if there is such a thing."

Seth's finger brushed against the side of her mouth, and Gwen's eyes flew open. He only grinned and licked his finger. "Missed some cream."

Gwen touched her mouth but didn't find anymore.

"What do you think?" he asked.

"I think . . ." She set the rest of the cream puff back into the box. "I'm going to gain a hundred pounds if I keep being your taste tester."

His mouth curved. "I like watching your reaction, and I don't mind watching you eat."

Heat flooded Gwen's face, and she hoped he wouldn't notice her blushing. *Eyes on the road.* "What's in it? Orange flavoring, or something more?"

"A little something more." His gaze flickered to hers, then returned to the road.

"So, what's the name of the cream puff?" she asked, trying to keep herself from staring at his profile and how it was obvious that while he might have showered, he hadn't shaved.

"I haven't decided yet," he said. "Want to come up with some ideas?"

"Hmm." Gwen looked out the window. "Summer puff? A Puff of Sun? Yummy Orange Puff? Seth's Puff?"

"Stop," he said with a laugh. "I think I'll just figure it out later."

Gwen looked over at him, unable to keep the smile off her face. "They weren't that bad, were they?"

His eyes connected with hers. "Do you want me to sugar-coat it or tell you the truth?"

Gwen laughed and shook her head.

"Tell me about those diamond earrings you wore last week," he said.

She released a slow breath. Seth had a good memory. And he was persistent. And . . . after all the time they'd spent together, did she really have a good reason to keep holding back? "They were my grandmother's," she said, "who died when I was fifteen. I was already going through a hard time at that age, so her death only made things worse. She was my favorite person in the world." Surprisingly, tears didn't fall as she spoke of her grandmother this time. Gwen wanted to stop talking, *knew* she should stop talking, because if she didn't, then the whole ugly story would come out. "I ran away. Not too far—only three blocks to one of my friend's houses. When her mom got tired of me living in the guest bedroom, she sent me back home."

"Did your parents ground you?"

"That would have probably been better than what they did do," Gwen said. "I mean, they were afraid I was going to spontaneously combust if they said something wrong. It was like egg shells had been strewn in every room of our house. I told them I was cancelling my birthday bash they'd been planning, that I didn't want any gifts, cake, candles, or cards. Nothing." She shrugged. "If my grandma had to be confined to a casket, I didn't want anything around me either."

"I'm sorry about your grandma," Seth said in a quiet voice.

She nodded. The old lump was indeed forming in her throat. She inhaled. Exhaled. Then swallowed. "When I woke up on the morning of my birthday, I found a small jewelry box on my nightstand. No note. No card. I knew it was from my parents, and I almost threw it out. Instead, I opened it. The minute I saw the earrings, I knew they'd been my grandma's." Her eyes started to burn, and she blinked rapidly. Breathed again. "I wore them every day for a year. I even slept in them." She brushed at the single tear that had escaped.

Seth rested a hand on her shoulder and squeezed lightly. "Your grandma must have been an amazing lady."

Gwen looked over at him. The weight of his hand was warm and solid on her shoulder. Comforting. "I think I was heading for a teenage meltdown no matter what. Her death brought it on faster."

Seth moved his hand and steered the car off the next exit.

The drive had gone by fast; they were already near the homeless shelter. "Is there a story behind all of your earrings?"

"Not any so interesting," Gwen said, her emotions calming. "Most of them I get on clearance."

Seth flashed her a smile. "You're resourceful. I like that."

"You do?" Gwen asked. "I mean, I thought you liked the high-maintenance women—you know, like Cynthia."

Seth chuckled as he pulled into the parking lot and stopped in a space at the far end.

"What's so funny?"

He put the car into park, leaving it on, and turned toward her. "You don't think *you're* high maintenance?"

"Not even close." She held out her hands. "I do my own nails." She touched her hair. "Natural color." She ran her hands down her blouse. "All real."

He had the decency to redden.

Then she pointed to her shoes. "Five dollars on clear-ance."

"I'm not talking about looks or clothing."

Gwen stared at him. "That's the *definition* of high maintenance."

"That's *one* definition." He lifted his hand and tugged at her braid, then let his hand rest on her shoulder again so that his fingers grazed her neck. "What about the woman who immediately rejects a man because of his upbringing—something he has no control over?"

She opened her mouth to reply, because she could see exactly where he was going with this—but he cut her off.

"What about the woman who refuses to get a car that can make it up a gentle incline—"

"Your house is on a *massive* hill—"

"What about the woman who refuses to take a night off work to go on a date?"

"Seth—"

"Shh. I'm not finished." His thumb arced a line along her collarbone.

She stilled as waves of warmth traveled through the rest of her body.

"What about the woman who turns down every guy who asks her out?" he continued. "Or the woman who stays up all night to make sure her homeless friends get Fourth-of-July cupcakes?"

"That's not really—"

He moved his fingers to her lips as if to hush her, and she stopped talking. "What about the woman who teases me every day yet won't go out with me?"

Gwen's heart was racing, and she heard the truth in his words . . . although they were still ridiculous. "Are you finished yet?"

He lowered his hand, and the corners of his mouth turned up. "I'm just getting started."

"I think you should take your own advice and stop making lists."

He gave a quiet laugh. "I will if you will."

She exhaled, long and slow. His hand was back on her shoulder, his fingers warm against the base of her neck. "You have a deal," she whispered.

Seth tilted his head, and she knew he wanted to kiss her. But he was doing that infernal waiting thing. So Gwen leaned closer and brushed her lips against his. He didn't move for a moment, then slid his hand behind her neck and drew her closer. And kissed her slowly.

Everything inside Gwen buzzed as she kissed him back. Seth had cracked her walls, and she wasn't sure how she felt about that. But right now, she let herself get lost in his warmth and touch.

Sixteen

It was usually the woman who wanted to define a relation-ship. *So, where do we go from here?* Or, *how do you feel about me?* Or, *are we going to be exclusive?*

All these things Seth wanted to ask, but all these things would probably send Gwen packing. Yet, something had changed in the car on the way to the homeless shelter. Seth felt it, and he was pretty sure Gwen did too. The kissing had been great and kept getting better, in his opinion, but that wasn't what had changed. They'd finally connected at a deeper level.

Standing next to her in the serving line again while she chatted with her homeless friends made Seth both proud of and in awe of her. Not only was the chemistry between them intense, but she was like a breath of fresh air in his life, as well as to the people around her. Everyone she spoke to left with a smile on their face.

The food *du jour* was chicken enchiladas, which looked pretty impressive, considering they'd been made *en masse*. When Seth had suggested whipping up a green chili sauce to go with it, Gwen had shushed him and told him in no uncertain terms that he wasn't the chef in this kitchen.

Seth loved her sassiness and had wanted to grab her and pull her into a kiss right in front of everyone, but then he thought better of it. At least for now.

Gwen nudged him when the line had dwindled and Mac was walking among the tables, dishing out seconds of enchiladas. "You look pretty hot," she said. "And I don't mean the attractiveness kind."

Seth turned to look at her. "Yeah, it's like an oven in here." He noticed the sheen of perspiration on her forehead as well. "Should I take off my shirt?"

She smiled and placed her hand on his chest.

His heart about leapt out.

"Tempting, but no." She moved past him and filled up a paper cup with water and ice, then handed it to him. "We can't have our workers passing out on the job."

He grinned, then gulped down the water. When he finished, he said, "I always look hotter than I really am."

Gwen arched a brow, and he laughed.

"I mean, like when I used to play sports, I was always the kid with the red face." He shrugged. "I can see you don't have that problem."

"Oh, I'm pretty sweaty right now," she said. "I just bear it like a lady."

Seth moved a strand of hair from her moist face. She didn't move, which he took as a good sign. "So, is the shelter getting an air conditioning unit soon?"

She wrinkled her brow. "It was like this last summer, so I doubt it."

"Do you think they'd accept a donation of an air conditioning system if I arranged it?"

Her blue eyes widened. "Are you serious?" Then her eyes narrowed. "Are you going to get your dad involved?"

"I should be offended," he said, "but I'm going to let it slide. And no, I'm not going to get my dad involved. I'll do it myself."

"But . . . it will cost thousands, and I thought you were living with your parents to—"

"It will only set me back a few weeks," he said. "Remember all those fabulous desserts I'm inventing? The profit margin is healthy, especially since I've convinced Pierre to order local ingredients versus imported."

"If we weren't standing in the middle of this kitchen, I might kiss you right now."

Seth rested his hands on her hips, risking a bit of PDA. "Kitchens are kind of our thing."

This time, her face did redden. "Well, Mr. Owens, I can't argue with you there. But you are quite sweaty. And if you move any closer, we're definitely going to have an audience." She neatly stepped away from him.

Seth resisted the impulse to grab her hand. They cleaned up the kitchen together, and Seth chatted with Mac while Gwen made her rounds to say goodbye to those who were still hanging around. Mac was highly in favor of a new air conditioning system.

"Thanks, man," Mac said. "I appreciate your help, and I'm glad Gwen has a friend."

Seth was surprised at the comment. "Gwen seems to have a lot of friends."

Mac rubbed the side of his neck. "Not any who have her back. She needs someone like that. She's always helping

145

someone else, you know, and sometimes I wonder who is helping her."

"True." Seth cut a glance over to Gwen, who was currently laughing with Jerry. "She's a tough woman."

"Tough on the outside," Mac commented.

Just then Gwen turned and saw Seth and Mac watching her. She said goodbye to Jerry and strode over. "What's up?"

"We're extolling your virtues," Seth replied.

"Really?" She looked to Mac for confirmation.

"Yep," Mac said. "Lots of virtues. Dozens." He chuckled and turned away. "See you kids next week, and I'm hoping the place will be a good twenty degrees cooler."

"Count on it," Seth called to Mac as he pushed through the back door.

"You told him?" Gwen asked, meeting his gaze.

"I did."

"Do you think the install can happen as fast as next week?"

"I have a few connections."

She rested her hands on her hips. "Oh, really?"

"Really." He tugged at one of her hands and linked their fingers. She didn't pull back. "Let's get out of here. I have something I want to show you."

"Air conditioners?" she asked, walking with him outside.

"Nope," he said. "A surprise."

"Wait." Gwen tightened her hold on his hand and tugged him to a stop. "Is this a date?"

He paused, enjoying the way the breeze moved the strands of hair away from her neck. It was hard to be this near her and not touch her. "It can be a date. Or not. It's up to you."

"Will you buy me dinner if it's a date?"

He grinned. "Definitely."

She started walking again, still holding his hand. "All right. I'll stop guessing, and you pay for dinner."

Seth tried to breathe normally, but his heart was racing. This was different. A good different. He unlocked and started the car with his key fob so by the time he'd opened her door, the air conditioning was blasting through the vents, trying to undo two hours of heat.

Gwen slid into her seat, and Seth walked around to the driver's side.

The farmer's market wasn't far from the homeless shelter, and Seth had only been to it a couple of times. He wasn't usually able to make the drive, but he'd remembered that it was open on Wednesdays and Saturdays.

"Here we are," he said as he pulled into the dirt lot that doubled as a parking area. The stalls were set up at the edge of a park with towering trees, so at least there was plenty of shade.

"What is this? A swap meet?"

"A farmer's market."

Gwen smiled and turned her gaze on him. "You brought me to a farmer's market?"

He shrugged. "Yep. What were your other guesses?"

"Oh, I don't know . . ." Her eyes gleamed. "Maybe a seafood restaurant by the coast that takes three months to get a reservation, or maybe a stroll through some eclectic art museum."

"I'm not sure if you've underestimated or overestimated me," he said. "But I'm a pretty simple guy."

"More like myopic."

"Yeah—myopic," he said. "But you like food, right? And you're hungry?"

"Yes to both." Gwen opened her door, and by the time

Seth climbed out and walked around the car, she'd already stood and shut the door.

Seth led her to a booth that sold woven bags, and he bought a couple, then handed one to Gwen. "In case you see something you want to buy."

She took the bag, and they started browsing the different sellers that had set up booths, simple stalls, and a couple who were selling produce directly from the beds of their trucks.

"Do you like eggplant?" Seth asked when they reached one of the sellers.

"Not particularly," Gwen said, but she was curious enough to pick one up.

"Most people don't even know it's in the dish they're eating," Seth said. "It doesn't have a strong taste."

"Then why use it?" Gwen asked.

"It adds a greater constitution to a dish," he said. "Besides, it's healthy."

"Good to know." Gwen set the eggplant down.

Seth added an eggplant to his bag. The whir of a juice machine caught his attention. One of the vendors had the right idea to make smoothies on the spot, and, predictably, there was a line at the booth. "Want a smoothie?"

"Sure," Gwen said, and when it was their turn in line, Seth ordered two.

"This had better not count as dinner," she said, after taking the first sip from the straw.

"Don't worry, you'll get your dinner." Seth reached for her hand, and she linked her fingers with his. He could definitely get used to this.

They continued to browse. Well, Gwen browsed, and Seth loaded up on produce. He had some more ideas to try, nothing with dessert, and maybe, just maybe, Gwen would agree to let him cook lunch for her tomorrow.

"What's this?" Gwen picked up a passion fruit melon.

"If you don't know, you need to try it," he said, adding it to his bag. "Passion fruit smoothies are the best."

"*Passion* fruit? Really?"

"I didn't name it," Seth answered. Since his bag was full, and he'd also filled up Gwen's, he said, "Let's go eat. I don't want you wasting away." They walked back to the car, and Seth set the bags on the back seat.

As they drove to their next destination, Gwen asked, "When did you know you wanted to be a chef? I mean, really go for it, culinary school and all?"

"One summer my dad hired a chef to cook for one of his parties," he said. "Usually he'd had the parties catered, with the food prepared off premises. My parents had used cooks from time to time when they were at home for longer stretches, but I'd never seen a trained gourmet chef in action. I sat on the kitchen barstool most of the night watching him do his magic."

Gwen smiled. "Magic, huh?"

"Pretty much." He slowed the car and turned the next corner. "I've only been to this place once, but I was impressed. I hope you like Thai food."

"I think I like most foods, although I'm not a fan of sushi." She gave him a sideways glance. "Please tell me you're not one of those sushi freaks."

"Not a sushi freak, although I do like it—maybe I can change your mind."

Gwen exhaled. "If anyone could, it would probably be you. But for now, I'm totally up for some chicken massaman."

Seventeen

Seth was reeling her in bit by bit, and Gwen could literally feel the pull toward him. She'd wanted to sit next to him at the Thai restaurant, but without a crazy woman named Valentina, there was no real excuse. And although Seth had made it clear time and time again that he liked her, she wasn't about to drape herself all over him. So she stayed on her side of the table and asked him questions about his time in Paris.

Seth had been right: the Thai food was delicious. But she managed to talk him out of offering a Thai dish at the restaurant. "Thai food is not the same at a regular restaurant. You need the atmosphere, the waitress who speaks broken English, the décor on the walls . . . it's all part of the ambiance."

Seth nodded. "You're probably right."

Now they were in the car driving back to Pine Valley as the summer sun sank behind the western hills, casting the sky into a riot of colors. The air conditioning was on low, and Gwen felt relaxed, even sleepy. But the last thing she'd do was fall asleep in Seth's car—because what if she started snoring or drooling?

The car suddenly listed to the side, and Seth let off the gas, gripping the steering wheel with both hands. "Hang on," he said as he eased onto the shoulder of the road.

Gwen sat up straight, suddenly alert. "What's going on?"

"Feels like a flat tire."

"You're kidding."

Seth put the car into Park and climbed out, then walked over to the tire on the front passenger side. Gwen climbed out as he squatted to examine the tire. Even from her angle, she could see it was flat.

"Dammit."

Gwen laughed; she couldn't help it.

Seth looked up and frowned at her.

"Sorry." She raised her hands. "It's just that your Mr. Perfect Car isn't all that reliable."

Seth rose to his feet, his brows still furrowed, which only made Gwen laugh more.

"Do you know how to change a tire, boss?" she asked. "Or should I do it?"

"I can change my own tire," he muttered.

So Gwen leaned against the car, her arms folded, while she watched Seth change the tire. She'd never seen him in a sour mood, and she found it quite entertaining. She was also impressed that he really did know how to change a tire. Fifteen minutes later, they were on the road again.

"So . . ." Gwen started.

"Don't say it," Seth bit out. "I had the tires rotated and balanced a couple of weeks ago."

"You probably ran over a screw or nail at the homeless shelter, so it was only a matter of time. Or maybe it was that gravel area by the farmer's market."

Seth gave a short nod.

A few moments passed in silence, and Gwen began to wonder why a flat tire would put him so much out of sorts. He was overreacting. Maybe this could be his one great flaw that would make it easy for her to stop dating him.

"Hey," she said. "Are you all right?"

He nodded, but his jaw was clenched tight.

Since he was driving with his left hand, she slid her hand into his right hand. "I'll stop teasing you about it if it will make you feel better."

He didn't smile or laugh. Instead he exhaled, and his fingers curled around hers. "My best friend flipped his car in high school because of a flat tire. He didn't make it."

Gwen looked over at him, her throat tight. "Wow. I'm so sorry. Was it a Mercedes?"

"No . . . a Land Rover."

Gwen took a breath. "Your car is definitely the safer car out of the two. For one thing, it's not top heavy."

"Yeah. I know," Seth said. "That's why I got it. But what if you'd been driving like you did a few weeks ago—would you have known what to do?"

"Let off the gas," Gwen said. "Steer slowly to the side of the road."

Seth glanced over at her. "Yep. Good."

Gwen fell silent, deciding to let his emotions play out.

But when they arrived at her place, Seth was still quieter than usual. For some reason, it didn't annoy Gwen like she thought it would. She wanted to somehow help him, console him. But it had been years since the accident, so how did she go about it?

"I think you need some processed sugar and tons of preservatives," she said as Seth pulled into her parking lot. She didn't know if he was going to drop her off in front of her building or park and walk her to the door.

But she had his attention now.

"That sounds toxic," he said, and his tone was lighter than it had been.

Gwen spread her hands. "I've been eating the stuff for years, and it hasn't affected me."

Seth quirked his mouth.

"Well, I'll let you be the judge of that," she continued. "If you dare, you can come up and try what I have in the freezer. Or you can go home and wash all your vegetables, then watch Netflix by yourself."

"Netflix?"

She shrugged. "Or whatever restaurant owners do on their nights off."

Seth pulled into a parking spot and turned off the car. "You're on."

For some reason, this made Gwen's heart soar. She'd managed to distract him, and now that she had him coming into her place, she second-guessed her motivations. It would put them in a private situation—after they'd already kissed a few times—and after Gwen had been letting her guard slip more and more.

"I can't guarantee the sterile state of my kitchen," Gwen said as they walked to her door. "But I probably keep most of the health codes." She unlocked her front door and flipped on the interior light.

"Then you're lucky I don't work for the county health department," he said, his tone even lighter.

Gwen led the way to the kitchen and flipped on another light. Then she opened the freezer and pulled out a carton of red velvet ice cream.

"That looks like it will do some damage," Seth said with a straight face.

"I hope you don't mind eating out of the carton." Gwen opened a drawer and pulled out two spoons. "It's better that way, and I'm sort of a purist."

"I don't mind." Seth grabbed a spoon and dug out a rather large scoop.

Gwen watched in awe as he popped it into his mouth.

"Not bad," he said after a moment, then dug in for another scoop.

"Hey." Gwen clinked their spoons together, knocking his to the side. "Save some for me." She scooped up a similar-sized bite and put it in her mouth. Then the brain freeze struck. She dropped her spoon and cradled her head with a moan.

Seth laughed.

"Not funny," Gwen ground out. She kept her eyes closed until the pain passed, and when she opened them again, Seth was washing his spoon in the sink.

"Giving up already?" Gwen asked.

He flashed her a smile. It was nice to see that smile again. "I'm kind of full from dinner. Not that this isn't really good."

Gwen put the lid on the carton and set the ice cream back in the freezer. "Admit it, this is too low-class for you."

Seth turned off the water and crossed to her. He stopped right in front of her so that very little space was left between her and the fridge.

"I think I'm going to make you ice cream tomorrow," he said in a low voice, his fingers brushing against hers.

"Oh, really?"

"Really."

"You know," she started, "you don't always have to one-up me in the food department. I mean, we can eat fast food

155

once in a while. Or ice cream out of a carton. Maybe even a Twinkie."

His mouth quirked. "I'm not opposed to Twinkies. They're kind of an American tradition." He tugged at the edge of her shirt, and the ends of his fingers rested on her waist. His hazel-green eyes seemed to look right into her soul. "And you might be able to talk me into fast food on occasion."

"You'll have to prove it," she said, in a more breathless voice than she intended. "I'm not sure I'll believe it until I'm a witness."

"Deal." Seth's hands moved behind her waist and pulled her flush against him.

"You know, not everyone can date a gourmet chef," she said. "Some of us have to settle for store-bought."

"I'll cook for you anytime you want."

It was perhaps the most romantic thing anyone had ever said to her. "What about the rest of civilization? Maybe you could start boxing up some of your creations and shipping them out."

Seth chuckled. "That would defeat the purpose of using fresh ingredients."

"Yeah, you're probably right." Gwen's heart pounded at his nearness, and she only wanted him closer. She moved her hands up his arms, then rested her hands on his shoulders.

"What are your lunch plans tomorrow?" he asked, his gaze moving to her mouth. "I have a recipe I want to try in my kitchen."

"Should I be offended you don't want to cook here?"

"Don't be offended." He kissed her then, and she wondered how it could keep getting better and better. His kisses were slow, as if he was cherishing each and every one. One of his hands moved up her back, and goose bumps spread across her skin.

She moved her hands behind his neck, finding his skin warm.

When he pulled away, so they could both mercifully breathe, she said, "Are you making me ice cream?"

He chuckled. "I was thinking more of a vegetable soup that would be paired with eggplant breadsticks."

"Ew."

Seth laughed and pulled her into a tight hug. "Don't jump to conclusions without trying it first."

Gwen breathed in his clean spicy scent. "All right, boss. I'll withhold judgment until tomorrow."

He released his grasp but kept her in his arms. "Did you just have a birthday?"

Gwen felt the warmth drain from her face. She knew what he was talking about without turning around. On top of the fridge, she kept a small basket with birthday cards in it—birthday cards and other letters her parents had sent her. Even though she wasn't on speaking terms with her parents, she hadn't thrown out the letters her parents had sent. She hadn't opened them either. She'd stopped reading the letters because they only made her angry. Instead she'd stashed them on top of the fridge and mostly forgotten about them.

"My birthday was in March," she said, thinking of how to change the subject. Well, she could always start kissing him again.

"You don't open your mail?" He released her and moved around her. "Oh. They're from your parents?"

The return address labels on them made that clear. Gwen chewed on a fingernail—a habit she'd long since kicked, she thought. "Yeah. I told them to never call me again, so they write me instead."

When she didn't elaborate, Seth turned to face her. His

eyes were intent on hers, yet filled with compassion. And possibly understanding. Except he didn't understand.

"What happened between you and your parents?" he asked.

She released a sigh. "It's a long story." She faked a yawn. "And it's late."

He stepped close to her and ran his fingers across her jaw, then behind her neck. She stilled and felt the light caress spread throughout the rest of her body. "You don't have to tell me, but if you want to, I'm here to listen. And I won't judge you."

The irony of his statement made her eyes sting. She turned from him and walked into the living room. Sitting on the couch, she grabbed one of the throw pillows and hugged it against her chest.

Seth didn't move from his spot in the kitchen for a moment, as if he was undecided about what to do. Then he joined her on the couch and draped his arm behind her.

Gwen leaned against him and rested her head on his shoulder. "So . . ." she started in a quiet voice.

Eighteen

$\mathcal{G}$wen was finally opening up to him, and Seth wished he could help her in some way, comfort her. Even though her issues with her parents had been going on for years, the pain in her voice was still raw. Sitting on the couch together, with his arm around her, was a start.

"After my grandma died," Gwen continued, "and after I returned home after running away, things didn't get much better."

"I'm sorry," he said. "The teenage years are hard enough without having to lose your grandma."

She nodded. "My parents never changed, no matter what I talked to them about. They kept up the façade of always trying to keep up with the neighbors. It seemed that they'd do anything they could so their friends kept thinking we had the perfect little life. My home life was no refuge, and I had tired of the same attitudes at school and among my friends. I guess I buried myself in schoolwork twenty-four-seven."

Seth brushed his fingers against her shoulder. "You had to have pretty good grades to get into Stanford in the first place."

"But still, it was my parents' dream, not mine."

"I can relate."

"Yeah." She peered up at him. "But somehow you're still speaking to your parents."

"I'll be the first to admit it hasn't been easy."

"You're a stronger person than I am, I guess."

"Hey." Seth lifted her chin so that she was looking at him. "You're the strongest woman I've ever met."

She raised her brows and smirked. "You're just trying to get brownie points."

He lowered his voice. "You don't like compliments, do you?"

"Not really."

"Well, then . . ." He kissed the edge of her mouth, then pulled back. "I'll take any brownie points you want to give me."

She linked their fingers and looked down at their clasped hands. "I think my biggest flaw was thinking that the grass would be greener on the other side. Once I was moved out to go to college, life only became more frustrating."

Seth listened as she told him about her college roommates and their lifestyle. She told him about the drunk parties, the guys crashing wherever, whenever, and the academic cheating going on.

"I guess I learned pretty quickly not to trust anyone." Gwen shrugged, although Seth knew she was being far from flippant. "Both my family and friends only cared about themselves and creating some sort of image they felt obligated to uphold. I didn't get why they were all chasing some unrealistic ideal."

Seth was quiet for a moment. Most people were chasing something, but he could see where Gwen was coming from. "I think it's the motivations that are bothering you. I mean, what's your motivation to go to a five-star restaurant every day to serve food?"

Gwen met his gaze, and he was tempted to kiss her again.

"Now we're going to psychoanalyze me?" she asked.

Seth smiled and brushed a bit of her hair from her forehead. "I'm curious."

"Okay," she said. "Um. I *don't* like being a boss. I like the flexibility. I like the hours. I like the variety. No two nights are the same."

"Fair enough." He paused. "And what about next year, or five years from now?"

She straightened and tugged her hand away from his. "Are you trying to get me to reveal my five-year plan?"

"Do you have one?"

She scoffed. "You sound like my parents."

He grasped her hand and drew it toward him again. "Maybe they're not so bad, then."

Gwen narrowed her eyes, but she didn't pull away. "You've never met them."

He knew he was taking a risk, but he'd taken a lot of risks with Gwen. "I hope to meet them someday."

She stared at him.

"I mean, I hope that you'll reconcile," he continued, "you know, after you read their letters. Then you can introduce me."

"Seth . . ."

"I know." He brought her hand to his mouth and kissed her knuckles. "I've jumped about ten steps ahead."

She gave a small smile. "Well, if I ever reconcile with them, I'll give you a call."

"And I'll answer that call."

She laughed. "I'm sure you will. You keep following me around."

He turned her hand over and linked their fingers together. "Am I bothering you too much?"

She exhaled softly. "Not so much anymore."

He laughed. "*What?*"

"I mean, I guess you're growing on me, and . . . you're not who I thought you were."

"Hmm." Seth moved his hand up her arm, then settled his hand on her shoulder. He brushed his thumb against the pulse of her neck. "So, are we going to keep hanging out?"

The edges of her mouth turned up. "Maybe."

"I like your 'maybe' a lot better than your 'no.'"

She lowered her lashes and said in a coy tone, "Well, you did name a dessert after me."

"I should have done that months ago," he whispered, then moved closer. She didn't move, so he closed the distance and kissed her softly. It was a light kiss, but he lingered, and she kissed him back, keeping things equally tame.

Despite their barely-there kiss, the temperature in the room seemed to skyrocket. When she drew away, Seth felt as if he was living in some sort of haze.

"*Months* ago?" she asked.

Seth blinked, trying to recall what she was asking about. Oh, yeah. "Christmas Eve, to be exact. You were hard not to notice, but I wasn't looking to date anyone. Then you came into work wearing red heels and Christmas ornaments for earrings, and I couldn't help but pay attention."

Gwen grinned. "They weren't Christmas ornaments—just little earrings painted to look like them."

He kissed her temple. "Whatever."

"And if I remember right, you were really grumpy that night."

"You remember that?" He looked at her in surprise.

"What was wrong?"

"Um, not sure, it was a while ago."

"Yeah, I agree," she said. "That's kind of a long time to be interested in someone without asking them out."

"I guess I'm good at waiting." He winked, then ran his other hand up her back. He leaned in for another kiss.

But she placed her hand on his chest, stopping him. He put his hand over hers, knowing she could feel the rapid beat of his heart.

"I think you should leave now," she said, but it was with a smile.

"You're right," he said. "My thoughts aren't exactly pure."

Her cheeks tinged pink. "Yeah, I'm guessing that. Nothing about me is easy."

Seth chuckled. "I wouldn't have it any other way." He moved to his feet before he could talk himself out of his resolve.

She stood and unexpectedly leaned in and wrapped her arms around his waist.

He didn't hesitate to pull her closer and rest his chin on top of her head. This was nice.

"Thanks," she said in a quiet voice. "The shelter was fun, and everything else. Even you asking nosy questions."

"I should be thanking *you* for spending the day with me."

She drew away and looked up at him. "You're welcome."

He didn't want to leave, but more than that, he didn't want to push this new relationship too fast. He wanted Gwen to be sure about him, to trust him, and to feel comfortable sharing anything she wanted to. So he released her and stepped away.

Moments later, he was in his car, texting her. *Lunch tomorrow at my place? No parents allowed.*

She replied before he pulled out of the parking lot, so he glanced at his phone to read it.

I'll be there.

Seth wasn't sure if he stopped smiling the whole way home. He didn't know if he'd be able to sleep now, but he didn't care. Some things were better than sleep.

When he arrived home, he unloaded the bags of vegetables and washed them all. Then he pulled out his laptop and started to type up a couple of recipes he'd been mulling over. Gwen had been right about not including a Thai-specific dish on the menu, but what if it was *inspired* by Thai food?

He wasn't sure what time he'd finally crashed, but he was glad he'd set his alarm, or he would have slept in. Something about Gwen was affecting him. He couldn't remember ever sleeping past 8:00 a.m.

By the time Gwen texted him that she was at the bottom of the hill, he'd taken his car to the shop to get a new tire and had returned home to start on lunch preparations.

"Hey there," he said when he arrived at the bottom of the hill.

"Hi." She climbed into his car, dressed in a light blue sundress and white-and-blue earrings that looked like miniature clouds. She also smelled like sunshine.

Seth wondered if they'd reached the stage in their relationship where he could greet her with a kiss. But she was looking down on her phone, distracted with something else. In fact, she seemed out of sorts.

"Is everything okay?" he asked.

She looked over at him, her blue eyes connecting with his. "I opened my parents' cards and letters last night after you left."

Surprise jolted through him. "Really?" He parked in the driveway and turned to her to give her his full attention. "What did they say?"

She looked past him, and he wasn't sure how to read her. Did the cards make things worse? Or was there hope?

He waited, unsure if he'd been too nosy.

Finally, she said, "The first couple were apologies for not letting me choose what I wanted to do after high school." She shrugged.

"That's a start, right?" Seth said in a quiet voice. He took her hand.

"Yeah." She still wasn't looking at him. "The next ones were more casual and friendly, as if we were regularly exchanging letters—all one-sided, of course." Her gaze flitted to his, and he nodded encouragement for her to continue.

"The last one was kind of surprising," she said.

"How so?"

"They're moving." She adjusted something with her hair. "Or they probably have by now. It was the last letter I received, and it's about two months old."

"Did they say why they're moving?"

Gwen blinked rapidly, and Seth's stomach knotted. She looked like she was holding back tears. He grasped her hand.

"They said that I was right, and when they started learning about the problems other families around them had, they realized that our problems were pretty small. My desire to make choices wasn't the worst thing in the world." She gave a sad smile. "They said they want a fresh start in a neighborhood where neighbors actually help each other rather than judge each other."

She leaned her head back, exhaling. "It's weird to think I can never go back to my childhood home. Not that I was really planning on it." Her fingers tightened around Seth's. "It's also weird that my parents could be living in a new house, and I have no idea where it is."

"Their cell numbers would be the same, right?"

She nodded.

"And it sounds like a good change overall," he added.

"Yeah." She looked over at him, the sadness mostly lifted. "I'm starving. I hope you cooked me something."

He laughed. "Be careful what you ask for."

She smiled, then released his hand and opened the door of the car to climb out. He joined her as they walked toward the house and up the front steps. Before he opened the front door, she said, "Thanks for encouraging me to read the letters."

He gazed down at her. "I'm glad you did. Maybe . . . Well, I'm not going to boss you around."

"Ha. I don't believe that for a moment." She stepped forward and wrapped her arms about his waist, surprising him. "Thanks, Seth."

He pulled her close and inhaled lemons and sunshine. This day was starting out pretty much perfectly.

A car came up the drive, and for a moment, Seth didn't move, until he realized it was his parents.

Gwen drew away and looked over at the car. "Are you expecting anyone?"

"I'm not, but it seems my parents are home a day early." He suddenly wished he'd taken Gwen somewhere to eat. The kitchen was in shambles, and that was sure to set his dad off. Coming home a day early wasn't a good sign of how his dad's latest business deal had gone.

Sure enough, his dad climbed out of the car, and by the glower on his face, Seth knew exactly what type of mood he was in.

Nineteen

Gwen had only met Mr. Owens briefly when he came through the restaurant, and then again at the short interchange at the Fourth of July barbeque. But the man coming toward her now appeared as if he was about to barrel through the door.

"Seth," he barked.

"Hi, Dad."

Mr. Owens stopped at the top of the steps, and his gaze slid to Gwen's. "What are you doing?"

Although he was looking at her, Gwen knew the question was for his son.

"Making lunch, are you hungry?" Seth said.

"No." He continued past them, opened the door, and went inside.

"I'm so sorry," Seth's mom said, arriving in her husband's wake.

Fortunately, Seth seemed to take after his mom in personality. Mrs. Owens paused on the porch and faced them. "You're Gwen, right? One of the waitresses?"

"Yes," Gwen barely managed to say when Seth cut in.

"Don't apologize for Dad," he said. "Whatever deal he lost doesn't excuse his being rude to my girlfriend."

Gwen snapped her gaze to Seth. *Girlfriend?* When had that happened? Didn't there need to be a discussion about it first? Her pulse rose another notch as she saw the surprise on Mrs. Owens' face.

"I'm sorry," Mrs. Owens said, recovering her surprise nicely. "Things went sideways with Coleman's bid. He underbid like we told him to, but then several of the board members voted against your father and chose the Feltons."

Seth exhaled. "Dad's got to learn that under-the-table deals go south at some point. He shouldn't have told Cynthia's dad to underbid."

Mrs. Owens' cheeks pinked. "Well, business can be complicated, dear. You know that. I should get in and see if your father needs anything." She paused. "It's nice to see you again, Gwen." Then she disappeared inside.

Gwen was speechless. She didn't know what to say—about either Seth's declaration that she was his girlfriend or his accusation toward his father.

"Sorry." Seth shook his head, then looked at her. "Sorry about this. Hopefully, they'll not join us for lunch. Things will be strained."

He reached for the door to open it, but Gwen caught his hand, stopping him. "Girlfriend?" she asked.

He scrubbed his other hand through his hair. "Yeah, uh, that sort of slipped." Leaning close to her, he said in a quieter voice. "Do you want me to take it back?" His eyes searched hers.

Gwen's instinct was to say yes, but for some reason, she didn't have the heart. "I'll let you know."

His gaze softened, and he pulled the door open. "After you."

Gwen knew her way to the kitchen, of course, and neither parent was in sight, so she took courage and walked in.

Once they were in the kitchen, it was as if a load had been lifted from Seth's shoulders. He was more relaxed, and Gwen was glad to see it.

"So . . ." She eyed the array of veggies that she recognized from the farmer's market, and a bag of brown rice, a steaming rice cooker, along with several bottles without labels that must have been homemade sauces. "Looks like you changed your mind about the vegetable soup."

Seth bent and retrieved something from a lower cupboard, then set a wok on the counter.

"Stir fry?"

"Better than stir fry." His gaze connected with hers, and he raised his eyebrows. "Do you want to chop?"

"Sure." She moved to his side of the counter, and they stood side by side, chopping one vegetable after the other. It wasn't the standard peppers, onions, and carrots, though. They cut up eggplant, cantaloupe, and kiwi, along with red pepper, broccoli, and water chestnuts.

Once everything was chopped, Seth dumped in thin strips of chicken he must have cut up before, and the wok sizzled to life. He added sauce from one of the bottles, and the fragrance blossomed. Gwen leaned against the counter, watching Seth in his element. He was like an artist as he added each type of vegetable to the wok at certain times.

The diced cantaloupe was the last to be added, and the scent got even better. Gwen's stomach literally grumbled.

"Try it?" Seth asked, spearing a chunk of meat and one of the veggies.

She smiled and moved toward him.

"Careful, it's hot." He blew on it before he offered it to her.

Now Gwen's stomach was fluttering for a different reason. She took the bite, and it was still hot, but also delicious.

"Good?" he asked.

"You're magic," she said and leaned toward him.

He met her halfway and gave her a soft kiss. It was sweet, and a warm shiver traveled through her body. They weren't even touching anywhere else, but it was like she was wrapped in everything Seth.

The sound of heels clicking on the wood floor brought them apart.

"Oh, uh, Seth dear," his mother said.

Seth blinked, then turned to face his mother. "Yeah?"

Gwen was sure her face was red as she looked over at Mrs. Owens. She and Seth had barely started dating, and now his parents had witnessed their hug on the porch, and now a kiss. Mrs. Owens just smiled, although there was something in her eyes that Gwen couldn't read.

"Your father wants a minute with you," she said. "He's in his office."

Seth exhaled. "After lunch. Why don't you join us?"

His mother hesitated but kept the smile on her face. "We have a dinner appointment in a few hours, so we're fine."

Seth nodded. "All right."

His mother turned and left the kitchen, her clicking heels fading as she went into another room.

"What's going on?" Gwen asked in a quiet voice. "Things seem pretty tense . . ."

"Sorry." He grasped her hand and looked down at their

linked fingers. "There are a lot of layers here—and none of them are pretty."

Gwen took a step closer. "Well, if I'm your girlfriend, don't you think you should tell me?"

His eyes refocused on her. "My dad won't eat when I cook at home. He'd rather eat takeout than something fresh from me."

"That's ridiculous."

"It's his way of getting his point across that he never approved of my culinary sabbatical." He shrugged. "And he's still set on reuniting me and Cynthia—that's why he's always trying to kiss up to her father, so that they'll keep a favorable impression of our family even though I've broken up with her."

Gwen stiffened. "So, me here isn't a good thing."

Seth slipped a hand on her waist. "You being here is the best thing. My dad needs to face reality."

Gwen tilted her head. "And reality is . . ."

"Reality is that we're dating now, and maybe, eventually . . ." He leaned close to whisper in her ear, his cheek pressing against hers. "I'll stop there for now, because I don't want to scare you off."

Gwen smiled against the warmth of his skin. Seth could pull out all the charm when he wanted, and she was falling for every bit of it.

Her stomach chose that moment to protest.

Seth lifted his head and chuckled. "I'd better feed you."

He grabbed a couple of bowls from the cupboard and loaded up the brown rice, then topped it with the steaming stir fry. They sat at the counter next to each other, shoulder to shoulder, as they ate.

"This is really good," Gwen said as she finished up. "Is this another potential restaurant menu item?"

"I might try a few variations, but it's promising." He nudged her shoulder. "Want to do something after this? Out of the house?"

"Like go to another farmer's market?"

"You choose." Seth rose and collected their empty bowls.

Gwen smiled. "I'll clean up, since you cooked. You can go talk to your dad."

"Are you sure?" He paused at the sink before rinsing out the bowls.

"Yeah, then we can get out of here."

He grinned and set the bowls in the sink. "Sounds like a plan."

After Seth walked out of the kitchen, Gwen scooped the rest of the stir fry into a storage container, then packed up the leftover rice. She scrubbed out the wok and the rice cooker, then put all the cooking utensils into the dishwasher. There weren't enough dishes to start it, so she wiped down the counter and put away the sauces.

When she finished, she was surprised Seth wasn't back yet; but she didn't want to hang out in the kitchen by herself when his mom might return any moment. So she decided to go outside and sit on the front porch. She'd text Seth so he didn't have to look for her. But first, she needed to find the bathroom. She remembered it was down the short hallway off the front entrance.

She moved through the kitchen, found the hallway, but before she went into the bathroom, she paused. Loud voices reached her—an argument that had to be between Seth and his dad. The voices were coming from farther down the hall, where Mr. Owens' office must be. The door was shut, but it was quite clear they were speaking about her.

Heart hammering, Gwen moved down the hall, closer to

the office. Everything told her not to eavesdrop, but then Mr. Owens said, "And you bring that trash in here?"

"Enough," Seth replied, his voice steely. "You don't know anything about Gwen."

"After all you had with Cynthia?" his dad continued. "You can't even compare the two women."

"I'm not comparing," Seth said. "Cynthia and I are never getting back together. I don't know where things will go with Gwen, but Cynthia is permanently out of my life."

"If that's true, then find a woman who's worthy of you, one you can have a future with," his dad said. "Stop messing around with waitresses. It's beneath you, and it's embarrassing our family and will jeopardize the restaurant's image."

"That's ridiculous," Seth cut in. "A job doesn't define a person."

His father gave a bitter laugh. "Keep telling yourself that, son. We'll see where you are in five years. Still living here, still paying off loans, no equity to your name."

Gwen wiped at her cheeks; she hadn't even realized tears had started falling. If Seth came out now, and he and his father found her listening and crying, she'd be mortified.

She turned and hurried down the hallway. Trying to not make any noise, she opened the front door. She considered sitting on the porch until Seth came out, but the tears wouldn't stop. The irony of all ironies is that Gwen grew up like the Owens family—a life of privilege and money—yet, she'd never heard anything so cruel as what Mr. Owens had said about her. Not even her own parents had ever been that cruel to anyone.

Gwen kept walking. Down the porch steps, along the driveway, until she was walking down the hill to Marge. Gwen was okay with her life being her and Marge for now. Marge might have her bad and good days, but Marge didn't break hearts.

Once Gwen was in her car, the tears had dried, and a new resolve had formed in her chest. She drove to the nearest park and stopped in the shade. She first sent a text to Seth.

I heard part of your discussion with your dad. And I have to agree with him. I don't fit in your life, and relationships are hard enough when parents are supportive. Please don't contact me. I'll see you at work, but that's it.

She turned her phone on silent, and about twenty minutes later, the texts started up from Seth. But she didn't open any of them. It was time to stop living in other people's lives and take care of her own. She pulled up another number she hadn't thought she'd ever call again. She pressed SEND.

On the second ring, it was answered.

"Hi, Mom."

Twenty

Three weeks had passed since the disastrous lunch at Seth's house, and since Gwen's phone call with her mom. Since then, Gwen had talked to one or both of her parents almost every day. They had a lot of catching up to do. And it was nice, which surprised Gwen. She hadn't gone to see them yet, because she was still getting used to talking to them again and including them in her life.

Although with every conversation, she couldn't help but remember how Seth had told her that when she was ready, he'd love to meet her parents.

Gwen had barely said hi to Seth at the restaurant since that final text. She'd called in sick for two days, and Seth had left messages and texted her several times; but she'd already said what she'd wanted to say. And it was the same thing she'd been saying from the beginning. He'd chosen to stay in his parents' world, and she would not make Seth choose between her and his parents.

She'd told Alicia what had happened, of course, and instead of trying to give her advice, Alicia had become a buffer at the restaurant.

At work, Seth had been respectful, although Gwen had half expected him to follow her to her car after closing. She'd caught his gaze on her more than once, but she kept her chin up and focused on the customers. Alicia had her back, and Gwen's relationship with her parents was on the mend. That would have to be enough.

But every night after work she returned to her apartment exhausted. Exhausted from pretending she was okay, that she could move on, that Seth hadn't meant anything to her. But she also had her pride. Mostly. So she'd call her mom, even though it was midnight, and they'd talk about nothing and everything. After talking to her mom, Gwen went to sleep feeling better.

Gwen would be seeing her parents today. She told them she'd come to their new house after the lunch hour at the homeless shelter. Gwen hadn't seen Seth at the shelter the past three weeks. It was just as well, although now there was a fully functioning air conditioning system to remind her of him. He hadn't forgotten about his promise. Of course not.

Since the August heat was pretty much at its worse, Gwen brought along a jug filled with ice for her drive to the shelter. Marge was grumpy in the heat, and there was no telling if Gwen's own air conditioning would work.

At the shelter, Mac greeted her with a welcoming grin. And although the question about Seth's whereabouts still lingered in Mac's gaze, he no longer asked.

"Taco salad?" Gwen said as she walked into the shelter's kitchen to see all the fixings set out.

"Yep," Mac said. "The taco meat is simmering. Can you scoop out the sour cream into a bowl?"

"Got it." Gwen opened the refrigerator. Two white boxes sat on the shelves. "What's in the boxes?"

"Oh, your friend dropped those off."

Seth. She lifted the lid off the first box. Inside were two dozen fruit tarts with golden crusts and glazed fruit nestled in a creamy custard. She swallowed against the dryness of her throat. "When did he bring these?"

"Right after I got here."

Gwen hadn't seen Seth's car when she drove in, so she knew he was long gone. She pulled out the dessert boxes and unloaded the tarts onto a serving tray. Seeing the exquisite desserts neatly lined up brought back memories of Seth and how he took so much care with his creations.

She missed him. But there was nothing she could do about it, or *would* do about it. When she saw him at the restaurant, an energy hummed between them, and she knew he was holding back from talking to her. He was respecting her wishes, giving her space. Waiting. Always waiting for her.

She had to find a way to take her mind off him, and it might take changing her job, but she was reluctant to go that far.

"Earth to Gwen," Mac said close to her ear.

She turned and smiled. "Sorry, I guess I'm tired." She looked past Mac to see that the lunch line had already formed. She got to work.

The faces were a blur, and although she greeted everyone and spoke with them, she could barely remember any of the conversations. By the time she left the homeless shelter, she was second-guessing her decision to visit her parents today. She sat in her car for a few minutes as the air conditioning made a feeble attempt to cool down the interior.

She pushed away the urge to call Seth, even if it was to thank him for the dessert, justifying it by the fact that surely Mac had already thanked him. It was time to move past Seth. To focus on her future, which meant reuniting with her parents.

Following the map app on her phone took her to a neighborhood several miles from where she'd grown up. The houses were well kept, but modest, and as Gwen neared the address, her pulse began drumming. Would they be watching for her car and come outside to greet her? Would they wait for her to knock on their door?

When she pulled alongside the curb, everything seemed quiet. The lawn had been recently mowed, and a riot of flowers grew in each flower bed. Everything looked ordinary. Gwen's eyes pricked with tears, and she closed her eyes for a moment, inhaling. Exhaling. A year had passed since she'd seen her parents. It wasn't so long.

Climbing out of the car, she squared her shoulders as she strode up the walkway. She reached to ring the doorbell, but the door opened. Her mom came out onto the porch, while her dad held the door open.

Her mom's hair was cut in a short bob, streaked with gray, but her blue eyes were the same. Her dad had changed the most, the wrinkles about his eyes more pronounced, and his once dark hair thinned and graying.

"Gwennie," her mom said, and in seconds Gwen was enveloped in a tight hug. Her mom smelled the same. Like department store perfume.

"Look at you." Her mom pulled away, scanning Gwen from head to foot. "You're beautiful."

The tears started, maybe because Gwen couldn't remember her mom ever calling her beautiful, or maybe because her dad was crying. She moved past her mom and hugged her dad. She closed her eyes as he held her. "I'm sorry," she said, although it was more of a gasp.

"No need to apologize," her dad said. "If anything, we're the ones who are sorry. We just want our Gwennie back."

After several moments, Gwen felt composed enough to pull away without breaking down again. She wiped at her eyes as her parents led her inside. They gave her a tour of the three-bedroom house.

"This is a guest bedroom." Her mom opened the door to a room that had the same bedspread Gwen remembered from her old bedroom. "You're welcome to stop over anytime. I also have all your things in boxes should you ever want to take them."

Gwen stood in the doorway, gazing at the bedspread. She remembered picking out the violet and black colors when she was about fourteen. They'd painted her bedroom walls violet to go with it.

"Are you hungry?" her mom asked. "I've got some chicken casserole in the oven."

"Sure, I'll have some," Gwen said, suddenly realizing she was famished.

She walked with her parents to the kitchen and helped her mom set out the meal while her dad pulled out a couple of photo albums.

"Now, I know what you're going to say," her dad said, opening the first album, "but it's not what you think." He slid the album over to her.

Gwen picked it up and slowly leafed through the pages. Her dad was right. The album was unexpected. The childhood pictures were there, yes, but so were bits and pieces of her schoolwork and lame attempts at art. She shook her head when she saw the angsty poem her twelve-year-old self had written when a dog had been killed in front of their house.

"You kept this?" she asked.

"We did," her dad said with a soft smile. He reached over and patted her hand. "We missed you more than you can ever know."

"I missed you, too." Gwen took a deep breath. "But I think it's great you guys are in this house. Strangely, it feels like home."

Her mom smiled. "That's nice to hear. I hope you'll consider it your home."

"I'm happy in Pine Valley." *Mostly.* "I have a good job, and I've made a life and friends there."

"Of course you have," her mom said. "Pine Valley is lucky to have you, and from what you've told us about Alicia, she sounds like a great friend."

"She is," Gwen said. She decided she needed to be the one asking questions, or it would be too easy to start talking about Seth, and she wasn't ready to go there.

The next couple of hours were filled with shared memories, laughter, and a few tears. When Gwen hugged her parents good-bye, she felt both happy and sad at the same time. Happy that these relationships had made it through all of their stubbornness, and sad that all of her parents' expectations had turned out so differently.

Climbing into her car, Gwen was glad she still had plenty of daylight to make the ninety-minute drive back to Pine Valley. Her heart felt light as she drove, and she realized she wanted to call Seth and tell him all about what had happened. But she couldn't, so she kept the radio on for company.

After she reached her apartment, she felt emotionally drained, and she ate a couple bites of her favorite red velvet ice cream, then climbed into bed with her clothes on. She was tired now, but tomorrow would be a better day. She'd be stronger than ever. But before she closed her eyes, she scrolled through the text messages on her phone and re-read the ones from Seth that she'd never deleted.

She was grateful to him for one thing: he'd encouraged her to reach out to her parents. She might have let those letters sit on top of her refrigerator for another year if he hadn't. Gwen plugged her phone into the charger and lay back on her pillow, closing her eyes.

Someone knocked on her door, but Gwen didn't move. It wasn't all that late, but unless she was expecting someone, she never answered her door. Another knock sounded, this one a little louder and more persistent. Even Seth would have texted her—but it wasn't like they were communicating.

A small seed of hope had already started to grow, though. What if it *was* Seth? She shouldn't want to see him, but if it was him . . .

She climbed out of bed and smoothed her hair as she hurried down the hall. She peered through the peep hole and recognized the man standing on the other side of the door. But it was the last man she'd ever expected to see at her front door.

Gwen unlocked the door and opened it.

Mr. Owens' lined face flashed with relief. "I was worried I had the wrong place." He wore a polo shirt and khakis, dressed down from how she usually saw him.

Gwen didn't move. Truthfully, she had no idea what to say.

Mr. Owens held up a paper grocery sack. "I hear you like lemons, and, well, these are almost ripe. I like to pick them before they're too soft."

Gwen glanced at the sack. *He'd brought her lemons? From his trees?*

When she didn't take the sack, he cleared his throat. "Uh, well, here." He set the sack on the floor next to her feet. "If you don't want them, you can throw them away."

183

Mr. Owens is nervous, Gwen thought. That much was clear.

"Anyway . . ." He rubbed the back of his neck, a motion that Gwen had seen Seth do more than once. "I owe you an apology."

Gwen exhaled.

"My son told me I was out of line, and I guess I was too bullheaded to see past my own nose," he continued. "Suffice it to say, after Seth moved out, I guess I finally understood how serious he was about you."

Gwen blinked. "Seth moved out?"

"Yes, a few weeks ago." His brows pulled together. "I thought you and he . . ."

"We broke things off," Gwen said. "I didn't want to cause contention between you and Seth."

"You heard our argument?" Mr. Owens asked.

Gwen nodded.

His face paled. "I—I don't know what to say."

She had never imagined in her wildest dreams she'd see a man like Mr. Owens acting so contrite.

"No wonder." He ran a hand over his face. Then his dark eyes focused on Gwen. "I regret everything I said that day. Have you ever said or done something you regret?"

"Of course," Gwen said in a faint voice.

"Can you overlook my bullheadedness and come over tomorrow night?"

Gwen stared at him. "What's tomorrow night?"

"It's our anniversary party at the house," he said. "Seth is coming—at least, he promised his mom. He's not speaking to me. I haven't seen him since . . . well, since that day *you* left first."

The man was rambling. It was pitiful, really. "I'm really sorry, Mr. Owens. I don't think I should come to your party.

Seth and I aren't seeing each other anymore." She took a breath. "But don't worry, I accept your apology, and I appreciate the lemons. I, too, have done things I've regretted. We can each move forward in our lives, with a clear conscience, and be better people for it."

Mr. Owens was staring at her now, his mouth open, as if she'd stopped him mid-sentence. "No. You don't understand. I came here to apologize, and I hoped to reconcile with Seth as well. But now I realize I must do much more."

Gwen folded her arms. "You've done enough. Thank you for coming over. I do appreciate it."

"Gwen," Mr. Owen said. "My son is in love with you. If I don't somehow prove how sorry I am, I don't know if he'll ever forgive me for driving you away."

Her ears buzzed, and she wasn't sure she'd heard Mr. Owens right. Seth was *in love* with her? And how did Mr. Owens know? Unless . . .

Gwen exhaled. "I don't think it's a good idea." She'd spoken, but it was like her voice was far away.

"Please come," Mr. Owens said. "If you can. This is not to appease my own guilt. I've been to the restaurant several times over the last few weeks—if only to make sure Seth was doing well. But I watched you, too. You have a way with people. You're genuine. You're a hard worker. In fact, you remind me of myself . . . before I made so many mistakes with my son."

He looked away for a moment, then continued. "We'd love to see *you* there. My wife would be thrilled, and *if* Seth comes . . . Well, he'll know that I am not such a horrible parent after all." Tears filled his eyes, and Gwen felt her heart twist.

No matter how brusque Mr. Owens' personality was, she knew he loved his son deeply.

She swallowed against the thickness of her throat. "I don't know if I can."

"I understand." He took a step back. "Seven o'clock, our place, if you can make it. Formal dress, but anything you have is fine." He took another step back, his gaze beseeching hers.

She watched him walk to the parking lot and climb into his car. She didn't know how long she stared after him, but finally she picked up the sack of lemons and took them inside.

Twenty-one

Seth shrugged into his tuxedo jacket, trying to resist the impulse to tug it off and skip the anniversary party. If it wasn't for his mother inviting him, he'd be sitting out this anniversary dinner, no matter how long his parents had been married. The fact that his father could celebrate a long and happy marriage, while he'd cut down the one woman Seth thought he had a future with, was not something he could forget.

Sure, his father had apologized over and over, but it was too late. Gwen had overheard his dad's rant, and she'd broken things off. Their relationship had been too new and tenuous to withstand such a conflict. That same day, Seth had packed up his things and by that night had them in a temporary storage unit. He'd stayed in a hotel for a few days until he could get into an apartment. It turned out a lot of single adults went through upheaval, and finding a sublease wasn't hard.

Truthfully, the space that moving out had given Seth between his parents had been good. He didn't think he could go for months and months, or even a year without talking to his dad . . . like Gwen had. He wasn't quite as stubborn as she was. Despite the fact that he was still nursing wounds, he smiled when he thought of her. Which was multiple times a day. His greatest fear was that she'd quit the restaurant; but so far she hadn't.

Of course, maybe seeing her so often was worse—subjecting himself to sweet torture on the nights they worked together. She hadn't replied to any of his texts or returned any of his calls, and he'd had to let her make that decision. Which meant that he'd let her make the decision about ending their relationship.

He'd never thought it would be easy; no relationship was. But he'd held out more hope with Gwen. It was all over now, and as he stared blankly at his reflection in the small bathroom of his apartment, he decided he'd have to figure out a way to move on.

The ringing of his cell phone pulled him out of his thoughts.

"Hi, Emmy," he said when he answered. He walked down the short hallway to the living room that was still stacked with boxes he hadn't unpacked. He'd picked up two lawn chairs that served as furniture.

"Are you still coming?" his sister asked.

"Yeah, I'm running late."

The relief in Emmy's voice was plain. "Good. Mom keeps asking about you, and it's driving me crazy. It's like you're going to make or break her anniversary party."

Seth released a sigh. He hated how the big blowup between him and his dad had affected his mom, and, well, everything. "I'm only going to stay for a few minutes, you know. Just making an appearance."

"I know," Emmy said. "However long you can stay will be fine." She lowered her voice. "Just get here."

Seth snatched his keys and wallet from the kitchen counter. "On my way."

Emmy hung up, and Seth walked out of his apartment, then locked the door. He hadn't even interacted with his neighbors, mostly because he didn't want to, but also because he practically lived at the restaurant. His apartment kitchen was a poor substitute for, well, anything. And he refused to use his parents' kitchen, even though he suspected his dad would be more accepting now. So he'd worked at the restaurant after hours, sometimes far into the night.

He climbed into his car and drove to his parents' place, mulling over the dessert line he'd been developing that could be frozen, and . . . shipped. Gwen had given him the idea, and if he could get it off the ground, then according to his projections, the business would turn a profit within a couple of months. The set-up would be minimal, since he had full use of the restaurant kitchen, and the only hard costs were the ingredients. Eventually, he'd have to hire someone to help; but for now, he liked being busy. It kept his mind off things like a certain woman who waitressed each night at his restaurant.

Seth turned the final bend leading to his parents' house. The place glowed against the evening sky, rivaling the sunset. Seth parked behind the long line of cars, then waved to Jon, who seemed to be serving as valet and usher for the night. Seth didn't bother walking into the house. Instead, he took the cobbled path that led around the house to the backyard.

As Seth stopped to survey the scene, he was surprised to see so many people. His parents had invited plenty of acquaintances. The two fire pits were already crackling and the conversation lively. Music provided a mellow backdrop, and several couples danced on the lowest deck.

Seth picked out his parents quickly. His dad stood with his mom, arm in arm, as they spoke to an older couple who looked familiar to Seth, but whom he couldn't quite place. Emmy was dancing with Jed, while Ryker hung on her leg.

Seth smiled as the kid persisted until finally Jed picked up Ryker, and the three of them danced together, making Ryker grin from ear to ear.

Then Seth's heart stilled. A woman stood near one of the refreshment tables, a drink in her hand, as she watched the dancing. Even though her back was turned toward him, Seth knew it was Gwen.

Her hair was pulled into a smooth chignon, exposing her elegant neck. Her pale blue dress dipped low at the back, then cascaded to the floor, and because there was a slit on the side of the dress, he could see that she was wearing red stilettos.

A hundred questions collided in his mind. First and foremost, what was she doing here, and why? He blinked several times, wondering if he was really seeing her or if his imagination had become more vivid.

Then the most extraordinary thing happened. His father caught sight of Gwen and crossed over to her, bringing his mom along.

His mom hugged Gwen. And his dad . . . grasped Gwen's hand, then kissed her cheek.

Seth felt as if the breath had been knocked out of him. Had his *parents* invited Gwen? She smiled and talked to them for a few moments, and Seth couldn't fathom how in the world Gwen seemed to be getting along with his parents just fine— and that she was *here* in the first place. Surely Emmy would have said something to him about this?

But when Seth found Emmy on the dance floor, it

appeared that she'd noticed the same thing, and looked just as surprised.

Then Seth saw Dave making his way over to his parents and Gwen. *Oh no.* Had Gwen come with *Dave?*

Seth didn't think so, because Dave greeted Gwen with a handshake. Seth watched as Dave tried to obviously flirt with her. She nodded as she listened to Dave, but Seth knew her smile wasn't genuine. Then Dave held out his hand, and even though Gwen hesitated, she took it.

Dave must have asked her to dance, and now . . . they were dancing.

Seth felt as if he'd swallowed a rock. Every second that passed with Gwen and Dave dancing was one too many. Seth wanted to know why she was at the anniversary party. But more importantly, he didn't want Dave near her, even if Seth *wasn't* dating her.

Seth exhaled and left the perimeter of the yard and walked toward the dance area. One or two people might have greeted him, but he didn't slow to return pleasantries. Moments later, he'd stepped around the dancing couples and laid his hand on Dave's shoulder.

"I'm cutting in," Seth told him.

Dave turned his head. "Oh, hey, Seth. Thought you weren't coming."

Seth felt Gwen's gaze on him, and there was nothing he wanted to do more than to meet that gaze. But first he had to get rid of Dave. "I'm here, Dave, and I'm cutting in."

Dave narrowed his eyes but decided to be a smart man. "Sure, sure." He looked at Gwen. "You know where to find me, sweetheart." Then he stepped away from Gwen, which was a good thing. The intense energy drumming through Seth would have made it really easy to pop Dave in the nose.

Seth stared after Dave as he wound his way around the

dancers and headed for the refreshment table. Then Seth turned to look at Gwen, who was watching him. Her blue eyes were filled with an expression he couldn't define. Was she angry, annoyed? Amused?

"Dance?" he asked.

She nodded. And then she stepped into his arms, one hand resting on his shoulder, and the other hand encased in his. He rested his free hand on the curve of her waist, and everywhere their bodies touched Seth felt like he was burning. The scent of lemon and vanilla tingled his senses.

Although he was dying to ask her what had brought her to the party, and what had possessed her to agree to dance with him, he said nothing for several moments as they danced to the slow music and he tried to comprehend the turn of events.

"I didn't know you were such a caveman." Gwen's mouth twitched as she gazed up at him.

Seth exhaled. "Dave brings out the worst in me."

"Apparently." Her gaze turned somber. "I didn't see you, and he asked me to dance."

"You came to see me?" Seth's heart rate sped up.

"Sort of," she said. "Your dad invited me."

Seth stopped dancing. "What?"

She hesitated. "A lot has happened."

"So it seems." He glanced past her to the greenhouse. "Can we talk privately?"

She shrugged, but he didn't mistake the agreement in her eyes. "Okay," she said.

"Come on." He grasped her hand. She didn't pull away, so he led her off the dance floor and toward the greenhouse. He was sure people were watching them, but he didn't care.

He opened the door, and Gwen stepped in first.

The interior was muggy, and Seth shrugged out of his tux

jacket. He was already plenty warm. Gwen moved a good distance from him and leaned against the table containing pots of herbal plants. The orange glow from the setting sun had transformed to violet, making Gwen's dress look even paler.

Seth walked toward Gwen and leaned against the table about a foot away from her. Without looking at her, he said, "Tell me what happened with my dad."

"He came over to my apartment last night to apologize," she said.

Seth looked over at her. "That's hard to believe."

"I know," Gwen said. "I was stunned. He even brought me a sack of lemons."

Seth glanced toward the lemon trees. "What did he say?"

She told him about the apology, and the more she talked, the more it sank in that his dad was truly sorry. He'd gone out of his way to try to make things better with Gwen.

"I think he expected to find you with me, too," she continued. "But he was surprised when he learned that we'd . . . broken up."

Seth exhaled. "Not really my choice."

Gwen's blue eyes connected with his, and Seth knew that none of his feelings about her had changed. In fact, they were even stronger.

"I know it wasn't your choice," she said in a quiet voice. "You did nothing wrong. It was *me* . . . I didn't want to be in a relationship where I came between you and your parents. I've had enough parent trouble to last me a lifetime."

"I get it." He might understand her reasons, but he didn't have to like them. "It's one of the reasons I moved out. I needed my dad to understand that I'd be making decisions about my own life, especially about the women I date. Even if things didn't work out between you and me, I needed to move forward without any emotional crippling."

She nodded. "So are things better with your dad?"

"They will be now," he said, brushing his fingers against hers. "A lot better."

A smile crept onto her face.

"In fact, I started a new business."

She laughed. " *What?* Don't you ever sleep?"

"Sometimes." He grinned. "I'm testing some frozen gourmet desserts to see how they hold up during the shipping process. About six of them have passed all tests, so I'm getting ready to launch the website."

Her eyes searched his. "You're an amazing man, Seth Owens."

"Well, I think I have you to thank for the idea."

She turned more toward him, slipping her fingers through his. "Before you launch, they will need my approval."

"Done." He paused. Her touch had to mean something between them was significantly different. "So, does all of this mean you forgive my dad?"

She didn't say anything for a moment, simply looked down at their linked fingers. Finally, she said, "Yes."

Seth's heart thumped. "Yes?"

She bit her lip and nodded, still not looking at him.

"Then . . . what does that mean for *us*?" He moved closer and lifted her chin. Her skin was warm beneath his fingers.

"It means that I'd like you to meet my parents," she said.

Words he hadn't expected, but words he was more than happy to hear.

"I spent a couple of hours with them yesterday," she continued in a tremulous voice, the line appearing between her eyebrows. "I think things are going to be okay between us.

They've changed; I've changed." She exhaled. "It was really nice to see them again."

"I'm glad to hear that," he said. "And I'd be honored to meet them."

She smiled, and it was as if all the burdens he'd seen in her eyes had melted away.

"Gwen," he whispered, cradling her face with both of his hands, "I'm in love with you."

Her smile broadened. "I know."

"You *know*?"

She laughed. "Your dad told me." She moved her hands around his waist, drawing him even closer. "That's why I came tonight. That, and to see what you looked like in a tux."

Seth traced her cheeks with his thumbs, then leaned in. When her eyes fluttered shut, he pressed his mouth against hers, tasting her warm sweetness. She kissed him back, drawing him closer to her, until he almost forgot there was an entire event going on outside of the greenhouse.

"Seth," she whispered against his mouth. "There's something else I need to tell you."

He lifted his head to gaze into her eyes. All he saw was contentment, so maybe it was a good thing. "Anything," he whispered back.

"I'm in love with you, too."

He could have sworn the earth stopped moving. He lifted her against him and spun her around. She laughed and kissed him while he was still holding her up.

"Stars?" he said, when he set her down. He'd just noticed her earrings were blue and silver stars.

She lifted her chin. "I was hoping you'd notice, because I plan to watch the stars with you tonight."

"My night is all yours." He leaned down to kiss each of her earlobes.

"Good," Gwen said, "because I'm planning on being a lot more bossy. You need to put your jacket on so we can rejoin your parents' party."

He released her, then pulled on his tuxedo jacket. "I thought you didn't like to be the boss."

"I changed my mind." She grabbed his hand and led him toward the greenhouse door. "First, we need to go mingle. Then, we're going to dance again. After that—"

Seth stopped her with another kiss, and for a few moments, she let him take the lead. Then before she could say another word, he opened the door. They walked back to the party, hand in hand. Seth's dad spotted them almost immediately and hurried over before anyone else could intercept.

"You made it," his dad said, gaze wary.

"I did," Seth said. "Gwen told me what happened."

"Are we okay, then?" his dad asked.

"We are." Seth stepped forward and embraced his dad.

His dad's hug was fierce, and when they drew apart, his dad grinned, the relief evident on his face. "Your mom is going to be so happy."

"Then we'd better go tell her." Seth reached for Gwen's hand. Their fingers linked, warm, secure. And Seth knew that whatever the future held, waiting for Gwen had been worth it.

ABOUT HEATHER B. MOORE

Heather B. Moore is a four-time *USA Today* bestselling author. She writes historical thrillers under the pen name H.B. Moore; her latest thrillers include *The Killing Curse* and *Poetic Justice*. Under the name Heather B. Moore, she writes romance and women's fiction. Her newest releases include the historical romance *Love is Come*. She's also one of the coauthors of the *USA Today* bestselling series: A Timeless Romance Anthology. Heather writes speculative fiction under the pen name Jane Redd; releases include the Solstice series and *Mistress Grim*. Heather is represented by Dystel, Goderich & Bourret.

For book updates, sign up for Heather's email list:
hbmoore.com/contact
Website: HBMoore.com
Facebook: Fans of H. B. Moore
Blog: MyWritersLair.blogspot.com
Instagram: @authorhbmoore
Twitter: @HeatherBMoore

MORE PINE VALLEY NOVELS:

Made in the USA
Las Vegas, NV
16 August 2022

53378973R10114

sharing anything she wanted to. So he released her and stepped away.

Moments later, he was in his car, texting her. *Lunch tomorrow at my place? No parents allowed.*

She replied before he pulled out of the parking lot, so he glanced at his phone to read it.

I'll be there.

Seth wasn't sure if he stopped smiling the whole way home. He didn't know if he'd be able to sleep now, but he didn't care. Some things were better than sleep.

When he arrived home, he unloaded the bags of vegetables and washed them all. Then he pulled out his laptop and started to type up a couple of recipes he'd been mulling over. Gwen had been right about not including a Thai-specific dish on the menu, but what if it was *inspired* by Thai food?

He wasn't sure what time he'd finally crashed, but he was glad he'd set his alarm, or he would have slept in. Something about Gwen was affecting him. He couldn't remember ever sleeping past 8:00 a.m.

By the time Gwen texted him that she was at the bottom of the hill, he'd taken his car to the shop to get a new tire and had returned home to start on lunch preparations.

"Hey there," he said when he arrived at the bottom of the hill.

"Hi." She climbed into his car, dressed in a light blue sundress and white-and-blue earrings that looked like miniature clouds. She also smelled like sunshine.

Seth wondered if they'd reached the stage in their relationship where he could greet her with a kiss. But she was looking down on her phone, distracted with something else. In fact, she seemed out of sorts.

"Is everything okay?" he asked.

He kissed her temple. "Whatever."

"And if I remember right, you were really grumpy that night."

"You remember that?" He looked at her in surprise.

"What was wrong?"

"Um, not sure, it was a while ago."

"Yeah, I agree," she said. "That's kind of a long time to be interested in someone without asking them out."

"I guess I'm good at waiting." He winked, then ran his other hand up her back. He leaned in for another kiss.

But she placed her hand on his chest, stopping him. He put his hand over hers, knowing she could feel the rapid beat of his heart.

"I think you should leave now," she said, but it was with a smile.

"You're right," he said. "My thoughts aren't exactly pure."

Her cheeks tinged pink. "Yeah, I'm guessing that. Nothing about me is easy."

Seth chuckled. "I wouldn't have it any other way." He moved to his feet before he could talk himself out of his resolve.

She stood and unexpectedly leaned in and wrapped her arms around his waist.

He didn't hesitate to pull her closer and rest his chin on top of her head. This was nice.

"Thanks," she said in a quiet voice. "The shelter was fun, and everything else. Even you asking nosy questions."

"I should be thanking *you* for spending the day with me."

She drew away and looked up at him. "You're welcome."

He didn't want to leave, but more than that, he didn't want to push this new relationship too fast. He wanted Gwen to be sure about him, to trust him, and to feel comfortable

She gave a small smile. "Well, if I ever reconcile with them, I'll give you a call."

"And I'll answer that call."

She laughed. "I'm sure you will. You keep following me around."

He turned her hand over and linked their fingers together. "Am I bothering you too much?"

She exhaled softly. "Not so much anymore."

He laughed. "*What?*"

"I mean, I guess you're growing on me, and . . . you're not who I thought you were."

"Hmm." Seth moved his hand up her arm, then settled his hand on her shoulder. He brushed his thumb against the pulse of her neck. "So, are we going to keep hanging out?"

The edges of her mouth turned up. "Maybe."

"I like your 'maybe' a lot better than your 'no.'"

She lowered her lashes and said in a coy tone, "Well, you did name a dessert after me."

"I should have done that months ago," he whispered, then moved closer. She didn't move, so he closed the distance and kissed her softly. It was a light kiss, but he lingered, and she kissed him back, keeping things equally tame.

Despite their barely-there kiss, the temperature in the room seemed to skyrocket. When she drew away, Seth felt as if he was living in some sort of haze.

"*Months* ago?" she asked.

Seth blinked, trying to recall what she was asking about. Oh, yeah. "Christmas Eve, to be exact. You were hard not to notice, but I wasn't looking to date anyone. Then you came into work wearing red heels and Christmas ornaments for earrings, and I couldn't help but pay attention."

Gwen grinned. "They weren't Christmas ornaments— just little earrings painted to look like them."

to uphold. I didn't get why they were all chasing some unrealistic ideal."

Seth was quiet for a moment. Most people were chasing something, but he could see where Gwen was coming from. "I think it's the motivations that are bothering you. I mean, what's your motivation to go to a five-star restaurant every day to serve food?"

Gwen met his gaze, and he was tempted to kiss her again.

"Now we're going to psychoanalyze me?" she asked.

Seth smiled and brushed a bit of her hair from her forehead. "I'm curious."

"Okay," she said. "Um. I *don't* like being a boss. I like the flexibility. I like the hours. I like the variety. No two nights are the same."

"Fair enough." He paused. "And what about next year, or five years from now?"

She straightened and tugged her hand away from his. "Are you trying to get me to reveal my five-year plan?"

"Do you have one?"

She scoffed. "You sound like my parents."

He grasped her hand and drew it toward him again. "Maybe they're not so bad, then."

Gwen narrowed her eyes, but she didn't pull away. "You've never met them."

He knew he was taking a risk, but he'd taken a lot of risks with Gwen. "I hope to meet them someday."

She stared at him.

"I mean, I hope that you'll reconcile," he continued, "you know, after you read their letters. Then you can introduce me."

"Seth . . ."

"I know." He brought her hand to his mouth and kissed her knuckles. "I've jumped about ten steps ahead."

of the same attitudes at school and among my friends. I guess I buried myself in schoolwork twenty-four-seven."

Seth brushed his fingers against her shoulder. "You had to have pretty good grades to get into Stanford in the first place."

"But still, it was my parents' dream, not mine."

"I can relate."

"Yeah." She peered up at him. "But somehow you're still speaking to your parents."

"I'll be the first to admit it hasn't been easy."

"You're a stronger person than I am, I guess."

"Hey." Seth lifted her chin so that she was looking at him. "You're the strongest woman I've ever met."

She raised her brows and smirked. "You're just trying to get brownie points."

He lowered his voice. "You don't like compliments, do you?"

"Not really."

"Well, then . . ." He kissed the edge of her mouth, then pulled back. "I'll take any brownie points you want to give me."

She linked their fingers and looked down at their clasped hands. "I think my biggest flaw was thinking that the grass would be greener on the other side. Once I was moved out to go to college, life only became more frustrating."

Seth listened as she told him about her college roommates and their lifestyle. She told him about the drunk parties, the guys crashing wherever, whenever, and the academic cheating going on.

"I guess I learned pretty quickly not to trust anyone." Gwen shrugged, although Seth knew she was being far from flippant. "Both my family and friends only cared about themselves and creating some sort of image they felt obligated

Eighteen

*G*wen was finally opening up to him, and Seth wished he could help her in some way, comfort her. Even though her issues with her parents had been going on for years, the pain in her voice was still raw. Sitting on the couch together, with his arm around her, was a start.

"After my grandma died," Gwen continued, "and after I returned home after running away, things didn't get much better."

"I'm sorry," he said. "The teenage years are hard enough without having to lose your grandma."

She nodded. "My parents never changed, no matter what I talked to them about. They kept up the façade of always trying to keep up with the neighbors. It seemed that they'd do anything they could so their friends kept thinking we had the perfect little life. My home life was no refuge, and I had tired